WAVE MECHANICS

Diana Cobbold is an American novelist now living in Massachusetts. She has worked as a film and theatre critic and began writing fiction several years ago. Set in California and Hawaii, WAVE MECHANICS is her second novel – and the first to be published in England.

Evening Faces

Diana Cobbold

WAVE MECHANICS

ARENA

An Arena Book
Published by Arrow Books Limited
62–65 Chandos Place, London WC2N 4NW

An imprint of Century Hutchinson Limited

London Melbourne Sydney Auckland
Johannesburg and agencies throughout
the world

First published in Great Britain by Arena 1989

Filmset by Deltatype, Ellesmere Port
Printed and bound in Great Britain by
The Guernsey Press Co. Ltd,
Guernsey, Channel Islands

ISBN 0 09 958200 7

FOR MY MOTHER

. . . et felicissima matrum
dicta foret Niobe, si non sibi visa fuisset.

Niobe would have been thought of as the most fortunate of mothers, had she not believed it herself.

Ovid: *Metamorphoses* VI. 155

Probability waves . . . was an entirely new idea. It referred to what was already happening, but had not yet been actualized. It referred to a tendency to happen, a tendency that . . . existed of itself, even if it never became an event.

Gary Zukav: *The Dancing Wu-Li Masters*

LESSONS

1

KATE: November 4, 1949. My seventeenth birthday, and
          Jenny's giving me a party. My parents are dropping
me off on their way to the movies, but because it's so hard to see,
my father takes it slow down Quintara Street. For three days
now the city has been out of focus and creepy under one of its
fogs, so that the houses on the hills, their roofs hidden in drops of
water as thick as smoke, look only half built.

'I hope Jenny's mother doesn't let the party go on too long,'
says my mother from the back seat. 'You have to study for your
exams.'

'She won't, Mom,' I say. 'She's very conscientious.'

My mother doesn't like me going to parties. She couldn't
have any more kids, and since I'm the only one, she and my
father are always scared something will happen to me –
especially at parties. To keep me safe, they try to isolate me,
damp me down, defuse any exotic ambitions. We live out on the
avenues in one of those houses that were built in San Francisco
before the war – a raw block of stucco that looks like it should be
the servants' quarters of a hacienda – and growing up I was very
busy. From day one my parents fed all kinds of information to
me – how to spell desiccate; the difference between segment and
section; the rule for remembering the twelve labors of Hercules;
what *Mene Mene Tekel Upharsin* in the book of Daniel means –
and then pulled it all out of me again. It was like being the only
contestant in a marathon quiz show.

By the time I got to high school I was primed, brainwashed,
ready for some big-time action. The first week at Merced, I
came home right away so I could be alone with my new books,
run my hands over the prosperous pages, scan the action, figure
out how fast I could learn the math so I could take my time with
the English, slow down and enjoy the lurid words. I had the
house to myself because my mother teaches grade school and
doesn't get home till late.

'Are the brothers going to be there?' my mother says, alert as always to any possible threat of molestation to her daughter.

'I don't know,' I tell her, which is true. Friday nights Peter usually has a date, and I don't see why this one should be any different.

Peter Hollander had been a senior when I came to Merced as a freshman, and even before he or his sister Jenny ever spoke to me I already knew them, at first by sight in the corridors, and later with the intimacy of longing. The first time I saw him I stopped to adjust the heft of my books as he passed me in the hall. Above the odor of old apples and flattened egg sandwiches left in lockers I caught the scent of his starched white shirt, the sun in the blue sweater knotted around his neck. There was an intensity about him as if he was sheathed in light. I turned to watch him, and right away my body began to change. I started to shiver, even on the hottest days. For a long time after that my parents dropped out of my life almost as if I'd killed them, and I've never stopped being sorry.

I became a hunter, searching for tracks and signs, planning my days around the times when I could be certain of seeing him in the halls, on the field or in the cafeteria. Whenever I came near him the encounter took on a fantastic quality, like the sighting of a gryphon or a unicorn in the forest.

Jenny Hollander was in my class, and every time I saw her laughing with her friends, I wondered how anyone so powerful could be so nice. In Home Ec my stuff came out better than hers, and sometimes I let her have a taste. She started to wait for me after class, and by the end of our sophomore year we were best friends. She lent me her cashmeres, and when I wore them I could feel myself smiling just like her.

For a long time, though, she didn't ask me over to her house, so I used to amuse myself by imagining her with her three brothers. With a little erotic thrill I tried to imagine what they'd looked like as babies, whether they'd all been born with that peculiar flawless maturity, smooth, numinous, already sexually inviting. On the last day of December, I lay in bed listening to the distant delirium of late night stations; hot-eyed at midnight, I wondered what the Hollanders did on New Year's Eve.

I never mentioned Peter to Jenny because my feelings about him either leapt or slumbered in a part of me too private and incoherent to expose to somebody else. We went to all his games together, but I didn't follow when she went down to talk to him afterwards. He was the quarterback, and held his head like a prize he'd just won; his passing game was arrogant, and they called him the Prince. Even after he graduated and came back to the stadium, there was a stillness in the crowd when he arrived, a reverence in the way his old teachers spoke to him.

On the streetcar coming home from school I began to dream about what he looked like when he was asleep. But only a little, because I knew it was self-defeating to dream all the time about somebody who would never have anything to do with me. Sometimes I tried to picture his life the way it would be if it was written about in a book. Jenny had told me that her parents didn't go out much, which was surprising because I knew the father came from one of those old society families you read about in the papers. 'She'd rather be with us,' Jenny said. But although I saw Jenny constantly, she didn't talk a lot about what she did with her family when they were alone, so I had to piece it together from the little bits of information she gave me, assemble them carefully in my mind the way that other people paste photographs of their families in a scrapbook, so I could keep my own record of their unseen lives.

There were a couple of moments when I got really near Peter, sometimes within arm's length. I sat across from him at dinner once when Jenny finally asked me to spend the night. And when she and I lay talking on her bed, he came in to joke with her before going out. He smiled at me, but he didn't actually say anything, not even hello, and I've never said a word to him. So I'm not expecting much tonight, but expecting nothing in a house where he might show up seems better than expecting a lot someplace where there's no chance of seeing him at all.

I want my parents to drive off, but I can hear the motor running as I go up to the door. Halfway, I turn and wave, and my father takes the hint; the car disappears suddenly into the fog, as if into a bank of clouds. The Hollanders' house stands by itself, a square of rough gray wood and glass floating on the dunes. It's the kind of house that'll look new even when it's old. Jenny opens the door. 'Hi, Kate,' she says and grabs my arm. 'Let's go to my room.'

Her mother comes out of the kitchen and smiles at me. Jenny has told me that her real name is Charlotte, but everyone calls her M.S., short for Mother Superior. She wears her hair in a braid down her back, pale as a river of cream. 'Jenny,' she says, 'I've got two cases of coke; is that enough?' We pass an open door, and I can see Henry Hollander reading in his study.

At Jenny's dressing table, I let her fiddle with my hair. 'I've got plans,' she says, 'but don't ask me. I've been working on them a long time and I want you to look good tonight.' Ever since she met me, she's been fascinated by my dark red hair, wanting to brush it, comb it, try it new ways. The attention my hair gets annoys me; kids point and strangers strike up conversations, interrupting my dreams. I haven't been interested in my own body since a man dropped dead in front of me on Market Street. He was walking toward me, and lurched at me so suddenly that I bumped into him. A man about sixty. I said, 'I'm sorry.' He put out his hand as if to ward me off, farted twice and fell at my feet. After that I saw that taking any pleasure in your own body is like falling in love with a known killer. But the Hollanders seem to be made of some stuff that's open, honest, durable, benign. They are the exception to every rule.

The first time I saw Jenny undress, her faultless body, the fairness of her skin, made me uneasy. I knew I'd be afraid to look like that. Naked in front of a mirror, she was blind to her own reflection, unaware of all that immaculate flesh just begging for the clawmarks of a wallflower world. She's full of unplanned affection, like a child, and her goodness anticipates goodness, so nice things always happen to her.

When Jenny finishes with my hair I follow her down the hall. I've always disliked the bleak airiness of this house, especially the enormous living room, almost empty except for a couple of chairs and a sofa as long as a train. The carpet is dusty white, like a desert under a winter sky. There aren't any pictures, not a single book.

The party is in the den. I watch Jenny dancing with her boyfriend, Bill Lewis, while from the other side of the room the middle brother Mark squints at me as if I'm tiny print. Several girls from school are there, and some friends of Mark's. When M.S. brings in a bowl of potato chips, a few spill to the floor and the youngest brother, Eric, who's being allowed to watch the older kids from the edges of the party, steps back with a crunch. 'Get me a broom.' M.S. points. 'So I can clean up this shit.' A strong face, almost a statesman's face: long straight nose, eyes high up and set wide. She's tall, and I suspect she never checks on her good looks, that she knows they're always there, like the sand and the sky and the water.

To me she seems both more, and less, than other mothers: more because she brandishes her love for her kids, brings their lunches to school so they'll be fresh, and because once, when the principal suspended Mark for smoking in the john she told him to go fuck himself; less because she's either abandoned or never developed any feminine characteristics. Not for her the card parties and evanescent teacups, the weighty tablecloths and candles stern as pikestaffs that other mothers affect. She glances at me and I get the feeling that if she touches me – or even thinks about me – some kind of current will go through me, give me a fit and leave me thrashing. For a long time after I first met her, I didn't like to stand too close. She bends to sweep under the table and I see Mark pat her bottom, hear her laugh.

When Peter comes in, Mark and his friends surround him like an honour guard. He looks like a different, enchanted aspect of his mother: taller, blonder, but still her, a miracle that she has made. He's very tan, and Jenny has told me that he spends a lot of time down at Santa Cruz, riding a surfboard. With her eyes on me, Jenny goes up to him. My hands begin to shake. As she and Peter come toward me, everybody's watching. I feel as if we're lit by footlights. Jenny stands between us, arms folded, smiling first at Peter and then at me. Outside the dunes rise like snowbanks, and the seals are quiet down in Kelly's Cove.

I say, 'I hear you walk on water.'

2

PETER: It's the first time she's opened her mouth to me,
           Jenny's little friend. A surprise, hearing her up close
– nice vanilla voice that strokes me in all the right places. But
she's always had great legs. Jenny's over there giggling with Bill
Lewis. A pain in the ass. Now that she's pulled it off, she doesn't
know what to do next.

About a year ago, I tell Kate, I'm out at the beach running,
and I meet this guy Keoki. Keoki Makaina. He's a Hawaiian,
from the big island. Must weigh two hundred and fifty pounds,
and the first time I see him he's tucked up into a wave like a fish,
slaps right down the front of it, and bellies into the beach. It
looks great, and when I ask him what it is, he tells me it's
bodysurfing, and if I can get my hands on a car he'll show me
something really fantastic.

A couple of days later we cruise down to Santa Cruz in M.S.'s
blue convertible, a couple of redwood boards sticking out of the
back like straws from a soda. Keoki's borrowed them from the
cousins he's staying with in Chinatown. When I help him load
them into the car I figure they must each weigh close to a
hundred pounds. Round noses, square tails. Brutal, like
battering rams.

On the coast highway we hit a cold fog, but Keoki doesn't
seem to notice. Arms folded, he stares straight ahead.

'What's Hawaii like?' I say.

'In Hawaii, everybody find what they want to find – good
more good, bad more bad. In Hawaii, every bruddah look in
your face; on mainland, bruddahs and sistahs look other way.'

'How long are you here for?'

'I go back in three days.' He yawns and pulls up his shirt. 'I
know judo, black belt. Say you put brick on *opu*.' He slaps his
belly, big as the barrel of a tree. 'Hit with hammer. Brick get
busted, but *opu* plenty good.'

'I believe it,' I say. 'Just so it doesn't slip and get your pecker.'

I watch from the deserted beach while he paddles out. By the pier gulls nick the skin of the water, hunting for sardines. Keoki is on his knees, big arms sculling. Fierce scent of eucalyptus drifting down from the cliffs, and I can smell the woods up north, see our tent in Mayesville. Every summer when we were little, M.S. took us camping, left my father to shift for himself in the city. I chopped her firewood, she rubbed my sore back and fried our hash in a pan as big as a shovel. I loved to watch her slamming pots on the Coleman stove or putting up the tent. She swore a lot, but it just seemed like an extra language she wanted us to learn, better from her than from strangers.

Half a mile offshore, Keoki straddles his board. A wave bumps up and he gets to his feet, skimming across the water, coming diagonally at the beach. Beautiful, dangerous and dignified: a maharajah on the back of an elephant.

I throw the other board in the water. 'Hey,' he calls, 'you learn paddle first.'

'Listen, I want to *ride* this son of a bitch.'

'No, *you* listen, *haole*. No learn paddle, you get bad wipeout, mebbe drown. If no do what I say, no show you.'

'Okay. Where do we start?'

'You learn *paddle*. Lie down on board; lift chin. Like this, bruddah.' He raises his head. 'Put arms in water, pull hands back like *fork*, no sideways like knife. Need da kine *power*. In big surf, look for . . . water *halula*.' With the flat of his hand, he traces a line on my board. 'Da kine sleepy water.'

The sky clears by noon. In Martignetti's on the pier, the long-haired, long-waisted waitress takes our order. The chowder is pink and creamy, and there's fresh hot bread. 'Plenty *wahine* in Hawaii,' says Keoki, staring at the waitress' ass. 'Plenty women. Mainland women look like mad aunties.' I slide a tip under the saucer, and Keoki wipes his mouth. 'Now you ride one wave, we see what you can do. What I show you, no many *haoles* know – my cousin say mebbe few guys in L.A.'

Our boards slip easily over the kelp idling in the water. Ahead of us the first wave is breaking. I lift myself up on my hands and the water fans easily between me and my board. I'm not quick enough with the next one and I get a headful of water. I cough and choke, but two waves ahead Keoki doesn't see me.

The only time I've ever really thought about drowning was one night in the tent at Mayesville, my light and air sucked up, my lungs slack, empty as popped paper bags. 'Sit up,' says M.S. quietly so the other kids won't hear. Her hands on my shoulders pulling me out into the light from the lantern. 'You were jammed down in your sleeping bag.' She runs her fingers through my hair. 'Stop that whimpering. You're safe; you've got me for a mother, haven't you?'

The next day she gives me a shovel. 'See that clearing over there? Go dig a hole about two feet deep, about this big around.' She makes a circle of her arms. 'That's the latrine. And *nobody* shits any place else.'

I've just finished digging when M.S. comes out of her tent. 'Peter,' she says, 'don't move. There's a rattler behind that rock. Lift the shovel and bring the blade down hard, right behind its head.' I raise the shovel. The snake is very beautiful, its buzz and whirr like the crickets that put me to sleep at night. '*Now.*' The snake swings it eyes towards me. 'Do you *hear* me?' M.S.'s voice flattens the grassy sound of the snake.

So fast I can't stop her, she grabs the shovel and, neat as slicing cucumbers into a bowl, she cuts off its head. Jenny screams. I turn away so M.S. can't see me crying. 'Pick it up,' she says, 'and hand it to me.' With my eyes closed, I hold out the snake like a gift, its body folded, end to end. 'Watch this,' she says. Swinging it like a lariat, she gives a whoop and lets it fly smack dab into the trunk of a tree. Running down, its insides are light red and a tender creamy yellow, as if it was very young.

'We stop here,' says Keoki, and my heart jumps. He's maneuvered his board so we're only a few feet apart. 'Now. You sit plenty far out, find *your* wave: mebbe last wave in set, mebbe second last, you learn pick for *you*.'

'How can you tell what's a good wave?'

'If shoulder – green part – no broke yet. If it look like it hold you up good, then paddle hard.'

'Then what?'

'If you lose board, no come up right away, or board crack your head. You find place now.'

Bright swells are forming. On my knees I stroke deep and

glance over my shoulder. Above and to my left is a thin line of foam. I pull again; the nose of my board dips, and the tail rises. I'm dropping down, and the hard momentum of the descent is unexpected: the wave has caught me, and not the other way around. When it starts to break up, I'm pitched headfirst off my board.

It's like being pressed under a mattress. I try to push for the top, but the whitewater brewing overhead drags me along. I let it take me where it wants, and surface thirty feet from the board. Treading water, I see Keoki drop down slick on a wave and clip toward the beach; at the end of the ride he steps back and the nose shoots up like the prow of a ship. 'Hey, you son of a bitch,' I shout. 'You'd have looked pretty funny if I never came up.'

'I know you come up. This just practice.' He doesn't smile. 'Now you stand up, ride,' he says when we've paddled out again.

'What's the surf like in Hawaii?'

'On big island where I live is place with one fine wave. Wave so tall, make you *pupule*.' He taps his forehead. 'One time after wipeout I plenty scared, I say, shit, this next wave coming big as mountain. Then I see this *is* mountain; I mixed up, turned toward shore.' Swells are wheeling in and he gets to his knees. 'Remember – when bodysurf, curl up like baby; on board stand up like man.' He scratches into the wave, half hidden at first by the hump of water, then tall and ingenious ahead of the spray.

After the set goes by, the water has a sour look. I rub my arms to keep out the cold. Something splashes and I see the shiny head of a seal; bandy whiskers dripping, it glides toward me, snorts, dives, swims between my legs. Suddenly it surfaces in a half twist, shoots a couple of feet out of the water, and slaps its flipper down splat on my board.

Behind it a wave is sweeping up. The seal nudges my wrist with its nose and I put my hands in the water, pulling hard. The board hesitates, then drops smoothly. In a crouch, I get to my feet, but I can't tell how fast the board is moving. What happens if I fuck up in tons of cold water? As I bend into the ride the seal swings away, going over the top. I look back: behind me a white scar – a sign, a proof that I exist – on the curve of the wave.

I slide all the way in before the board loses momentum and I fall off. Outside, another set is beginning to line up, and I can see the seal hanging like a teardrop in the water.

3

KATE: It's late in the day and Peter is waiting for me on the beach. He's built himself a hut not far from Kelly's Cove, where tourists eat foggy lunches and old seals lie shiny as kelp on the rocks. He's asked me to meet him out here, so I suppose you can call it our first date. There's an oily smell on the breeze, and the sand is the colour of ashes. My pace is even, but my legs are stiff; I know he's watching me. His blond hair is visible a long way off, and I begin to have inklings, premonitions. The ends of my bandana snap in the wind.

'I'll make a fire,' he says.

I help him gather kindling, and he jams it in spokes under a log. Flames hop out, the glow casting a racy light on his naked shoulders. When he slips a sweater over his head, the curves of his arms and back are as smooth as deep-sea animals.

'You know a lot about making fires,' I say.

'M.S. taught us when she took us camping.'

'Not your father?'

'He only came up on weekends. Except during the war when he was on Tinian; he helped plan the drop on Nagasaki.' He takes some carrots from a paper bag, puts a pan of water on a grill. 'Mark and Jenny don't know.' He holds up a newspaper-wrapped bundle. 'I caught this perch a little while ago. It should be nice and fresh.'

'I'll rinse the carrots,' I say. Kneeling, I dip them in a little wave. It's a small act, but it feels significant, as if I'm not going to have to depend on faucets or sinks or running water any more because everything I will ever need is right here on the beach. He takes the dripping carrots, cuts them with a penknife into chunks and drops them into the pan.

'What is it about surfing?' I say. 'The speed, or what?'

'I guess it's that what you *can* do gets to be more fantastic than what you can't. I like to paddle in after the last ride and know

I'm going to live another day – with my arms and legs, with everything going.' He pours rice from a Mason jar into the pan with the carrots. 'No bullshit: every time you come up after being wiped out, it's like a blind man getting back his sight.'

'I've never met anyone like you,' I say. 'It's like I'm reading about you in a book.'

'Don't say that.'

'Why not?'

'People see me, the way I look, and try to make me into something I'm not.' He goes into the hut and comes out with a blackened skillet. 'Does your name come from a book? Are you "Kiss me Kate" from Shakespeare?'

'No, from Katharine Hepburn. My mother likes to go to the movies.' I watch him sink the pan with the rice and the carrots into the ashes and put the skillet on the grill. 'It's neat being on the beach, but I never learned how to swim.'

'Why not?' The light on his face is like a mask.

'I've been so busy reading, I guess I just never got round to it.'

'What do you read?' With a paint scraper he scoops fat from a coffee can and drops it into the skillet.

'Right now, Joseph Conrad. Guys all cooped up in a boat, rolling close together in a storm. One of them is dying and the sailors love him and they hate him – he could be their father. It seems like they're either the first people in the world, or maybe the last, like they were hatched from a speck of mineral on a reef somewhere, down by the Cape of Good Hope. They're only alive and thinking when they're on the water. And the ship thinks, too. Everything is connected to everything else: the men, the words, the ship, the weather.'

'You really like that stuff. Most girls wouldn't.'

'It's funny, but sometimes life on that ship sounds really cosy, except everything they see and do doesn't have any limit, just like the water. Even when the storm stops and the guy finally dies, you get the feeling that it's all going to keep happening, and you're going to be sailing with them for the rest of your life.'

'For someone who doesn't know how to swim, you seem pretty interested in the water.'

'It's not just the water, it's the people.'

'Yeah, but guys on *ships*?' He lays the neatly gutted fish in the pan.

'Why not? My favourite is Billy Budd. He's a friendly innocent guy – a sailor – and he's so good nobody can believe it. But in the end they hang him, which is really kind of ironic.'

Peter tilts the pan to spread the fat. 'He sounds like my seal. Did he have big brown innocent eyes?'

'It says he was "welkin-eyed".'

'What the hell is that?'

'It's like the sky. My parents made me learn a lot of weird words when I was growing up.'

'Didn't they ever let you have any fun?'

'They never let me forget I was the only one, and now I think they'd love it if I was suddenly a hundred years old, right now this minute, so they could prove they did it – you know, got me through life safe and sound.'

'My old man is ape-shit on safety.' He pokes at the fire with a stick. 'That's why he's sending me to college, even though he knows I can't hack it and never wanted to go. What's safe for ten thousand other guys isn't safe for me – do you know what I mean?'

'Yes,' I say. 'I do.'

'I don't know. My head works better than my mouth, and whenever I try to explain something, it comes out sounding half-assed.' A flurry of fat heightens the fire, and he lifts the pan. 'When I was little I was always warm and clean, and everything felt good – even my clothes didn't weigh very much. But the thing is, I didn't ask for all that, and by the time I was six I knew none of it was for free. I knew I was going to have to find a way to *buy* trouble or I wasn't going to make it; that I had to put everything up for grabs or it was all going to be taken away. It's funny – now that I'm not a kid anymore, my mother really digs it whenever I put my ass on the line. When I played football, I never got the great feelings I do surfing; whatever play you call, you know all these people are watching, and there's never any real danger. But riding a surfboard you can drown alone.'

'If my mother knew all that,' I say, 'she'd never let me play with you.'

He reaches over and pulls my arms out from under me. Unpropped, I topple back, but as I fall he catches me, turning me so I lie face up in his lap. When he bends down, I go right under, as if giving myself up to surgery that can save my life. He stops the kiss before I do; embarrassed, I sit up.

We eat the fish and the rice and the carrots off cracked plates, and when it gets cold he wraps me in his sweater.

After that he doesn't give me enough time without him to wonder when I'll see him again. Under the outdoor lights at Fairfax we dance, holding each other in constantly shifting experimental grips. (Peter's white shirts dazzling, emblematic; ceremonious as a suit of armor.) Go with Jenny and Bill Lewis to the movies, where we whisper in the loges; afterwards in the ladies' room Jenny and I chew quick sticks of gum before going up to park on Twin Peaks. Watch Dirty Joe score for the Shamrocks with a few gingerly taps of his stick as if the puck is a red-hot checker; in seventy-degree weather, sing 'Baby, it's Cold Outside' on the way home. On gray afternoons, walk to Playland, eat Bull Pups and It-Bars and chocolate-covered bananas on a stick; thread our conversation over and under the amplified fat laughter from the Funhouse, the grind of the rollercoaster on the rise, the screams and volleys of its descent.

In June, in the clarity of spring, I cut bonds, tidy friendships, make amends. The Hollanders have invited me to spend the summer in Redwood Creek.

4

CHARLOTTE: Believe me, I never forget that she's infil-
trated us. I just don't have a bead yet on
what she wants. I watch her getting close to my children and I
wonder what she'll steal, store up, carry away. She's not as
pretty as Peter's other girls and I don't know why he bothers
with her. But of course I know what she wants from him: his
face, his grace, his big beautiful arms, his dreamy head. She
draws him in with her stories, asks questions, and he never sees
what she's doing. With all that red hair, she's definitely a
stranger, the last of some wild disbanded tribe.

I sprinkle flour on the table, slap down a ball of dough. The
kids – and Kate – will be home from the beach soon. Have to get
these pies done, some shirts ironed for the boys, and a couple of
blouses for Jenny. Hank's coming down from the city tonight;
needs some clothes ready to take back up on Sunday. The kids
call me Mother Superior – which is true, and it shows they're
grateful. I've never given them any reason to doubt that my love
for them is as reliable as time. I don't believe in letting them do
anything for themselves – mainly because, whatever it is, I can
do it better than anybody else. And because I want their lives to
be perfect now. As perfect as they are. They'll have plenty of
time later to learn how to work.

I turn on the radio. ' . . . beautiful day here at Seals Stadium,'
the guy says, as if everybody doesn't already know it. I reach for
my rolling pin. Only four, but already it's getting dark in the
kitchen; our cabin is so deep in the woods, we're completely
surrounded by trees. The creek passes by at the back, roaring
through the summer, chilling us all as it goes. Hank bought this
land five years ago, right after V-J Day, and we built the cabin
the following spring. When it was done I was tempted to sell the
house in the city, yank the kids out of school, and live all year
round here in Redwood Creek.

It's a tiny town, almost a frontier town. At the head of the one street sits Davy's Bar – deep and serene at noon, but feisty at night. It's a short, wide street, open-ended, so it's easy to see everybody who comes and goes. On all four sides, hills and big formal trees, a lot of land nobody has ever set foot on. Up by the pool, a couple of summer cabins like ours. Not neighbours. Far apart. Which is the way I like it. In San Francisco we used to live near the park, and when the kids were little they were always asking to play with the Irish kids down the street. I told them no, I wanted them to stick together. But sometimes I couldn't prevent it.

Once I had to go into their house to get Peter. Dark furniture; smell of cabbage and mildew. The mother, still in bed, had just had her eighth kid. Over in one corner a white enamel basin with something in it that looked like stewed tomatoes. Blood, I think, from giving birth. Bright cheap statues of the Virgin all around the room, and a crooked crucifix over the crib. The six-year-old, who was Mark's age, grabbed my skirt. I could smell the crap in the poor kid's pants – I don't think she ever changed him. He kept making little noises, uncontrolled groans of excitement or pleasure, as if he was coming all the time. I squeezed Peter's hand and took him home. Why he should have to be around blood and defectives I didn't know, when I always took such pains with my children to keep them clean and fresh. Right after that we moved into our house at the beach and, to my relief, none of the other families out there had any kids their age.

I roll the bottom crust a little thin and it tears in the middle. 'Shit,' I say, wondering if I can patch it. A sound on the gravel outside. Could that be the kids home already? No, it's quiet again, and I know it was some kind of animal. They're amazingly bold in these woods: not enough humans yet to make them cautious. The kids will be hungry when they get here. Up every morning at six, they take the Studebaker into Santa Cruz. Peter is teaching them all to surf and Kate, tired and shivery in the early morning, always goes along; in an old sweatshirt of Peter's, she reads on the beach. They're back by nine, and at ten I drive everybody up to the pool, where Peter's the lifeguard. While I do my shopping in town, Jenny and Kate play canasta under one of the yellow umbrellas. Kate doesn't go in the water, but my children, brown as bread, swim laps or practice the butterfly stroke. Every year they win the local swimming competition and people like to watch them train.

Hank comes down every weekend, and on Sundays Kate and the boys sleep in while Jenny and I go to Mass. After supper the kids play hearts or go to the dance up at the pool, and everybody's in bed by midnight. The boys each have a cot at one end of the sleeping porch, and Jenny and Kate share an old double bed at the other. I have the only bedroom.

I wet the tear in the crust with a couple of drops of water and pinch the edges together. The light filtering in through the trees is the color of rust, and makes the kitchen look like an old photograph. Here in the California woods everything is hidden, camouflaged by trees. But on the Nebraska prairie where I grew up you can see your friends and enemies coming at you. The prairie is so big that when I was little I actually believed that if I ever got to the end of it I'd be on the edge of the world, in danger of falling off. Windmills popped out of the earth like daisies, and I thrived on the isolation; I didn't even like going into Bellamy, where Papa ran the general store. On cold nights my sisters and I lay pressed together in our big bed, hearts seething at the coyotes' cries. Sometimes we fetched our younger brother, wrapped him in our warmth. Lucas was the only boy, and all our hopes had been for him. Beautiful Lucas, dead at the age of seven.

'So far,' says the announcer smugly, 'he's given up a double and two walks.' I don't like him; I think he's biased. I turn the dough.

Every inch of my childhood, every memory, was shaped by the weather. Clouds like blackened buildings shot up into the sky. Heavy rains beat down the gardens, and always by summer two or three people were lost in quick-rising streams. Our house danced to the sound of thunderclaps; lightning could bore a hole in your roof.

'And he's safe,' brags the announcer. 'On deck Ferris Fain pinch-hitting for Clement Easley. . . . '

Why, do they always say pin-*shitting*? I look at the clock. Any minute now the kids will be home from the beach. I love the blue prairie my children ride. But when I came west at the age of eighteen everything about California shocked me. It was surprising to find a city where the houses sit as tight on the hills as a comb on a rooster's head. In Nebraska, when my father drove us home in the buckboard after a fair, the lights of a farmhouse could seem very near, but it took us so long to get there that the house might have been in Tibet. The land was bare, and sometimes when it shimmered in the afternoon light, I thought that the earth had tipped and I was walking on a sunset sky.

Pies in the oven, I go out on the porch to shake out the kids' sleeping-bags, pick up. Jenny's rosary has fallen between the floor-boards and gently I pry it out. Darling dainty Jenny; hair streaming like the light from a star. 'Here's the pitch . . . hit deep. . . . ' I stick my head around the door, trying to hear the radio in the kitchen. ' . . . and Hunsdorfer delivers a beauty into left field . . . I think it's gone . . . it's out of here!' My Seals losing, and the announcer can hardly hide his glee.

Dirty shirt under Peter's bed, Mark's shorts on a chair; blouse and bra of Jenny's on a hook. Rubbing their clothes over my nose and mouth I suck in their sharp and different smells. Just being near my kids, touching any part of them, gives me as much pleasure as sleeping with a man. Every time I have a baby I like to stroke its body, hold it in the palms of my hands, bite its buttocks as a mother cat does her kittens.

But no more babies now. Sometime I regret all the screwing Hank and I have done, see my pleasure in it as a kind of weakness. But when I'm honest I'll admit that the real reason I'm ashamed is because I loved the way it felt and the babies it brought, but not the man who screwed me. He's good-looking, smart. When he married me I was a file clerk in his office. I thought that I loved him. But as soon as my first baby came, I discovered what love really is.

5

KATE: There's a kink in the coast at Santa Cruz so that late in the day the sun slopes behind the mountains instead of into the sea. The afternoon is humming, spinning, smooth as a top, and as I turn the pages of my book I'm conscious of the changing pattern of Hollanders, like birds settling on the swells. Cars stop on the cliffs now so people can watch, and strangers come down the sandy path to ask me about them; who they are, what they're doing. I say that Peter learned to ride the water from a Hawaiian, and that they wax their boards to keep their feet from slipping. I try to answer kindly, controlling an arrogance that's new in me. At the end of every afternoon Peter sits on the beach with me, and talks about the Japanese current that warms the water and the Humboldt current that cools it; about the seal he calls Billy Budd who surfs with him out at the point.

I don't like to admit this, but I've already sacrificed a lot of what I am, just to be with Peter. (Some of the changes – I guess – are for the better: in my new role as Peter's 'girlfriend' I've stopped mending my slip straps with safety pins, and sometimes I remember to shave under my arms.) Basically I've become an amnesiac, truly living for the moment, dumb to what I was, helplessly kidnapped from my past. I know that I used to exist in a different world, and I know that I exist right now, but I can't tell you what I was then or how I manage to stay alive now, when or what I eat, how many hours of sleep I get. My grades are still good, but I study mechanically, without any flair or passion, and when I get an A I'm not excited or surprised. I've trained myself to concentrate even when my mind isn't on it (which it isn't), because I owe it to my parents to get a scholarship to Berkeley, and I will. But my real mind and energy are no more engaged than if I was packing fruit in a cannery in San Jose. I've started to regret all the time I spent studying, the years of silent wrestling that now seem selfish and petty, lacking in imagination. For years my mother told me that I should 'bring' myself to the 'right man' fresh and pure, as if I was a drink of water. But nothing I studied, and nothing my mother said, got me ready for Peter. The only thing I could 'bring' him that he would understand would be to do something crazy like putting myself in some kind of physical danger and coming out of it without a scratch.

A wave hits the pilings under the pier and shoots to the side. I stick a marker in my book and close it. Water is always unreasonable. Once, Peter got me to straddle a board just off-shore. He sat next to me, and after a wave had broken further out, he pushed my board into the foam so it would take me in. On my stomach, my face close to the edge, I could see bubbles fanning across the water, like wildflowers in grass. But the board tilted, almost chucking me off the nose, and Peter said I better not go out again until I learned to swim.

Mark props his board against the bathhouse and, without looking at me, goes into Martignetti's. He never speaks to me unless he has to. Jenny apologizes: Mark is very shy, she says. But I notice he spends a lot of time talking to Georgia, the long-waisted waitress. Her father is old man Martignetti.

Eric runs up the beach, calling me. 'Hey, Kate, Billy Budd's out there, and Peter wants us to watch.'

I think about Peter's seal every day, dream about him most nights. How far up and down the coast does he wander? What sea-forests and valleys does he know? What murky illuminations? Does he slap sides with a dolphin, a whale? Glide among fish more mysterious than planets, twinkling and poisonous pinpricks of light? Does he lie in the hard black water and puzzle with his snout the inconstancy of the moon?

The fog is in, and my suit is cold and damp. I can't wait to change, but Peter stays out with Billy so late we don't get home till six.

M.S. comes out to meet us. 'You kids are late; Daddy's already here. For Christ's sake, Eric, I'll unload that board. You're scratching the car.'

Jenny kisses her. 'We saw Billy Budd ride with Peter. He

made Peter wait out four waves before giving him the go-ahead. It was neat.'

'How big, Peter?' says M.S., Eric's board balanced on her head.

'Seven, maybe eight foot.'

Mark sips from a bottle of milk. 'I got a ding in my board.'

'I'll fix it later,' she says, 'if you've got some varnish. Don't bother my ass with it now.'

He wipes his mouth. 'Why's she so witchy?'

'Seals lost in extra innings.' His father has come out of the cabin with a bourbon and water. Blond and symmetrical, he looks exactly like his wife, but even though people say he's a famous lawyer, it's hard for me to believe he's very important.

'Hey, guys – hear that? Seals lost. Everybody cater to M.S., or I won't get my board fixed tonight.'

While Jenny washes her hair and I change in the bedroom, M.S. deploys her dinner pans on the stove. Every night I offer to help her, and every night she runs Jenny and me out of the kitchen. Jenny tells me that her father has offered to get M.S. a maid, but that M.S. said that she could do by herself what needed doing, and a lot more besides. I try to imagine an M.S.-trained maid answering the phone: 'Hollander residence – what do you want, you creep?' Or: 'Mrs Hollander is not at home to you; you give her a pain in the ass.' I look up, surprised at the sight of myself in M.S.'s mirror. On the porch Peter and his brothers are playing blackjack, and I can hear Henry Hollander in the kitchen talking to his wife: 'That's some headlight she's got on her forehead.' Jingle of ice in his drink.

'Yeah, with that red hair.'

'But why does she have them? None of ours do.'

'She needs a good dosing out with castor oil, that's all.' The icebox door snaps to.

I don't like the way they talk about me, the way they never care whether I can hear them or not. I want Peter a lot, but not enough to listen to his parents size me up like a piece of livestock they're buying for the barn. I open a drawer and slam it.

'You've got to get the kids out of the way tonight,' says Henry Hollander. 'Last week I was so horny I stuck it in a jar of jam.'

'Well, I hope you threw the jam out – we don't need any extra vitamins.'

On the word 'vitamins' I come out into the kitchen. Let them wonder how much I heard of *that*. 'Hi,' I say, smiling. 'Is everybody out on the porch?'

After dinner Mark lays down some kindling, while I try to finish my book. M.S. comes out of the kitchen. 'You aren't putting the wood down right,' she says. 'Toss me that piece.' She jumps. 'Watch what you're doing – it got me right in the snatch.'

Henry Hollander folds his newspaper. 'There's a fly in here, and it's not going to go away. Can one of you kids get it?'

'Don't kill it,' says Peter.

Mark looks up. 'I see it; give me the paper, Dad.'

'What's this shit about not killing flies?' M.S. says. 'I hope you never have to defend yourself, Peter.'

'That's got the son of a bitch.' Mark tosses his father the paper.

'I defend myself in the water every day.' Peter lights the kindling. 'And if I had to, I know how to kill a man with one blow.'

'That's neat,' says Eric. 'How?'

Slowly I close my book.

'You hit him with the side of your hand. Here.' He points to his Adam's apple. 'Keoki showed me; he's a black belt.'

'And he's got a black skin,' says M.S.

'M.S. hates niggers.' Mark throws another stick into the flames.

'No, I don't,' she says, and everybody laughs but me. 'You kids better get ready. It's almost nine.'

As we're climbing into the blue convertible, Henry Hollander puts an arm around his wife. 'Take that money I gave you,' he tells Peter, 'and buy everyone a hamburger in town after the dance.'

M.S. smiles. 'And take your time: your father wants to show me his French tickler.'

The sun is a long white line on my shins. I sit on my towel watching Peter giving swimming lessons at the shallow end of the pool. M.S., carrying a stopwatch, runs up and down on the other side. Mark is swimming laps, and through the loud-speaker Vic Damone is singing about a love that can't happen again, telling us it was 'once in a lifetime', a 'thrill divine'. He sounds sad, like he might slit his wrists, but people go right on laughing and playing cards. On a breeze, the hot scent of bathing caps and baby oil – smells I always associate with that first wide-open summer; with young fruit and new grass, with bodies that don't give any clues about what will happen later.

'Two tenths better than yesterday,' M.S. says when Mark climbs out of the water. 'But you're still swinging your ass like a goddam wrecking ball. And watch your hand entry. We'll try it again when I'm done with Eric.'

Off-duty, Peter has been trying to teach me how to swim. 'Here,' he'll say, throwing some pennies into the shallow end, 'see if you can pick these up.' But the water fights back like a tough piece of steak. 'You see how hard it is to get to the bottom,' he says. 'Your body is naturally buoyant. Don't tense up and you won't sink.' But before I met Peter I'd never been in more water than our tub at home will hold. I've never even thought about swimming, and when I look at that cement casket full of water I have my doubts. Water is not my element or habitat.

M.S. drops her towel down beside mine and puts her stopwatch in the canvas bag she always carries. 'You know, Kate, it must be pretty embarrassing for Peter: he's the swimming instructor – and his girlfriend can't even swim. Think about it.'

'Why should he be embarrassed? There are far worse things than not knowing how to swim.' I think of her bookless house, her sweeping ignorance of art, of history, of ideas.

As if she hasn't heard me, M.S. tugs on her braid. 'It's funny,' she says, 'I can never get over how much both Jenny and Peter look like my brother Lucas: especially Jenny.'

Whenever she mentions her brother, I'm surprised: she's so full of energy, so complete, I can't imagine her parents having enough protoplasm left over for another kid. 'Does your brother still live in Nebraska?'

'No, he was careless. He died. A long time ago.' She moves her towel into a circle of shade under an umbrella. 'I'm getting a hot box from sitting in the sun.' On the edge of the pool Jenny is talking to Eric. 'Aren't my children beautiful?' She points.

I nod. I don't know what to say.

'Jenny was such a dimity, dotted-Swiss little girl, but I was a big kid, not dainty at all. When she was born, she was so beautiful the nurses couldn't believe it. I had my first three babies as close together as a rabbit drops its turds. Peter was the only one who wasn't exceptional right away. He was a sad little baby, and he puked a lot. But he had a prick you wouldn't believe, always peeing in my face.' Under the next umbrella, a woman snaps the leg of her two-piece Mabs, and I wonder if she can hear. 'I used to be embarrassed when I changed his diapers and one of my girlfriends saw him. He was just like a man. They'd turn away.' She looks at her watch. 'I've got to get some groceries. Those kids open the icebox so much, I'm surprised they don't all get pneumonia.'

When Peter and I are walking back to the cabin, I say: 'Have you been to Nebraska?'

'No.'

'Have your grandparents ever come out to California?'

'No.' He kisses my bare shoulder. 'M.S. never writes them, or gets letters. I'm not even sure they're still alive.'

On my last day in Redwood Creek, I get up early. Jenny and Peter are still asleep, but Eric is standing on the porch listening to the birds. He's smiling. I dress and go down to the creek. The water is so fresh and clear it seems no more than a strong wind blowing over the rocks. A huge pine flashes against the sky, but further down the needles are a cold green, as dark as the bottom of the sea. Peter has told me that as a kid he spent a lot of time with these trees, that he thought of them as mystical beings ('ghosts' he called them) who came out to shine on him every day, but disappeared into the dark at night.

Mark is coming down the hill. When I left the cabin he was in the kitchen with M.S. He picks up a pebble. 'I don't like strangers,' he says. 'Strangers who live in my house.'

'I'm not a stranger – not to Jenny and Peter.'

'Yes you are.' He flips the pebble into the air. 'And you always will be.'

6

CHARLOTTE: I've always taken the spotless bodies of my children for granted, and when I see the little bruise on Jenny's arm I'm surprised. The other kids are already gone, and she's in the kitchen putting on a blouse, drinking some orange juice and eating a piece of bacon. 'Where did you get that?' I say, pointing to the bruise.

'I tripped over a rock last Saturday when we were down in Santa Cruz.'

'If you get bruises, you're being sloppy – be more careful.' I look at the clock. 'You're going to be late for school; I'll drive you.'

'Thanks, Mom, but I'll make it – don't worry.' Undoubtedly she's planning to meet her boyfriend, Bill Lewis, en route. Yesterday he gave her his football medal to wear on a chain around her neck, and she showed it to everybody – at least three times per person – last night. After she's gone, I fill up the pail, get my cloths and brushes from under the sink. It's Wednesday, my morning for doing the floors. On my knees, I shut my eyes intermittently as if praying; I'm seeing Jenny's bruise. It's strange that I can't remember finding a bruise on one of my children before. They were born flesh-perfect and, after an old age that will rest on them no more heavily than a snowflake, they'll be lowered, beauty intact, into their graves. But I've always regretted that the loveliness of my children is so public. I want to lock it up, keep it from the eyes of undeserving strangers; preserve it, no matter how. I never wanted to bronze any of my babies' shoes, but rather the whole kid. And I wanted to do it when they were older, at the hot spurt of maturity. I dream of four unchanging testimonies to my powers of creation.

I dip a cloth in the hot water and wring it out. I like scrubbing floors, getting rid of any unidentifiable grime the kids bring into the house. They go barefoot most of the year, so I keep the floors like silk. A baby could crawl around this house, swing its naked buns, without picking up a single splinter. I smear soft soap on my cloth and scour a small crack I discover in the corner of the dining room, but it's so superficial I can't even feel it with my fingers. Alone, my arm as well-trained and hardworking as any pitcher's, I think about the years when my children were very young. I do this a lot. I concentrate on one kid, retrace his personality from babyhood, examine in my mind every thread of his texture – where it began, when and how it became woven with another strand, and whether or not I can spot it among all the other threads today. I worry about Peter's monkish calm and passivity – but I've seen different threads. When he was seven and Mark six, Peter liked to bring me bunches of wildflowers. Mark laughed at him, called him a sissy. One day, Peter put down the flowers and, without a word, beat the shit out of him. I straighten up as the phone rings, and I can feel myself smiling.

'This is Officer Nolan from the San Francisco Police Department,' he says. 'Could I speak to a Mr or Mrs Hollander?'

'This is Mrs Hollander – what do you want?'

'I'm calling in reference to your daughter Jennifer. . . .'

'What about Jenny?' I say, maddened by his caution.

' . . . who was involved in an accident. . . .'

'Where?' I say. 'What kind of an accident, goddam it, and where?'

' . . . and has been transported to City Hospital. . . .'

I'm in my car in thirty seconds. I drive right out in the middle of the street, and on the way I scrape two cars, one at a red light and one moving, but nobody stops me. Jenny's on a gurney right outside the emergency room, and there's a cop with her writing in a notebook. No doctors or nurses, just the cop. 'Mrs Hollander?' he says. 'I'm Officer Nolan. I talked to you on the phone. . . .' His pen is in position on the pad, as if he's going to take down what I say, but I ignore him and tuck a strand of hair behind Jenny's ear.

'Hi, Mom,' she says. 'I'm late for school, so I guess you're going to have to write me a note.' She's talking okay, but her eyes are a little fruity.

'What happened?'

She blinks. 'It was like a bomb. . . .'

A young-looking doctor comes up, puts his arm around my shoulder. 'You're the mother?' He takes me several paces down the hall. 'She's okay,' he says. 'But she was lucky. There was an explosion on Mint Street – gas company doing some kind of excavation – and a couple of pieces of metal from one of the trucks hit your daughter. A few small lesions in the tissue of her left arm, and a good-sized one in her left leg. We'd just like to keep her here overnight to make sure there's no concussion, nothing internal. But she's going to be fine, just fine.'

After they take Jenny up to her room, I call Hank. 'Tell the kids they'll have to shift for themselves tonight and get supper,' I say. 'I'm staying here with Jenny.'

'The whole time? They'll kick you out,' he says.

'Let them try. I'll come home when I want to, and not before. I want to make sure everything's all right. When Mark had scarlet fever, that doctor didn't know his ass from a hole in the ground – I was the one who got the kid well.'

While I'm waiting for the elevator, I stand next to the cop. 'I was at the scene of the accident,' he says, 'and I don't believe it. Four men working on the site, real big explosion – a directional blast – and not one of them gets so much as a hangnail or a splinter.' He bends toward me, almost, you might think, as if I was going to explain it. 'And your daughter's halfway down the street, and she gets a piece of shrapnel, direct hit.' As I step into the elevator, he says, 'Even after writing out the report I'm not sure whether it was a freak or a miracle.'

Upstairs, Jenny has been tucked in bed as tight and neat as a bar of soap in its wrapper. 'I'm going to stay for as long you want,' I tell her when we're alone. She nods, but she doesn't say anything, which makes me think she's suffering a little from shock. I sit on the bed and take her hand. The hospital is so quiet, I can hear a foghorn croaking out in the bay. When the fog is really thick, it's impossible to see the dunes or even the other three houses on my street, and I like to imagine that only my children and I exist.

Jenny's mouth is open and she's panting a little. The cop said the accident was a freak or a miracle. Obviously a miracle, because here she is. But in a sense a freak: chunks of man-made crap coming at her because of the sloppiness of strangers. Of dumb hairy *idiots*. Glass and bricks and metal landing as thoughtlessly as a handful of jacks. And she only a little girl, clean and sweet right up to her eyes. A little girl walking to school.

The nurse said she fainted when they brought her in. I try not to think about how she looked. Her weakness was so public: was her mouth open while she was unconscious? I shudder, unable to believe that she could lose control over something as manageable as her own body. The Japanese are realistic about disgrace – it's easy to understand why they committed hara-kiri in the war.

'God, I want to go home,' Jenny suddenly says.

'You will. I'll make you some persimmon water. It'll heal everything right up – I learned it from my mother.' I draw back the covers, and put my lips to the little bruise on her arm. 'Soon,' I say. When I smooth the pillow, it's wet, and I realize she's been crying. 'Don't be afraid, darling. You've just got to be tough. If you don't trust what I say, try trusting in God.'

'My leg hurts.'

'Just relax. Remember: you've got your family on your side. We're all here to help you.'

'And Jesus.'

'Yes, and him too.'

'I'm too tired to pray.'

I take the beads from her fingers. 'Okay. Then I'll do it for you. Now try to relax.'

Jenny turns her face to the ceiling. A tear rolls down her temple, dies in her hair. How beautiful she is: Lucas given to me again.

Corinne and I are on one side of the table; on the other Abby sits next to Lucas' empty chair. Papa is cutting his meat, knife harsh. Mama rests her hands on either side of her plate, palms upturned, head dropped forward as if she has been unsuccessfully guillotined. I'm aware that Abby is watching me. Papa has looked at no one since Lucas died; and this is the first time Mama has eaten with us, having come out of her room only once, two days ago, to go to the funeral. The skies of early evening are still grey, the dirty petticoats of yet another spring storm to pass over Bellamy.

Corinne hands me the corn-bread and our fingers touch; I wonder if she draws hers too quickly away.

The storm has passed, but the tick of the clock in the parlour beats against the walls, a solid invisible rain. Lucas in his teak and satin nest tamped down in the ground. And, less than a mile from the house, in the space and privacy of the prairie, the wind circles Cathedral Rock. I imagine myself there, queenly on its rise. Cathedral Rock is a high blunt tower of stone set among a cluster of other less aggressive stones. It's an anomaly, geologically inexplicable. Whenever I approach it, the stones seem to lack colour, no matter where the sun is in the sky. The land around it is uncommonly still; and from a distance it's like an early photograph, a significant and somehow mysterious moment stopped out of time. Papa lifts his head, and when I understand that he is looking at me and at nobody else, I know that he is thinking that I went with Lucas to the rock on the day that he died. But he doesn't know all of it; how that night my head ached as if my soul was swollen, ready to burst behind my eyes; and how, the next morning my skull felt thin and damaged.

Papa blinks and his expression is hidden by the twitch of his lids as completely as his chin is hidden by his beard. The kerosene lamp is a mournful torch at the center of the table, its light painful, like sun striking ice. I try to concentrate on an earlier, more natural light: the pale prairie mornings when Lucas and I, up at dawn, chased red-tailed hawks as if they were butterflies.

7

KATE: My throat tickles, and I cough. I toss the French book
          onto the pile of papers at my feet. I've caught a cold
and been out of school four days. Christmas less than a month
off, and I'm trying to make up as much work as I can. I have a
job at the Post Office sorting mail for the holidays, and have to
be free and clear. But I can't study. I haven't seen or heard from
Peter in over a week. Jenny called me on Tuesday, but since
then nothing. And I've made it a rule never to call her. Even
after the summer in Redwood Creek, I don't want them to think
I worry, or chase Peter. I've sworn never to make a fool of myself
over him like other girls I've seen, girls with eyes as meaningless
as puddles reflecting an empty sky. I don't know why Peter
hasn't called; we haven't had a fight. But still I'm afraid that
tomorrow, when I go back to school, Jenny, out of respect for
our friendship, will have to tell me the truth – that Peter has
found somebody else.

My mother comes into the room rubbing lotion on her hands.
'Why don't you take a break? Berkeley doesn't care whether it's
an A or an A+.'

'You always say they really look at the transcript.'

'Believe me, you're fine. Going out with Peter seems to make
you work harder, which is more than I expected.' She strokes
some lotion under her eyes. 'Do you like his *family*?'

I tap my pencil on my book. 'They're different,' I say. 'They
throw a lot of food away.' My mother nods; she isn't surprised.
'It amazes me,' I say, knowing she wants more, 'but I don't
think they ever believe they'll come to an end.'

She goes downstairs and I look at my watch. If he's going to
call, it will be now. I draw a rocket-shaped surfboard in the
margin. I want to kiss his teeth, sweet as milk. His smell is
always in my nostrils, and I lie down with him in dreams; press

against him, put my lips in his hair; breathe in the fresh but ancient aroma of sunlight and salt. Being kissed by him is like being raised from the dead. Now maybe I'll never see him again. But even though I know the pleasure would be so great that I might pass out – swoon the way women do in old novels – I can't let him open me up as though we were married. I know he's done it with other girls, but something tells me that if I let him, I'll lose him, so it's better right now to make him use his imagination.

'Kate. Come set the table,' my mother calls from the foot of the stairs. I go into the kitchen and find her talking to Peter. They both look tired. My mother says, 'Go into the dining room, the two of you. Kate, set an extra place.'

I take the plates from the sideboard and begin putting them on the table. 'Peter, what is it?' When I look at him, he backs away.

'They've cut off Jenny's leg.'

'But why?' I whisper. Nothing in all my life of reedy dreaminess has prepared me for anything like this.

'Gangrene. Black blisters as big as a plum. She got hit in a gas explosion – an open main on the way to school. I was going to call you.' He puts his hand over his eyes. 'They cut this morning.'

'Did she . . . know?' I can see the doctors stunned and diminished by their own diagnosis.

'No. They had to take the whole leg.'

My father comes into the dining room. He touches Peter's shoulder, hands him a glass of bourbon and goes out again. 'M.S. is taking it hard,' Peter says. 'I've never seen her like this.' He closes his eyes and takes a sip of the whiskey. 'They're all at the hospital.'

When I'm alone later, I go carefully over Peter's words, trying to remember in the sounds and stillnesses anything that will make me believe that Jenny won't die. But he'd said, 'The doctors were crying when they came out of the operating room,' in a voice so low I could hardly hear him.

I'm taken by surprise when, two days later, Peter tells me M.S. wants to see me. Will I come to the hospital? 'Why?' I say, my voice trembling.

'I think she wants you to try to get through to Jenny. She's doped up, and in a lot of pain.'

When Peter and I arrive at the hospital, a nurse tells us that M.S. and the others are in Jenny's room. 'You two'll have to wait until they come out; we've let too many people in as it is.' She glances at Peter. 'Your mother can be very insistent.' Above the flawless uniform her face is pricked with pimples, the scars of old pimples, and blackheads. She points to a bench against the wall. 'You can wait there.'

I'm cold as we sit outside Jenny's room. Patients in wheelchairs glide past, creating a slight steamy breeze. Other patients in bathrobes of grey towelling stroll by; occasionally a nurse's shoe screeches on the linoleum. I want to get up and walk out. I want to go somewhere safe, want even to be in a cemetery; hospitals are full of hideous options, but cemeteries are full of peaceful facts. Jenny was innocently favoured until they trapped and hobbled her. She didn't know what they were doing to her on the operating table; perhaps didn't know even now. What was it like? Her honest breathing. The knife. The blade caught in the grain of the beautiful blind skin.

M.S., wearing a hospital gown, opens the door of Jenny's room. When she takes off the mask, her face is trembling. Henry Hollander, along with Mark and Eric, comes out a few seconds later. They're all wearing gowns. No one speaks, and Eric leans his head against the wall.

When she sees Peter and me, M.S. comes to sit with us. She puts her hand on my knee. 'She's said your name several times. But she hasn't asked for Bill Lewis at all. He calls every night, and I've told him he can't see her.' She taps her index finger on my thigh. 'I want you to go in there. She hasn't recognized anyone since she came out of the anaesthetic. I'm hoping maybe she'll know you.'

'I won't know what to say,' I murmur.

She leans across me, talking to Peter. 'She's still pretty doped up. The doctors are in there now, but you can go in. You'll have to put on some of this gear first.' She touches her gown. 'I'll get a nurse.'

When we're ready, M.S. opens the door. 'You're not supposed to touch anything,' she whispers as we go in.

The light is obscure, and at first it's difficult to see. I don't want to see; to have my faith in the Hollanders destroyed, my beautiful gods toppled and crushed like statues in a ransacked city. A peculiar odour hangs like a curtain in the room, and Peter winces. Gangrene smells like sour bread. Two doctors are bending over Jenny, their hands on her arms. She's grunting, wriggling, trying to sit up. A white screen stands at the foot of the bed. When Peter and I walk in, the two men glance at us, but continue to hold her down. The scene is shocking, like an interrupted rape.

One of the doctors says, 'Be a good girl, Jenny, don't thrash like that. If you lie still, we'll raise the bed so you can see your visitors.'

She groans and pulls one arm free.

They're cranking up her bed now, still trying to pin her arms. 'If she doesn't calm down, she's going to hurt herself,' says the other doctor. He pushes her against the pillow, turning her head so she can see Peter and me. He holds her by the jaw.

At first her eyes seem unfocussed, and for several seconds the room is silent. Then she stares at me and begins to scream. I can't move until one of the doctors touches my shoulder. He says, 'You better go.' Peter stays a few minutes longer, and kisses M.S. when he comes out.

Jenny's delirium, Peter tells me when he calls the next night, is caused by the gangrene as much as by the drugs they're giving her. And, as they'd expected, she's beginning to experience 'phantom limb', the sensation that she still has a leg, neat as a sausage, attached to her left hip. The chief surgeon told M.S. that gas gangrene was rare off the battlefield, and that it was frequently fatal. The infection has spread to Jenny's liver, and they're trying to control it with drugs and X-ray treatments. 'But they've warned us that the X-rays could make her sterile,' Peter says. 'Give her cancer by the time she's thirty. They just don't know.' And then: 'They've got no other choice.' Jenny was lucid that morning. And remembered screaming. She talked to Peter about it. Would he please tell me she was really sorry, and did he think I would forgive her? In bed later, I'm conscious of my own legs, heavy, stretched out straight; grounding me in my fear. I'm both afraid of Jenny and for her: mid-tide in her pain and sinking, she faltered only at the thought of hurting someone else.

I visit the hospital regularly several times a week; but Jenny, in and out of morphine, doesn't always know I'm there. Sometimes now I find Bill Lewis holding her hand, looking at her fingers with a frown. Often I sit alone while Jenny sleeps.

One of the nurses comes in carrying a small tray. She glances at the lopsided body under the blanket. 'You should hear her when she's coming out of it sometimes. She talks. Has these long conversations with. . . .' She looks at the door. '. . . Jesus. One of the night nurses heard it too.' Jenny sighs in her sleep. 'She has these chats with him, says she'll die now if he wants her to. Then – and this is the creepy part – she *waits* for his answer. Standing right here I've heard it. She says, "Do you want me now?" Then there's this long pause like she's listening. And then she says, "But I need *time* for that." Or: "If that's what you want." I tell you, it's enough to make you join the mackerel-snappers.' She rolls Jenny on her side, so she's facing me. 'I've got to give her a shot, and it's easier when she's under. Half the time, she doesn't feel a thing.' She takes a syringe from her tray. 'Getting her johnny open without touching the dressing's not an easy trick. There we go.' With a quick breath, she pushes the needle into Jenny's bottom. 'Isn't she a beautiful thing?'

For me the worst part of each visit is the smell like spit fried on metal (outside the X-ray room), and whiffs of urine on porcelain (everywhere). But I don't mind it on the days when Jenny is awake and we can talk, always in low voices, as if we're in danger of being overheard. She's weak, and sometimes I don't stay long. But I like to hear her making plans for a weekend at Santa Cruz when 'this' is over. Or worrying that the cleaners have ruined her plaid skirt, and which of her other ones do I think looks good with the blue sweater Bill gave her. Do Peter and I miss them in the loges? I don't tell her that on Saturday nights we park the Studebaker at the beach, where I smoke a lot of cigarettes, and Peter watches the whitecaps form, icy lips on the steep dark water; where we hold each other, and kiss, huddled together as if stranded in an open boat. And are silent about Jenny.

I don't like to talk about her: to my parents, to anyone at school – and especially not to Peter. The backbone of my life, the length of its upright structure, seemed to collapse when Jenny lost her leg. But after the first awful days, her glory grew tranquil, more assured. And I, uneasy, wonder if she knows what might be coming after. Because, as the gangrene continues to seep through her tissues and veins, Jenny seems actually happy. Has she discovered near the snowy plains of death something that makes her long to lie there blissfully white forever?

M.S. is usually at the hospital when I arrive. In blue or grey suits and black blouses, her braid coiled like an important rope on a ship, she's either talking to doctors or running errands for Jenny. She's begun to speak fatefully, in the permanent tones of an oracle, always ready to brief visitors on Jenny's condition. Three weeks after the operation, as I'm coming down the corridor, she pulls me aside, out of the way of a passing gurney. 'Tell me, do you think she's looking better, or just about the same?'

'I think she's stronger today. In fact, she was sitting up when I left.'

M.S. is breathing hard, and I can see that her skin is dry. She squeezes my arm and smiles. 'You know, they're giving her all these weird new treatments. I just hope they don't hurt her in some way we can't tell yet.' She starts to walk away, but turns. 'Thanks, Kate. You've been terrific about coming to see her. I know it's a long way on the streetcar, and I really appreciate it.'

8

CHARLOTTE: I like to encourage Kate's visits. Jenny responds well to her, and if I could I'd cut Kate up, boil her, dole her out to Jenny like medicine, by the spoonful. I have no shame. As I go down the hall the young doctor who gives Jenny the X-ray treatments passes me and waves. His chin is too small, and I suspect him of some furtive weakness.

The odour of blood and ether and antiseptic. Breathing through my mouth, I hurry to Jenny's room. Before the operation, the chief surgeon had put my hand on Jenny's leg. 'Feel that.' The skin had crackled. 'We call it crepitation: it's gas, trapped in her tissues.' When they wheeled her out of the operating room, I saw that Jenny's tan had vanished; the flesh they'd left her was as thin and white as Communion. There was a strange scent in the room; helpless, Jenny has smelled. How does Kate like it? Kate the naïve, who smells of white flowers. Well, let her. The final smell is always a stink.

As Kate said, Jenny is sitting up. But her eyes are closed, her head dipped. I bend to kiss her, rearrange the pillows. 'Hi, fluffy duck. How are you feeling?' I put my hand on her cheek. 'I'm sure your temperature's down. Have you got your period yet?'

'No. But don't worry.' She opens her eyes. 'You look beat.'

'It's too damn hot in this hospital – I'm sure it's unhealthy. I brought you some Kotex, just in case.' I open the shopping bag. 'I'll feel a lot better when you menstruate; it'll show your body's getting back to normal. Here's some cake I made this morning.' I bring out a wedge-shaped package. 'I wish I could bring all your food. That soup yesterday tasted like they'd boiled a rat in it.'

Jenny smiles, but doesn't answer. At the foot of her bed, the sky, crossed by the lines of the window, hangs like a painting.

'You'll be out of here soon, sweetheart, I promise.'

'I know I will. You don't have to promise.' The hair around her face is stringy with sweat.

'We're all waiting for you, and that's why you're going to do it; families are strong, stronger than one person alone. A family is the only thing worth having.'

The chief surgeon, in a grey tweed suit, comes in; nods to me. He sits on Jenny's bed and takes her hand. 'How's my darling girl?'

Jenny cocks her head and looks up at him. 'I'm better. I told you I would be.'

A nurse I haven't seen before seems confused to see the doctor there. 'I was just . . .' she begins.

He stands up. 'That's fine. You go right ahead.'

'Are we feeling better today?' Timidly she takes Jenny's pulse. 'Almost time for our medication.'

'Why,' I say, when the nurse has gone, 'does she talk like a Siamese twin?'

The doctor raises two fingers in a V and grins at Jenny. 'You're on the ball. I like people who do what they say.'

'Can I speak to you a second?' I ask him.

We go out into the corridor, where he glances at his watch. 'It'll have to be quick. I've got a meeting in five minutes.'

'You know what I want. In a couple of days it'll be Christmas: can I take home a present to my family, tell them Jenny's going to make it?'

He seems surprised. 'I thought Dr Sprague had talked to you.' He hesitates, as if embarrassed. 'We're a little more optimistic now.'

'What are her chances? Is she going to make it?'

'Well, there's still some infection, you know; and always the possibility of complications. We've had to take some pretty extreme measures. But – you can see for yourself – she's getting stronger. Her body's putting up a hell of a fight, and her attitude is good – I should say excellent. She's remarkable.' He picks at a hangnail on his thumb. 'I'd say right now her chances are better than fifty-fifty. . . .'

After three weeks, only fifty-fifty. I drive home toward the beach, and a sun that slips quickly down a thinning sky. So this is my reward for going to confession, to Mass; for praying regularly to that impotent son of a bitch. I'll drop him like a hot potato. But for Jenny's sake I'll keep up appearances, go to church, play all the games they've invented for the meek and the dumb and the hurting.

9

PETER: On Christmas Day I visit Jenny in the hospital.
          'When are you going to Santa Cruz?' she says. She's
pale. Lying down.

'Maybe today. Why?'

'Because you haven't mentioned Billy since my accident. If
he lets you get close, give him a kiss for me, right on the snout.'

'I keep thinking,' I say, squeezing the metal bars of the bed,
'it's so weird you were the only one hurt.'

'Yeah. M.S. says in this family we always have to do things
different.' Leg aslant under the blanket, she sits up. 'The worst
thing is, I really miss going out on my board.'

The last time Jenny and I went surfing, we had an argument
because she thought she could save my life. Mark and Eric had
gone up to Martignetti's to drink coffee and talk to the waitress,
Georgia. Down on the beach I said, 'I'm going to catch a couple
more curls before we go.' I threw my board into the water.

'It's getting dark,' Jenny said. 'You shouldn't go out alone.'
She was shivering.

'I'll just get one. Go on in; you're freezing.'

'If anything happened, nobody would know.'

'Don't be dumb. Put your clothes on, get warmed up.'

'No.'

'You're a determined bitch. Did you know that? What the
hell do you think you'd do if I did get into trouble?'

'I could pull you out if I had to,' she said. 'Here comes
something.' A blue-black line of water rising behind her, out at
the point. 'Let's go.'

'That's enough,' I told her, holding on to her arm. 'If I got
wiped out you'd be alone out there. Thanks for the offer, but I
don't want that to happen.' The sun was almost down. I was
glad she'd stopped me, embarrassed at being glad.

Boards under our arms, we went up to the car. 'Watch out,'

Jenny said. 'There's some rocks, but you can't see them.' She
stumbled, fell to her knees.

'Did you hurt yourself?' I helped her up. 'It's so goddam
dark.'

After I leave the hospital I tie my board on top of the '42 Ford
my father bought me. Jenny seems to be improving, but it's so
slow it hurts to watch her. I roar along the avenues, double-
clutching at intersections, trees flashing their ornaments
through big bay windows, wreathes hanging on every door. My
own house is as bare as a butcher's block. I shoot the lights at
every stop; when I hit the Bayshore it's almost empty and I'm
up to sixty, board whooping in the wind.

I haven't been surfing for three days so I feel like somebody
stranded in the desert, half dead from lack of water. And three
days is the longest I've ever gone without seeing Billy Budd.
Every afternoon after my last class I drive down to Santa Cruz,
sit on my board and wait for Billy. And every afternoon he meets
me out at the point. I don't know how he does it, but he always
manages to surface behind my back. A hiss, a snort, and I spot
his blue-gray flippers twisting and turning, maybe to catch the
light. Sometimes he circles my board, plays a game with me
before we get down to business. Or I sense that he's close by, but
the water around my board isn't moving. Next thing, Billy's
round eyes and the rusty patch on his forehead loom up, the rest
of him dropping straight down, swaying with the current. It's
easy to imagine him weaving from fathom to fathom, fish
crossing his path like falling stars.

Once he shot straight up and came down in a half gainer.
Proud of himself, he swam up to me and laid his muzzle on my
knee. When I bent down I could see my face big as a sun in his
eyes, and, no bullshit, I could feel him thinking so hard it was
almost like a voice, saying, 'I love you, I love you.'

When I hit the outskirts of Santa Cruz I slow down. Santa
Cruz is known for its jumpy cops, and M.S. gets pissed off if I
pick up a ticket. Whatever else she does for Mark and me, she
never pays for our tickets. She does just about everything for us,
but I'm not sure what she wants in return. She moves around a
lot, swinging her braid. Likes things she can grab, feel, handle.

Has strong fingers, stand-out muscles in her arms – she prays strangling her beads. She should have been a jockey or a pilot or a stevedore, something that needs a lot of guts and adrenaline.

Whatever she does, it isn't for any easy or obvious reason. Even before Jenny's leg, our Christmases weren't like other people's. She doesn't believe in presents or trees. Every holiday, depending on her mood, she serves us funny-feasts: macaroni and cheese at Christmas, Spanish rice at Easter. Mark gets embarrassed when other people talk about their turkey and gravy and mashed potatoes. But other times, for birthdays or some family celebration, we get steak or leg of lamb.

When I was a little kid the only thing she did like other mothers was to carry a purse. I could probably reconstruct my entire childhood by picturing M.S.'s old purses. The one I remember best was a brown alligator she had when I was four or five. She used to let me play with it, stick my hands in its mouth, pinch the beads of fluff I found in the bottom, wrap old sticks of gum around my fingers. Cool smears of lipstick in the corners because she never puts the tops back on; a small bottle of perfume, radiating like a star. In the bag she carries now, a comb, keys, bandages, Mercurochrome and her stopwatch. Sometimes when she forgets to draw the string, I see her tampons. Kate never carries a purse. I used to think a woman without a purse was less of a woman: a purse is like a woman's belly, full of liquids and tricks and shapes, with uses you can only imagine.

I untie my board, paddle out with relaxed hands and a strong pull, the way Keoki taught me. A small set is coming through, but I'm not interested. I want to see Billy. In the last hour the fog has socked in, and I straddle my board and shiver. I'm wearing an old Pendleton to keep warm, but now it's getting wet and it sits on my back like a sheet of ice.

The beach looks just as cold. Deserted. Nothing except, down deep, rotting rubbers and broken glass. Last summer I could pick out everybody from my board. M.S. easy, the darkest tan. Kate's long hair luffing in the wind. Just six months ago. And Jenny still in one piece. I used to sit out at the point and watch them, a sound like radar pinging in my head. It was always the same: Mark feeling up Georgia in the shorebreak, M.S. waxing Eric's board; Kate and Jenny bullshitting further up the beach.

Every time one of them changed position, I knew it brought us a little closer to the end. The end of what? It was like when you're coming; you want it to last forever, but the second it starts you know it's almost over.

Did we have too much or not enough? What I don't understand is, why something like Jenny's leg didn't happen before, for instance all those times M.S. took us up to Mayesville. There she was, a woman alone with four kids in some pretty wild woods. Bears. Wolves. Rattlers. She didn't even have a gun. But in all the times we went camping, not one of us even came down with a case of poison oak. She's so gutsy I wonder why she needs the prayers and beads and stuff – I'm not even sure how much she believes in all that Catholic routine. My theory is, if you're Catholic, shit is more likely to happen.

In parochial school they told us we were being punished for our sins, but that covers a lot of territory, so how can you tell which ones? After class Father Moriarty takes me into his office, puts that purple thing around his neck and asks me if I know any dirty words. Fuck. Shit. Cock. Cunt. Had any dirty thoughts. I put it to her, Father, maybe fifty times, my prick licking, slipping in like a wet eel. He's got B.O. Does the church make them take pills to smell like that so they'll never get laid? Make them wear robes so nobody can tell when they're jacking off? A kid I knew in grammar school had an aunt who was housekeeper at the rectory. She fed them potatoes and custard and Cream of Wheat; no spicy foods, so they didn't get overexcited. The way he talked I used to think his aunt tucked them in every night, rain pattering on the windows, shiny black shoes under the beds, teddy bears and nice clean sheets up to the chin.

But they must know something about women. A couple of years ago when Father Ryan came to the house I heard him talking to M.S. about her 'marital obligations'. 'Did he mean what I think he meant?' I asked her the next morning, when we were alone in the kitchen. 'He wants to make sure your father's getting enough pussy,' she said, peeling off strips of bacon and dropping them into the pan. 'I felt like telling him that not only do I do my duty, but more often than not I do it a couple of times a night.'

Nobody can tell M.S. anything, but when I met Kate's

mother I thought she could use a few lessons. Not more than forty, but she's got grey hair. Keeps brushing it out of her eyes and smiling, like a little girl in a party dress. But if you watch the way she sits, she presses her knees so close together they've got to have notches.

One time she invited me over for dinner. Before we eat, Kate's father pulls down the blinds. Bright as noon, but he pulls down the blinds. Kate told me he works with sheets of figures all day, adding up money that other people make. He keeps looking over his shoulder, like he thinks the Feds are watching, like they even want to see what's on his plate.

'How's your French, Kate?' her mother says, when we haven't been eating more than a minute.

'Fine.'

'I meant the subjunctive. Are you still having trouble with the subjunctive?' She's talking to Kate, but she's watching me.

'I don't think Peter is interested in my grades,' says Kate. Her face is red, as if she's just been caught wetting her pants.

She didn't like having me there, and her mother never asked me over again. But crazy as the stuff is that M.S. gives us to eat, she likes to ask Kate to spend Thanksgiving with us, or Easter. I'm not sure it's a compliment. 'Poor thing,' she says. 'She's so thin.' Like she's talking about an orphan.

Ever since Jenny's accident Kate's been sexier, more alert, as if a single mistake could cost her her life. She's full of curiosity, great at finding new ways to put her hands and mouth on me. But she'll only go so far. I get the feeling she carries around inside her all the characters in the books she's read, that she's protected by the ghosts of people I'll never know. She talks to me about what she's reading, tells me tales about tales. Her voice excites me. Sometimes it jumps right out, like it has three dimensions. Sometimes it's got no weight at all, goes everywhere, like the wind. Once when I was listening to her, she said I have a medieval face like one of the knights in King Arthur's court.

She's stubborn, comes at you with all guns blazing. I'd hate to be a book she didn't like. Reading and drinking milkshakes, she waits for me on rainy days at the Buttercup. Her mouth is very red through the bottom of her glass, and I like the way her lips take hold of that river of banana and cream. A faint down on her cheeks, and I can see her collarbone thin as a coathanger in the opening of her dress. She wiggles a little across from me in the booth, and when she bends toward me, the part in her hair shows healthy, pink, from all the thinking underneath.

So far, it's all been child's play, and the serious stuff's only in her mind, but sooner or later I'm going to give her something to feel, instead of the crap some old-fashioned writer comes up with. She's remembered every thrill she's ever read, and she's got a lot of energy, so whoever gets her into the sack's going to have a big responsibility. But I'm going to work my way up there, find out what she's hiding, feel her insides squirm and flutter like a newborn animal.

Something – maybe a fish – splashes by the tail of my board. It isn't Billy. I've been out here over an hour, but no sign of him. The temperature must have dropped about ten degrees. Teeth chattering, I take off my shirt and let it fall into the water; it sinks slowly, a flag without a breeze. I slap my hands together like flippers and throw back my head, but when I bark, the call is harsh and artificial. At last I paddle in.

A sign on the door of Martignetti's says CLOSED, and I remember it's Christmas Day. Out on the pier a couple of fishermen pass me, speaking Italian, lighting cigarettes. I lean on the rail, looking out over the barren harbor, and Billy doesn't seem very far away. A flock of gulls streams into the sky. I walk out to the end of the pier and it's so still you can almost hear the cod flapping their fins in the water. Below me a fishing dory is tied up. Lying on the bottomboards is a seal, whiskers crisp in the slack muzzle. I jump down into the boat. I can see the hole; it's been shot through the neck. I kneel by the comma-shaped body, sniff the spinach smell of seaweed still on its coat, run my hand over the head as smooth as a child's. On its brow I see the rusty patch like a diamond.

10

KATE: I lie on Jenny's pink quilted spread and wait for her to
          get dressed. Next to me her clothes have been laid out,
sleeves angled like a model's arms, awkwardly chic. M.S. has
arranged them herself, trying maybe for a new ideal of beauty,
based on phantom limbs. In a private conversation, she's asked
me to spend the night with Jenny as often as I can. My
schoolwork is suffering, and M.S. annoys me when she treats me
like one of those paid companions rich old ladies take with them
to Europe.

'Is she finished?' Carrying a large towel, M.S. goes into the
bathroom without knocking. Through the open door, I see
Jenny reach from the shower for her crutches, and M.S. wraps
the towel around her, as she might embrace a lover.

Jenny pushes her away. 'Afraid I might get a good look at it?'
Leaning on one crutch, she tightens the towel around her
breasts. 'Don't worry, I've seen all of it: I took a mirror to myself
the day I got home.' Three stabs of her crutches and she's sitting
on the bed next to me. 'Let's go to Jeanette's after, okay?'

M.S. opens the door of Jenny's closet and brings out the leg.
'What's it going to be? High heels or low?'

'You must be crazy. I'm not wearing heels to a movie.'

'Okay. Just wanted to know. It takes a while to screw on the
high-heel foot, and it's a hell of a lot easier to do it off you than
on.'

Friends of Henry Hollander, engineers at Cal, have designed
and built the leg for Jenny. M.S. helps her buckle the wide
leather strap around her waist. I've seen Jenny do it alone often
enough, but I think she wants to make it up to M.S. for yelling at
her in the bathroom.

Jenny and I sit between Peter and Bill Lewis. They'd all wanted to see *Across the Wide Missouri*, but I don't like Gable's coarse teeth, his dirty moustache, the big rat ears. Next to me Jenny's cold custom leg squatting in the darkness. She's used to it now, but I never will be. It tags behind us to class, and down the street to the Buttercup after school; waits languidly to be taken to the senior prom, although Bill hasn't actually asked her yet. I didn't have any feelings about the leg at first, except to hope that like any other labor-saving device it would make life easier for her. But although I wasn't conscious of it, I probably expected it to perform miracles and give us back the life we had before. Maybe that's why I hate it so much now, when its concealed meaning is so plain to me.

Right after Peter told me he'd take me to my prom, Jenny said I had to buy a dress. 'I already have one,' she said, 'but unless I go with you, you'll never get anything decent.' On a Saturday morning we took the streetcar downtown, the leg stiff and straight as a soldier marshalling us through the crowds. I was all set to buy the first dress I saw, at the Emporium, but Jenny said it was too much like every other prom dress. In Livingston's, exhausted, I begged her to stop for a sandwich and a cup of coffee. She agreed on condition I tried Magnin's next. I don't shop there much: the prices are way out of line, and all the marble, the chandeliers and mirrored pillars make me feel I ought to pay admission. But I promised. I just wanted to sit down. In the last hour I'd noticed that when she moved, her body seemed heavy, except for the leg, which continued to pump her smartly along. She closed her eyes as we stepped into the elevator at Magnin's, and I thought maybe she didn't like small spaces. On the third floor, she talked me into buying a yellow dress, soft, with a skirt like a slender bell: on sale, half price. She went straight to her room after we got back. When I came in, she was lying on the bed. Her blouse and skirt were on the floor, and there were streaks of blood on her slip. I knelt beside her and began to unbuckle the strap. Where it had bitten into her body, the flesh came away in strips, like the feathers of a bird caught in the rain.

We wait in front of the movie while Bill brings the car around. Usually Peter takes his, but tonight Bill has insisted on driving.

'Less time to make out,' Peter whispers, 'but that's his problem.' Bill opens the door for Jenny, and with the leg she takes a long time. She sits down, facing Bill, and pulls her natural leg inside, so the dead one sticks out like an oar. Laughing, she puts both hands on it and lifts it onto the car. Not looking at her, Bill holds the door, his eyes on the people talking in little groups outside the movie.

Jeanette's is crowded and noisy, and we get the last booth. Bill says, 'I'm going to go apeshit on the onion rings tonight.' When our order is ready, the waitress has to clear the aisle before she can get to our table. I'm sitting by the window, and I see that it's begun to rain, the wet reflections of light like daubs of paint in the street. In another booth, four girls are whispering, staring at Peter, who sits across from Jenny on the aisle.

'When are we going swimming?' he asks her.

'I don't know. When do you want?' She splashes ketchup on her hamburger.

'Whenever you're ready.'

'How about tomorrow? M.S. is taking me to confession. We can go out to Fleishacker's right after.' She turns to me. 'Want to come?'

'Sure.' I'm looking at Bill.

'How the hell do you know what's going to happen?' he says to Peter. 'Maybe she'll sink.'

'For Christ's sake, Lewis, I know what I'm doing.'

I take out a pack of cigarettes, but it's empty. I crumple it, and Jenny hands me one of hers. Lifting her skirt, she runs a match up the side of the phony leg, from calf to knee, lights first my cigarette, then hers. The girls in the booth across from us stop talking, and Bill pushes his plate away. When he goes to the men's room, Peter and I finish his onion rings.

Outside, Peter says, 'Why don't you let me drive?' Bill hands him the keys and looks away while Jenny gets in the back.

They're quiet on the way home, and Peter doesn't go up to Twin Peaks. I look in the mirror to see what they're doing, but the angle is wrong.

11

CHARLOTTE: I don't bother to kneel or cross myself when I slip into the pew; Jenny is safe in the confessional so she can't see me. Nowadays when I go with her to Mass, I find myself forgetting my part, coming in late or limp, missing my cues in rituals I've performed since childhood. Since the leg, Mass seems about as potent and holy as tossing salt over my shoulder or avoiding the cracks in the sidewalk. But Jenny likes to believe she has a Catholic mother, so I'll be whatever she needs, do whatever she wants, including going to confession if I have to. Or rather, I'll let Jenny see me going into the box. It's funny how each kid wants something different from you, something secret. They don't tell you what it is; you have to guess. And if you fail, the kid fails. But they never tell you.

When Jenny came home from hospital I hated the idea of her sleeping alone, suffering alone in the pink quilted bed of her childhood. She never had a miserable moment in her life until, membranes intact, she went to the hospital and came back sliced and handled. That first night I insist on staying with her, even though she doesn't want it. I lie on my back, listening to her breath, the rustle of her skin against the sheets. When my children were babies, I spent hours counting their inhalations, their exhalations, monitoring my riches. During the night Jenny slides her right hand over her stomach, her left hip. The movement is slight, but I recognize it and catch Jenny's hand with my own, as it falls into nothingness. In the morning she says, 'Sleeping is private; leave me alone.'

I learn to step back, to watch without seeming to watch, to be ready for any thrust by the enemy, chaos; to be alert with plans of counterattack like any prudent general with the good of his troops at heart. I wait, ready always to hand Jenny what she needs, drive her in the Studebaker wherever she wants to go, play cards with her when she's bored. I try to seem circumstantial. Every morning I pray to my own new god, a grim image of myself that flares just to the right of me, a little out of true, like a double exposure; a god I approach as an equal, who always grants my wishes, helps me pull something off. Even so, I take no chances. I scrub the house, wash the food in detail, change daily the sheets on Jenny's bed; allow nothing to touch her that isn't fresh from the line, disinfected by sun and salt air.

During my last period, I noticed that the blood was slow and mournful. Maybe it's beginning. But I was born to be a mother, and I'll die one, and no skinny trickle can make a difference. Menstruation is nothing more than an inconvenient symbol, telling me what I already know. Monthly blood is blood without dignity; circumscribed blood, flowing in limited amounts at a specified time. Blood that lacks the dramatic spurt, the beauty, of a man's battle wound. I don't care if I dry up; I hate wearing those mattresses between my legs. The thing is, certain processes in my belly — unique adhesions, cohesions, fusions and combinations — have produced my children. Nobody else could have done it. I'm bound by nothing, I know my own strength. I could mother lions and mountains, madmen and monks. I've made four perfect creatures, not only beautiful outside, but inside too, right to the backs of their blue-eyed souls. And all those prissy-prick doctors with their white hands and coats couldn't destroy even one of them.

As she comes out of the confessional, Jenny's rubber-tipped crutches suck at the church floor. An angel on a pedestal, she's no less beautiful on one leg. And yet the Church expects her to go into the box saying, 'Bless me, Father, for I have sinned.' And they want her to kneel, when kneeling's no longer possible in any decent way.

I cross myself in case she's watching. Father Ryan called the hospital nearly every day after she got sick, to ask about extreme unction. As if the Church had decided that Jenny would die, and didn't want to be caught short or proved wrong. I'll never forgive him for that. He only stopped talking about it the last week she was in the hospital. Oh, my eyes have been opened, and they'll never be closed again. As I go into the box, it's commission not confession I want; massacre, not Mass.

When Father Ryan slides open the grille, I don't ask for his blessing. 'I'm here because of Jenny,' I say, 'and only because of her. I'm certainly not here to confess, but I do have a couple of things to say. The Church gives you all that shit about putting God first, and I used to feel guilty because I never admitted that I love my children more than God. But it's true. And it's lucky I did put my kids first or I wouldn't have any left.'

'I'll pray for you, my daughter.'

'You've got no right to pray for me; I didn't ask you to. You used to pray for Jenny, and look where it got her.'

'The Church understands your sorrow, and forgives you.' Dusty black of his cassock straining against the grille.

'Look, I've got to stay here a minute, so she'll think I've made a good confession. Read a book, if you want to. I've shot my wad.'

12

KATE: When we get to Fleishacker's, I can hear the animals
in the zoo; the whistle of the children's train as it
makes its rounds. Mark and Eric have come along, a sign that
this is serious business. Jenny wears one of her brother's old
shirts over her bathing suit, and I feel lighthearted, almost
giddy, when I see she's left the leg at home. On crutches, her
body sways a little, as if it's caught in the currents of a mild
wind. She sits on the edge of the pool, dangles her foot in the
water, while Peter practices some dives off the high board. I'm
nervous, as if it's me, not Jenny, who's going to do it. I can't sit
still, so I stroll down to the other end of the pool, which is
crowded with swimmers and splashing kids. Peter once told me
it's the longest pool in the world. From that distance, Jenny and
her brothers look tiny and unimportant, but of course that isn't
true. The accident confirmed something in them they already
suspected: that they were different, superior to the rest of us,
and would stay that way forever.

Jenny takes off the shirt; she's been waiting for me to come
back from my walk. She's got on a two-piece suit, and M.S. has
sewn a patch inside the left leghole, so that the line over the
empty socket is perfectly straight and smooth. She looks fine, as
if maybe she comes from a neater, simpler species. I sit down
between Mark and Eric, and immediately Mark moves away.
Jenny stands at the edge of the pool. She throws down the
crutches, and now Peter's arm is around her waist.

She bows her head. Eric grabs my hand and squeezes it; his
feet tap the cement in a fast, soft rhythm. Mark bends forward to
watch, and I hear a curious clicking at the back of his throat.

'No shit,' says Eric. 'I think she's going to do it.'

'She's going to fall on her keister if Peter doesn't get her in the
water.' Mark laughs, but not as if he thinks it's funny.

The three of us are sealed into position, absolutely and

forever, until Jenny can move and free us. She stretches out her hands, fingers touching, palms down. Peter says something and she twists her face up to smile at him. We wait, and the sun settles on us lightly, like an old quilt. Peter steps back. Hands together, Jenny drops forward in a deep oriental bow; her foot lifts, and she's in the water. When she surfaces, she doesn't look at us, but brings her arms up and her shoulders forward in a strong slow beginning of the butterfly stroke.

My pulse is thudding in my throat, as if I've had a narrow escape. I start to say something, and Eric pulls me to my feet. Roaring with an incoherent excitement, he lifts me up, puts me down; kisses me, his mouth frank and wet as a dog's. But Mark is impersonal and cocky: 'Pretty neat trick for a girl with one leg, but I guess if you can't swim, you wouldn't see the point.'

Jenny has trouble getting out of the pool, and Mark shows her how to use her arms to swing her body up onto the cement. I watch her laughing with her brothers and it seems almost blasphemous ever to have wondered if her luck had diminished with the amputation. As she shakes out the drops of water that cling like blossoms to her hair, she seems more charmed and able than ever.

Later Peter takes her over to the high board. They're arguing about something, but I can't hear what it is. Jenny pulls herself up the steps, with Peter close behind; holding on to his arm, she hops out to the end of the board. She hesitates a couple of seconds, but her dive is clean; a twist in mid-air, and she enters the water facing the board.

Bill Lewis is standing on the other side of the pool. I can't tell how long he's been there. 'How about that half-gainer,' Peter says to Mark. 'Her balance was maybe a little off; she's got to learn to compensate.' Bill is coming our way, and Mark and Peter stop talking. Looking neat and freshly showered in chinos and a T-shirt, he greets us with a silent lift of his hand.

When Jenny's ready to come out of the pool, I give her the crutches. She's done two more dives. One of them, to my untrained eyes, seemed very good, the other awkward. Bill stared as if he had trouble seeing her, although he was very close to the board. 'Well,' he says. 'Congratulations.' I think he's embarrassed. He touches her shoulder and I walk away.

As we come out of the entrance to the pool, I'm pretty certain

I see M.S.'s blue convertible ease away down the street. But I don't mention it. Jenny says, 'Do you and Peter want to meet us at the Buttercup? I have to go change first.' Bill's hand rests lightly on her neck, just under her hair.

Two sailors are coming towards us, and we step aside to let them pass. One of them is very drunk. He stops to stare at Jenny. 'Hey,' he says to Bill, 'what's it like to lay a one-legged cunt?'

Mark smiles, and walks on. Shrugging off Bill's hand, Jenny catches up with him. The sailors seem to be waiting for something.

'Come on, Bill. Let's go.' Peter takes his arm.

'Hey, asshole: I asked you what it was like. With the gimp.'

Bill hits the sailor once, in the face. The sailor takes off his hat, smooths his hair, puts it on again. He swings at Bill and I hear a soft crack. Bill kicks the sailor in the groin, and when he falls, his friend kneels beside him.

Blood is running from Bill's nose and mouth. For a second I see him as he'd been at the pool: young and clean, choosing to stand in shadow while we took what was left of the sun. Snot mixes with the blood, and he's crying. He comes up to me like a little kid reaching for its mother. 'Kate,' he sobs, and I take his hand. Mark, Eric and Jenny are watching us. A drop of blood falls on my arm, but I don't wipe it off. I don't want to draw attention to it.

'Let's get out of here,' Peter says, the way he always does at the end of a bad movie.

Bill is looking at him. 'You're going to let him say that?' he whispers. 'What's the matter with you? Don't you care about *any* fucking thing?'

13

CHARLOTTE: In my open convertible I drive down the main street of Redwood Creek; past the post office and Frank the Barber; past the Norwegian Bakery, Green's Hardware, Davy's Bar. Sunlight as thick as milk covers the dusty pavement. Ted Green calls hello and I wave back, my braid warm as a dreaming animal against my neck. 'I'll be over to get some sandpaper for the kids' boards,' I tell him, and go into Danny's Cash Store whistling 'It Had To Be You'. I take the basket Danny hands me, pleased as always by the smell of cardboard and gingersnaps, by the dimness, the wide-boarded floors and walls.

'How're the kids?'

Danny asks me this every day of every summer. One of the first things I thought after Jenny's operation was, 'Now I can't go into Danny's any more.' But she wears white dresses now and dances with her brothers under the colored lights at the pavilion, and the nights are like a clear black river. In the mornings, she paddles out at Santa Cruz on her new lightweight board.

'Fine, Danny, the kids are great.' I take down a sack of flour. 'I saw your grandson the other day. He's a good-looking little kid, but he ought to get rid of those warts. Tell Sally to rub them with dandelion milk.' Papa stored his meal in barrels around the stove and there was a smell of raw cloth from the bolts of cotton and gingham and muslin he kept behind the counter. Whenever I come in here I think of Papa. Is the store still there? Or has it been blown down? Superseded? I reach for a box of Oxydol and shudder. How Corinne and Abby had hated me.

It is very hot. I stop stirring to wipe with my apron the sweat between my breasts. Corinne and Abby are talking just under the kitchen window, but I can't hear what they're saying. I tidy my blouse. I've been careful with myself, not letting anybody notice how much my breasts have grown since Lucas' death. Conscious of the hired hand working in the garden nearby, Abby stalks a listless chicken, a hen who has laid only ten eggs in the last month. She scoops it up and, holding it by the head, begins to twirl it gracefully, peering at the man over the feathers of the choking bird as a belle might flirt behind her fan; two final shakes, and she drapes its body around her neck. On his knees by the tomato vines, the man watches, mouth open, whether from lust or adenoids it's hard to tell. I begin stirring again, the mortal smell of lard seeping like a stain into my clothes, my tissues, my hair. Usually we make soap in the spring, leaching the winter's ashes with water to get lye. But Lucas died in March, and the faithful beat of the house has become erratic, like a heart with palpitations. Yesterday Mama spoke to the neighbors for the first time since the funeral. The tenth of August: Papa's birthday. There was a picnic down by the river. All around us the cornfields crackled, stalks dry and elderly swaying in the heat. The women hugged my mother, shiny as a crow in her mourning dress. We ate cold beef and cornbread, strawberry shortcake. I wanted to lie on the river, float downstream in my best clothes. In the middle of the afternoon, the sun was so bright, the fields and sky so yellow, I felt I was suffocating in the yolk of an egg. Only when knives and forks and dishes were being put back in the basket did I realize that, like my family, the neighbors spoke to me only when passing food, or asking me to help.

Abby comes into the kitchen. She dances past me humming 'Artists' Life', the chicken encircled like a small partner in her arms.

'Where's Mama?' I say. 'If you make a mess with that chicken, you're going to get it.'

'She's lying down. And I'm not going to "get it".' With a thick piece of string, Abby ties the chicken's feet together and hangs it on a nail over the sink.

I stir the soap, watching her. The crease between my breasts is wet again, the sweat seeping down my belly. A tin can now hangs by two hooks from the hen's jaw. Abby is holding a knife.

Corinne takes an apron from a hook behind the stove. 'Want me to help, Abby?'

'No.' Abby opens the chicken's mouth. A rash and blazing slice, and its blood burbles into the can. Abby's face dapples with pleasure. 'Now,' she says to Corinne, 'you can put the water on to boil.' My two younger sisters work silently, their backs to me.

I put down the spoon. 'Corrie: take over for a while, I'm tired.'

Abby frowns, but says nothing. Corinne's voice wavers. 'Shall I, Abby?'

I pick up the spoon, tap the bowl in the palm of my hand. 'Don't ask her, just do it.'

'Mama told you not to boss us.' Abby comes right up to me. 'And you don't own Lucas anymore either.' She flicks hot soap onto my cheek. I don't move, and Corinne, biting the corner of her apron, puts herself between us. Abby steps around her, backs me up against the stove. 'Isn't it clear that the three of us matter less now, and you least of all?'

I dip the spoon into the soap. I'm calm. My heart is hard to them now, but I'm calm. 'You never mattered anyway,' I say. 'Either one one of you. I took care of him.' The soap swirls in the pan at the faintest movement of my wrist, like the whorls I had made in Lucas' soft little soul with the strength of my own desires. Once when he was a baby I gave him a piece of pear. He licked the fruit slowly, as if he were blind; lapped it, tapped it, probed the world with his tongue. I knelt to kiss the little gobbets of pear from his chin. His body was very warm, and when I touched him I felt my stomach contract, a sensation both pleasant and painful that I would later associate with my menstrual periods. The pear still in his hand, he put both arms around me and, lifting himself off the floor, kissed me on the mouth.

Now when I go to Cathedral Rock, Lucas often comes to me in images so whole and real that I can almost hold him in my arms. I love to lie on the rock, my face to the sky. On bright mornings the grasses below quiver in the sun; on windy afternoons, they hiss and foam like a fast-moving river. Dense with savage events and memories, the rock feels top-heavy, fallen out of time. I rest my cheek on its glossy surface, and trickles of dust as dim as the years before I was born shift in slow spirals under my eyes. Even flat on my back, I'm invulnerable: no one ever comes out here. An eagle beats so close that I can see the gold of its throat. When I turn my head, Lucas is stretched out next to me, his hair young and pale under the wild feathers of the bird. The eagle swoops and I roll over, my body between Lucas and the lecherous claws, the pulse-seeking beak. As if I'm bald, I can feel on the back of my head the vile pecks, the contamination of its assault.

Some days Lucas appears to me, some days I'm alone. But the eagle is always overhead, pounding the air until it's shiny, colored, electrified. At times when I lie dreaming, I open my eyes and the eagle is very near, turning his talons in the sun. There had been an eagle in the field the day I first saw Lucas, watched each slippery piece of him come out of blood and darkness and water into the light.

'I saw him being born,' I say.

'*You sneak.*' Abby is almost screaming. '*You hid in Mama's room when she was having him. You always have to be in on everything.*'

'*The water's boiling, Abby,*' Corinne says timidly. '*We can dress the chicken now.*'

I concentrate on the strokes of my arm, the graceful folds left by the spoon in the heavy liquid. Sullenly, Abby gathers up the hen. I pity her. More than Corinne, almost as much as I did, Abby had wanted to possess the baby. But I'd stayed close to him, nuzzling his life with my own. I'd been with him during the only two agonies he had ever endured: I'd seen him being born, and I'd seen him die.

Apron around my finger, I dip between my breasts and wipe the sweat. Poor Abby, never the sister of eagles, but only of hens.

The mean dull body of the chicken seems to flame for an instant as it falls into the boiling water, like a comet hissing into the sea.

'These 'cots down from Cupertino: nice and fresh.' Danny leans on the counter.

I take a bite. 'They're fresh okay, but they need about two more days.' I toss the apricot into my basket. Six cantaloup; two dozen oranges; three pounds of plums; six avocados; two lettuces. And because Danny looks hurt, two pounds of apricots. I'll put them in a bag for a couple of days under the sink.

At the meat counter, I have to wait. Fred is old and stubborn: even though the woman ahead of me has said the lamb chops don't need trimming, he fusses and pares as though he's giving them a manicure. But his meat is good. I can afford to put anything I want into my children's mouths, and I'm very particular about meat. It must be dark red, wet and springy. I'd love to line them up, feed them myself, measure what each one takes; keep a file I can refer to later if one of them starts to flag. I buy nothing without sizing it up: cradle every chicken, heft each potato, every pear. No lightweight aces its way into my basket.

I've heard that foreigners haggle over prices; there's something shameful in that. Even if Hank didn't make so much, I'd be glad to pay whatever they asked. Like a full tit, the California soil gives us what's rich and pure, and I grudge it nothing. More than once I've told Hank I'd like California to secede, to pull back her skirts from the spindly states that cling to her.

We'll have steak tonight, with onions and gravy. For Jenny. She's regained most of her weight since we came down to the cabin, and things seem pretty much back to normal. She still hasn't tried to stand up on her board, but she'll get her confidence back in time. The business of the prom was a setback I hadn't foreseen, and if I ever get my hands on Bill Lewis, I'll kill the son of a bitch. I should have known what he was like when I met his parents. The house in Saint Francis Woods, Hank and I invited to dinner as if the kids were already engaged. Pink stucco, wrought-iron balcony. 'Fake spic,' I muttered to Hank as he rang the bell. Mrs Lewis in a long dress. Dinner in the dark, with candles. Afterward, coffee in piss-ant cups. I should have known when I met his parents that Bill has a blank between his legs where his balls ought to be, flat and smooth as the crotch of one of Jenny's old dolls.

14

KATE: Beaches are about bodies. The surfers and their girls
         are playing volleyball, and when one of them jumps
up to make a spike, I want to believe every homegrown
California myth I've ever heard. Especially the one that goes:
'In California you grow up beautiful and you stay beautiful;
anywhere else you rot.' Only Mark's girl, Georgia, seems
different; although she has the most beautiful body of all, I want
to bury her in the sand so she won't corrupt the rest of us. It
doesn't matter if you're a man or a woman, whenever she's there
you think about sex. I see their faces. But, strangely, the kind of
sex she makes you think of doesn't promise beginnings of love or
of life, but only endings. She's a venereal disease, and I hope she
doesn't travel beyond Mark. I think Peter's safe, but how can
you tell who'll get sick in an epidemic?

I'm lying on my stomach, and all I have to do is lift my head
and I can see what's going on in the water. Jenny's proning out
some little stuff close in, but Peter and the others are out at
Steamer. In the parking lot Barney Tillotson is waxing his
board. He spent last Christmas in Hawaii, and talks to Peter
about the surf he's seen at Makaha, Makapuu and Haleiwa –
beaches with warm vowels that lap at you. He's a math major at
Stanford, and I don't think he has a girl. When he comes out of
the water, he sits with me. His face is always sunburned, and
Mark calls him the lantern.

The beach is more crowded than usual. For one thing, it's
Saturday and the college kids are down, and a lot of soldiers
from Fort Ord are checking out the pier looking for girls. I guess
most of them are about to ship out for Korea. They're always in
groups, laughing; poor scurrying faces. Barney tells me he'll
probably be safe because of his eyes, but that a lot of the guys in
his class at Stanford will get drafted. Peter's going to graduate
from the University of the West next year, but he never

mentions the war. The soldiers hang out in the back booth at Martignetti's, and try to talk to Georgia. She never smiles or answers, just keeps on taking their orders, bending so close that her boobs nudge their shoulders.

When the surfers have money, they can buy a bowl of clam chowder for fifteen cents. Sometimes Barney orders a cup of tea without the teabag; when the pot comes, he shakes some ketchup into the cup, fills it up with hot water to make soup, and helps himself to the oyster crackers. On Saturday nights the surfers build fires on the beach, and there are Gallo parties with bread and half-raw horsemeat. Some of them bring sleeping bags, but most of them pass out on the hard sand till dawn, and paddle out for an early ride. When they're in a hurry, they throw their boards off the point and jump in after them.

I sit up, spread some Sea and Ski on my nose. Jenny's squatting on her board like a yoga, leg bent under so she's resting on her foot. By the pier gulls are diving for sardines, each one touching off a circle when it hits the water. At the window tables in Martignetti's you can see the food wriggling in the orange joints of their mouths.

Barney props his board against the pier, and slumps down on my towel; he hands me his glasses. 'Great night, had a great night last night; really neat. Checking out the behavior of complex functions near singularities. I'm so excited, it's so goddam beautiful, I think I'm going to die.' He watches some San Jose kids coming out of the water. 'Those two jack-offs keep trying to go left on a right slide. Somebody's going to get killed and I hope it's them.' Words pop through his lips like bullets, his chin is never dry. 'You look terrific with a tan.' He strokes my arm. 'Too good-looking just to hold my specs. I wish it was something else.'

'Before you go out,' I say, 'you can put some of this stuff on my back.' Two girls in prissy white blouses and pedal pushers are spreading a blanket near the volleyball net. I point. 'See that girl with the dark hair? She looks just like Olivia de Havilland in *The Heiress*.'

'Where?'

'There. By the net.'

He's rubbing my back. 'I don't see her.'

'God, Barney.' I hand him his glasses.

'Oh, yeah, she does. Sort of.' He caps the bottle. 'Have to get another prescription; too much reading, cracking the books. But I'm sure as hell not going to stop now. Contour integration is better than a frigging comic book.'

The dark-haired girl comes up to me. 'D'you all know,' she says, 'is there a ladies' room round heah?'

Barney points to the pier. 'Sure there is, lady; heah in California, we take a leak every day.' He starts down the beach. 'Jenny's coming out.'

I watch him hand her the crutches, slip her board under his arm. Whether I'm the one to help her or somebody else, I'm nervous till she gets onto hard sand. She's always sulky the first few moments out of the water, and swings herself up to her towel without a word. 'When your eyes are full,' she'll say if somebody's staring, 'open your mouth.' Or she waits till he walks by and, quick as a fang, trips him with a crutch.

Our conversations since the prom are different. Jenny wants to talk, and I let her. Sometimes it's about Bill Lewis, and the way it used to be, but never about how it is now. I don't ask questions or interrupt. In the silence afterwards we're closest.

I suppose, if I wanted to, I could hate Bill Lewis; everybody else does. Well, maybe not the Hollanders: except for Jenny, nobody even mentions him.

I don't know when it first occurred to me that Bill wasn't going to take Jenny to the prom. But I think she knew even before he stopped calling. I didn't want to ask about it, but once when she was quiet I heard Mark say, 'What's the matter, got a bean up your ass?' And then later, to Peter: 'Christ, then *I'll* take her.'

Jenny called me two days before the prom. 'Peter says you guys aren't going because Bill didn't ask me. Listen, that's crazy. I don't want to go with anybody, I just want to stay home. But I'll never forgive you if you don't go.'

I couldn't tell what Peter was thinking as we walked up the steps of the country club, but his mouth was so sad I wanted to touch it. I wasn't happy the rest of the night. Not just because Jenny wasn't there, but because when I looked at Peter on the steps, I had the feeling I'd taken something away from her.

The country club was cool and dark, a little balcony with a

wrought-iron railing overlooking the dance floor. I didn't like the room; it smelled of old cigars, and when I touched the walls, they were damp and slippery. I began to get a headache. The band was loud, there were little fishy-tasting sandwiches without any fish, and the punch was sour.

'Let's go outside,' I said.

We'd almost reached the long doors that led to the terrace, when I saw that Bill Lewis was there, with a girl I didn't know. Somebody had told me he'd been taking out a girl from Lowell. I'm not sure why he'd brought her. It seemed a perilous contradiction to the idea that he dropped Jenny because he didn't have any guts, which is what most people thought. But most people hadn't seen him swinging at the sailor. I'd realized then that he had an impractical bravery, but bringing a Lowell girl instead of Jenny to a Merced prom was worse, some kind of dim-witted derring-do. I knew the looks she'd get, the remarks on the dance floor – or in the ladies' room, if she was dumb enough to go there. And I had no idea what would happen to Bill, if they ever got him alone.

I don't think Peter saw them till we came back inside. He pressed his hand into my back hard when we were dancing, and all of a sudden he led me off the floor. Bill and his date had just passed close by, so I guess he didn't want any encounters. None of Jenny's friends said anything about Bill, but everyone looked tense. By the end of the night, I was grieving. This was our senior prom; this was the romantic arch through which we were supposed to pass, out tight-skinned beginnings on one side, our flabby mitigations on the other. And we couldn't even say we had a good time.

Toward the end of the night, Peter and I stopped dancing, but as we stood by the punch table, some of my friends danced by, the girls' shoulders like soft damp baby bottoms, the boys straight-backed, eyes cautious, as if waiting for important news. Earlier all the girls' dresses seemed fresh and exciting, even though they were a lot alike. But now the decreed spaghetti straps seemed designed to injure, the ruffles to unbalance; when they danced to 'Castle Rock', they looked like wobbling tops.

'Can we go?' I said. The band had started to play 'Goodnight, Irene'. On the dance floor, groups of kids suddenly began gliding all in the same direction, the way they do in musicals.

When the floor cleared, I saw that Bill and his date had been isolated over in one corner of the room. They danced alone. I hoped that Bill would lead her off the floor, but I didn't really think he would. He pulled her closer. Over the music, I thought I heard a twittering or cackling. Bill looked up the same time I did. Above us, some kids were leaning over the balcony. I saw in his expression everything happening all over again, the amused way the sailor had hit him, the astonishment on his blood-slicked face. The song ended, but Bill and his date just stood there. The cackling was very loud; even the bandleader stopped to look. Then, gently, from the balcony, they began to drop the chicken feathers, like a fall of dirty snow.

Jenny stops to talk to some of the volleyball players over by the bathhouse, and Barney puts her board down near my towel. 'Catch,' he says, tossing me his glasses. 'Hey, I almost forgot – I've got a book for you in the truck. *Gargantua and Pantagruel*. It kind of reminds me of Saturday nights on the beach.' He flings his board into the water, and on his knees begins the long pull out to Steamer Lane. From where I sit, his shoulders seem to spring directly from his behind; when they paddle like that they look like humpbacked midgets.

In the morning the water was as white as a glacier; now it's an inkstain blue. But I know that by the end of the day the fog will have sucked the shine out again. Georgia is looking for me, and I shut my eyes; maybe she'll think I'm asleep. She always comes to sit with me, spreading her towel so that it touches mine. I wasn't expecting her on the beach yet. Mark had just come in for a beer, and I thought she was still with him. I don't like it when she puts her face so close to mine that I can feel her breath. When she props herself on her elbows, her halter is so loose you can see her big brown nipples.

She puts her hand on my shoulder, gives me a little shake. 'No dozing on the job.' Carefully as ever she puts down her towel. 'How come you're not reading? You've had that book three days – that's a record for you.' Whenever Georgia talks to me, she whispers, or touches me to get my attention; but to everyone else she speaks in a normal voice. I think I'm supposed to be her confidante, although it always strikes me as the kind of friendliness prizewinners give to runners-up.

Her tan has a cold dusky cast, as if she got it under a haunted mushroom, or by the light of the moon. I've never seen her without a tan. She doesn't shave under her arms, and when she comes out of the water, the hair looks shaggy, consequential. She lies on her stomach, and turns her head; our faces are only a few inches apart. 'That's some cute pre-med we've got out there,' she says. 'Mark tells me his name is Terry. Did you get a look at those pecs? Man, I'd love a nice sloppy bite. Are you guys going to stick around for the party tonight?'

Saturday nights at Santa Cruz. Mark and Georgia drinking and murmuring just out of range of the rest of us. Girls with long shiny hair coming up to Peter, but, after I make myself apparent, falling back to the other side of the fire. In the daytime these same girls wrap themselves around him like paper on a package whenever they think I'm not looking. When it doesn't make me laugh, it makes me puke. They drink the wine too fast and talk about Georgia. Everybody talks about Georgia. She and Mark always go down the beach early; then she slips out into the dark again with somebody else, while Mark waits, cosy, like a father who trusts his daughter to be home before midnight. When she comes back to the fire, he pulls her into his lap. 'I don't know why she doesn't get knocked up,' I heard one of the San Jose guys say, 'with all that screwing.' And Barney said, 'Maybe sand is a natural contraceptive.'

I know Barney never goes down the beach with her. But except for him and Peter I can't be sure who doesn't, and who does. 'Doesn't Mark mind?' I said once to Peter. He frowned: 'I don't think he has a mind right now.'

Georgia closes her eyes. 'I feel like getting a heat on. Maybe Mark can scrounge up some bourbon.' She squeezes my hand, which is lying palm-down on the sand between us. 'Have you and Peter ever done it? Never mind – you don't have to answer. God, I love it. It makes my skin real smooth. And I feel like I'm strong. You know what I mean? Not beautiful, but strong. Like a man is strong.'

15

KATE: About a week ago, we were all jammed around a
          window table in Martignetti's, and Eric suddenly
pointed: 'Jesus, look.' Fifteen miles away, and blue-black with
shadows, the mountains were crisscrossed with thin orange
tracings like the lines on a map. Some of the lines were
beginning to blur into others, as if the ink had started to run. A
fire had broken out in the Santa Cruz mountains, and later it
spread to Valley Basin, about ten miles from Redwood Creek.
That night Peter and Mark went into town to volunteer. Ted
Green, who owns the hardware store, organized the volunteers,
and, along with the others, they were all taken out to Valley
Basin. Mark coughed too much in the smoke, and only lasted
the first day, but Peter spends every afternoon out there, and
sometimes part of the night, clearing firebreaks with the
convicts who've been brought in.

Right away when I saw those orange lines, as if the
mountains, corrupted, were splitting open, I knew I had to go
up there. I get bored sometimes, lying on the beach listening to
Georgia. I get tired of reading, of living in somebody else's
words, by somebody else's design. I want to go out and bump up
against the world. Smell it, feel it, watch it jump through hoops.
I want to see cause and effect. The first few days Peter went out
to Valley Basin, I didn't say anything; he was tired, he got back
to the cabin late, and I knew we'd have a fight. But on the fourth
day of the fire, when he's getting ready to go, I say, 'I'm coming
with you; I want to help.'

'See you later,' he says. He kisses me. 'Ted would never let
you. Anyway,' – he squeezes my upper arm – 'firefighting, you
need a lot of muscle.'

'If you don't think I can handle the equipment, I can help
clear brush. I really want to come.'

'Ted thinks women are about as helpful in a forest fire as a can of gasoline. But I'll take you down into town with me and you can try. Bat your lashes; it's worked for women before.'

I bat and plead, and finally, outmaneuvered in front of his men, Ted tells me I can hand out food and coffee.

'I can't believe you got away with it,' says Peter as we jump out of the truck in Valley Basin. 'Just don't ever try any of that crap with me.'

From time to time Army trucks unload more equipment and prisoners, and I set out the food under wet canvas in the bed of the pick-up. Eating a doughnut, Ted Green tells them all to stay close to the breaks: 'This here's a crown fire and it jumps through the tops of the trees like a buggered monkey. Don't get caught underneath.'

Somebody calls Ted, and when I'm alone with Peter, I say, 'I want to see the flames up close. Just for a minute – I won't get in the way, I promise.'

He takes me to a spot where the fire has joined two lines of trees, a perfect nave forming a hundred and fifty feet above our heads. 'Don't come any further,' Peter says. 'You can watch from here.' My hair shooting straight up in the draft, I see him walk into the flames; appear and disappear again, spraying water from a tank strapped to his back. The fire shifts and changes as senselessly as a dream. Fire can take the shape of anything. It can destroy a forest and build the shape of a church in five minutes on the same spot. Build it bigger, clearer, transcend every principle of architecture in a few flawless seconds. And then the church passes, takes on a different form, another radiance, deeper in the forest, until there's nothing left but the meekness, the purity, of ashes.

Peter signals me to move back. It's possible that right now I'm in danger, but the flames are as beautiful as a garden, and for a long time I've wanted to know how it feels to be really afraid. Fire is a solid, more earth than water; when a stand of trees goes up, not a pinprick of darkness can be seen through the flames. A tree just before the fire gets it seems only a shadow, faint as the imprint of a fossil embedded in rock. The smell of resin makes me cough, and when I take a step forward, leaves and small twigs give way under me, although they've felt only the breath of the fire. It's as if the sun has been flung to earth.

'For Christ's sake.' Peter drags me back. 'You said you wanted to watch the fire, not marry it.'

Sparks vault; saplings sing with the heat and vanish, carried up by fire-ghosts, hot streams of air, which, although you can't see them, are as terrible as the flames. The men push further into the forest and the fire soars, wheeling around them like a fast red sky. Plants are bright with life as they disappear, and I wonder if fire is essential nature, a spirit which has created the world in its own image.

I bring Cokes to Peter and one of the convicts; they're clearing brush, part of a detail that's been sent to widen a break at the foot of the mountain. The convict is a frail-looking man who fells as many trees by himself as the rest of them do in pairs.

'What're you in for?' says Peter.

'Burked my wife.' He straightens up, his arms filled with vines and leaves, and looks at me. 'But I got lots of Christian love for ever'body else, including your girlfriend here, so don't get your bowels in an uproar.' Late in the afternoon just before Peter and I go home, he and another convict escape. They're making their way into the dry foothills when the wind volleys some sparks across a break; encircled, they're dead in minutes.

We drop down beside Danny and Ted Green, who are waiting for the truck to take us all back to Redwood Creek. 'I heard the sons of bitches screaming,' Danny says. Danny owns the grocery in Redwood Creek. He slaps Peter on the back. 'Your old man may not be paying for this education, but it's worth a few bucks.'

Frank, the fat barber who gave Peter his first crewcut, joins us with a bottle of bourbon. He offers us a sip, but I shake my head. 'Nice to have you around,' he says shyly. 'Makes me less of a coward if I think a young lady's watching.' His left hand has been badly burned. We sit in the shade of a flaming mountain, where the shrubs and grass don't cool but conduct the heat erratically, stinging my forehead, my chin, the length of my arms; drying my eyeballs so that it's painful to blink. I've never been so happy.

Ted takes the bottle from Frank. 'Will you ask your ma,' he says to Peter, 'was that a seven-sixteenths wrench she got from me the other day? I forgot to write it up.' The whiskey jumps like a toad down his throat.

The fire is so intense that its faint shifting reflections blur the shadow of the mountain. 'If this keeps up,' Danny says, 'I'm taking Pat to her mother's in Santa Rosa. We're only about five miles from there.'

'Yeah. I keep worrying about my garden, and Ginny gets pissed off.' Frank rubs his face with a forearm. 'She says I don't care about the house. But, damn it, I got the best zucchini I ever had.'

Ted tosses the bottle to Peter. 'Buying your fertilizer somewhere else these days, Frank?'

'My own clippings. Don't take long to get ten pounds with the summer people down.'

'You using hair?'

'Why not? It's all good protein.'

As the truck taking us home crosses the bowl of the valley, the hot air rumbles and shakes. 'I hope that's the goddam fire,' Ted yells to Peter, 'and not the San Andreas.' The sound grows fainter and the mountains dim once we're on the main road. But I imagine that behind us I hear the snuffles of small animals bolting, bark popping and creaking, frightened heads pulped against trees. I think I smell fur burning, like the first cooked meal.

16

PETER: It's an ideal wave, cresting slowly, shoulder quiver-
            ing like mint jelly. I take three strokes and start the
slide. As the spray hits my face, dark drops of water run into my
eyes, down my cheeks and chest. Blinking, eyes stinging, I pull
out over the back. In the shadow of the cliffs Mark and a couple
of pre-meds sit their boards in Steamer Lane. Mark cups his
hands. 'You're striped,' he calls. 'Like a jailbird jigaboo.'

I dunk my head, rub the side of my face. My hands are raw
and blistered; when I put them in the water, they sting as if
they've been cut. Dark, ashy water drips from my hair. Every
day after fighting the fire, I take my board out. Sometimes I'm
too tired even to ride, but I like the feel of the wet wood, my legs
cooling in the water.

Kate was really stoked, up there in the fire. Almost the
happiest I've ever seen her. I know love when I see it, and this
was love. We hustled and heaved, we sweated and grunted. We
came crawling out like babies, crapping in our pants, and she
loved it. Not because of the pain or the destruction, but because
our chance of dousing it was an off bet, harder to imagine than
anything in her books. All the long shots she knows are on
paper. We did put out the fire in Valley Basin, but not before it
broke out again higher up. For a few minutes we thought we'd
beaten it; for a few minutes anything seemed possible, and
that's what she wanted to feel.

A little way off from Mark and his friends, I rub salt water on
my arms and listen to their gossip. Santa Cruz is busier these
days, with students and itinerant surfers from San Onofre,
Malibu or Windansea. A couple of weeks ago a kid from San
Jose went on a surfing safari, checking out every inch of
accessible shoreline from Santa Cruz to the Mexican border. He
came back with southern gothic tales of hot curls starting at
Point Conception, where the water is totally deserted, on down

to the crowded currents at Hermosa and Redondo Beach. He finished with a visual aid: the shark-nibbled arm he got on a three-foot wipeout in the Tijuana Sloughs. Personally, I've never wanted to surf south: L.A. and its sandy ghettoes seem more like truck stops, convenient for a quick bite (the kid's arm was proof of that), but without any real class. And I don't like the L.A. hotdoggers, all the fancy spinning, carving, dropping, climbing, riding the nose. But anything over five foot, they disappear to ball and drink until the water is palms up again.

I'm more patient with the Sunday surfers: depressed doctors or stockbrokers, their bellies spread under them like a second body when they paddle prone. They come out and talk to us, ask us how to ride. When they take off they breathe hard, and the water slips uselessly through their fingers; they get up too early or too late, stumble down the face of the wave like Chaplin on a flight of stairs. They ride flatfooted, big defenseless children, and I'm always afraid one of them will have a heart attack.

I know one thing – I'm not going to be like that. By the time they hit thirty, most guys have wives, kids, they're settled into their jobs, and the big things are already over. Around thirty, most people die. But that's not going to happen to me. I'm not about to spend my life inside some office where the stuff you touch is born dead and the people you work with have already died.

I spit on my hand and inspect the gray gob. My mouth is bitter and tastes like I've swallowed iodine. I spit again, in the water, wondering if I'll ever clean the smoke out of me. Barney paddles out; he sits next to me, waiting for his first ride of the day.

'. . . last semester . . . buddies with . . . really bitchin' . . . they found him in his room . . . got so drunk he died. . . .' Pre-med voices. Boards so close together, a goldfish couldn't swim between them. '. . . totally glassy . . . stalling in the green . . . see me take gas?' They talk shop through cracked lips, boards rocking gently in the water.

Since the migration from Stanford, there's a lot of conversation out here. I'm sitting a little way off, but I can still hear them. To them, surfing is just an extension of life on the beach, a one-note pleasure like drinking, balling and pissing in the sand. Barney is the exception; for him surfing is just another way of calculating the possibilities of infinity.

When Barney's out, you have to hustle if you want to get on a wave. He can't see more than a few feet in any direction, but he can hear what the water is doing, and he has a reputation for taking off on anything. He likes to ride alone. 'Christ,' he'll say, 'I'm stoked, I'm really stoked, I've gotta take a kook. This is lousy, shoulder won't hold up, but I'm gonna nail it.' And take off on the best wave of the set. Or he'll wait until something is about to drop at just the right angle, and boards are swinging into position, but nobody's paddling for it yet. 'Outside!' he'll yell. 'The real pisser's outside!' When we turn to look, he's got the wave to himself.

I like Barney's energy, his ass-in-a-basket rides. (But his enemies have a question: do you call a man brave if he mistakes the light of a train in a tunnel for the lamp on a miner's hat?) Barney has said that my own style doesn't give anything away. He's probably right. But eventually for all of us it's going to be the same. Because, sooner or later, something in the water is going to zap you, show you and everybody else what you really are.

Nice clean little wave whistling toward us. About eight foot. Barney is starting to paddle, but I let it go; the one I want is still outside. Arms and legs tumbling like puppies in different directions, Barney stands at the critical moment. From where I sit, I can see only his head and shoulders, the rest of him hidden by the wave. It's a nice steep hook, but nobody else takes off. Mark, Eric and the pre-meds are sitting together, laughing. The wave collapses. Barney straightens his board, and rides the soup. Swinging his fists over his head he dances a little jig. The pre-meds lean forward. As the elastic gives way and Barney's trunks drop to his ankles, one of them snickers: 'Textbook episiotomy, though I say it myself. He shouldn't leave his gear lying around.'

'Maybe you fucked up his trunks,' I say. 'But you notice he finished the ride.'

On the beach people are waving towels, and a girl swims out to Barney.

17

CHARLOTTE: From the cliff, I watch my sons racing on
their boards, like warriors in canoes. If they
catch a wave out at Steamer, they ride for five minutes, for
almost a mile. They're the stars. But I've written the play;
produced and directed it. I'm also the perfect audience. The
other surfers, and the kids on the beach, are only there to hand
them something, speak the odd line, or form part of a crowd
scene, no more important than the extras in a Cecil B. De Mille.
I park the Studebaker so I can see the beach, but I'm too far
away to pick out Jenny or Kate.

I often come out here just to sit under the eucalyptus and
watch them. Coming into Santa Cruz over the Graham Hill
Road, I've invented a little game I play every time I drive past
the cemetery. In what situations could we die together, as a
family? Earthquake, fire, plane crash, avalanche, car off a cliff,
sinking ocean liner, bomb, faulty can of soup. All good
possibilities. But the best one actually happened to a family in
Monterey. I read about it in the papers. Three kids were playing
outside, and when their ball rolled under the house, one of them
went to get it. When he didn't come out, his brother crawled in
after him. The little sister, after calling for help, also disappeared under the house, followed by her father and mother. A
neighbor who was watching called the police, and they were all
found dead in a nest of rattlers.

I like the thought of dying with Hank and the kids, our bodies
stacked in a single coffin, locked together stiffly, curve snugged
into curve. If we all went at once, it would mean something,
deny importance to the living, make death seem like an act of
choice and companionship. I don't like to think of one of them
dying without me, of a batch of my blood dripping out tame and
lonely.

My children have become my partners, my peers. Hank, on

the other hand, is no longer my husband. He comes down from the city more often now because he's afraid to sleep alone. He'll be waiting on the porch when I get back from Santa Cruz, walking around with a glass, waiting for me to fill it with ice and bourbon, the way a baby carries around an empty cup. But I still screw him most nights. Once, when I tried to refuse him, he began to sob and tug at my nightgown. It's easier to screw him. He's good at it, and when I don't think about him, but only about what he's doing, it's almost the way it used to be.

I recognize Mark's stance: left foot forward, left hand out in front, right arm up, slightly bent at the elbow. On the small ones, he looks even better than Peter. I'll have to remember to tell him that.

When I get down to the beach, Kate is sitting with Georgia, and I honk. I put down the top of the convertible while she gathers up her things. There'll be a nice breeze at the top of Graham Hill. I've noticed before that Kate takes forever to leave the beach; shakes out her towel several times, flutters the pages of her book; brushes off her shoulders, her arms, the backs of her legs, as if the grains of sand are lice. I have a mental picture of Kate standing in a monstrous shower, water rinsing her ceaselessly clean. Kate's a hypochondriac, although not the sort to get the significant disease she fears, to die thrillingly with pomp, but doomed I think to grow old and ugly, to suffer the impersonal pains of age.

'Thanks for the lift.' Kate tosses her book and towel into the back. 'I want to wash my hair before they get home and use up all the hot water.'

'Why don't you drive, get some practice with the clutch.' I open the door and slide over. I've been teaching the girls on weekends, using Hank's car because it has an automatic shift for Jenny. But sometimes I let Kate try the convertible. 'Let it out slowly; remember, you've got to watch both sides when you're backing out. God, what a lot of soldiers these days.'

'I know. I look at them and think, in a few days they'll be shooting at you in Korea.'

'Not my kids. They've been brought up for better things than that. Let them take the Okies and the niggers.' I lean forward. 'Look at that bastard changing lanes; he ought to be picked up for vagrancy.'

'Barney told me Max what's-his-name was drafted – you know, the big tall one, who always wants to use Peter's board.'

'They won't take that kid; he's a psycho. Stoplight coming up, check your mirror.' On Kate's knee, a little vein, young and helpless as the soft spot on a baby's head. Strange girl: seems to be reaching out to you with one hand, fending you off with the other. I want to put an arm around her, explain that life isn't a thought you examine, but a series of forward movements; that each day is a single completed act. And that in spite of what the Church says, the important things are only what you can see. She never takes her nose out of those books, except to watch Peter or talk to Jenny. As if life plain and simple isn't good enough; that before it can be taken seriously it has to be pressed flat, like a flower, between the pages of a book. We start up the Graham Hill Road, and in the cemetery the shadows of tombstones, like rays of twilight, begin to darken the grass.

'What do you mean, he's a psycho?'

'You know he stayed at the cabin before you came down.' Today, looking at Georgia on the beach, I'm sure Mark is screwing her. Which is fine, good for his health. 'Careful,' I say. 'Stay on your side of the road.' Georgia looks healthy and moist: you can tell she has good pink insides, not like some girls I've seen, pale and dried-up like coyote shit dropped in the sun. 'He's nuts all right. One day he came back from Santa Cruz early, before the other kids. I went into town shopping and left him alone in the cabin.' We're coming to the top of the hill, and on either side of the road trees grow out of cliffs that are the color of brass. A long wind is sweeping through the leaves. 'Okay, now put it into second. When we start down, don't ride your brakes, and don't take the curves too wide.'

'So what happened?'

'Eighty-degree day, he builds a fire in the fireplace. Just keeps piling on logs whether they burn or not. When I get back there aren't any left in the box. Tap your brakes as you take this curve.' Georgia is unstoppered, a good sport: she's the kind to have heavy, easy periods, and life will make its way into and out of her with very little resistance. 'I get back to find the rug – nice little white hearthrug I just bought – is on the fire, sparks jumping like Jesus. He just sits there on the floor smiling . . . tap the brakes, I said . . . and, if I hadn't rolled the rug up. . . .'

18

KATE: I quote what Bill Lewis wrote in my yearbook: 'Lots of people have been trying to read my mind this year, but you came closest. Watch out they don't read yours wrong. Maybe I'll see you at Cal next year.' Which is pretty near the mark. Sometimes I do feel M.S. is figuring me. But when I try to catch her at it, she's always looking the other way. All day I've been trying not to think beyond the minute. I know if I let myself, I'll see the future, and I don't want to. Now that Jenny and I have graduated, this will be our last true summer together. In the fall we'll leave the cabin, step out of the cradling shade of the redwoods, and the larger shadow of M.S's wings. We'll stand in the sun and grow old.

In a practical acknowledgement of what this means, M.S. has begun teaching Jenny and me to drive. I've always liked to watch M.S. behind the wheel of a car. Sometimes she drives me up the Skyline to see my parents or to bring down something I've forgotten. I like sitting low in the convertible, the Skyline cutting canyons in the rock, its sloping bends and curves moving us as fast as the currents of a river. Reflections of leaves splash like big raindrops on the windshield. Ball of her foot snug on the pedal, calves not hanging but hard. The legs of a hunter, they know their purpose: walking, stalking, squatting, waiting, winning out.

But now I'm at the wheel, barreling down the Graham Hill Road near the end of the summer. My body seems to have slowed down in an effort to avoid time. The car, on the other hand, feels light, furtively empowered, as if taking me against my will into the winter to come. I shift into second.

'. . . nice little white hearthrug . . . sparks jumping like Jesus. . . .'

The gearshift, dull and skinny as a witch's finger, jerks in its socket.

'He just sits there on the floor, smiling . . . tap the brakes, I said . . . and, if I hadn't rolled the rug up . . . slow down, damn it. . . .'

'We popped out of gear,' I say. The wind, now cold, blows into the open car.

'Hit the brake,' says M.S. 'We're freewheeling. But don't slam it.'

I press down, but there's no response, no resistance – nothing – even when I hit the floorboard. It's shocking, what it must be like to fall out of an airplane. I see Peter and the others pounding on a closed coffin; weeping, wiping each other's tears. And Henry Hollander, in black, leaping into a bonfire.

'Try pumping them,' says M.S.

I don't know how fast we're going now, but I can't keep the car in my lane. As we take a curve, I'm way over the line. Behind the windshield of his gray sedan, a man's face is drawn back flat, as if I've already hit him. M.S.'s voice without expression: 'Go around him, to the shoulder.' His primitive frown as I plunge toward him. Pull left, left, left; muffled shudder of the Studebaker in sandy dirt, the sedan creeping past me up the hill. My hands, begging, on the wheel; not too hard. Jog to the right, straddling the white line, still picking up speed. My foot striking the brake again and again, a match that refuses to light.

'They're gone,' says M.S. slowly. 'Try the emergency.'

Left hand grabs the brake; holds it like a pistol; draws it, creaking, hot. M.S. silent. The car shivers once, lightly. (Jenny bending over Peter's arm, hands together in that deep Oriental bow. We sit on the bench, watching. Her foot leaves the cement and as she enters the water the meaning of her body is both intimate and profound.) Put in clutch, drop it into gear, any gear. Give it a little gas. Gearshift up; down; jiggle it, jiggle it. Engine maybe in high now; my hand on the gearshift, holding it steady. M.S. still silent. We're coming around the last curve, two-thirds over the line. (One day behind the bath-house, I see Mark's white buttocks, pitching; Georgia's hair spread like a shiny animal dying on the sand.) Clutch in quick, hit the gas. Slam stick up, try for second, engine grinding. Clutch caught neat in its invisible slot, Studebaker whipping back as if snagged on a fisherman's hook. Our heads flop and dangle.

M.S. draws up her right leg, which has been stretched out

stiff. She touches my hand. We're in second, gears howling, streaming down the last of the hill. The road is straight now. We skim across the railroad track at the bottom and the car starts to slow down where the road rises and widens after the crossing. We coast to a stop under some trees.

I can hear M.S.'s breathing. As if I've got something to say, I turn to her; she lets go of my hand. I look into her eyes, and the pupils have a reddish glow, like a radio when you leave it on in a darkened room.

'Let's go,' she says. 'I know where there's a gas station.'

I shift into low, surprised she hadn't wanted to take over. Slowly, I let the car out onto the road.

'That kid really is a creep,' she says. 'I come home to find my rug on fire, the cabin about to go up in flames. And him just sitting there mumbling, "Christ, it was so beautiful I didn't have the heart to put it out." '

19

KATE: I stand up to my waist at the children's end of the
          pool, and listen to Jenny on the cement above me.
'You're lifting your head too much,' she says. 'Your lips should
barely crack the water. Try breathing out of the corner of your
mouth.'

Careful not to range into deep water, I begin to swim again,
staying close to the side. Whenever I lift my head, her foot is just
in front of me, waiting for me to catch up. In the mornings she
swims right before my lesson, and each print of her foot on the
cement is flanked by two damp circles from her crutches, like a
couple of half dollars that have given up the ghost. I see that foot
when I close my eyes at night: wide, with a bald big toe, the nail
sunk almost to the quick. A hard brown foot, the ankle maybe
grown thicker, taking all the weight now. A foot that abides.

For a week I've been practicing in the children's pool, ever
since the day I brought the car down the Graham Hill Road.
That night I'd been restless, irritable. 'What's the matter?' said
Peter.

'I don't know.' We were on the porch eating dinner, and M.S.
came out of the kitchen. She didn't sit down, just folded her
arms and watched us. 'This afternoon,' she said, 'up on Graham
Hill, Kate saved the Studebaker. The brakes went, and she got
it down without a scratch.' She spoke slowly, even formally, as if
making a speech.

Henry Hollander put down his drink. 'She saved you, not just
the goddam car. Did you ever think of that?' It was a new idea,
that I was her savior, and I chewed and turned my head
carefully, preening in their attention. Just before we went to
sleep, I said to Jenny, 'I want you to teach me how to swim.'

'That's better,' Jenny says at the end of my laps, 'but you're
not finishing out your pull.' Balanced on one crutch, she lifts her
free arm and shows me the stroke dry, the movement of her

muscles so smooth that it seems without beginning or end. 'This way. Don't stop short.'

'Got it,' I say.

'Your head was lower in the water – how's your breathing?'

'Okay.' I don't like the breathing part. Ever since I can remember I've hated to think that underwater it's always dusk, and since you can't talk or breathe, every minute down there must be like death, whether you drown or not. In the mornings before it gets crowded I lower myself into the stock-still pool. The water is tight and even, an unbroken seal; there isn't a sound. But when my feet prick the surface, I think I hear roaring, a heavy gallop that rumbles the walls of a cave. In Greece, they sacrificed maidens to a bull in the labyrinth; and the water seems to shake and heave, as if I've disturbed a sleeping animal down there. I never say any of this to Jenny, but I keep my eyes closed whenever I put my face in the water.

Pulling the full length of my arms, I swim for Jenny again. Two widths of the pool and I wait, treading water. 'You're ready,' she says, swinging away on her crutches. 'Tomorrow, it's the diving pool; right out in the middle. Better tap out early.' I can hear her laughing. 'And a couple of Hail Marys wouldn't hurt.' ('I want you two girls to take my room,' M.S. had said to me early that summer. 'She needs more privacy now.' In the night Jenny's silver rosary presses against me, a string of icy peas. Certain shapes are on her tongue, between her lips: grace, blessed, womb, sinners. A few mild archaic words, whispered, the begging not original, only repeated in the dark. This seems to me a reckless way to plead with a great power, but Jenny's expectations are always more real to her than anything bad that happens, so I don't see how she can lose.)

I practice again for luck at the end of the day. They've closed the pool early so the pavilion can be used for a wedding reception, and we're the only ones left. A long table has been set up in the pavilion, and paper streamers belly out from the rafters. As I climb out of the pool I can see Peter in there arguing with Mark. Mark jumps up on the table. It's dark inside and I can just make out his tan back and yellow trunks, a crowd of champagne glasses on trays.

On the way back to the cabin Peter is laughing. 'What's so funny?' I ask.

'Mark,' he says. 'Pissing in the glasses. California bubbly.'

20

CHARLOTTE: I slip a tire iron between the shell of the abalone and its tough pedestal of meat. Eric went diving in Monterey today and came back with his arms full. Too many to eat fresh, so I gave some away up at the pool. With a paring knife, I scrape at the sticky black film that coats the meat. Jenny comes into the kitchen. 'Tomorrow,' she whispers, 'Kate's going into the diving pool. First time in deep water.' When the meat is pale and clean, the color of rubber bands, I slice it into thick circles. In the other room I can hear the kids talking; everybody but Kate. I spread the slices on the table and, using an old coffee pot filled with sand, pound each one tender. No way of knowing what will happen once we put Kate into the diving pool. She seems so powerless, her fingers thin and insufficient; yet they'd stayed on the wheel of the car.

Peter comes out to cut himself a hunk of cheese. 'Kate will have to do it early,' I say, 'before the pool's open; you'll have to let us in. That way, if she doesn't pull it off, nobody outside the family will know.'

'I thought you didn't care what people think.'

'She could easily push the panic button, and we'd have to haul her out. I'd care if they thought your girlfriend was a gutless little twist.'

'She's not my girlfriend.'

'What is she then?'

'Something else.' He hacks off another piece of cheese, opens a box of Saltines.

'I don't see the attraction.'

'The reasons I like her you can't see.'

I crack some eggs into a bowl and beat them with a fork. 'Everything in this world depends on what you can see. What you can't see isn't important.'

'You say it's good for people to have guts, but you can't see guts.'

'Don't be stupid. You can see whether somebody's got guts or not by everything they do. People are only interested in what they can see. If you can't show it to them, they don't believe it.'

'Tomorrow if Kate gets scared in the pool, I'll know she tried, and that's important even if she doesn't swim so somebody can see it.' He puts the cheese and crackers on a plate and takes them into the other room.

For a few seconds the kids are so quiet I can hear the creek, its beat as intimate as the rhythm of my heart; in those few seconds the creek dropping and the rising of the dusk seem natural manifestations of my own pulse. I dip a slice of abalone in the egg, draw it through some crumbs and drop it into my skillet. Tomorrow I'll know about Kate and whether the car was just a fluke. I'll find out whether she's leaf or tree, squall or storm, crust or core.

21

KATE: Everyone talks a lot at dinner. We eat on the porch,
             sitting close together in our small circle of light.

'What's the matter, Kate? You sick?' Eric is watching me.

M.S. taps his wrist with her fork. 'Leave her alone. You know she doesn't eat much.'

'Pie for dessert,' he persists.

'I know,' I say, smiling. I like Eric because he believes everything he hears, and trusts in everything that happens. His affection is serene, and his simple responses never fail him. At school they call him the Id, short for village idiot, but everybody likes him.

Peter is talking to Jenny, his powerful head at the center of things. When he yawns he puts his hands behind his head, and I want to kiss the pale skin under his upper arm where the tan stops. I'm not the only one who likes to touch him. Jenny and M.S. dip their hands in his hair, run their fingers down his back; his father and brothers jab at him, but they're more kisses than punches. I think we touch him for luck.

'Can we get a T.V.?' says Eric. 'They're really bitchin'.'

'Don't do it,' Mark says, 'unless you want him sitting around all day, drooling and going ape-shit.'

M.S. scrapes and stacks our dishes. 'I'm not going to get one, for the simple reason that I don't want a lot of strangers in the house, freaks I don't know. Our business is with each other.' She brings out one of her full buttery pies. 'When are you going to look for something bigger?' she says to Peter.

'What do you mean?'

'Leave the chicken-shit surf to the chickens. You've got to ride something big, something nobody's tried.'

'It's not that easy.' Insects thump at the screen.

'Look, all I'm saying is, you've outgrown Santa Cruz like you outgrew diapers; it's time you moved on somewhere else.' She turns to me. 'Kate. About tomorrow, remember: if you're not afraid, you'll always see it coming at you. But if you're gutless, you'll get it from behind – and that's the worst way to go.'

After dinner we talk and play cards, lying around on the cots. I have the feeling that, like the soldiers at Fort Ord, we're still in boot camp but soon we'll be called up to the front.

I dream all that night that it's morning, that the sun is coming through the porch screen, falling on the bed; that the creek is growing fainter as it always does in the early light. And I see the diving pool, a blank unbidden blue, twelve feet deep. In the morning my eyes ache.

Peter lets us in early, and M.S. jokes with him while he puts the lock back on the gate. I hear the squeak of Jenny's crutches as she ships herself up and down, waiting by the pool. Eric sits at one end, his feet in the water, and Mark scratches his belly. With a clack Jenny tosses down her crutches, and I know M.S. is coming, that now it can begin.

'Come on, Kate,' Jenny says. She dives in.

Holding on to the rail, I go backward down the steps, lower myself up to my neck. The water doesn't move and I'm delicately suspended, as if held in the heart of a bubble. Afraid of the beast-dark fathoms, I look down, but it's blue all the way to the bottom. As I let go the railing, Eric jumps in. 'In case you need me,' he says. And Jenny glides up on my left. I'm only going to swim a few yards, and they don't trust me not to panic. Other people get thrown in by their parents when they're babies, but I have two bodyguards at the age of nineteen. 'I don't need you,' I say, but they wait, treading water. M.S. calls, 'What's the delay?' and Peter is watching at the other end of the pool.

As I take my first stroke I know I'll do it, the way I knew I'd go up to the fire in Valley Basin. Keeping my head low in the water, I see Jenny each time I take a breath; her body moves quietly under the surface, which streams past yellow in the sun. The water brushes my arms lightly, like the sleeves of a silk gown. I can see the other end of the pool coming at me and I hear myself giggle, see the bubbles rise. With a little shudder, the water gives me up, and Peter reaches for my hand.

'Good, Kate.' M.S. hugs me as I'm taking off my cap. 'I'd like to do something for you,' she says. 'Something special.' But she's looking at Peter.

That night we have leg of lamb for dinner. Lamb with mint jelly, peas, mashed potatoes and gravy; there's ice cream with chocolate sauce for dessert. The lamb is the tip-off. M.S. always gives us lamb when she's happy.

But Peter is late. He's been firefighting again up in the mountains, and doesn't get home until we're nearly through dinner.

'You're drunk,' says M.S. 'I can smell it.'

He smiles, leaning on his elbow in the doorway.

'You've been drinking with those idiots Ted and Danny,' she says, slicing more lamb.

'I'm not hungry. Barney's coming later, and I thought we'd have a little celebration for Kate up on Muscatel.'

'What's Muscatel?' I say.

'Muscatel Mountain, the hill up behind the pool. When we were little we used to take our sleeping bags up there every summer.'

'What about Lester?' says Eric. He glances at me. 'Lester's a mountain lion: Lester the molester. We hear him every year. They even write about him in the paper.'

'Kate won't mind Lester,' says Peter. 'I'm going on up now. The rest of you can wait for Barney. I'll take a couple of lanterns with me because, God knows, I don't want to build any fires.'

'Wait a minute,' says M.S., and brings out two bottles of wine. 'Here. To celebrate Kate's swimming. You kids always drink that rotgut down on the beach. Don't tell me, I know. But this is good stuff. At least, Danny says so, and he sure as hell charged me enough.'

22

PETER: Most of the time I can hold my liquor, but when I get to the top of Muscatel the bourbon starts coming into its own. I've been happy lots of times before, alone in the woods, but right now it must be the booze that's making me feel so outstanding. What I mean is, there've been other times when I've felt like this, when I've sensed some kind of language outdoors and figured I was pretty close to understanding it. But right now I'm on the edge of something really great. It's not that an animal twitches its fur in any special way, and I'm the only one who sees it; or that leaves send out little green signals, and I've got the only key to the code. But I think I observe the woods with fewer body movements than other people; that I'm quieter inside and out. Animals – and I'm pretty sure plants and trees – have a center inside them that responds to stillness and an open mind, and that's why sometimes I get into some pretty wild stuff.

M.S. thinks I'm too sensitive; she calls it delicate, which pisses me off. Even when I was a kid she let me know it. Once on her birthday, Mark and I tried to see who could come up with the best card. I drew mine, with lots of birds and hearts and flowers, but he bought his down at the drugstore. The next day I was taking out the garbage and I saw mine torn in pieces, but when I came back in, Mark's was still in the window over the sink. 'How come you threw out my card,' I said, 'but you kept Mark's?'

'I was going to talk to you about that,' she said. 'Your card was nice, and I know you took a lot of trouble with it, but drawing is for old people, or people in wheelchairs, people who have a lot of time. You should be busy doing what it is that boys are supposed to do. Flycasting, or shooting a rifle.'

I stand the two lanterns on a rocky ledge; we'll use them to light the clearing later. Dusk is hanging from the branches, but through a gap in the trees I can see out into the valley. A few rays of sun still spoke the sky, the fingers of an upraised hand. In the Santa Cruz mountains the fire is still burning, and the shadows down in the valley are a cloudy red, as if it'll never be night again.

When my head clears a little, I lurch into the woods. Tall ferns brush my legs, and the ground is warm, soft with the seeds and droppings of redwoods. An owl hoots. A bad news sound, like hearing what day you're going to die, or when the world's going to end. The light under the trees is thick, the color of maple syrup. Ahead, a monster redwood shoots up maybe three hundred feet. I stumble towards it, put my arms around it, feel against my chest the steady swing of its pulse, the big slow life inside. My temples ache with all the quick booze, but I wander further into the woods, sniffing and listening (it's too dark now to see much), like an Indian looking for a good meal. Behind me something rustles, and when I turn, a patch of sky shows where the top of the monster redwood was. 'Holy shit,' I whisper. I'm dizzy, I blink, but the gap where the tree was is still there; the redwood is bending towards me, branches running like rivers on the ground. Hard to tell now between the different kinds of darkness, between ground and tree and sky. I reach out to the big beast trembling in front of me, but instead of branches I feel the cold veins of a fern. When I look up, the line of trees is unbroken.

23

KATE: Barney swings the beam of his flashlight on Jenny and
        Eric, who are coming up the path behind us. 'We're
only about halfway,' he says to Jenny. 'Give Kate your crutches
and I'll carry you up on my shoulders.'

'Don't be an asshole,' Jenny says. 'I've climbed Muscatel
before.'

'If you're worried about snapping my back, don't. Everybody
knows I'm spineless.'

'I said I don't want to.'

I nudge Barney to shut up, and we go on ahead, watching for
undergrowth so she won't get tangled. 'It's not that big a hill for
her,' I whisper. On one side of the path are trees; on the other a
cliff. Straight up, the moon simmers in a clear sky. At a twist in
the path, I hear stones rattle down the side of the cliff. 'Why
don't I like it here?' I say.

'Because it's the perfect spot for an ambush; for Indians or
robbers or rapists. Lots of interesting things you can do in the
woods. I want to bring my books up here sometime; it'd be a
great place to read.'

'For the kind of books I like,' I say, 'you need a warm house, a
rainy night, a big lamp over your shoulder, and meatloaf and
potatoes in the oven.'

'I could bring my books over there too. I can do math
anywhere, even on my board. Math is like an invisible gas: you
can't smell it or touch it or see it, but it's everywhere – in cars, in
operating rooms, even in stars.' Whenever he talks about math
it's like there are hundreds of words in his mouth, all wanting to
be noticed at once.

'Calm down,' I tell him. 'You'll have a heart attack before we
get to the top.'

'Kepler said geometry is God, but he didn't mean God is a big
cube or trapezoid or anything. He meant that geometry was

here before the world got started; before nitrogen or lightning. So maybe it created us. Isn't that a great idea?'

'I guess so. But words were going too; as ideas, I mean, even if nobody said them. Maybe words are God.'

'Wrong. There're lots of languages but no one language is truer than any other. Geometry is universal. People never believe anything is real unless they can measure it, and get this: geometry measures reality, but it can't be measured itself.' He loops a strand of my hair around his finger. 'If Jenny won't let me carry her up, how about you?'

'Stop it, Barney.'

'I want the feel of you on my shoulders. Why won't you let me?'

'I wish you'd get things straight sometimes,' I say.

'I don't want them straight; I want them wrapped around my neck.'

Peter has lit one of the lanterns and he's rubbing his hands over it as if it's an open fire. Although he's been waiting for us, he seems surprised when we step into the light.

'Nice little joint you got here,' says Barney. 'I dig the green and brown wallpaper.' And when Jenny pours some wine into paper cups: 'Jesus – glasses yet. Everybody's putting on airs.'

Jenny holds up her cup. 'Here's to Kate. She swam today when she was scared. Here's to her guts.'

'Yay Kate,' says Eric, and everyone drinks. When Peter kisses me I can smell the bourbon.

Barney says, 'Ever notice that if you reverse the "c" and the "a" in scared, you get sacred?' He's cracking peanuts, putting the shells in the pockets of his jeans.

'What's the name of that place in Hawaii you told Mark about?' Eric is lying down, a cup of wine balanced on his chest.

'Peanuts,' says Barney, picking a shell from his teeth, 'are maybe the most complete creation in the universe. You mean Sunset Beach? I only saw one guy who was any good, and he was a *haole*.'

'What's a *haole*?' says Jenny.

'A white man.' A thin cry from the cliff above us, as if a baby is waking from a nap.

'Lester,' murmurs Eric.

'He's telling us he's around.' Peter cracks a peanut. 'But he won't show himself. If we ignore him, he'll go away.'

'What would happen if we chased him?' I say.

'You don't want to get him frightened or angry.'

Carrying a rolled-up sleeping bag, Mark trails Georgia up the path. Georgia kisses everybody and takes a drink from the bottle of wine. As if the rest of us aren't here, Mark unzips the sleeping bag, puts it down just out of the circle of light.

The lion calls again, but faintly, and Georgia says, 'What the hell is that?' Mark straightens up, listening.

'Lester,' Jenny says. 'Peter told you about him.'

'Oh yeah, the lion. Well, I don't care what he said, I don't want to see him.'

'I checked out Sunset once,' Barney says, 'when I was driving around the island. I know I couldn't handle it – fat, mushy-looking stuff. It looks like a lot of power after the drop, but if you screw up it's a long swim.' He rolls his cup between his palms.

'Keoki says the whole North Shore is big and crazy,' Peter says. 'Who was the guy surfing Sunset?'

'Some Marine, and one of the locals told me – '

'What's that?' says Eric, as gravel hits the ground near where Mark and Georgia are drinking in the sleeping bag.

'Don't get excited,' Mark tells him. 'I saw Lester and I threw a rock.'

'I don't want any more big animals breathing down my neck,' says Georgia. 'One is enough.'

'You dumb kook,' Peter yells at Mark. 'I told you never to do that. What is it with you?'

'This Hawaiian,' Barney goes on, 'told me the Marine's an M.P., the terror of Hotel Street. When the locals see him paddling out at Sunset on a stormy day, they go a little nuts and start chattering about *kahunas* and spirits and *mana*.'

Peter gets up. 'I'll be back,' he says. 'There's a tree I want to see.'

'You don't have to use euphemisms with us,' says Barney.

'It's not a euphemism.'

'As they say in the movies,' I murmur when he's gone, 'I wonder what he meant by that.'

We all sit around drinking and talking on the blanket, but it's hard to ignore the sounds coming from the sleeping bag. Barney is pulling the cork from the other bottle when the lion calls again. Mark jumps up. 'Take it easy,' Barney tells him. 'You heard what Peter said.'

'I don't give a shit what he said – I don't want to keep hearing that cat.'

Georgia whispers something, and he laughs.

'Can I have some more wine?' Eric holds out his cup.

'Watch it,' says Barney. 'You're still sweet sixteen.' But he fills it halfway.

The moon has grown smaller, as if it's being squeezed out of the sky, and in the woods a shadow throbs, but it isn't Peter. When the lion calls, I shiver, as if it has pressed its lips to my ear. Peter said it was full-grown, but its cry is young and sulky as if it knows already it'll never get enough of what it wants.

'Fucking thing's probably jammed.' In his jockey shorts Mark is standing by the sleeping bag, and at first I think he's holding a stick. But when Barney says, 'What the hell are you doing?' I see it's a gun.

He fires twice before Barney gets to him, but from where I'm sitting I can't see anything on the ledge.

'You dumb son of a bitch,' says Peter. None of us has seen him come out of the woods.

Mark hands the gun to Barney, and pulls on his jeans. 'M.S. told me to bring it,' he says. 'Because of the girls.'

Knocking down dirt and rock, Peter begins to scrabble up the side of the cliff. From a toehold, he grabs enough ledge to pull himself up onto his elbow, and bellies his way across to where the ledge begins to wind upwards again, disappearing into other crevices, other cliffs. He runs his fingers along the rocky shelf. When he drops back down, he holds out his hand. 'That's blood,' he says.

'Point of the exercise.' Mark looks pleased with himself.

'If you got him in the leg, he won't be able to hunt; he'll starve to death.'

'Give me back the gun,' Mark says. 'Maybe I better go finish him off.' With a slow shimmy, Georgia eases herself out of the sleeping bag; completely naked in the moonlight, she's even more beautiful than she's ever been half-clothed in the sun.

'Dummy,' she whispers. 'Everybody knows a wounded animal is dangerous.'

'Where do you want me to put this?' Barney says. Holding the gun, he's standing right behind her. Eric snickers, but Peter is still looking at the stain on his hand and I wonder if he's thinking about Billy Budd.

24

KATE: When we get back to the cabin, Jenny doesn't come to
               bed right away. I hear her out on the porch. Mark has
taken Georgia home, and in the kitchen Peter and Eric are
finishing off a pie.

M.S. comes into the bedroom while I'm taking off my bra.
She glances at my breasts and smiles, as if she's been thinking
about them. I reach for my pajama top and she sits on the bed.
'You were terrific today,' she says, 'at the pool.'

'Thanks.' I want her to leave, so I can finish getting
undressed.

'There's nothing important that doesn't take guts: living,
dying, getting married, bringing up kids. Even crossing the
street takes some kind of guts.'

Holding my pajama bottoms in front of me, I slip out of my
pants. But when I step into the pajamas, I see that she's looking
between my legs. 'So your pussy's red too,' she says. 'Cute.' She
notices my face and laughs. 'You are a baby, aren't you? Don't
be embarrassed. With that body, you and somebody else are
going to have a very good time.' She stands up. 'What I really
want to tell you is, I measure people by the quality of their guts.
And today, for the first time, you registered on my machine.'

'I wouldn't have shot at the lion,' I say.

'Lester? You think Mark shouldn't have done it.' Her hand
on the curtain, she stops in the doorway. 'Well, in a way you're
right – but only because he missed. Mountain lions aren't good
for much, and if Peter had shot him, he wouldn't have missed.
But Peter would never shoot, and you have no idea how much
that worries me.'

After I'm in bed, I hear the squeak of Jenny's crutches. She
comes in and undresses, but goes right back out onto the porch
again without speaking. I turn out the light, wondering what I
could have done to make her mad. The creek is running hard

and cold just under the window, but inside the cabin everything is quiet. In the faint starlight, I see the curtain in the doorway ripple, as if somebody's passing a hand over it. I sit up, thinking it's Jenny, but then Peter opens the curtain.

He sits on the edge of my bed. I can't smell the whiskey any more, and his face in the starlight is serious. 'What do you want?' I whisper. He lies down, pressing against me, and I can feel the inside of me opening up slowly, joyfully, the way a hand unclenches when a pain has gone, and the absence of pain feels better than anything you can remember.

'You better not let M.S. catch you,' I say. 'Where's Jenny?' Our lips are about an inch apart.

'Tonight, a redwood bent down, bent all the goddam way down, branches floating like a crazy band of angels, and put its head at my feet.'

'What do you mean? When you were drunk?' I hear somebody moving in the other room.

'Up on Muscatel, and I wasn't that drunk. I went back to look for signs after, check out the bushes, but I couldn't find anything.'

'Was this when Mark shot at the lion?'

'Yeah. Before, when I used to surf with Billy, and now with this tree, it's like I keep getting previews of something fantastic, but I don't know what it is.'

'You've got to get out of here. I don't want any scenes with M.S.'

'You won't have any. She knows.'

'Where's Jenny?'

'She's on the porch.'

'M.S. said you could sleep with me?'

He picks up my hand. 'Because you were really great today; she knows how scared you were. So she said we can do whatever we want tonight.'

'You mean make love?' I'm still conscious of somebody in the next room.

'If you want to.'

'I don't believe she said that.'

He rolls onto his back. 'Well, she did.'

In the sleeping bag, Georgia's breath had beat out a steady rhythm as if the sound was being squeezed out of her. And Mark had snorted. 'Maybe,' I say, 'you misunderstood her.'

M.S. comes in without knocking. 'This is just for tonight,' she says. 'Don't get any ideas beyond that. I've put you both in the same bed, and what you do about it is your own business. Kate.' She bends forward as if trying to find my face in the dark. 'Peter knows what he's doing. So if I were you I'd just go ahead and have a good time.'

'Goodnight,' says Peter.

'Okay, I'm going. Have fun.' She drops the curtain and I sit up listening.

'Don't worry,' says Peter. 'She's not eavesdropping. What do you think she is?'

'I don't know,' I say. 'But I think you better get out of here.'

'Why? You want me to stay – you wouldn't kiss me like that if you didn't.'

'If M.S. wants to give you a whore, why not Georgia?'

'Georgia's got nothing to do with it.'

'I guess now that I can swim she thinks it's okay for you to have me. Why doesn't she just put me on a platter, stuff an apple in my mouth? Or is she giving *you* to *me* as a prize for being a big girl?' He doesn't answer and I know I've hit on something. 'She thinks she can just step in . . . that just because I've passed some kind of test I'm good enough for you to – '

'Keep your voice down. This is between us.' He sits up and I turn my back. Sliding his arms around me, he pulls me up against him, his hands flaming on my breasts.

'It's not between us,' I say. 'Your mother is calling all the shots. She had to come in here and let me know she was behind it. Do you really want me, or are you doing it because she said to?'

'Do you want me to show you?' He licks the back of my neck.

'What if I got pregnant?'

'You won't. M.S. bought something for me in Santa Cruz.'

'Without even telling you?'

'This afternoon.'

She would have confided in the clerk – 'For my randy son' – laughing as she picked up the little package in her tight brown fingers. I shudder. 'Leave me alone,' I say.

He turns me so we're face to face. 'I want to spread your legs like live wires, and teach you some good common feelings.'

'I feel common enough now. I thought we were close, but if we were, you wouldn't have let her do this.'

'I never told anybody the things I told you – I guess that's close. Sometimes I think I let you get too close. What she did tonight is incidental, because I've wanted to make love to you since that first day you came out to the beach.'

'It's not incidental.' I'm crying. 'She's ruined everything.'

He gets up and the feeling I had in my belly when he kissed me leaks fruitlessly away.

'Do you want me to go?'

'Yes.'

'Are you sure?'

'Yes.' My mouth is half-buried in the pillow. When I lift my head, he's gone.

Twisted at the waist, my left arm bent under, I lie on the bed the way I've fallen. In my mind the faint steps of his going pass along endlessly, through boxes, crates, cells, rooms, chambers, the sound widening as the house stretches to receive it. A little nick as the screen door falls to.

I lie watching the long curtain in the door, the pattern of roses very pale, as if they've been bled white. Behind it there's a little disturbance: a breathing, a hissing, a rubbing – a friction of skin. Not of normal skin, I feel, but skin that is cold. I'm not even sure I hear it, because it's so quickly covered over by a line of silence, the way ice forms over a pond.

I wake again around the time when the stars lose their light, but before the sun begins to shape the sky; at the moment when night dulls down to the color of old bones. M.S. is standing just inside the curtain, her pupils glinting the way they did when we came down the Graham Hill Road. They're copper, like an animal's eyes when you surprise it at dusk.

25

KATE: On a hot day in September, my parents take me
across the bridge to Berkeley. My room is on the
second floor, and all the chairs have shiny orange covers. Before
they leave we take a walk around the campus and when we pass
my mother's sorority she says, 'That's my room, the top one on
the left.' But I know I won't rush. I've been around the
Hollanders too long to care about trying to please a bunch of
strangers.

I share the room with another girl, but she's never there. Her
boyfriend is a grad student, and he and some friends have
rented an apartment up on Northside. I spend a lot of time in
my room, alone with my books and the shiny chairs. I don't try
to make any friends because that would take me away from the
things I want to remember. At first it's easy: if I just shut my
eyes I can see Peter walking up the beach with his board, salt
drying in a fine web on his arms and face; I can reach out and
touch him, my lucky charm. But by the middle of October I
can't see him any more, and that's when I first realize that even
people who are alive can die. I don't know why I forget him first,
before Jenny or M.S. or the rest. Not just what he said or the
way he moved, but details of his body I thought I'd always
know. What's left is a sensibility, a feeling about him that has
seeped into my genes and chromosomes, changed their nature,
so I can never be the way I was before.

In the afternoons sometimes I walk down Piedmont past the
sorority houses. Through the open windows I can hear the girls
inside, laughing in the rich gloom; in hot weather they sit on the
lawn, brushing their hair. I miss Jenny, but I don't want to. I
took the bus home the day after my fight with Peter, and since
then she hasn't called me once. But when I see these girls, hear
their conversations like bright strands of yarn that come
unravelled as fast as they knit them together, I long for her. She

knows about silences, and how they make talk stronger; we've been silent, we've allowed each other secrets.

Barney calls one night from Palo Alto. I talk to him on the downstairs phone, barely protected from passing ears by a large philodendron. 'Where are you?' I can hear music.

'A bar. I got your number from your mother. How's it going?'

'My midterms didn't set the world on fire.'

'No? That's why I called: I thought I saw a glow in the sky.' Somebody says, 'Hang up, Barney, and buy me a beer.' Barney puts his hand over the receiver, and when he comes on again, I can hear guys laughing. 'Kate, are you there? These assholes are driving me crazy.' More loud noises from the jukebox; a trumpet, and drums like enemy fire. 'I saw Peter in Santa Cruz last weekend. He said he hasn't seen you.'

'No.'

'Don't you want to know how he is?'

'All right, if you want me to ask: how is he?'

'I don't want you to ask, but since you did, he's okay.' A crackling near the receiver as if he's opening a bag of potato chips. 'How about you?'

'I'm fine, hanging out with George Eliot. I thought about you the other day.'

'You did?'

'I'm doing a paper on her, and I've been reading so much I started to get these headaches. I had to get reading glasses.'

'You could have borrowed mine.'

'How's Kepler?'

'Who?'

'The geometry nut.'

'I haven't kept in touch.' His voice is loud: 'Listen, I've got to go. Maybe I'll call you.'

After Christmas I watch miserably as Dorothea marries Mr Casaubon, and the chill of his rectitude glazes her body and imagination. The days soften into April, and I spend a lot of time walking around the campus or studying by Strawberry Creek. One day when I pick up my mail there's a note from Jenny in short round writing: *I think we better talk. If I don't hear anything, I'll be there Saturday morning around eight.* The first thing I think is, the Hollanders always do things early. And then, that I shouldn't see her because she might tell me something about

Peter. But when I realize it's only Tuesday, I wonder how I'll ever make it to the end of the week.

Friday afternoon as I'm coming out of Dwinelle Hall, I see Bill Lewis in the plaza. He stops, and his friends go on. 'I was wondering when I was going to run into you,' he says. 'I saw you in the distance a couple of times, but you looked like you had a lot on your mind.'

'I probably did.'

'I hear you and Peter broke up.'

I nod. 'Seeing you is kind of spooky. I just got a letter from Jenny and she's coming over tomorrow.'

His hand on my shoulder, he steers me across the plaza. 'I know a place on Telegraph.'

We take a booth in the back where it's quiet. 'I miss Jenny,' I say.

'She got a job working for a friend of her father's.'

'Doing what?'

'Some kind of secretary.' The waitress comes over, pencil cocked above her pad. 'Banana shake. Kate?'

'A chocolate Coke.'

'Jenny never wanted to go to college,' he says. He picks up an empty match folder somebody has left in the ashtray. 'Maybe you don't believe it, but I miss her too. I just couldn't hack it when she lost her leg, but not for the reasons they think.' It isn't easy for him to look at me, and when he does, I glance away. It's as if we each know something embarrassing about the other. 'She was just so damn *good* about it. And tough. She's just as tough as M.S. After the leg I could never tell whether she was being tough or good, so I never knew what she needed.' He creases the cardboard into tiny pleats. 'I'll probably never find anybody like her again, but in the end it just wasn't worth it.'

'It was worth it to her, but she'll never ask you to come back. It's not that she thinks she's a cripple,' I say, 'because she knows she isn't. It's the way she thinks she looks. She doesn't want to give you a hacked-up body. To her, being ugly is some kind of crime.'

'Back off, will you?' His face is very red.

The waitress puts down my Coke and his shake, and I can feel that my face is red, too. I'm telling him private things that Jenny has confided in me. I'm letting her down. I take a sip of Coke.

'I'm sorry. But I've never had anyone I could talk to about it –
outside the Hollanders, I mean.'

'I know.' Carefully he unfolds the cardboard, tears it twice
and drops the pieces into the ashtray. 'They like having people
like us around, but they can always get along without us.' He
sinks the straws into his shake. 'I have a feeling you'll go back,
but I won't. I never thought they were as perfect as you did.'

I was angry at that. For a while maybe I did think they were
stronger and stranger and better than the rest of us, and maybe
a little bit magic. But that summer I'd seen M.S.'s imperious
conceit, I'd watched her wreck Peter and me. I want to tell him
about it, but as he closes his lips around the straws I think how
young he is. I wear reading glasses, and he still looks the way he
did before Jenny lost her leg. I want to tell him about M.S. and
the night of the prizegiving, but it's a family matter, and Bill has
always been an outsider. My mean defenses up, I say, 'You hate
them because of the sailor.'

'I always felt I had to compete with them. In football, in
surfing, in just staying alive. But competing is following, and I
don't like to follow. So I tried to get the jump on them when I
decked the sailor.' He shakes his head as if for a minute he thinks
he's alone. 'But they didn't care; the sailor wasn't good enough
to be a goddam competitor, so they didn't care.'

Running my fingers over the dusty leaves of the philodendron, I
wait for Jenny downstairs. I don't know why, but I'm afraid to
be alone with her. When I see her get out of the car I grab my
books and run down the steps. 'Hi. I thought we'd go to the
library so I can take back some books and you can see the
campus.'

'Okay. Sure.' She's wearing the leg. I'd last seen it crouched
behind some clothes at the back of the closet in Redwood Creek.
She only wore it a few times last summer, to parties or dances at
the pavilion. Her face is very tan and her shoulders seem bigger,
as if she's been doing hard work. As we pass a couple of guys
they stare; I've forgotten what it's like to walk down the street
with her. I pat the red convertible: 'Nifty.'

'Yeah. M.S.'s new toy.'

She swings herself easily, blonde and discrete, as if she knows and likes the looks she's getting. On the steps of the library, I can feel my everyday habits, all the acts and thoughts and minor sensations I depend on for comfort and protection, slipping out from under me. Relaxed and willing, my body is reverent, opening itself up to her alien strength the way it did that night with Peter, before I found out that M.S. had planned it. I'm responding to his lovemaking now, months later, in the presence of his sister. Maybe this isn't Jenny at all, but an avatar who will carry me off, make love to me with Peter's face hidden beneath its features.

I take my books up to the desk and Jenny glides through the stacks, trailing her fingers over the titles as if by touching them she can learn what's inside. The scent of grass and sweet hot flowers comes in through the windows; inside, a smell of new paper, old dust and leather, wooden shelves warming in the sun. Even during the misery of last fall, I'd loved being in that room. I watch Jenny run her hand along the books as a kid drags a stick along a picket fence, and I almost believe that life has finally surrendered, accepted my terms.

'That's a neat place,' she says on the way back to the dormitory. 'Like a church. Everything holy and straight and tall. Whenever I see a library I think of you.'

We take some coffee up to my room in paper cups. Jenny lights a cigarette and turns on the radio, wheeling through flags of music. A man says, 'The temperature here in the Bay area . . .' and she snaps it off. I sit on the desk. 'I've missed you,' she says, and gives me a hug. She picks up her coffee. 'Peter's going to Hawaii.'

'That figures,' I say. 'When?' We're only a few feet apart, and I wonder if she can see that I'm shaking.

'Sometime in November. Barney got him this job teaching swimming in Santa Cruz, at the Dolphin Club. Barney met the guy who owns it when he was in Hawaii. He's going to open another pool over there, and if Peter does a good job this summer, he's going to send him to Honolulu.'

'Sounds like just what he wants,' I say. I've never quite believed Hawaii is real. I picture it as no more than a whisper, a radiance in the path of the Pacific, an island invented by Matson.

'Yeah. But it'll all fall through if he gets drafted; he loses his student deferment when he graduates.' She leans against the desk. 'Why did you break up with him?'

'Why did he let me?' I'm furious at the question. 'And why did you go meek as a lamb out to the porch when you knew M.S. was going to send him in to me?'

'I thought you wanted it,' she whispers. 'Right there in the cabin, with all of us knowing.' I feel as if I'm just waking up; our faces are so close that she's a blur, the way a dream thins out in the morning. 'M.S. said that was what you wanted,' she says. 'I stayed away because I didn't know what else to do.'

'Never mind. It's over.'

'No, it isn't. Peter wants you back.'

'If he wants me back, why doesn't he say so himself?'

'He won't talk about it.'

'Then how do you know?'

'Because he doesn't look at me any more, even when we're surfing. I make him think of you. But if he came up here after you, M.S. would say he was weak. So now,' she drops her head, 'I think he's screwing some friend of Georgia's Saturday nights on the beach.'

'I don't know what you want me to do about it.' (His hands on strange indifferent breasts, breasts not a part of me. I asked him once if he'd slept with many girls. 'What do you want?' he said. 'I'm not Francis of Assisi. And even he had a few lapses before he converted.')

'Come down to Santa Cruz.'

'He doesn't want to see me.'

'Yes, he does, he just won't admit it – the same way he wouldn't talk about Billy.'

'What happened to Billy? Peter never told me.'

'Some fishermen shot him. Seals eat their fish.' She took my arm. 'Come on. Get your suit and let's go. By the way, Mark really did hit Lester that night. Just like Peter said, he couldn't hunt anymore, so he started raiding people's garbage. The sheriff sent some hunters up to Muscatel, and when they killed him, they found an open wound in his leg. They said he was nine feet long from his nose to the tip of his tail.'

We drive down to Santa Cruz through heavy traffic, passing two nasty accidents on the way. The crosscurrents of a warm wind draws our hair into our eyes and mouths, and Jenny puts on a bandana. She drives with one hand on the wheel, the other resting on the dummy leg. Ahead of us the Bayshore is dull and dusty as a dirt road; above, inflexible, the sun crackles over our heads. I want rain – cold seasonal rain, like they get in New England – and short black days to remind us we're going to die. Jenny has put the top down and I can smell the clams at low tide, rotting in the sand like bad teeth.

'I saw Bill yesterday,' I say, still feeling guilty, 'and we talked about you.'

The wind whips some sparks from her cigarette, and she hands it to me. 'I haven't thought about him for a long time.'

'He thinks about you.' I smear the stub in the ashtray.

'Poor Bill,' she yells over the wind. 'He likes things to be average, ordinary, normal, and we were always letting him down.'

At Santa Cruz she drives out to the point so we can watch the surfers out at Steamer. 'There's Peter,' she says, and honks the horn. He's sitting off by himself, and when he spots the car he waves. I don't think he knows I'm there. When he lifts his arm I can see the beautiful nude shadow underneath. 'By the way,' Jenny says, 'when you see M.S., don't mention Hawaii. Peter hasn't told her yet.'

There are more surfers out than I remembered. A couple of them are wearing rubbery black vests – wetsuits, Jenny calls them – that some guy has just invented to keep them warm when the temperature of the water drops. Mark is out. And Eric. But I don't see Barney. 'He's been studying,' Jenny tells me. 'Cramming like crazy.' I've forgotten how good they look, big and calm and reckless, the long shine hitching up behind them.

26

CHARLOTTE: On the beach I'm towelling my hair, drying
off after a swim, when I see Jenny getting out
of the car. This morning she told me she was going over to
Berkeley, and I suspect that Kate will be with her. Undoubtedly
Kate will be with her. Yes, there's Kate, hair hanging down in
those irregular ripples; Kate, skinny-legged and sharp-
shouldered in her old one-piece suit. 'Hi, Kate,' I say. 'What a
surprise. Long time no see.' Never let it be said that I'm
unforgiving.

'Hi.' Kate holds out her hand.

A strange gesture and – even stranger – I find myself kissing
Kate's cheek. 'How's Cal treating you?' I say. Jenny has gone
up to Martignetti's for some cigarettes, and Kate and I are
alone.

'Fine. It's big though, and sometimes you're afraid nobody
knows you're there.'

'How do you think Jenny is? Don't you think she's looking
good?' Eric has brought his board in, and he's running up the
beach.

'She looks great. But I've never seen her when she didn't.'

'Well, in the hospital her skin was blotchy, but that was
because they kept it so damn hot. No, I meant, does she seem
happy?'

'As far as I can tell. Why?'

'I'm worried about her. She takes her board out every day but
she hasn't tried to stand on it since the leg.' In a way it's a relief
to have Kate back: someone I can talk to about the kids. Kate
cares about Jenny and Peter almost as much as I do.

'What makes you think standing is even possible?'

'I can't tell you, I just know.'

'Kate! I thought that was you on the cliff.' Eric grabs her
hand. 'I came to get you.'

I follow them down to the water. Arms hugging the rails, Kate lies down on Eric's board. 'Have a good time,' I say, as Eric kneels alongside her and begins to paddle out. At the first stripe of whitewater I can see Peter waiting, and they make the transfer so fast I doubt Kate got wet. Kate is ungrateful. But the kids keep bringing her back, so she might as well stay. And this time I'll make damn sure Peter marries her, brings her into the family where I can keep an eye on her.

'Where's Kate gone?' says Jenny.

As I point, a flock of gulls shudders up from the water like bits of paper rising from a fire. Hard arms wheeling, Peter swings his board around the end of the pier, with each stroke bending nearer to Kate, who lies quietly between his knees. 'I think he's taking her to the other side,' I say, 'where there aren't so many people.'

27

KATE: Naked, Peter sits at the deal table. He leans forward, shading his eyes, checking to see if the mist in the valley has burned off. Disguised and shifting in their own shadow, the mountains seem more in the mind than in the eye, as if they haven't yet reappeared with the day. An unstopped sun is already with us in the room, and I pull the sheet over my head. In the bent and angled early light, we're pinned like butterflies behind the glass wall of the room. For a wedding present, M.S. has given us two weeks in the mountains, mountains not far from the sea. Late in the day we can see the blaze of the Pacific, in some places pinched to a trickle by the mountains; in others, flared like a girl's skirt when she's dancing.

I sit up. 'Come here,' I say. Peter kneels beside me on the sheet. 'Closer.' I reach out, cupping him in my hands. 'That's funny.'

'What?'

'How quickly it changes its shape.'

'Do you like it?'

'Men are so obvious.' I take his fingers. 'Feel me.'

'You're wet.'

'But looking at me you can't tell; you have to search.'

'I'll make the coffee,' Peter says. He pulls on his jeans. 'And I know how to make good oatmeal; M.S. showed me when we went camping.'

'No thanks. Just coffee.' I slip into a kimono I bought in Berkeley. 'God, it's only seven. Do we have to get up this early?'

'I like to see the sun. Go back to bed if you want.'

I lean against the stove, watching him. The muscles in his back are so hard he looks like he's been fired in a kiln; but when he turns on the faucet, they tense and shift under his skin a little so you can tell he's human. And, faintly, I can smell his delicious sweat. I can't believe we've been in bed together all night, but already I'm taking it for granted as if I *deserve* him, and all the good things he does to me. 'This is the longest time I've been alone with somebody outside my family,' he said yesterday. 'I guess I've always avoided it.' I'm beginning to realize he's a solitary, always has been, and that here in the mountains with me he's going to know the friendship of a stranger for the first time. This has the odd effect of making me feel that whatever we do is being seen and judged by an invisible audience – his family? – and that our smallest act is crucial. He's excited by my intensities, the rash testament of my responses. 'You wouldn't mind if we did nothing but make love,' he'd murmured. 'I didn't think there was anything wrong with that,' I'd said. 'You don't talk much.'

He puts his oatmeal and my coffee on the table. 'When we go to Hawaii you can wear lots of sexy island things.'

'Maybe we won't go.' Ever since Jenny told me Peter could get drafted, I've been worrying about the war. But up here I concentrate on the tidiness – the tidedness – of our days together; everything we do begins in the morning and ends in the night. A perfect circle is impossible, but whatever it is we have up here, I don't want to step outside it. When we lie in bed, sometimes under an old quilt we took off the sofa, there are only two sources of light: the fireplace, its flames as short as grass, and the stars like freezing crosses. 'If you get called up, I guess I could get a job, but my mother wants me to go back to school.'

'No point in thinking about it now. If they don't take me, Mike will definitely send me to Honolulu. He says a couple of people told him their kids really like me. I taught a sixty-year-old woman to swim last week. A rich old lady, and she's going to tell all her friends.'

'I can't believe it. That you'll be drafted. Or die. I wonder if war widows go crazy, jam things up inside, bloody themselves, so they can remember what it was like to make love.'

28

CHARLOTTE: When I've finished cleaning out the fireplace, I begin stripping the beds. Labor Day.
Another end, plainly marked, of our life together in Redwood
Creek. Then the joggle-ass ride back up to the city with our
sheets and towels, and the boys hanging their shirts in the
windows like Okies. But this time Peter won't be coming with
us. When he and Kate come down from the mountains, they'll
go to their little apartment in Santa Cruz. Kate's mother
wanted her to wait until she graduated, but I knew she
wouldn't. Jenny was maid of honor, in blue silk. More beautiful,
more radiant than the bride. They could have taken the nice
three-room I found them down by the water, but Kate made
Peter take the one at Pleasure Point. Paint curling from the
walls thick as potato peel, for God's sake, but she wants it
because it's old.

I tie the sheets in a bundle and open the door of the closet,
which smells of stale ashes and wet wood. Hiding at the back, a
couple of pairs of dirty disfigured sneakers, and on the floor a
sleeping bag has grown mold the color of pea soup. I take the
bag outside and lay it on the grass. Hank is sunning himself on
the porch, but as I come back up the steps, he opens his eyes and
squeezes my bottom. 'Before we hit the road, how about letting
me fill up your tank?'

'I've just stripped the beds.' His lips are cracked and dusty-
looking; too much sun and bourbon. But if I don't do it, he'll
start weeping, and the kids'll be back from the beach.

I spread my legs wide, make it easy. As far as I'm concerned
it's over in seconds, a narrow shiver right up my middle, bright
and unbearable, as if someone has rubbed the rim of a
wineglass. Under my fingers, the many little excremental crusts
that his skin throws up now he's nearly fifty. He's slower, he's
always been much slower.

'Turn on your stomach,' he whispers.

'I'm not some goddam dog.' But in order to save time, I do. A long red hair is caught in a button of the mattress. Maybe right now, Kate opened up like a baby sparrow begging for food, and Peter lambasting the hidden skin. Maybe she's already pregnant. Hank increasing his speed; it won't be more than a minute. But whatever he pumps up there is going to die lonely. My insides are as empty as the beach at the end of summer. No movement, just a few hopeless creatures washed up by the tide; no undulations, my womb like the sand, flat and lifeless and hard. There'll be no more companions. No slick wet baby whorled up inside me, its brain moistened by my thoughts, my blood. A man is sucked dry by screwing. But a woman becomes richer, warmer, her bones more flexible, teeth shinier, heart stronger. Always the chance of a baby. But my halls are deserted now, no more new faces; my circle of friends is complete. Kate'll have a baby though, I'll see to that. I try to picture the two of them as they are at this moment. If I can see them in my mind's eye, I can move them as easily as my own body. I'm sure I can. Once, I wanted Corinne to do something nice, bring me a surprise; but in my mind I wasn't specific. Sure enough Corinne came back from town with a pound of cherries, like a bag full of dolls' hearts.

I shut my eyes, concentrating: for a few seconds I see Peter and Kate. Then Hank shivers and flops out of me.

29

KATE: Lying on the sofa, I'm nearly asleep, and my book, half-closed, slips down between my legs.

'The surf,' Peter says, squinting through binoculars. 'I think it's up.'

'Who cares?' I murmur. 'We're in the mountains.'

'Good-looking little ground swells, but I can't see the break from here.'

'What difference does it make?' I sit up. 'You're here with me.'

'I was thinking about that last night. I'd like to live in the mountains, but I know I couldn't do it. I need the speed and panic of surfing.'

'I wonder if M.S. doesn't push you into it, make you a fanatic.'

'Barney surfs a lot, and you don't call him a fanatic.'

'What's Barney got to do with it? I don't surf with him, you do.'

'I know. But I always think of him as your friend.' He strokes the top of my head. 'I hear he's applied to grad school. He's safe all right – there's no way the Army'll take him, with two cracked marbles for eyes.'

'Whenever I worry about you being called up, I wonder about M.S. Isn't she ever afraid? Doesn't she have nightmares like the rest of us? Even that time on Graham Hill, I didn't know what she was thinking. Just once, I'd like to see her sweat something out. She scares me.'

'She'd love to hear that. She likes to keep the troops crapping in their pants. Just don't think about the war. Maybe they'll sign an armistice; maybe I won't go.' He pulls me up. 'Come on – I just had an idea.'

Not far from the cabin, a long stem of light comes through the tops of the trees. The leaves are deep green, they smell juicy, and they don't make a sound under my hips, my hair. But my cries dazzle the dark parts of the forest, like the calls of a bright-colored bird.

Only the fire, almost horizontal now, gives any light. Through the glass wall, the sky is grainy-looking like a snapshot magnified a hundred times. 'Fog's in.' He dips his fingers into a pool of my hair. 'First time I haven't been able to see the stars.'

'I know.' I'm lying on my back, eyes open.

'I don't think it'll burn off. Tomorrow's our last full day; we ought to leave around noon on Wednesday.'

'Will you be sorry?' I draw my knees up under the quilt and with my movement I detect on myself the young odor of earth after it has been heavily wetted with rain.

'What's the matter? You haven't said much since we came back from the woods.'

'I feel funny.'

'What do you mean?'

'My neck.'

'Let's see.' He touches the small swelling behind my left ear. 'Maybe you bumped against something. You know, this afternoon.'

'I don't think so. My head aches and my legs are prickling.'

In the morning, he dresses quietly. When he comes back from his walk I'm sitting up, hugging my ribs, breasts pushed out passionless. He picks up my kimono. 'Here, get this on.' He puts a match to the kindling. We didn't need a fire the day before, but overnight the fog has mobilized, pressing against the walls of the cabin as if it's the only vacuum left in the world. His clothes and hair are wet.

'How are you feeling?' he says. 'Your eyes are red.'

'I'm cold,' I say, and he kisses me. I feel as if some spirit or illumination has died out under my skin.

'Your lips are hot.' He touches my forehead. 'You practically burn my hand.'

'Maybe I've got the 'flu.'

He feels behind my ear. 'The swelling's as big as the ball of my thumb. Do you have a sore throat?'

'No.'

'You better stay in bed; we'll leave first thing tomorrow.'

I don't drink the coffee he makes, don't want anything to eat. I doze on into the afternoon, while dim currents of fog lap at the glass wall. At the table he studies his atlas and an old globe somebody's left up here, trying to predict the ways in which the configuration of the Hawaiian Islands might bend or break the shape of the water. I read some place that the Pacific can flap like the hair on your head, in gales sent down from the Aleutians; or be drawn up into a violent cramp by an earthquake in Japan. When the water sucks out before a tsunami hits, a boat tied up at the pier can dangle like a yo-yo at the end of its string.

Half unconscious, I get out of bed, and sit on his lap. 'I'm still cold.'

'No wonder. You haven't got much on.' He carries me back to bed. When I lie down I can smell the fever, my sweat on the sheets. He covers me with the quilt, two of his shirts, a sweater of mine, and a pair of chinos. We didn't bring any coats. 'I don't want you to get up again. I think you're pretty sick, and there isn't even an aspirin up here.' He tosses more wood into the fire. 'So you have to wait until I can get you back down the mountain. It's too late to start now because of the goddam fog.'

'Will you have to take me to the doctor?' I have trouble looking at him, and shut my eyes. When I turn my head, he says, 'The left side of your neck is purple – like the beach right after the sun goes down.' He sounds confused. 'We'll go home to M.S.'

'I want to go to my mother's.'

'She won't be able to take care of you.'

'They can get a substitute.'

'Don't worry; it's probably some kind of 'flu. M.S.'ll know how to deal with it.'

He gives me a glass of milk, a glass of water. In the firelight my body beneath the quilt and shirts slopes like a mountain under low-lying cloud. I open my eyes every few minutes to make sure he's still in the room. I've never been really sick before, and I've never had a husband. Marriage is both a commonplace and a mystery – for a man, literally a shot in the dark. There's no way of telling what we bring to each other inside ourselves. I'll always be a stranger to him because I'm a woman; no matter what he does to me, he'll never know my body the way I do. And I come from a long line of people he's never seen, all unknown quantities until they reappear in the faces of our children.

He spins the globe again, and turns a page of the atlas. When you first look at the Pacific on a globe, it seems more like a map of the sky, the tiny spatters of islands like stars centuries away. A half-turn, and the Atlantic, though full of the ghosts of perilous convoys, of dead romantic wars, hangs down feeble as an old man's beard. But there are sharks in the Pacific, and queer-patterned poisonous fish; coral sprouting like big pink cauli-flower. And not a speck of land to stop the swells coming down from the north until they hit the Hawaiian reefs, loud and neat as oil drums down an alley.

In the evening he roasts some hotdogs in the fireplace, heats up a can of Franco-American spaghetti. It's all the food we have left, except for a box of Rice Krispies. But we began with steaks and butter-stuffed chicken. For me, making love and cooking are two parts of the same act. Sometimes I get right up and go to the stove, kimono aflap, parting and naked underneath. In Redwood Creek I was always modest; but up here I like my nakedness to transform everything in the cabin into an exten-sion of my body, a curve or crevice that demands or offers itself to him.

He cuts up a hotdog on a plate with some spaghetti. 'Why don't you try and eat this?' He puts an arm around my shoulder, but I shake my head clumsily, cheeks slapping the pillow, like a child who's lost control.

In the morning the fog is stationary, patient in its purpose. Peter tells me we'll have to get down the mountain with a visibility of twenty feet. He packs the car and, using a pile of clothes for a pillow, makes a bed for me in the back seat.

'Why do my lips stick together?' I whisper.

'Fever. You're probably dehydrated.' He helps me into a sweater and a pair of pedal pushers. But my legs ache so I can't put on shoes. My head unsteady on his shoulder, he carries me to the car. 'Please,' I say, as he covers me with the quilt. 'Don't take me to the hospital. I don't want them to cut me up like Jenny.'

As he backs out under the trees, drops of condensation heavy as the bodies of oysters whap the top of the car. The landscape is shifting without a sound. It's no place I know: France, maybe, or Switzerland. Trees I don't recognize are begging us, arms outstretched. Peter has to put his head out of the window to make sure he's finally on the road. In the back, I whisper to myself under the quilt. It feels like a giant hand is pushing the fog against the windows, the way a murderer stuffs a pillow over his victim's face, and I resist the temptation to fight for breath. The wipers, pathetic, scrape the glass.

'Kate,' he says softly, 'are you all right?'

A long time after that he pulls over to tuck the quilt around me, and I open my eyes. 'I know where you're taking me,' I whimper. 'And they're going to cut off my head.'

I sit up at the sound of the traffic as we come into the city. 'You've been out of it since we left the cabin,' he says, 'and if I take you home to M.S., she'll never let me call a doctor. So I'm going to take you straight to the hospital.' From Twin Peaks I can see the bay shining like a penny in the sun. But for the last two days the sky has been blank, the sun has turned a blind eye, and I wonder whether the sickness is a direct result of the afternoon he took me into the woods; and whether because of what we did in the leaves, we've between us popped that thing out behind my ear, blackened the side of my neck as if a fire leapt there.

He carries me up the steps of the hospital, and at Admitting they call for a gurney. A doctor presses his stethoscope to my breast, lifts my hair to look at my neck. When a nurse begins to wheel me down a corridor, Peter walks alongside. With a slow circle of my tongue I wet my lips; my face feels dry and puffy, as if I've turned forty in the back seat coming down from the cabin. The corridor is dull green, slaked with antiseptic. At a set of double doors, the nurse says to Peter, 'I'm sorry, but this is as far as you can go. Until the doctor can make a diagnosis, he wants her in isolation.'

30

KATE: There are bars on the window. I think when they
            brought me in they started giving me big doses of
penicillin or some kind of antibiotic. I've been here two days
now, and my head is clearer, my temperature's not so high. I
ring for the nurse.

'I want to see my husband.'

She shakes her head. 'You're in isolation. I've got a polio in a
lung, and two meningitis plus a possible third down the hall.
Nobody comes in here without special permission.'

As soon as she leaves, I feel for my ring. I'd told Peter I'd
never take it off, and somewhere I heard that when they think
you're dying, the nurses steal your jewelry. I lift my head. My
neck doesn't hurt so much, but I can still feel a runnel of fever in
my chest. And my arms ache, as if I'm a fly and somebody's
trying to pull off my wings. They wouldn't let me see Peter, or
my parents. I guess there are only two ways out of here: one is to
die; the other, to pretend to get well. I remember with shame
visiting Jenny in the hospital, and how I left each time with a
little sense of superiority when visiting hours were over.

Early the next morning a doctor comes in with two interns.
'Dr Geagan first diagnosed encephalitis,' he says, as if I'm not
there. 'Comatose. Elevated white count.' He glances at me.
'How are you feeling?'

'Fine,' I chirp.

He asks the nurse to bring him a mirror. 'Look,' he says,
whisking the hair back from my neck. He holds the mirror so I
can see the skin, a faint gray-green, as if somebody's standing in
my light. 'There was a bump there when they wheeled you in.
And your skin was the color of a thundercloud. At first I thought
somebody had given you a whack, but your temperature was a
hundred and six.'

Peter told me that when Jenny got sick her leg turned almost black. My throat is dry, and I drink some water while the interns watch me.

'To be frank,' he continues, 'we don't know what the trouble is. There are anomalies, but the medication's brought most of them under control. We'd like to do some more tests, and a series of X-rays. You're still running a low-grade temperature and we want to find out why.'

My mother has left some of my books with the nurse, but I don't feel like reading. I lie on the stiff bed, listening, smelling out danger. I don't relax even at night, when there are no nurses' voices, no chime of metal dishes or squeak of gurney wheels; no sound human or mechanical. And yet nearby I perceive the solitary gasps and haemorrhages; on still sheets the unembarrassed bowel movement. And down in the basement the stained and freezing flesh; the special ones, the mysteries, cleavered like chickens in a market.

The tests and X-rays tell them nothing. I still have a fever – just under a hundred most days – and a prickling in my arms and legs. The day after the tests are complete I hear Peter whispering my name. I sit up. Evening is coming in at the open window, and I see his face beyond the bars.

'Come here,' he says, 'but don't make any noise.'

I swing my feet into the paper slippers. 'Where have you been?' I whisper, pressing my face close to his. 'I dream about you.'

'The bastards won't let anybody in. I've been hassling them for a week.'

'I want to go home,' I say, my voice small and irritating, a child asking for candy.

'You're going to. M.S. gave me hell for taking you to the hospital. The doctor says he'll probably let you out tomorrow if you promise to stay in bed. No getting up, no walking around. M.S. wants to take care of you.' He runs a finger up and down one of the bars. 'I take my physical in two weeks.'

'Oh God,' I say. 'Everything's over before it's started.'

'Don't panic. At least I'll know where I stand.'

'Do you miss me?'

'I have to go in a minute; there's a cop walking around.'

'Why can't you say you miss me?'

'I don't know.' He takes an orange from his pocket. 'This

rolled out of M.S.'s grocery bag and it reminded me of the sun from our window in the mountains.'

I fall asleep holding the orange. In a dream I feel it flash in my hand, radiating a bright heat like a picture I saw of the bomb over Nagasaki.

M.S. puts me in Peter's old room, and Mark moves in with Eric down the hall. He's in his last year of college and comes home late from the city, sometimes not till after dinner. Peter drives up from Santa Cruz to see me on Saturday evenings, as soon as he can get away from the Dolphin Club. But Mike always wants him back down by the next afternoon. He's given up our apartment in Santa Cruz and now he sleeps at the cabin in Redwood Creek.

I don't weigh much, and I sleep a lot. Sometimes I wake up to find M.S. sitting on the other bed, watching me. I remember Peter telling me how she sat with Jenny just before her leg got cut off. I thought I'd feel better when I got out of the hospital, but I don't. In isolation I had the feeling that hospitals were like God: too big to comprehend, they held the answers to life and death. But now that M.S. has taken over, her intensity makes me feel more helpless than ever. I don't like to be alone with her, and I'm relieved when Jenny comes home from work.

Today Peter went for his physical. But even though I wanted to stay awake till he came home, I fell asleep; the sickness seems to cut off my strength like a tourniquet. I just now discovered he's back, because I heard him telling Mark about it out in the hall. Swathed in my fever, I listen to their voices drift intermittently, like a conversation overheard through a summer window.

'I'm not worried,' I hear Mark say. 'They'll be just as dumb when they get to me. But I have to admit yours are worse.'

'When the doctor saw them he put me in a different line.'

'Did he ask you what they were?'

'I told him, but he had a hard time believing me.'

I sit up as Peter opens the door. 'I'm not going,' he says. 'They didn't take me.' He bows his head as if to grieve or pray, and I reach for his hand. 'The sergeant said, "Get out of here, and don't ever let me see you again."'

'Why? What did they find wrong?'

'You know those knobs on my knees? And these two things.'
He points: on each instep a bump like a petrified blister. 'The
doctor said they were some kind of housemaid's knee; he told me
I wouldn't be able to get through basic in G.I. boots. But when
the sergeant heard I got them paddling on a surfboard, he said I
was a motherfucking rich kid still playing with toys, that I
couldn't get off my knees and fight like a man.'

I put my lips to his hair. Before I married him, I associated
that kind of blondness with magic. With ancient Greek feats of
strength, with sublime and legendary couplings – the screened-
in beauty of movie stars. Or with the gentle beard of Jesus. Now
I see it less as a mystical privilege, or blessing, and more as a
responsibility, a talisman given me for safe keeping.

31

KATE: Before Peter drives back down to Santa Cruz we talk
        about going to Hawaii. 'Now that you don't have to
worry about the Army,' I tell him, 'there's no reason why you
can't take the job Mike offered you.'

'He wants me to start in November,' says Peter, 'and I'm not
going to chance it. What if we get over there and you get sick
again? There's not enough time for you to get well.'

After he goes, I'm feeling really low. Flat on my back, I pick at
the chenille spread, wondering if I can shake the fever in two
months. When Peter asked me to marry him, I felt as though I'd
won a battle fought on the edge of a cliff, and then looked down
to see where I might have fallen. But now I'm not sure the
marriage is such a victory. Except for the first week of our
honeymoon, I've been sick all the time, or in the hospital, close
to death. I've never thought much about death before. In the
movies it hits nice elderly people who wear cardigans and die
sweatless in their sleep when the wind blows out a candle. But in
the isolation ward I wrestled with it. Fat and smelly, it sat on
me, buttocks riding my breasts till I couldn't breathe; then flung
itself off me with a giggle. Now when I move, cords of pain
tighten on my arms and legs. My hair is dull, the color of old
leaves, and I'm so limp I wonder if some of my ribs are missing.
M.S. glides in and out, bathing my face and neck and back, but
I won't let her bathe me all over the way she wants because
sometimes she looks at me as if she knows all the things Peter
and I have done together.

At night I think of him sleeping alone. I hear the stream
behind the cabin, feel its breath rise, chilling the sheets on the
bed I once shared with Jenny. I told Jenny I didn't think I was
going to shake this thing, but she has as few doubts about my
ability to survive as she had about her own. I don't mention my
fears to M.S. because once I heard her tell Henry Hollander

that the only time a married woman should stay in bed is when she's just had a baby.

'I tried knocking,' says Barney. 'But you didn't hear me. M.S. told me you were awake. Are you?' He bends over me, a couple of books under his arm.

'You're a surprise,' I say, glad to be diverted. I don't like lying there thinking of the ways I'm failing Peter. Conscious of my flat and tangled hair, I sit up. 'Can you hand me that comb?'

'Sure. Do you want me to comb it for you?'

'Thanks, but no thanks. It's such a mess it'll take me hours. It's great to see you, Barney.'

'I'm not sure it's great to see you. I'll tell you in a minute.' He tosses me one of the books. '*History of Western Philosophy*. You'll love it. Or, if you don't, you should.' He drops the other one in my lap.

'*Kiss Me, Deadly?*'

'Some trash to keep you dumb and sexy. Peter will thank me.' He sits on the bed. 'I saw him in Santa Cruz yesterday, and he told me you were sick. What've they done to you? You look like you've been locked in a castle with a lot of vampires.'

'I've never seen you in street clothes,' I say. 'But you look kind of good.'

'Yeah. Well, I'm sorry I couldn't make it to the wedding.'

'I didn't mean that. I just meant . . . you look impressive in a jacket.'

'I'm in training for the eastern seaboard,' he says, flapping his lapels. 'I leave on Friday, and I'm getting my equations all psyched up for M.I.T.' He pulls back the covers. 'Move over.'

'What are you doing?'

'Getting in so we can talk.' He plumps one of the pillows and leans against the headboard. 'Now. What have you got to say?'

I glance at the door, remember the night in Redwood Creek when M.S. came into my room. Feverish and silly, I say, 'Oh, to hell with it,' and draw the comb through my hair. 'Did Peter tell you Mike wants him to manage the pool in Honolulu?'

'You'll love it over there.'

'Peter says we won't go if I don't get better. They've put me on big doses of aspirin.'

'You look different. I guess being in isolation's like being in prison, or a monastery. You're not the same when they let you out.'

'Tell me something,' I say.

'Like what?'

'Something interesting.'

'Well, let's see. I just read a really bitchin' book. Schrödinger. Physicist, Nobel in the thirties. About the statistical tendency of matter to go into disorder . . . is that your foot?'

'Go on,' I beg, placidly raking the tangles in my hair.

'He says something I like to think about on a good day out at Steamer. You've got two premises, okay? One, that your body operates as pure mechanism, according to the laws of nature; and two, that you know by experience that you initiate and control its acts. Not only that, but you can predict the effects of these acts. So if you believe this, you also believe that every day you take full responsibility for your life. So. What does this mean?'

'I don't know,' I say. 'But I'd like to.'

'Schrödinger says the only possible inference is that if we each control the motions of the atoms of our own bodies – and we do – then we can each say, "I'm God Almighty." He doesn't mean it as blasphemy, just a way of proving the existence of God.'

'The thought of you as a god cheers me up.'

'I'd be a great god, kind to all my concubines.'

'What he says is fascinating if you take it personally.'

'Exactly.' He unhooks my comb, which I've absentmindedly left hanging in my hair. 'But life is hard. Who can you believe? Far from thinking we're each our own god, the Hawaiians have witch doctors or *kahunas*, who can pray people to death. And there's another kind who can cure you. They call in a *kahuna* the same way we call a doctor; no autonomy there, either way.' He puts his head on my pillow and watches me comb my hair.

'Do these things really happen, or do the Hawaiians just think they do?'

'They happen all right. I got some books on it when I was over there. It has to do with *mana*, some kind of psychic energy. It's sort of like sex appeal; either you have it or you don't.'

'How can you tell if you've got any?'

'You must have one hell of a lot. Your legs are burning up. I can feel them from here.'

'That's the fever.'

He takes off his glasses and peers into my eyes. 'What are you looking for?' I say.

'Nothing. Just an excuse to get close to you.'

'You're plenty close enough.' The muscles of his right eye are weak, so that it doesn't focus directly on me, but on something just slightly to my left. 'Has a *kahuna* ever really killed anybody?'

'Well, sometime in the nineteenth century, I forget when, King Kalakaua wanted his sister Princess Likelike out of the way, and he had her prayed to death by a *kahuna ana'ana*. Next thing, there were thousands of tiny red fish in the harbor, so many they changed the color of the water. A couple of *haoles* saw it too. The Hawaiians, who were scared shitless, believed that whenever these fish appeared, it meant somebody in the royal family was going to die.' My combing hand slows. 'Right away the princess got sick, but the *haole* doctor didn't take it seriously, and he told her she'd be better in the morning. But he told people later he didn't like the sight of the old *kahuna* crouching at the foot of her bed.' I bend closer, drawn by his unbridled eye. 'Her servants started to shriek so loud you could hear them all over Honolulu, and when the doctor came back a couple of days later, she'd had a relapse. The place was knee-deep in *kahunas*, so he resigned from the case, and right after that she died.'

'It's breathtaking,' I say, 'and scary.'

'Stick with me, kid, and you'll be wearing diamonds.'

'I can see all those tiny red fish leaping up, like a fire in the water.'

'You're a great audience.'

'That's what a T.A. told me. He said I was the ideal reader, gullible and fantastic.'

'What an asshole. Do you miss Berkeley?'

'Not much. But when the T.A. heard I was dropping out to get married, he said, really prissy, "I'm afraid I can't offer you my congratulations." He told me my paper on Eliot was, to quote him, "quite original". He said if I stuck around, he thought I might do something really good.' I hear Jenny's crutches in the hall; she always takes the leg off as soon as she gets home.

'Hi,' she says, coming in. She stares at Barney. 'I know what it is: you look smarter without your glasses.'

'That's because I am.'

She throws herself on the bed. 'Aren't you hot under the blankets with that jacket on?'

'Not to mention his shoes,' I say.

'I must have a sexy voice,' says Jenny. 'When I answered the phone at work today, a guy asked me out. Sight unseen. For all he knows, I've got two heads.'

'Or one leg,' says Barney.

'Bang,' she says with a giggle, putting the tip of the crutch to his temple.

I'm the first to see M.S. She's standing in the doorway, with half-closed eyes, thinking hard, as a coach might watch a losing team. 'Get your ass out of there, Barney,' she says.

'It's not my ass you should worry about.'

'Well, whatever it is, I want it out of there when I come back.' She slams the door.

'What a grouch,' says Jenny, getting up. 'I better go calm her down.'

Barney puts on his glasses. 'Back to the math mines – children's hour is over.' He tucks me in and takes my hand. 'Well, as they say, "This is goodbye." You'll get to Hawaii, don't worry.' He puts my fingers to his lips. 'I'd like to do more, but I don't kiss too good. Write home once in a while. And don't take any wooden *kahunas*.'

I cry a little after he leaves. Seeing him reminds me of last summer in Santa Cruz, when the only times I knew I had a body were when the sun glanced off my skin or Peter touched me. With the memories come sweat and a headache. When M.S. takes my temperature it's a hundred and one.

'No more visitors until Peter comes up this weekend,' she says, 'if that's what it does to you.'

32

PETER: Ten miles out of Redwood Creek my Ford breaks down, but the lettuce farmer picks me up a couple of minutes later. At the time it seems like a miracle. The Skyline probably doesn't get more than ten cars a day, which is why I like to take it up to the city. When the sun's out, my wheels slick over the shiny straights and curves like I'm polishing a mirror. Just trees, mountains, hills and valleys, and the Bayshore a long way off. Sometime I'd like to talk to Kate about my feelings for this road, but I probably won't because when I love something this much, I fuck up when I try to talk about it. The truth is, I always think there's a chance she'll compare my words to the ones in her books, or to somebody else's, like maybe Barney's. Practically everybody I know uses words either as a weapon or a shield, which leaves me the only one undefended. In my head there's a real zoo of incredibly interesting shapes and creatures, but whenever I try to talk about them, they come out sounding like deformed orphans, which doesn't make me look too bright.

It's an old truck, with lettuces under canvas at the back. When I get in I can smell them, fresh and green as creekwater. The farmer is rough-skinned, has shiny black hair. 'What's big good-looking kid like you doing on back road? Road for farmers or cowboys.' He laughs and guns the motor.

'My car just died on me,' I say. 'Never had any trouble with it before, and it was really pissing along, but I guess they always run best just before they crap out.'

He nods, as if I've said something important. 'Yes, that is the way.' In second, he takes the small grade that winds up and around a big outcropping of rock. 'You married, kid?' A wooden cross hangs from his neck.

'Yes.'

He too is married: he has five kids, and his wife, she has big breasts and a nice sloppy belly. (I can't do the accent.) There was a good crop this year, and he's saved enough to take a trip home to Mexico. Would I like a stick of gum?

The dry grass at the side of the road is a feminine pink, soft and flattened by the wind; ahead of us, the sun bobs low enough to shine directly into our faces. I blink and the after-image is a whirling disc, like a buzz saw. As the road curves, the hills line up, peak after peak in the distance. At the Saratoga summit, the shadows are beginning to blur and mingle with the trunks of the trees. 'I see deer cross here sometimes,' says the farmer. 'They wild and beautiful, and I drive slow.'

'I see them late at night on the road in Redwood Creek,' I say. 'Once some drunk coming home from the pool hit one and I heard him laughing about it with the cops.'

The truck slams into a rut and jumps hard; he pulls over. '*Las lechugas*,' he says, opening the door. With small quick hands he tightens the canvas over the lettuces. '*Bueno*.' He gets back into the truck. 'No little ones lost.' He guns the motor then switches off the ignition; lifts the wooden cross and kisses it. The long grass rustles in the wind. 'You, kid,' he says, putting his hand on my leg. 'You want good blow job?'

A hawk glides near the cliffs, feathers shining in a late jet of sun. On the wind are the faint traces of its scream. I've decided to cut across wooded country and later, where the road curves, join it again. M.S. won't worry, but Kate will, and I don't want to wait for a hitch if I can make good time this way. The chances of another car are slim, so I'll get as far as I can before dark, and try again in the morning. If I have to walk all the way to the city tomorrow, it's going to take me most of the day. Simpler to have stayed with the truck, but I couldn't take the farmer's pleading. 'You big kid, beautiful. Last chance for me.' Stringy little fingers. Incredible that they should be so strong, so full of ballsy lust. I knew I wasn't in any danger, but on the other hand I didn't want to stick around. For a minute though I didn't think I was going to get off so easy. I was walking along the highway when the truck came back, and I wondered whether I should sprint into the woods. But he was smiling and held out a paper bag. 'Here. Lettuce sandwiches. My wife make them. Lots of the lettuce and butter. Best sandwich in world.' Knowing it was his dinner, I said no, but he sticks the bag in my hand. 'You maybe get hungry waiting,' he says.

Right after he leaves, two vultures (V-shaped, as in vultures make you vanish) begin soaring in wide circles over the highway, old scars in the orange sky. Wings leering, they hover, not committing themselves. As soon as I can, I abandon the highway and begin to walk a straight line that'll put me back on the road about ten miles further on. In thick forest it's not easy to keep your bearings. The tops of the trees close over my head like fathoms, and I can hear small movements, the rustling of leaves, of low bellies slipping over stones. I can hear the effects but I can't see the causes. It's surprising how much secret life goes on in a forest, as primitive and fabulous as anything underwater. A forest is as different from treeless land as the mountains are from the sea. Unlike us, trees are happiest when they're together; they don't need the prestige of isolation. In a forest of redwoods all marching together I feel like I'm in the Army. I try to stand up just as straight, so it doesn't look like I'm relaxing in front of the troops.

I was going to dump the sandwiches, but now I bite into one and finish it. Two more to go. Some cookies and an apple. It's weird: when the farmer gets hungry up around Daly City he'll think about me, the way right now I'm thinking about him.

I zip up my windbreaker. Not much chance it'll keep me warm after dark. The sun's nearly gone, and the afterglow looks as cheap as the red candles I remember from church. Only M.S. and Jenny go now. Recite their female sins for some arthritic, dry-balled old priest. For Jenny, I think the church is a way to health and life, and I can't blame her for that. But I'm not sure what M.S. gets out of it now. The only thing I remember about church is how surprised I was when I found out that people fart there the same as they do any place else.

A second of silence as the sun goes down, as if something big has missed a beat. Here in the woods I feel like the last survivor: no machines or music, no way to make a sound except with my voice. Should I go on, or rest here until daylight? I take out another sandwich. The light still coming through the leaves looks like blue mold when it hits the ground. Dead ahead, some rabbits are watching me from behind a fallen branch. They're frozen into position, hoping that if they're quiet enough I won't notice them. I crouch down, pull a piece of lettuce from my sandwich and scrape off the butter with a twig. The lettuce in my open palm, I lay my hand on the ground. I'm motionless for so long that two of the rabbits hop out, and one of them gets up on its hind legs, head swivelling. Slowly I edge the lettuce closer. Their nearness, their wildness, their lack of fear are different from anything I've seen in a woods animal before. The one who's been checking me out hops right up to my open hand. A flash of pink nostril and it bites into the lettuce, banging its teeth together like little bricks, eyes popping as if it's stunned. After it takes a few bites, a couple of the other rabbits come out from behind the branch and start to nibble at the lettuce, one of them resting its paws on the flat of my fingers. Whiskers flicker, dusting my palm. When the lettuce is gone the rabbits begin to play, running at each other in quick charges, practicing sudden starts and stops, wily turns.

I lean against a tree and watch them. In November I'm going to take Kate to Hawaii. The doctors say she shouldn't get out of bed, but she's going to come down to Santa Cruz with me and swim in the cold water. Forty-five degrees will race her blood, tighten her muscles, lower the fever. Doctors don't have all the answers. It's just as easy to believe that she'll get well swimming in cold water as staying in bed; or that trees bend down and wild rabbits eat out of my hand. What I believe by myself is just as true as what everybody else believes together.

I might as well stay here until it's light enough to move on without bumping into the trees. For now I stretch out on the ground, watching the rabbits leap and graze in a tribal pattern of fuzzed and crazy forms until the daylight goes and the woods are completely dark.

33

KATE: Feverish and irritable, I haven't slept much. Peter called a while ago and Eric went out to 19th Avenue to pick him up. His car broke down on Skyline and he had to spend last night in the woods. When he didn't show up for dinner M.S. wasn't worried. 'Maybe the surf was up,' she said, 'and he got carried away at Steamer. He won't be home till tomorrow now.'

This morning when she came to see if I was ready for breakfast I kept my eyes shut. But she didn't close the door right away, and I had the feeling down my spine I always get when somebody's right behind me. I knew she was watching me because I've caught her at it several times before. There's something about the way she does it that disgusts me. I'm sure she thinks about my body a lot, almost the way a man does when he wants to go to bed with you, and that she takes advantage of the times when I'm asleep to think those things about me.

While we wait for Eric and Peter, she sets up her ironing board by my bed. 'Now,' she says. 'Pay attention. When you do a man's shirt, you begin with the cuffs. Keep them tight so you don't iron the wrinkles in. Now the sleeves, stretch them absolutely flat – always do the sleeves before the shoulders. Next the collar. Lay it out, do the front first, then the back.' She smooths the iron in a half circle under the collar, tightening the shirt over the ironing board in short jerks. 'Now you do the right panel – like this.' She bears down hard. 'Now the back. Think of each part as a piece in a puzzle. Go all the way around, left panel last. You better watch while I do a couple more. Peter should be home any second – why don't you put on some lipstick?'

'I'm so pale, it makes me look worse.'

'Suit yourself. See the way I stretch the sleeve so I don't iron tucks in it? Any woman who can't iron a good shirt is a half-assed idiot. Why don't I wash your hair for you?'

'No thanks, I'll wash it myself.'

'You've been kind of fretful the last few days. Anything wrong?'

'I'm sorry if I'm not exactly the way you think I should be.'

'Don't get all pissed off. I was just wondering if there's anything I can do. The best thing would be for you to get pregnant. Peter's probably nervous about the idea of touching you while you're sick, but I'm going to clear everybody out of the house tonight. I really think a baby would cure you.'

I lie down and long for my mother. She's come to see me here only once; she sat grimly at the foot of the bed while M.S. gave her coffee and cake. My own mother, but after the flashy presence of M.S. she seemed a disembodied stranger. I wanted to run my fingers over her face, read it like Braille. There's so much I can't tell just by looking at her: what does she really think of M.S., of Peter? Does she still love me, after the way I've left her so completely? Can she ever understand how much Peter has opened up my life? She wore a hat, and that hurt most of all. Didn't take it off, just ate a little bit of the cake, and didn't touch the coffee. When we were alone, she said, 'The terrible thing that happened to Jenny, all that bad luck. I worry about you. And the youngest one, Eric – he's awfully slow, isn't he?' Just before she left, she kissed me and, when she went out with M.S., I had the feeling I'd never see her again.

'Here's Peter,' says M.S. She unplugs the iron and piles the shirts over her arm. 'I'll send him right in.'

I watch the door like a beggar girl in a fairy tale waiting for a prince to happen. Whenever Peter shows up, I almost believe my regulation suffering is over, even though I know I'm not virtuous enough to deserve a perfect ending.

There are bristles on his chin, and his hair is wild; when he kisses me I can smell pine needles and the sleepy pelts of animals. 'I hate it when you're gone,' I say.

'I'm not going to be gone any more. You're coming down to Redwood Creek with me.' He yanks off the covers and swings my feet to the floor. Kneeling beside me he pulls my night-gown over my head, and I feel the cool, cool air against my skin.

34

CHARLOTTE: When the bus pulls out for Redwood Creek,
                        I wave and both the kids wave back, Peter's
face a little behind Kate's. She's put some lipstick on, but she
was right – she's still pale. I've double-parked in front of the bus
station, and I take off just as the cop car comes out of the alley. I
swing round the corner onto Market Street, and I'm heading
home. I drive slowly, watching the drunks and the tight-assed
young sailors in the arcade. Peanut shells, candy wrappers and
old newspapers are dream blue in the shadows of the buildings,
but the arcade lights are hard and complicated the way they are
at midnight. San Francisco is a tough town, a man's town, and I
love to move around in it. The arcade excites me. I want to fire a
rifle in the shooting gallery, eat some of that hot deep chili, and
fuck a stranger on dirty sheets to the beat of a neon light. I like
Market Street because my children will never end up here. It's
like letting yourself enjoy a horror movie because you know it
can't happen to you. But tonight Peter told me he was going to
Hawaii. Are there arcades in Hawaii? Why is it that at any
moment the child you love most is the one you're most in danger
of losing? He was a little jungle-eyed when he came home, took
Kate onto that bus as if he cared about nothing else. Kate's
arms and legs are so rickety, God knows what her womb is like.
Paltry probably, with freckles. Not a day goes by but what I'm
conscious of the fine blue forest of arteries that feeds my own
womb. When Kate gets pregnant I'd like to reach right in and
snatch the fetus, plant it inside myself, where at least it'll get half
a chance to grow, to come out into fresh air and sunlight.
    A colored soldier and his woman walk close together, his arm
around her waist. The woman's legs are long under a bright red
nylon skirt, her feet lascivious in ankle-strap shoes. If Peter and
Kate have a baby in Hawaii, it'll grow up foreign in a land of
niggers. I've been close to a nigger only once. He'd put his hand

on my leg, his pink palm cracked and lifeless, the skin on his arm oily and smoky-looking, like meat left in the oven too long. I was eight years old, and I'd gone with my family in the buckboard to a fair. Lucas had been a baby, and Mama had carried him from animals to vegetables, his chin bobbing on her shoulder, blue eyes staring at me as I follow just behind. Pumpkins the size of carriage wheels, radishes big as a fist; champion rams with balls hanging down like five-pound sacks of meal; a parade of carthorses, feather-legged, prancing prim as spinsters; four-inch squares of fudge and penuche, the sugar turned to cream in your mouth.

'I want to pee, Mama,' I say.

'There's an outhouse behind the horse pull. Come right back; I'll be at the jams and preserves.'

There's a long line ahead of me: a woman hanging on to a child with one hand, with the other sweeping up wisps of long hair that have come unpinned; men slouching, hands in their pockets, sweat-faced in the sun. I can't wait. I plunge into the field behind the outhouse, arms revolving, almost swimming in the dry yellow grass. I've played in prairie grass before, and know how easy it is to get lost, but I want to get away from the people. If I don't make any turns, I'll be able to find my way back to the fairground. When the sounds of the fair are blurred by the wind running through the grass, I lift my dress and hook my fingers into the top of my drawers. As I'm about to squat I see through the stalks the dusty soles of a man's shoes, toes pointing to the sky. Curious, I part the grass. A man is asleep on the ground. His skin is very dark, almost black, and, although I've never seen one, I wonder if he could be a nigger. His head, matted with tight gray curls, is resting on a knapsack. I bend down to get a better look, and he opens his eyes, grabs me by the ankle. He sits up. He's wearing a dark suit, torn and covered with dust; underneath the jacket his chest is naked. My legs are trembling, and I'm angry that he's able to sense my fear with his fingers. 'Pretty little white girl,' he says. 'Please don' tell 'bout me. They be like to kill me.' His eyes are uncontrolled, the whites flickering like ghosts; saliva in the corners of his mouth, a mad dog. 'I jus' passin' through, I be hoppin' the freight tonight. Mus' promise not to tell 'bout me.' I feel something trickle down my leg, and I know I've lost control. My water spashes onto the black man's hand; when he lets go of me, I start to run.

Flying dust grates my mouth and throat. Dry blades of grass flash in the sun, and I'm beating my way upstream in a river of knives. I run in another direction. The grass whicks at my legs, in some places cutting deep. I'm lost, and the black man will hear my frenzy. I'll run in circles, right into my death at his hands, hands hard and hungry as a crocodile's mouth. I scream, and the sound of my voice frightens me more than the man's hands. But I scream again: 'Papa, Papa.' I'm running first in one direction, then another, the grass in places flattened completely by my backtracking. I hear my name, Mama's voice, and run in what I think is the right direction. But I've lost it. I stop, out of breath. Overhead the sun chiming and pealing and booming, its strong brass rays like the pipes of an organ. 'Charlotte! Stay where you are; keep yelling till we find you.' Papa. I'm less frightened now, and wait humbly in the grass, calling, till old Mr Hoffman tracks me, and leads me back to the fair. Mama kisses me, and I begin to sob. 'I think it was a nigger,' I say. Papa kneels and takes my hand: 'Where?' I point to the grass behind the outhouse.

People stand silent at their picnic tables, families close together, protecting their jugs of lemonade, their beans and sandwiches, coffee and pie. Dogs are nervous, circling. A wind bends the corners of a tablecloth, flattens the women's skirts against their legs like the draperies of old statues.

Papa says, 'A nigger here? What was he doing in the grass?'

'I think he was sleeping, Papa.'

'Did he try to touch you?'

'He grabbed my ankle.'

Papa bows his head, and a few of the men step forward as if something might be expected of them. 'I mean, anywhere else?'

'No, I told you. Just my ankle.' In a way, I'm sorry he didn't, because I sense that Papa is about to go into one of his electrifying rages, and I want something to cover my humiliation, the spectacle of my terror. 'I think he's going to get on a train.'

'I can have him picked up,' Papa says. 'I'll talk to Tom Anderson, and he can nab him when he tries to hop the 8:05. I'm sure that's what he'll try to do.'

Papa picks me up, and I put my arms around his neck. I've never been frightened before, I'll never be frightened again. But in the grass the nigger has dirtied me with my own filth, and I hope they'll hurt him.

IN THE PEACOCK'S TAIL

35

KATE: Over my head, the shrieks of the mynah birds glitter
                 in the tops of the complicated trees. But in his
carriage Hans Lucas is quiet. I like the walk from our apartment
down to Beretania Street, the smell of ginger, plumeria, pikake,
and a greenery so enchanted that every house behind it seems
not quite ordinary, like the house of the giant at the top of the
beanstalk. I cross the street with brown and yellow women who
say '*Wikiwiki*' to their children, and wear long flowered dresses
as if going to a coronation; with kids going barefoot to school –
proof that nothing in Hawaii is fierce enough to hurt you.

When we got off the plane nearly a year ago, I felt wonderful,
better than I ever had in my life. A sweet sticky wind lapped at
us, and even though there were clouds and mist on the
mountains, right away I sensed a perennial noonday light. Our
apartment was cool with tatami mats; when you pulled up the
bamboo blinds you could see all the way down to Waikiki. Our
landlord, Akamu Kanazawa, had put a bowl of mango and
papaya on the table, and in the kitchen, smelling like dried
brown flowers, was the kona coffee he'd left us. '*Aloha nui kakou*,'
he said. The first day, with all that fruit in the house, we
borrowed Mr Kanazawa's car and drove out to Wailuku,
picked a pineapple straight from the field, peeled it with a
butcher knife, and ate it with the juice dripping down our arms.
As we walked back to the car big drops of rain fell from a sunny
sky, and the fields steamed like Judgment Day and the rising up
of souls.

The day I went into labor, we had driven out to Makaha. The
sand there is clean and coarse, lightly colored, as if the clouds
over Tantalus have been pounded up by the sea. I spread my
towel and waited on a beach empty and new, like the face of an
unmarked clock. We had left Honolulu early. Roads were being
widened and repaired, and on the way out of the city we'd

passed some workmen drilling near a sign that said 'Big Hole'. There was an air of ritual and hilarity, as if it was not the roads of civilization being built, but an *imu* for roasting a pig. Some of the men were Hawaiian, or part Hawaiian, and very fat. On the mainland I'd always thought that obesity came from the workings of a furtive mouth, but in Hawaii fatness seemed a part of health and hardiness. We took the Nuuanu Pali Drive and, as we passed the rain forest, a sad wisdom made me blink. It was like looking at a young and lovely girl: you couldn't imagine the uses that age and men might put her to, but you knew the marks of death and desire would soon begin to show.

At the top of the Pali, Peter got out of the car. The cliff face falls away a thousand feet, and a pair of binoculars is bolted to a metal stand. You can see the coastline, Kaneohe and the little town of Kailua. That day there were storm clouds on the Koolau Range. 'Want to look?' said Peter; he was checking out the surf.

'I'll stay here,' I said. It's always very windy, and the wall doesn't quite come up to my hip. Our landlord's wife, Mrs Kanazawa, told me that in the battle of Nuuanu, King Kamehameha cut down his enemies at the top of the Pali, or forced them to jump off the cliff. She said that some of the men who jumped were blown back up, but I don't know if this is true. And that sometimes old bones are dug up at the bottom of the cliff. She told me that a lot of Hawaiians don't like to go out alone at night because they see ghost-warriors lighting their way up the mountainside with kukui-nut torches. I got the impression that ghosts are as necessary as water to the Hawaiians, and that on the island there are at least twice as many people as you can see.

'Flat as a coat of paint,' said Peter, getting into the car. 'Let's try Makaha.' He put his hand on my stomach. 'Think he can take the ride? You're not due for two weeks yet.' He headed back into Honolulu, and out of town again the other way. I had become used to the fact that my fortune and whereabouts were largely dependent on storms I'd never seen; on wind, evaporation and barometric pressure. Sundays, and afternoons when Peter could get away, I went with him like an altar boy who does what he's asked and doesn't question the knowledge or intentions of the priest. His job at the Mahimahi Club –

mahimahi means dolphin in Hawaiian – was ideal, because he could set his own hours. And when he was there, he worked hard; he liked teaching people to swim and dive, and he was very good at it.

The beach at Makaha changes a lot from summer to winter. On that afternoon in April, the shore was wide and flat as a plain, but I discovered that in October, when storm water begins to erode it, the foreshore steepens hard. I sat up as Peter dropped down into a bright little valley; at the end of the ride he waved. He didn't paddle on his knees because the water there is so warm you don't have to. I had hated even the summer water in Santa Cruz. When I was still sick and Peter told me he wanted me to swim in the cold water there, I had shuddered: in early fall it can drop down to the mid-forties. I don't know why I didn't say no. Every day after he finished work, I swam laps while he timed me. I wanted to swim in the pool, but he said I should go into the sea. Every day the water took my breath away, every night I was hot again with the fever. After the laps once I cut my foot on a piece of glass, but I was so numb I didn't notice it until I saw the blood. Peter was always waiting with a towel, and I argued with him every time I came out of the water. 'I'm going to tell the doctor,' I screamed. And another time: 'You're trying to make me into the image and likeness of your family. It won't work.' But when he wrapped me in the towel, it was wonderful, like closing all the windows when a heavy rain begins. And the next day I would swim again. We slept closer together, and sometimes Peter would lift my arm. 'You're getting definition,' he'd say. 'Here.' Touching one of my muscles. One night I didn't have the fever any more.

In November, just after we got to the islands, I discovered I was pregnant, had been pregnant all the time, even while I was sick. I told Peter I was sure it had happened that day in the leaves. The first thing he said was, 'I want to take you to Waikiki. I want you to try it. On your stomach, before you get too big.' He brought me there late one day when the beach was deserted, and only a couple of people were out. 'Take my board, I'll watch you from here. When you see a wave, paddle hard and hang on. The surf is nice and small, and there aren't any drunks or flying boards.' Peter never surfed Waikiki; it wasn't big enough.

The water is mild and fragrant like Chinese green tea. And when it's low in the sky, the sun is enormous, as if you could float right down into it. I lifted my arms to paddle the way Peter had shown me, and it was hard to tell when they broke the surface of the water, it was so silky, and only slightly thicker than the air. When I got outside, the other surfers, beach boys I think, didn't pay any attention to me. A few lights had come on in the hotels, and I imagined the tourists hurrying to their rooms, the slung cameras like badges on their shirts; the smell of gin and broiling meat in the dining rooms; the torches that would later be lit; and, in their whites, the sailors a light drift of snow on Kalakaua.

Out there it was quiet and I was suddenly conscious that I was in the middle of the Pacific, far from the ramparts and strongholds of a continent. The beach boys were looking over their shoulders, so I lay down on my board and craned my neck. The shadow of a wave, arching like the back of a cat, bristled at me from behind. When they paddled, I paddled – but not fast enough, because they took off, while my board slid down the back. I never thought it would be so hard to catch a wave, only that it would be tough to ride it. The sun sank abruptly, the way it always does in the tropics; the board was slippery, there was nothing to hang on to. Now, if a wave came, I might not be able to see it, and I could lose the board. I didn't know how far out I was, but I didn't think I could swim in if I had to. Slowly, piecemeal, I paddled and stopped. Hugged the rails whenever I heard a wave hissing behind me. Let it pass underneath. Paddled again.

Ahead, the lights of Waikiki were reflected in the water like bits of broken glass, but they didn't seem to be getting any closer. I think I was about to panic when I heard Peter calling. He was swimming out. After he brought me in, we sat on one of the benches where the old men play chess on Kalakaua.

'I started thinking about sharks,' I said, 'as soon as the sun went down.'

He closed his eyes: 'Not at Waikiki.'

I felt my baby move then for the first time. I was glad that he was going to be born in Hawaii, that the first Hawaiians had put their boats into the water and, star-fired on long currents, had floated to those islands that not even a blind optimist could have imagined.

The day Hans Lucas was born, Peter stayed out a long time. As I sat on the unscratched beach, the baby pooling up life inside me, a sudden throb of its body drew mine into a pucker, and I knew I was in labor. After the next contraction, I stood up and looked around, as if I expected somebody to be there. I was two weeks early, and I didn't know how soon it would come. Slow and flatfooted, I went up the beach to our old station wagon and opened the door. I pressed hard on the horn, and one of the surfers straightened up on his board. Peter swung around, put his hand to his ear in a mock attempt to hear me. 'God *damn* you,' I said. 'Why don't you come in?' I leaned further into the car, jabbing the horn staccato with my fist. I felt a hand on my arm. A Hawaiian had parked behind me in a failing, rusty jeep, but I hadn't heard him drive up over the noise of the horn. He glanced at my stomach: '*Keiki* coming?'

'I'm in labor,' I said. He was the biggest man I'd ever seen, his skin dark and shiny as a porpoise.

'Which one your husband?' He pulled his board out of the back of the jeep.

'The one on the left,' I said, pointing.

His arms rolled through the whitewater like the wheels of a train. When he was over halfway, Peter waved and began paddling in. I waved back, but I saw that he hadn't been waving at me. As their boards met, the Hawaiian put his hand on Peter's shoulder, and they talked a minute before coming in to the beach. Peter was very excited. 'Let's go,' he said, sitting next to me in the front seat. 'Keoki's going to drive. He can get there quicker than I can.'

Keoki started the car before Peter closed the door, but he didn't drive recklessly over the country roads, just very fast. Pressed against his packed black arm, I closed my eyes, yielded to his presence. By then I'd figured out who he was. I'd seen only one or two other Hawaiians like him: with their big pure features, their calm mantle of expression, they looked like a small band of oracles cast ashore by an ignorant king.

Car swaying as we came around a bend into Nanakuli, Keoki

said, 'My father and mother live here now; come over from Hilo last week.'

'Your father still a fisherman?' said Peter. His watch on my lap, I was timing my contractions.

He nodded. 'I fish with him in morning, help Auntie Lilia in afternoon. That's my mother. Make leis for sell airport.'

I winced and sat up straighter. Keoki glanced at me: '*Da kine opu*, hurt bad?'

'Yes,' I said, and he put his hand on my stomach.

'You okay, I see that. Auntie Lilia help with plenty *keiki*, get them born. She one *akamai wahine*, remember old ways. She know things jus' by lookin'.'

'I know what you mean,' Peter said. 'Sometimes M.S. scares the shit out of me.'

I was the only *haole* in the ward. A nurse said, 'Would you like to hold your baby?' In the bed across from me, a tiny Chinese woman smiled, but not as if she was used to smiling. 'He's very beautiful,' said the nurse, holding out Hans Lucas. 'I don't think I've ever seen one quite so flawless right after delivery.'

I was surprised he was so smooth. And so fair that I thought he might vanish. His features pulsed in transition, as if he was turning more perfect every second. At first I held him at arms' length, afraid so much beauty would either freeze or burn me. 'Go on,' said the nurse. 'You can cuddle him. They like to be held next to the mother's heart.' When I brought him close, he whimpered a little, and I wondered if it was because my heart was pumping so fast. I don't know what I would have done if the nurse hadn't been there. He was so beautiful I was afraid; I wanted to run out of the room.

A Hawaiian brought her baby over, hospital gown adrift on the tall fountain of her body. 'This is my fourth,' she told me, 'and all the time I've been in the hospital, yours is the one I'll remember best. I've never seen such a lovely head.' The Chinese woman went down to the nursery, and when she came back she offered me something from a box one of her visitors had brought. She didn't say anything, just held out the box. It looked like white candy. When I bit into one it was gluey and very sweet.

In the nursery the Hawaiian babies were steep and hard-looking, like chunks of cliff. They cried a lot to be picked up. The Orientals slept harder and kicked more; adept and imperial, they seemed to have an early premonition of pain which gave them some kind of advantage. Hans Lucas was the calmest, as if his body heat was lower, his needs less critical than the rest of them.

Keoki stayed at the hospital with Peter, and after the baby was born, Peter made several trips to the nursery, leaving me alone with Keoki. 'Do you see that woman over there?' I whispered, glancing at the Hawaiian. 'She told me the doctor let her have the umbilical cord, and she's taking it home with her.'

'*Da kine piko* cord.' Keoki leaned forward in his chair, hands on his knees. 'Old Hawaiians put *da kine piko* in one rock, so *keiki* stay close to land where he born.'

The afternoon she went home carrying her glass jar, I was nursing Hans Lucas. I wanted to watch her snug that birth-brown rope deep into a hollow, the beginning of his body tucked up in the earth just as securely as the scraps of it would be at the end. I hugged my baby. I wanted to apologize for not taking precautions, for not laying down for him a nice calm circle of cord.

36

KATE: I leave Hans Lucas in his carriage under a plumeria
            tree while I bring in the groceries. Steak and potatoes
and ice cream. M.S. is arriving in the morning, with Jenny and
Eric. She's fussy about meat, and I wonder if she'll notice about
the steaks. Hawaiians feed their cattle pineapple bran, and the
beef has a wild taste, more carnal than the meat on the
mainland. A Chinese cabbage like a folded fan, the ginger root
and squid, I'll cook later for Peter and me. M.S. doesn't like
experiments. She's rented a house up in Alewa Heights, but it's
hard to imagine her, straight-backed and spiny, her braid as
taut as the tendons in her neck, living among the Hawaiians.

  While I'm putting the things away, Peter comes in carrying
the baby. Whenever he isn't eating or sleeping or surfing, he fills
his hands with Hans Lucas. His head close to the shimmering
hair, he kisses him, whispering things I can't understand.
They're like two vines that having once touched grow round
and round each other until they become one plant. Peter's love
for Hans Lucas is something he can't help; it wasn't planned. It
just arrived with the birth, as if it had been growing all along
right next to the baby inside me. He loves him for the sake of
loving, his love an involuntary hymn. The baby's eyes are
shaped like an animal's, but their color is northern, always
changing, their light brightening or perishing, inconstant and
bodiless as a cloud.

  'You better get ready,' Peter says. 'I'll feed Hans Lucas.'

  The Kanazawas' daughter Amy comes to babysit. She's a
silent girl and, like her mother, looks more Hawaiian than
Japanese. 'Come in,' I say.

  She presses against the wall as if she's afraid to stand in the
center of the room, but when Peter comes in with the baby she
holds out her arms. 'Oh, I love him,' she says. 'Can I hold him
in my lap?'

Peter drives slowly out to Diamond Head; hard against the horizon, it looks like an ancient plow ready to ream the sea. We've been living in Hawaii for nearly a year, but still I marvel at the winds, the mountains, the immaculate clouds, the lordly light. 'You don't want to go tonight, do you?' I say.

'No. But she reminds me every day when she brings the kids to swim.'

'What have you got against her?'

'It's not her, it's the kind of people she knows. They own everything; measure it, buy it, change it, so it's exactly like them. Nothing bigger or smaller than their own ideas. I'm surprised they don't measure each other's pricks.'

'Maybe they do,' I say. 'Why are we going?'

'Because you want to. But before we even get there I know nobody's going to say anything to change the way I am, which is the only reason for meeting people. Nobody's going to say anything I want to hear.'

When Lucy Delano brings her grandchildren to the Mahi-mahi Club, she won't let anybody but Peter teach them. She regards swimming as an important social and moral asset in the islands, and she wants her grandchildren to have the best. She brings them nearly every day, and I think she's a little in love with Peter. I've seen her watching him, her slightly bald head bent forward as if he's somebody she's been wanting to meet for a long time. Walker Delano's grandfather got rich on sugar and roads, and the Delanos, along with one or two other *kamaaina* families, own most of Honolulu. You read a lot about La Tresca, the house they've modelled after an Italian palace, stashed with old and faded art, and enclosed inside a high wall, an island within an island.

At the gate, a man in gray uniform checks Peter's invitation. 'Was that a servant,' I say, 'or some special kind of cop?' Peter shrugs. On the way to the house he takes my hand. Drinks are being served on the terrace. Some of the older women are in brocade and others are wearing *pakemuus*, long fitted dresses with Chinese necks.

When I told Mrs Kanazawa we were going to La Tresca, she frowned: 'We'll have to get you a dress.' She sent me to Liberty House, telling me to charge to her account any dress I liked and bring it straight home. I chose a square-necked shantung. Just by looking at it she was able to cut a pattern and I went out and bought a couple of yards of lustrous staw-colored silk. By five the same day the original was back on the rack. She wouldn't let me pay her for the copy; she said she used to be a seamstress and didn't want to get out of practice.

Lucy Delano is waiting at the edge of the terrace; she puts herself between us so that Peter has to let go my hand. 'I know you teach,' she says, squeezing my shoulder, 'and I think you'll love the Kelways. He's head of anthropology at the university. There's Geneva, but I don't see Davis.' She takes me up to a woman with green eyes and short blonde hair. 'Geneva, this is. . . .' A fingertip to her lips.

'Kate Hollander,' I say.

'Yes. Well, Kate teaches, and I thought you two might get along. I'll just take Peter with me a minute; I want him to meet Frank Tayman.'

Geneva Kelway and I watch as she draws Peter into the crowd. 'That was fast, my dear,' says Geneva. 'I didn't even get to meet him. Is he your husband?'

'Yes. And I'm not a teacher,' I say.

'That's all right – I'm not either.' Her throat isn't quite firm, and I figure she's about forty. A hand shading her eyes, she smiles at me. 'I think Lucy fancies your husband. I know all about that sort of thing – I have a good-looking husband myself.' She flicks her fingers at a man talking to a girl in a backless dress. His face is smooth and tan, and the whites of his eyes are very clear.

Japanese maids in kimonos pass bowls of caviar, and water chestnuts wrapped in thin pieces of steak. They wear frangipani in their hair. 'I've always wanted to do that,' I say, 'ever since we came to Hawaii. But with my hair, it just looks like a bird dropped something on my head.'

'It's sensible to know one's limitations. It took me years to discover how frightful I look in a muumuu.'

'Is your husband English too?'

'Not bloody likely. I came over from England just before the war to stay with a cousin in Louisville and I met Davis at a Derby party, a few months before he went into the Army. He was terribly glamorous in uniform; related to Jefferson Davis, all very romantic.' She lowers her lids against the sun, head a little to one side, and I sense a state of graceful despair. 'Do you have any children?' she says.

'A baby. He's six months old.'

'What's his name?'

'Hans Lucas.'

'Delightful, quite masterful; I hope he lives up to it. I don't have any myself. I've never liked wet things clinging to me, but they're cute at a distance, like bats or lemurs.'

Her husband comes up behind her; he kisses the back of her neck. 'Sorry I was so long, sweetie. Here's your drink.' He takes my hand. 'Davis Kelway. I've been looking at your beautiful hair. Please don't ever cut it.'

Geneva sends him to get me a drink. 'Your husband isn't going to get you one because Lucy has him firmly in hand.'

The old woman has slipped her arm through Peter's and is leading him toward the house. On the way, she points to some people at the edge of the lawn, and gives instructions to a passing maid. 'I don't see any Hawaiians here,' I say.

'And you won't,' Geneva tells me. 'Chinese, yes; doctors and lawyers. And maybe some Japanese. But Walker thinks anything darker than yellow is bound to be sexy and sloppy and sticky; too risky for his Episcopalian bread and salt.'

'Come on,' Davis says. 'Let's go through the house.' He takes my arm. 'If you haven't seen it, you ought to. It's a young museum.'

The door leading to the library is open, and inside a man and woman are flipping the pages of a book; they turn when we come in and I can tell they've been laughing. Behind them shelves of books rise to the ceiling, bright and leatherbound, shining like pennies.

'Walker has an excellent collection of Chinese pornography,' Davis whispers, guiding us through another door.

The next room is like the inside of a display case: no furniture, nothing to bump into, just a parquet floor unfolding with the freedom of a meadow. Lots of jars and pitchers and jugs and urns. The centerpiece is a display of busts; mostly chipped, with long-nosed faces. 'For Walker, enough is never as good as a feast,' murmurs Davis, close to my ear.

Plonk, high on a pedestal on each side of the door, is a faded urn, red and two-handled; soldiers fighting mythical battles on the belly of one, slaves playing the flute on the other.

'It's like an early Capone,' snickers a man peering at one of the heads. Peter has come in with Lucy Delano and is just inside the door. Withheld, his eyes estimating something I can't see, he's letting her do all the talking. A wet breeze sways in through the French windows and I smell some kind of animal. Not dog or horse but a wild mainland smell, out of place in Hawaii. I've smelled that kind of wildness before, the first time I bathed Hans Lucas. When I undressed him I'd caught a faint furry odor like the floor of the forest in Redwood Creek. Even after I soaped him, it didn't come off. Now, whenever I hold him, I catch whiffs of something that's been growing in the shade for a long time.

People, noisy, bulge into the room; crush Mrs Delano against Peter, who steps back, the spurt of his back straight up, his shoulder lifting as if he's about to turn into a wave. What is it? I want to ask him. Why does our baby smell like that, and why haven't I asked you before? He brushes against one of the urns, and in their stale expensive sunshine the soldiers rock like leaves in a wind before they settle to earth.

'I want to show you something,' Davis says to Geneva as if it's a private joke; he takes her over to one of the marble faces.

Peter's looking bored, but when I go up to him, Lucy Delano grabs his hand. 'I have one or two paintings of the early Hawaiians that might interest you,' she says, ignoring me. When she leads him away, I follow right behind. She doesn't let go of him, as if she's afraid he might bolt, and I can feel her simmering at him as we go from room to greedy room. Everywhere, we pass through clumps of guests, most of them as indifferent and unknown to each other as strangers on a city street. Some, with anxious faces, stalk through the house as if hoping to find a revelation there. Toothy and dangerous, the middle-aged ones are clotted with self-esteem. The older ones are more relaxed; on the terrace their voices hum quietly over their drinks, as if they've always been old, calm and full of a pleasurable resignation.

'In here,' says Lucy Delano, taking Peter into a room of white wicker, paintings and tatami mats. If she knows I'm there, she doesn't let on. In front of a small watercolor she narrows her

eyes and tilts her head. 'It's a Mishiro; do you like it?'
Chrysanthemums at dusk, the soft spikes in the foreground a
dying explosion; up in a corner the prongs of a new moon.
'Walker picked it up in Tokyo on his last trip. It's supposed to
illustrate a couplet from the *Kokinshu*.' She clears her throat:

> 'Why did he die in autumn of all the seasons?
> In autumn one grieves for those who yet remain.

I used to know a lot of those.' She steps back and waves her
hand. 'Go ahead, I'm in your way.'

With his index finger Peter straightens the picture. 'It's a
pretty good painting. But I grew up in California, so I've never
seen a garden give up the ghost like that.'

'You don't believe in ambiguity, do you?' she says.

'In nature, maybe. Not in people.'

'I can't imagine anyone being ambiguous about you.' She
draws him over to a large engraving. On a square-nosed board,
a Hawaiian is paddling out alongside several other natives in
canoes; frigates lie newly at anchor in the harbor, and in the
background the mountains are shrouded and undisclosed. 'It
was done by one of Cook's sailors,' she says. In their decent,
virginal clothes the natives sadden me. Rocking on the edge of
their future, they're like children whose parents are about to
give them away, who soon forget the place where they were born
and learn the manners of strangers. 'You wish Cook hadn't
come,' she says, finally noticing me. 'But what you don't
understand is, it's not healthy for the gullible races to be left in
isolation.' She points to another engraving, two places down.
'Perhaps you like this one better.'

An ancient surfboard sleeps on the grass in front of a hut
which is woven like a good piece of herringbone. In the hut a
wahine pounds a piece of *kapa* while her husband, a chief in a
cape and helmet, looks on; brazen and serene, they're content to
be at the natural center of things, immortal.

'It's like one of the dreams I had every night about Hawaii,'
says Peter, 'just before we left the mainland.'

She glances at her breasts as if he's paid her an intimate
compliment. 'I'm glad you like it.' We stroll back through the
house, and I look for the Kelways. 'You must come to La Tresca
any time you want,' she says to Peter, as we come back through

the door with the urns. Davis and Geneva are standing just inside.

Guests crowd into the room. A man in a white dinner jacket spills some of his drink on Peter. 'My apologies,' he says. 'But I don't think gin stains.' He kisses Lucy Delano on the cheek. As Peter steps aside, the handle of one of the urns presses like a fist into his back. He turns and the air is charged with the color of blood, the color of money. When the urn hits, the pieces run chattering across the floor; close up I see that the red is thin and shabby, without power or substance.

'And behold the walls of the temple did shake,' says the man in the dinner jacket. He takes a quick look at the other urn. Geneva puts an arm around me, and Davis is holding both hands out, palms up, as if he'd tried to stop its fall. People gather at the back of the room, stepping wide around the pieces, as if they might still be moving.

'I was trying to get out of the way,' Peter says, 'and I backed into it. I didn't mean to break any of your things.' He kneels to pick up a fragment curved like a teacup, the handle still attached.

'It's all right,' says Lucy Delano. Kneeling, she faces him and I see the lines filled with make-up under her eyes. 'They're not really good pieces, and I don't want you to worry about it.'

'That thing was probably a couple of thousand years old, but I ride a surfboard, so you think I can't appreciate it. You invite me out here, so you can check me out like a chunk of marble or a goddam piece of canvas.'

'I just don't want you to be upset,' she says. Several of the guests are squatting behind them, picking up the pieces. 'Would it make you feel better if I made a scene?' She is hobbling over to Peter on her knees.

'I just want you to admit it was a disaster, and give me credit for knowing that I screwed up.'

'Please,' she says. 'Don't be angry. I'm really terribly sorry.'

37

KATE: Geneva puts a candle on the glass table. 'If we eat out here on the *lanai*, the men won't have to move.'

It's raining, so fine you can't hear it on the overhanging roof. Davis puts out his cigarette. I think he's waiting for us to go back into the house so he can go on talking to Peter.

A lamp like a low moon hangs down in the kitchen. 'Thanks for asking us to dinner,' I say to Geneva. 'It would have been awful to go straight home.'

'Just cold lamb and potato salad.' She spoons chutney into a crystal dish. 'I agree it would have been a mistake to take him home; he's in rather a state, I think. Could you just take this out to the table?'

The *lanai* smells of grass and damp cement. At the edge of the candlelight, Davis lights a match. 'Lots of *haoles* don't accept that idea,' he's saying, fresh cigarette in his fingers, smoke curving like a quill over his hand. 'We say that life is rational whenever we think we're in control, and that it's irrational when we're not. To a *haole* science is rational, but if a Hawaiian trusts a *kahuna* he's a lunatic. In fact no religion can claim to be totally rational, because none of them can give us complete control.'

'Do *kahunas* really have powers?' I say to Geneva in the kitchen.

'So they say, but nobody knows. I do hope Davis isn't boring Peter. He's writing a book on *kahunas*, and people at parties have started to run when they see him coming.' With precise almost imperceptible movements, she slices a handful of green onions. 'Does Peter look any happier?'

'A little.'

'What do you do when he's out surfing?'

'Read on the beach, play with the baby.'

'I work four days a week at the university library, which, thank God, keeps me sane most of the time. I don't have enough interests to stay tastefully at home with food or flowers, like a lot of faculty wives.' She rinses the knife, dries it. 'When we first came to Honolulu I got a job selling cosmetics in Waikiki. I absolutely adored it. The lovely colors of the lipstick, those delectable creams. And the women all trusting me, every one of them wanting to be beautiful for some man. The thing was, they thought I could do it. I'd suggest different shades of make-up, a new powder or scent, and when those women walked out of there they were undoubtedly prettier, and happy as clams. I felt wonderful. Talk about witch doctors: I was performing miracles every day.'

'Why did you quit?'

'When Davis started teaching, he didn't think it looked right for the wife of a professor to be working in a shop. I still miss it. I like to be up on all the new things. I'm a few years older than Davis, you know, and I'm at an age when one has to tart oneself up. I think if you really work at it, it's perfectly possible to look good almost to the end. As the magicians say, it's all done with mirrors, my dear.' She hands me a loaf of bread. 'Would you be a love and slice this?'

'Where's my viewer?' says Davis, coming into the kitchen. 'I want to show Peter a slide.'

'In your desk, bottom left. We're going to eat in a minute.' From a cupboard she takes down four plates. 'If he starts looking for a book, which is his usual tactic just before dinner, we may not eat for hours. I hope Peter is bearing up; Davis can be very earnest if you don't watch him. Is he all right out there?' she says, as I glance at Peter.

'I think he likes to be by himself.'

'He's gorgeous, isn't he?' she whispers, and we both stand in the doorway looking at the back of Peter's head.

Davis brushes past us. 'I found what I want,' he says, waving the viewer and a couple of books.

'I'm very susceptible to the way people look; I can't help it.' Geneva is stacking a tray with knives and dishes and forks. 'And I'm pretty good at guessing what's underneath. Peter looks like somebody who has things *happen* to him. Do you know what I mean?'

'Yes,' I say. 'Tonight was a great example.'

'Lucy told me she's going to send the pieces to a museum in

Boston to see if the thing can be mended. It was an extra-ordinary sight: Peter and the old girl kneeling face to face, as if they were being married in church, and all those people kneeling around them. Appalling the way she hung all over him when we were leaving.'

'It wasn't really his fault. That man in the tux crowded him. It's like his mother says: why are there always more horses' asses than horses?'

As I bring out the tray, Davis drops a slide into the viewer. 'We found this at the entrance to a burial cave,' he says.

'Who did they bury there?' Peter holds out his hand.

'Royalty and chiefs, the *ali'i*. At first we thought we'd found Kamehameha's tomb. The old fishermen used to believe that the jawbone of male *ali'i* had magical powers when it was made into a fish-hook; so to make sure their bones didn't get stolen, the *ali'i* had themselves embalmed and hidden in caves.' Davis hands him the viewer. 'And the *kahunas* were detailed to put heavy curses on anybody who entered the *ali'i* tombs. Interest-ing: just before the war a *haole* doctor took some bone specimens and artifacts from a sepulcher over on Molokai – and got hideously ill right after he left the cave. The Hawaiians I've talked to think only the fact that he was a *haole* kept him from croaking.'

'Where is this cave?' says Peter.

'Near Palikai.'

'On the North Shore?'

'In a field near the beach. The surf out there in the winter is damn near impossible – rips and currents and lots of coral. But, way back, the old Hawaiians used to play funny-buggers on the biggest breakers. Sometimes so many of them were out in the water there was nobody left to mind the store. The women surfed too.'

Peter hands the viewer to me. 'Does anybody surf there now?'

'Haven't the faintest.'

'Grub,' says Geneva, coming out of the house.

Inside the viewer, the figure of a man scratched in blue rock. Arms, long and gleeful, lifted; knees bent. Behind him bright sky or water, the color of stone. And, fat under his feet, a board. 'How old?' I say, still looking at the slide.

'Old. Eventually we hope we can pin it to a specific period.

The rock is too big to have come from anywhere else – so it's almost certainly a surfer at Palikai.'

Peter winks at me. His first surf in Hawaii had been at Makaha the day after we arrived. He had waxed his board and carried it down the steep foreshore. At his back the mountains, and palms beating like insects in the wind; beach and horizon empty, the sea as bright as a sword. Trades slapped offshore, and little crescents of foam wetted him as he paddled out. The drop down the eight-foot wall was sloppy and choppy; and on the second set he miscalculated the chop and wiped out. 'The swells are real shaggy,' he said when he came in. 'Not like the ones in Santa Cruz; and they break a lot further out. But the big difference is speed. They come from the open ocean, so they're heavier, more hard packed. They don't touch a goddam thing till they hit this reef, so everything happens faster. And after the drop, the water sucks at your feet like mud after it rains.'

On his next trip out to Makaha, he rode what became the first of many flawless waves: about ten foot when he got there, the shorebreak round as a hoop. Some coast *haoles* were out, and a Hawaiian we'd seen at Ala Moana. 'I've got a feeling this is going to be good,' he said.

Later he talked to me about that ride the way he always talks to me about anything important: in bed, face to face, our parts all touching, just before we make love. He stammered, reliving it, so it didn't all come out clearly, but with pauses, gaps and breathlessness: 'I'm paddling for it – drops of water clinging to the wax, jumping and sparkling right next to my face – drops rolling forward, lengthening like they were blown glass – wave's curling, whitewater cascading from the left – and safe, it's safe – I'm safe – still it hasn't broken – I'm sliding forever, right down to the bottom.' He slipped his hand between my legs, feeling me. 'I saw it all, felt it all, I didn't even think about it,' he said. 'But after I was paddling back out I suddenly realized I was in control the whole ride, and I wasn't even trying.'

For a long time surfing Makaha was like that for him. In one day he rode as many good waves out there as he'd ridden in a month in California. But after a while he told me that surfing Makaha was like a premonition of middle age. You had done all you were going to do, and nothing after that was going to matter, be any different or better. No more problems, no tension, no juice-giving complications – but simply, on these pert and domesticated waves, the rest of a safely spent life. A ratio, a certain proportion, was missing: he was afraid he'd never be afraid again. Surfing Steamer or Makaha, he had wanted to test his endurance, perfect his technique. But during his first spring in Hawaii, he had begun to believe in the possibility of a mysterious moral awakening in the warm sea mountains off the windward coast; to dream of finding a place that would make him feel good every day, a place where he would know that if he paddled out he might not make it back in; a place that would let him touch base – or whatever you wanted to call it – every minute. Nobody else he knew, except maybe Barney, felt like that.

All that spring he searched. He began to drive the island alone, slowly, mile by mile, inspecting every inch of the coast, his reckoning as clean as a jeweller's before cutting a diamond. He would start on the windward side, driving from Ka'a'awa to Punaluu, a distance of only a few miles. If he went too far or too fast, he might miss something. The day I had Hans Lucas he told me and Keoki he still hadn't found anything.

'You no find what you looking for till the winter,' said Keoki. 'Then we go North Shore. My cousin, he tell me is one big place there.'

'Sunset?'

'No. This other place. My cousin, he see it break one time before he go mainland, but he no see nobody ride there.'

In November the red-dirt pineapple furrows at Wahiawa were as hot as a grid on a city street. Keoki's old jeep bounced high on the road, and every few minutes Peter checked to see that the boards, wedged nose down in the back, were still secure. As we came over the hill into Haleiwa, Keoki pointed to the long arms of whitewater opening to the horizon. 'My cousin say when soup like that at Haleiwa, more bigger further up, at place where we go.' Down by the beach, he said, 'We park here, watch break.' Far outside, the lines of whitewater were lengthening, and I could see Peter's shirt sticking to his chest. 'If one big break here and Waimea, we gon' see something up the coast we never see before.' When he let out the clutch the jeep slammed ahead like a blow, and we bounced up Kam Highway, boards rocking, road whining under the wheels.

At Waimea, the shorebreak was big and fast, incoming waves colliding with the backwash, white turrets burning in the wind. 'I was out here twice this summer,' said Peter, 'and it didn't look like this. More like a baby's bath.'

'North Shore get the winter storm that make the *nala nui*. I hear two, three coast *haoles*, they try Sunset, get ass broke.'

From the canefields a smell of manure on the sticky trades, and salt blurred the windshield as the jeep bumped down a lane of fitful shacks and Quonsets. A mist hung offshore at Sunset Beach, but didn't soften the edges of the long symmetrical swells beating in, regular as the tick of a clock. 'It's bigger than anything I figured from looking at the map,' Peter said. When we got out of the jeep, he turned to Keoki. 'From this angle, what do you think?'

'Eighteen, mebbe twenty. Gon' be more bigger up-shore.' They were shoving each other and laughing. With Hans Lucas in my arms I walked down the beach. When I came back I could just see them squatting behind some bushes.

'I wish my mother could see the size of these sets,' Peter was saying to Keoki, as the ground thrummed under our feet. 'I think I just laid the longest cable of my life,' he said, and called to me to hand him some leaves.

A little further north, the sun was hidden behind currents of cloud, and the mountains had turned the color of the sea. From the road the fast swells seemed endless, unmoving and perfectly formed. They were the kind of waves M.S. had seen for Peter in her most fantastic dreams. In her letters to him she was loud and violent, a rabble-rouser: 'You say you're still surfing Makaha. Can't believe you haven't found anything better. There must be a spot on that smelly island where you can make a name for yourself. You're no better than the niggers that live there if you don't ride something they're too fat-assed to try themselves. The way you put it, the point of going *over* there was to get on something big. But all you ever say is that you went to Makaha or took Kate to Waikiki. Even a couple of the old ladies at the pool have been to Waikiki.'

'Round that bend is where we go.' Keoki handed me a scrap of paper. 'See where my cousin say turn off.'

'He's got an arrow by something called Lo's,' I said. As the jeep took the curve, I wondered if they would even paddle out. At least Peter was in good condition. When he'd been setting up the club in Honolulu and didn't get out to the country much, he'd found that he couldn't get through the day without the feel of salt water. Every evening after work he swam at Ala Moana, and practiced holding his breath under water, the sea so clear that the shadows of birds floated like leaves over his head. But it scared me that if he got wiped out in this stuff, he'd have to hold it forever.

To our left, a small store, nothing more than a few boards and a corrugated roof, and next to that a dirt road leading down to the beach. Some children and a naked baby were playing in the dirt by a sign that said LO'S GROCERYS in large wavering letters and, underneath, something in Oriental calligraphy.

Keoki took the dusty road slowly, smiling at the cries of the children, who ran with us a little way. As the jeep came over a little hill, a fine spray dappled our skins. On the beach side it was blowing, and the noise of the water was hot and loud like the blast of the fire in Valley Basin. Keoki stopped halfway down: 'Look the point.' Gray bluffs of water, edges crumbling into a dusty foam, toppled slowly as they approached the strip of land. 'They unwind nice and steady,' he said, 'just like line from reel.' He parked the jeep under some palms and he and Peter jumped up onto the hood.

Peter cupped his hands, calling above the wind and the shorebreak. 'It's about the same size as Sunset, but the walls are thicker, with a lot more juice. It's a scary place – like a technicolor movie that's gone back to black and white.'

Keoki nodded, squinting at the swells out at the point. 'We gon' watch, understand plenty before dip our dick in water.'

'Does this beach have a name?' I shouted.

'Palikai. My cousin father say the *po'e kahiko* ride here one time. Now nobody come.'

'What's *po'e kahiko*?'

'Old people of Hawaii.'

Peter said, 'I was just thinking about my first overhead at Steamer. It was terrifying, but I knew I had to do it. I'm not sure about this place.'

'We wait long time before paddle out,' said Keoki.

'My mother thinks I'm gutless.'

'My mother think I got plenty too much gut – all time *kaukau*, chow down.' He leaned against the windshield and stretched his legs.

'I'm going to take a walk,' Peter said to me. 'Want to come?' I wrapped Hans Lucas in a blanket and held him tight; I didn't trust that beach an inch. The sand, clean and prismatic, was the coarsest I'd ever seen; at every step, we sank to our ankles. On the foreshore the water shot up fast, cooler on my legs than anything I'd felt in Hawaii. Clouds and mist had closed in so tight they seemed appointed, but we could still see Keoki – silent and superior, apparent and powerful – beached on the jeep. The sets were consistent. 'A west swell,' Peter said, 'and they're breaking about every fifteen seconds on the outside reef.' Two sets later, he shouted at Keoki, who met us halfway between the jeep and the water. 'It's got to be damn near thirty,' he told him. 'The drop would be like falling out of a third-storey window.' The three of us just stood there watching; I'm not even sure our mouths were closed. 'The peaks are dumping straight across. It's completely closed out. The soup alone is bigger than anything I rode at Steamer.'

'The way that stuff break,' Keoki said during one of the lulls, 'and you no watch before you go out, never see your *wahine* or your *keiki* again. And maybe no paddle out place,' he said on the way back up to the jeep. 'We find out later.'

'If there isn't, you'd have to get out between sets.'

'This place got power. More better than anything on island, mebbe in world. In half-hour we here, that wave jump to thirty, close out; no can get in, no can get out in that stuff. Mebbe in other hour, jump to forty. We find out. Then we come one small day, ride first time.'

'It's down to twenty,' said Peter when the next two sets had come through. He shook his head. 'I never thought I'd hear myself say that.' Before we left California he'd told me the kind of surf he hoped to find in Hawaii, but none of it came close to what we'd just seen.

Keoki touched Peter's arm. 'Wave same last half-hour. Let's go that store, see what they have for chow.'

He started up the jeep but Peter said, 'Wait a minute, I just want to see this set.' Slipping through the mist, hills and valleys and shadows; whitewater flashing like lightning on the crests. Keoki turned off the ignition and Peter stood on the seat to watch. When the last wave of the set peaked, the soup curving all the way across was very white. 'It's like looking at the teeth of God,' he said.

As we sit down at Geneva's glass table, I can hear drops of water falling from leaf to leaf on plants invisible in the darkness of the garden. The rain has stopped but the moonlight is deflected by clouds. 'Shall we stay out here?' Geneva says. 'Or is it too damp?'

'It's just right,' I say. I can smell big wet flowers and island dirt. The soil in Hawaii is different from anything on the mainland. It looks and smells as if something supernormal is going on underneath; palpitating pink and blue roots maybe, or seeds that go blink in the dark and push up the stiff bright Hawaiian plants. You get the feeling that amazing stems and stalks and flowers are being invented every second under your feet.

Davis comes to the table holding an open book. 'I was trying to find a picture of a petroglyph, and I came across this marvellous passage about the first time the Hawaiians clapped eyes on the white man's ships: *Commoners and chiefs saw the wonderful sight and marvelled at it. Some were terrified and shrieked with fear. The valley of Waimea rang with the shouts of excited people as they saw the boat with its masts and sails shaped like a gigantic sting ray. One asked another, "What are those branching things?" and the other answered, "They are trees moving on the sea".'* Davis closes the book. 'It says they went into hiding and started to pray, but later some of them came out to welcome the white-skinned gods or ghosts. That must have taken a lot of guts.' His hands are small and manicured, but his wrists are rough-looking and very big.

'The Hawaiians are kind of like gods themselves,' I say. 'When I went into labor, Keoki – he's this Hawaiian friend of Peter's – drove us to the hospital. He put his hand on my stomach, and right away I was able to stand the pain.'

Davis unfolds his napkin. 'I've heard other people say the same kind of thing. The Hawaiians do seem to have some sort of calming influence on *haoles*, but I don't know why. It's easier to understand how their *kahunas* heal. In the early days of Christianity, the disciples healed all sorts of cases, if we can believe the Bible. But when Christianity got older, that first fervent purity was lost in the shuffle, so the healings got less and less common. I have a theory that the *kahunas* know how to tap that same source, perceive the same atoms of wisdom. They see or hear or feel phenomena the rest of us don't, and through some kind of inductive or intuitive process, they've figured out what to do with it.'

'Speaking of Hawaiians,' I say to Peter, 'were you telling Davis about Palikai?'

'No,' Davis says. 'I was telling him.' He turns to Peter. 'What about Palikai?'

'My brother's coming over from the mainland, and we're going to surf it. Keoki and I have been checking it out for the last couple of weeks, and we're just waiting for the right conditions.'

'Ah,' says Davis. 'So that's why you were so interested.' He seems annoyed.

'How long is your brother going to be here?' asks Geneva.

'My mother's rented a house up in Alewa Heights. She's bringing my sister over too. They're coming tomorrow, but I don't know how long they're going to stay.'

'It'll be nice for you to have them here for Christmas.' Geneva hands a tall narrow bottle to Davis. 'I'm not offering you any of these pickles,' she says. 'Davis has them sent from Louisville, and they're filthy hot.'

'How do you know you'll be able to handle Palikai?' says Davis.

'I don't. But I've been training for the wipeouts, I paddle fifteen miles every day, then swim a mile, down at Ala Moana.'

'Let's have coffee inside,' says Geneva.

In the living room two lamps are turned low, and the curtains in the big window have been drawn. Hanging above one of the lamps is a watercolor of Waikiki around 1900. I get the feeling that this is a stage Geneva has set for Davis many times. Peter sits at one end of a long red sofa. Across the room Davis is lighting a cigarette. 'Lichis in champagne,' says Geneva, coming in with a tray.

'Did you tell Davis how Barney measures waves?' I ask. I'm sitting on a zabutan at Peter's feet.

'How?' Davis says to me, when Peter doesn't answer.

'In units of fear. He says feet and inches aren't exact because they don't tell what you really want to know.'

'Witty chap.' Davis is watching Peter. 'I've seen them out at Makaha sometimes, and I'm curious. Once you've established that the waves are a certain height, and you can ride them that tall, it seems to me that everything after that must become a little repetitious.'

'No,' says Peter, and 'thanks' as Geneva hands him a goblet of lichis. 'It doesn't matter if it's the same size every day. The more waves you ride, the more you can appreciate the difference. And different beaches give you different waves.' He dips his spoon into the goblet, brings up some lichis and stops a few inches from his mouth. 'When you're on a wave, you're trying to scoff up some of that energy, make the planet work for you. One time, if you use it right, all the energy is at the top, at the lip, and it powers you straight down the fall line. Or sometimes one part of a wave curls over faster – maybe there's a rock on the bottom or something – so your board shoots right over it, like when a car skids on a patch of ice. You work this too, you use the power of this rock. And every time you buy some of that power you know you can get killed, even in the little stuff. A guy I knew in San Onofre broke his neck in four-foot surf. Every time you take the drop, it's like walking into an ambush: there's a lot going on out there you can't see. And,' he smiled suddenly, 'the more ambushes you survive, the healthier you get.' He drops the lichis back into the cup, puts it on the table. 'And the healthier you get, the bigger the waves you need.'

'The tourists snap pictures of them out at Makaha,' says Davis. 'Do you think one of the reasons they surf is to get all that attention? Surfing is a lot more public than, say, mountain climbing.'

'I can't say for anyone else, but if the surf was good, I'd ride it all day if I was the only person in the world.'

Davis leans back against the red and white flowers of his chair. 'I guess out there on the waves is one of the few spots left where you don't feel cheated. There aren't as many places like that as there were when I was your age.'

'Places like what?' Peter has put his hand on the back of my neck, the stroke of his fingers slow under my hair.

'Places where somebody hasn't got there before you. Most of the big adventures have already been had, most of the world has been found and explored. A few months ago they climbed Everest. Science is probably the only place left where a chance for adventure still exists – but it's pretty sedentary adventure, and it's only open to specialists.' Davis's hot southern voice is compelling. 'I can see, a generation or two down the road, when there'll be nothing left: everything plumbed, climbed, explored, set foot on. If not during your lifetime, then sometime soon, there won't be a spot that isn't full of the ghosts of earlier men. You won't even be able to think an original thought; you'll always be in the shadow of other men's ideas. I wonder if the kids growing up right now don't sense this and hate us on some deep level of consciousness. We've left them nothing to do except rebel. And worry about the unseen.'

'You mean God,' I say.

'I don't know what I mean. But the tragedy is, sweetie, that pretty soon the world's going to be used up like a giant condom.'

'This is *not* the kind of conversation me dear old mum foresaw when she taught me to hand round the coffee and brandy. Speaking of which.' Geneva offers me a glass, but I shake my head. 'Anyway, darling, what's all that got to do with surfing?'

'Just that surfing is one of the few ways still left to show you have a little guts. Although perhaps a somewhat limited way.'

'If I were Peter I'd be irritated,' says Geneva, glancing at me.

'He shouldn't be. I don't mean it personally. But surfing, like skiing or racing cars, is just a search for random personal pleasure. It takes guts, yes, but so does becoming a monk or going to war. And in war or a monastery there's a reason for being there, or you find one.' He crosses his right foot over his left knee, and I can see a snake's tail tattooed on his ankle.

Geneva stirs her coffee with a tiny blue-handled spoon. 'So that's why men are healthier and happier when they're fighting a war. Better than a sport, it's a philosophy. Two of Davis's best friends went into a decline right after V-E day, my dear, and only come out of it whenever they visit each other to talk over the good old days on Omaha Beach.'

I don't think Peter even hears her. 'I surf for one reason,' he says, 'and for one reason only. The drop. And I guess you could say surfing is a way of putting my mark on the water. But the water keeps changing, so I have to keep doing it all the time. No surfer I know makes any claims about anything except his own feelings. Brave is for other people, the drop is for you; brave is what you fake in public, but you make the drop in private, the way you're born and the way you die. People can see you while it's happening, but nobody knows what's going on inside your head.' The back of my neck is cold when he takes his hand away.

'That's pretty arrogant,' says Davis, 'but of course courage *comes* from arrogance. When it doesn't, it comes from despair. Sometimes you can learn it. Hemingway says that war is a great teacher, especially for a writer. Southern writers have known that for years, of course.' As he talks, Davis smiles or frowns or raises his eyebrows. He seems incapable of repose.

'My little kid has more guts than I do,' Peter says, 'and he hasn't been taught. His eyes are wide open; he watches everything, he isn't afraid.'

'But that's not courage. If you *know* what the risks are, and you go ahead anyway, that's a good definition.'

'My mother claims no matter how well you know the risks, you shouldn't show it,' Peter says. 'She doesn't think anybody, especially one of her kids, should admit he's scared.'

Davis holds out his glass to Geneva. 'Just before a battle a soldier is afraid; he knows it, he talks about it. So he's very active – eating and drinking and going to the whores. He likes to feel his whole body working; he wants to take an inventory of all his moving parts.'

'I don't know why we're analyzing it,' says Peter. He squeezes my shoulder and I know he wants to go home. 'Pretty soon it'll be brave to eat a Hershey bar or walk down the street.'

Before I can say anything, Geneva gives Peter another brandy and Davis starts talking to me. He'd fought in North Africa during the war, and in the medina he'd seen an American soldier castrated for lifting a woman's veil. 'She had the most perfect ears I've ever seen, like little gold petals.' As I stand up, he says, 'Everything about women fascinates me, sweetie; every little thing.'

Driving home, Peter gets stopped on Kalakaua for speeding. The sky has cleared, and the plumeria outside our bedroom window is the same color as the moon. He strips off all his clothes, and I think of the passage Davis read about the arrival of the early ships. Naked, he must look like how the Hawaiians first imagined the white man's god.

'I've never heard you like that before,' I say, getting into bed. 'I think Davis made you so mad you forgot you don't like to talk.'

'I wonder,' he says after a while, his mouth just above mine in the milky darkness.

'You wonder what?'

'If old Rhett Hemingway knows about this. Or *this*.'

38

CHARLOTTE: Peter is too tan. I don't remember him looking like that in California. But, luckily, his hair is lighter than ever. I take out a stack of sandwiches from my hamper and lay them on the blanket. Jenny and Eric and I have followed him out to this place so Eric can be with him when he surfs it for the first time. Kate has brought the baby and, sitting in the sand, she's feeding him, his head propped against her arm as she shields him from the sun. Down by the water, the rest of them are watching some stranger; I can't figure out why. And I can't understand why Peter is so panic-assed about surfing this place. He told Eric about it as soon as we got off the plane, but waited nearly a week before bringing us out here. He had a call this morning from some Hawaiian friend who's rented a house out here on the beach; more a shack really, I saw it when we drove past. He told Peter conditions were right for a first try, and they all left without finishing breakfast. But now they're here, they just sit around watching this other guy. And the Hawaiian hasn't shown up either – Peter says he has to help his mother out at the airport. Grubbing money off tourists, probably.

God knows, I don't like the tourists myself. In Waikiki the atmosphere's frivolous as a pajama party – matrons baby-stepping in frilly bathing suits, the men in Bermuda shorts, big bellies harder and more important than their peckers. I've been swimming at Waikiki only once. I don't like the idea of water that's lapped around thick Hawaiian legs seeping into any of the openings of my own body. And the house I've rented, though okay to look at, has cockroaches. I loathe cockroaches – sticky dates with legs – whether Kate tells me they're more common over here or not. And I don't like it after the sun has set, when tropical plants with leaves like the fingers of sick men scrape at the windows. Nothing's what it ought to be. The days seem twice as long as the ones in California, but just as you've almost given up hope that one of them will end, the sun clanks into the sea like a penny into a piggy bank.

And Peter's preoccupied. To the point that when he first drove us up to the house in Alewa Heights, without thinking he took a drink from the garden hose, got some of it in his lungs and almost drowned. If this is what marriage and fatherhood and living in Hawaii has done for him, better a poke in the eye with a dirty stick. But Hans Lucas is so luscious that holding him is almost worth the change in Peter. After a messy labor of thirty-six hours, nothing of Kate in the baby at all, exactly as if her genes didn't exist. If I'd been there for the birth, I could have talked to Kate, shown her how to do it. Ever since an afternoon long ago in my mother's bedroom, I've known I'd be good at having babies, cupping them inside myself, snug and hot, turning and honing them in my womb. I should have had Hans Lucas myself; arched my back, pressed down in the birth embrace, and shot him out of my belly clean as a cat.

I'm on my knees behind Papa's fat old armchair before the midwife even knows I'm in the room. A few hours ago Mama had said, 'It's time,' and sent Papa to fetch Mrs Froude, who delivers all the babies in Bellamy. Minnie, her tall silent assistant, is laying out the equipment on a white cloth she's spread over the chest of drawers: soap, jug and two washbasins, kitchen scissors, a box of matches, a glass of whiskey, squares cut from one of Mama's worn-thin sheets. The ends of her fingers are broad and flat as dominoes. Mrs Froude is talking to Mama, who is lying on the bed, knees drawn up. 'This one's going to be good and fast,' says the midwife, her hands on Mama's belly. Mama raises her head a little: 'Oh, yes. . . .' The yes is drawn out and sucked in again. Mrs Froude washes Mama between the legs with soap and water. She's standing at the foot of the bed now, so I can no longer see the violent red path at the quick of my mother, or the little hood that shields it, pointed and narrow, like the window of an old church.

Now that the snow has stopped, the afternoon has fallen silent, and the silence itself, the living thickness of the snow, throbs against the house. Outside, the white of the clouds and the sky is a faint green against the helpless white of the snow. The bedroom is no more than a reflection of the snow: white sheets and soap and basins and blankets, Mrs Froude and Minnie in white aprons, Mama in a white nightdress. A darkness is beginning to form in the sky, and on the ceiling of the room. Mama lets out a little growl, slow and bumpy as if she's being dragged across gravel. Mrs Froude lifts Mama's head, so she can sip the whiskey. Mama begins to groan, and when she turns her head, I can see that her mouth is open. 'Keep pushing,' says Mrs Froude. 'They're about three minutes apart.'

I sway with the sound. The room, the world, has been set to rocking with my mother's cries. Arms crossed, I hug myself, pinch my elbows, close to choking with excitement. 'I'm ready,' grunts Mama, and slowly the room beings to fill with color.

From Mama's hole, a little blood, and with it something clear, like rainwater. 'Here we are,' says Mrs Froude. A dark blister is straining against the opening, and the hole is bigger: the top of the baby's head. My teeth are chattering, and I'm afraid Mrs Froude will hear. I imagine I can feel my own hole opening, just like my mother's. When the baby's shoulders begin to show, I feel so good, I have to look away. Outside, an eagle skims the far fence. Behind him, the prairie. The bird seems a mistake, too weak to have been put down in a place where rocks always outlive feathers.

As if slammed out by a train, or carried on a wind, the baby shoots from my mother into the midwife's hands. Sprouting out of it, something like a snake covered with jelly. 'Good,' says Mrs Froude, in the way now so I can't see. 'You've got a beautiful little boy and you didn't tear.' She lays the baby on Mama's stomach, and picks up the kitchen scissors; I can hear the squeak of the blades as she cuts the shameful serpent cord. To make sure it's dead she burns it with a match. She reaches inside the baby's mouth and, with a square of sheet wrapped around her finger, dabs at the back of his throat. 'Now,' she says, giving the baby to Minnie, 'I want to get that afterbirth out of there.'

Like the sun brightening the sky, the blood pouring from Mama lightens the room. 'It's coming,' says Mrs Froude, pushing on Mama's stomach. Oozing, it slips out red and spongy, and round as a pie. As it lands on the bed, Minnie holds up my brother. He is covered with the white gobs of something I want to wipe off. But underneath it his body is slippery with health, and I know how important he felt to Mama when he was coming out.

He starts to cry as Minnie puts him in a little blanket. Before the cloth is completely wrapped around him, I see that the white gobs, traces of his fishy beginnings, are already sloughing off. And the room is warm because the baby is full of color, of every color, the color of life.

The stranger has caught a ride, but he doesn't look too good: splayed toes, big hunchy shoulders, knees badly bent – more like he's gunning down an enemy than sliding across a wave. But the kids are still watching him. 'I'm going down to the water,' I say, passing my hand lightly over the baby's head. 'Is he eating?'

'He doesn't like carrots,' Kate daubs at his mouth with a clean diaper.

'Well, don't worry. I never met a kid yet who licked his chops at everything.'

The stranger is riding the middle break. 'Why,' I say, going up to Peter, 'doesn't he surf the point break where nobody can see that ridiculous asshole stance?'

He doesn't look at me. 'I don't see how he gets his balance, but he really takes off in this stuff.

'I don't see you there. Or Eric. What are you waiting for?'

'Checking it out.' He smears some wax on his board. 'I think he's that Marine Barney told us about, the M.P. who surfs the North Shore. I saw a Kaneohe sticker on his car.'

'Those shoulders would block a tunnel,' I say. 'And he's got feet like rubber fins. I wonder if he's prehistoric.'

The stranger is coming in and Jenny and I go with Peter and Eric as they carry their boards down to the water. The stranger waits, standing in the shorebreak, watching us come. His eyes, in a young face, size us up, but his expression is old, as if he doesn't want to please or be pleased. My sons are dimple-kneed dribblers before this brazen man.

'It looks like a fast take-off,' Peter says. 'Pretty hairy.'

'You ever surfed here before?' asks Eric. The man nods. 'Anything we ought to know?'

He hefts his long board onto his shoulder. 'Why don't I let you college boys find out for yourselves?'

'You looked like fools,' I say when he's out of earshot. 'Like a couple of quivering queers.' I keep my voice down, but I've blocked Eric's way to the water. 'You don't ask other people, you get out there first. And you don't,' I say to Peter, 'tell a competitor he got a good ride until you get a better one.'

'He wasn't a competitor.'

'Everybody's a competitor. You'd figure that out fast enough if there was a shortage of food.'

'Maybe,' says Jenny, as Peter and Eric put their boards in the water, 'we look like we've got it all, so he doesn't want to give us anything extra.'

'Especially an advantage the first time out,' I say.

39

PETER: 'We should have waited for Keoki,' I tell Eric, as
we're paddling hard in a lull. 'But he told me if it was
coming up or crapping out we should get into the water fast.'

'What's it doing?' he says. 'I can't tell.'

'Nothing. But M.S. was hassling me, so we might as well try
the inside break until he gets here. I don't want to go outside
without him; we've been planning to surf Palikai together ever
since we found it.' When I first saw the car with the Kaneohe
sticker, I was really pissed off. Keoki's cousin and Davis Kelway
had both told us that nobody surfed it now, and Keoki and I
wanted to be the first since the old Hawaiians. But the M.P., the
hatchet of Hotel Street, had beaten us to it. Too late to change
that now, but maybe we can hack out an even bigger chunk of
that gruesome blue ice; and, when a set comes through, we can
march in the monster parade without any news from some
dicked-up Marine.

One foot on his board, Eric picks at a toenail as we wait in the
lineup. 'Eight foot, it looks like,' he says. 'We ought to be able to
handle that.'

'I'm not sure,' I say. If Makaha, to the west, gets an
occasional eccentric surge, what kind of jolt will light up this
place, far less protected by land?

Something is coming through. Eric paddles for the first one in
the set, but he's too late. To his right, I stroke twice and get to
my feet. I'm almost standing when the water begins to
straighten up like a man taking a deep breath. The wave is
completely vertical, pulling me up to the lip at the same time
that my board is slipping out into open air, empty space, my
skeg popping out of the water. Keoki told me that once at
Waimea a guy was caught in the hook like this and went over the
falls so hard he broke his back. Falling, remembering, I hit twice
on the surface before going under. In the spin-out my board

slams away and bounces high. It was an impossible take-off, the shoulder too steep, and the Marine with the feet like an indecent duck knew we shouldn't ride the inside break. The water dark and thick, a stormy sky, and I don't see the coral till it gets me, tabby talons scraping the back of my neck, hot as a woman making love. I roll with the turbulence and try to protect my head with my arms; probably not more than five feet of water over the reef – only a numbnuts would surf it, or a suicide. Another wave overhead. When it flips me, the coral runs its nails across my chest. Ten seconds. Lately I've started to count the time I'm under. I like to know my capacity for taking gas in a wipeout, as well as I know it swimming laps underwater. As the wave passes, I push off the coral, slicing the bottoms of my feet. I go up like a flare, hating the thought of daylight. M.S.'ll have plenty to say about wiping out on my first wave at Palikai, about the Marine not being dumb enough to surf inside. And Kate, since she's had the baby, panics whenever I lose my board. But the feel of the wall at my back was good; eight feet here powers you like fifteen anywhere else. When I come up there isn't much soup, and right away I get a clear breath.

40

CHARLOTTE: I carry Hans Lucas down to the water where
                      Kate and Jenny are watching. 'That's
Peter's board,' says Jenny. 'Riding the whitewater close in.'
Another wave breaks and Peter ducks under. When he comes
up, the set has passed and he swims for his board. He's taken a
bad wipeout, and it makes me want to puke when the both of
them start to come in.

   The stranger doesn't say anything, just stands next to me and
watches them drop their boards on the sand above the
waterline. The muscles in his arms and shoulders are jacked up,
as if he swings an axe all day, or lifts big blocks of stone. Peter
sees us watching and comes slowly up the beach. Eric, looking
angry, follows a couple of steps behind. I see blood on Peter's
chest, unmistakable evidence that he's screwed up in front of
this stranger.

   Peter goes right up to him. 'You cocksucker,' he says. 'You
knew I'd spin out on the inside break.' The marks are wild and
deep, as if somebody took a rake to him. 'You cocksucker,' he
says again, and I see that he's laughing.

   'Better get yourself a tetanus shot, man,' says the stranger.
'That coral is no joke.' But he's laughing too, and goes with
Peter to get his board.

   A few minutes later Peter's Hawaiian friend arrives. Kate has
wiped Peter's chest with a spare diaper, and he's gone back
down to the water still talking to the stranger. 'M.S., Jenny,'
Kate says. 'This is Keoki.'

   'Hi,' says Jenny from the blanket.

   'Keoki is Hawaiian for George,' Kate says.

   'Hello, George,' I say, still holding Hans Lucas.

   The rest of the afternoon Peter and the stranger talk surf,
while Eric listens a few feet away. In the hard sand down at the
waterline the Hawaiian traces a surfboard, and I see him hold

out his hand to Jenny. When she steps inside, she doesn't have her crutches, and he shows her how to balance herself, how to ride standing up. 'It gives me the creeps,' I say to Kate. 'His face is as black as a planet without a sun.'

41

KATE: I take a long time getting Hans Lucas ready. Wash him in perfect water, the temperature tested until it feels like a second skin; use only a little soap (Castile) because I don't like to take chances with his blondness. With cotton swabs I clean his ears, but there's never any dirt. I dry him on the kitchen table, my hands gentle on his slightly sticky skin, in the sweet crevices of his elbows, hips and knees. I always use the softest towels, and Peter says I treat him like a burn victim.

New Year's only a week ago, but this morning the temperature had already hit seventy by the time Peter left for work. I lower the bamboo blinds and put Hans Lucas on our bed, where I've laid out his clothes. He's a stately baby, serious, and doesn't move while I powder him and pin on his diaper. To draw on his shirt I have to lift his head and shoulders, because he isn't sitting up yet. His arms keep getting stuck in the sleeves because the index and middle fingers of both his hands are crossed, a habit he's picked up in the last month. I should say reflex, not habit. If I try to uncross them, they clamp right back together again. To get him to play, I tickle his foot but he doesn't jump, and when I put on his shoes he doesn't resist. There are times when I wish he'd have a tantrum, so dressing him wouldn't be so quick, and taking care of him so painless.

His mouth begins to stretch and quiver, the advent of a smile, a festival, an adoration, and it seems to me that the sea and the sky have come together in my baby's shadowless eyes. I touch my hair, feeling for the mantle of Mary, and wonder why he's found it on me. But when I bend down I see in his oversize irises the window, where a tree flickers through the blind, and not my face. He's still smiling, his head turned slightly to the side, and my received purity falls away, leaving me weak and almost angry, as if he's planned to hurt me.

*

Although I made the appointment before Christmas, I have to wait, Hans Lucas damp and dozing on my lap, for over half an hour. Across from me a man and his wife talk in quick whispers. I wish Peter was here, but since Thanksgiving he hasn't really gone anywhere except to work and the beach. I don't know if it's because of M.S. Ever since she's come over here she's been egging him on, calling every night to see if he's been out to Palikai, and how big it was. Sometimes, he gets up at five so he can surf a couple of hours before work. Weekends, everybody goes out to Haleiwa or Palikai, and M.S. takes pictures. When the prints come back, she brings them over, and they sit around measuring the waves with calipers. I'm tired and I go to bed early, but I can hear them in the living room arguing over an eighth of an inch. Sometimes even Jenny gets mad, when she thinks somebody has downgraded one of her little curls at Haleiwa. She's just signed on as a hospital volunteer, working with deformed and crippled kids. I went with her once. There were kids with sky-high heads and kids shaped like doughnuts. With a piece of chalk she drew the shape of a surfboard and pulled them inside, the way Keoki did with her. She told them if they could walk to the nose they'd drop down into enchanted water, surf like the old Hawaiian kings. A couple of them actually took a few steps.

Mark has come over from the mainland. He and Eric have got jobs part-time driving tourists around in beach buggies with pink and white striped awnings. After work they surf with Peter at Haleiwa, and sometimes at Palikai when it isn't too big. But over ten foot, Mark doesn't like Palikai, so Peter surfs it with Eric, Keoki, or Axel Webber, the Marine from Kaneohe. 'There goes Tsunami Sue,' Axel said to me once when Mark was carrying his board down to the water. 'He'll whip out his invisible ruler, and if it's an inch above his cut-off point, he won't get wet.' 'Too much chop,' Mark said, a few minutes later, as he came back up the beach. 'I'm going to check out Haleiwa.' Axel smiled at me. 'Good,' he said, when Mark had gone. 'This place is enemy territory, and guys like that are just its meat. It knows them, and it smells them coming.'

Axel is older than Peter. He fought in the Pacific during the war, and then re-upped. At night he patrols Hotel Street, picking up the drunk and disorderly, many of them, he tells

Peter, out to kill or be killed, not to mention the others who fight the M.P.s for sport. Days, he's supposed to get some sleep, but most of the time he goes out to Palikai with Peter, and sleeps only a couple of hours before hitting Hotel Street. Sleepless and drinking and fighting, but never a mark on him. He always looked rested. In a way, he reminds me of M.S., because he doesn't make allowances for things to go wrong. Once when I was making dinner, I heard him tell Peter about the time he got stranded on a reef in the Tarawa atoll. He was a frogman on some kind of reconnaissance and missed the pickup boat. Because of the Japanese he couldn't go ashore, so he stood on the reef for twenty-four hours, up to his neck in water. The way he talked, he didn't think it was luck that the boat came back, only what he expected. He tells Peter a lot about himself – how his mother ran off when he was four, and left his grandmother to raise him – but never when I'm in the room. I want him to like me, and maybe I try too hard. He never says anything personal, except once on the beach when I was bouncing Hans Lucas on my lap, he seemed to notice me. 'You've got good-looking legs,' he said, 'for such a skinny chick.' Another time, when I was reading, he picked up my book. 'What's the matter,' he said to Peter, 'is she smart or something?'

The nurse calls the couple across from me. Hans Lucas shifts in my arms, and I smell musty earth, the burrow of an animal. I bathed him just before we left, and changed his diaper, but it hasn't made any difference. I hold him tight, waiting. When the door opens I'm next, and they tell me to go right in.

Afterward I go to Geneva's because I don't know what else to do. I call her from a drugstore around the corner and she says, 'You mustn't be alone. I'll put the kettle on, and tea'll be ready by the time you get here.' I've been seeing a lot of Geneva. She's somebody to talk to when I don't want to listen to the Hollanders, or go to the beach. I like her frankness, and the feeling I get that she's already survived some of the troubles that might be coming to me. She seems to have all the right social and serious responses, or maybe it's just well-learned English manners. On days when I stay late, Davis comes home and hands me books. 'Read this,' he'll say. 'It'll change your life.'

The night I invited them to dinner, M.S. dropped by with Eric and brought some surfing pictures. Later Davis said, 'You were embarrassed when they showed up, weren't you? Look, it's honorable to talk about books – don't any of them read?' I don't like it when he talks like that about Peter. 'They do things,' I say. 'I can't do anything at all.'

'I just walked in when the phone rang,' says Geneva when she opens the door. She tries to take Hans Lucas, but I won't let her. 'He has this awful smell,' I say, 'and the smell is part of it.' I start to cry, and she holds me and Hans Lucas, patting us both until I stop choking. I stay with her until we hear Davis's car in the driveway. 'Don't tell Davis yet,' I say. 'First, I have to talk to Peter.' I think Davis can tell I've been crying, but all he says is, 'You're looking wonderful, sweetie; I love your dress.'

Peter isn't home. He'd said he was going to Ala Moana with Keoki after work. Hans Lucas begins to whimper and I can tell he's hungry, so I give him his supper right away. When he's finished I put him in his pajamas and rock him in my arms on the sofa because I'm afraid to put him down for the night. I watch it get dark, see the lights come on in Waikiki, the dusk breathing evenly on the water. When Peter gets home he goes straight to Hans Lucas's room. 'In here,' I say. When he turns on the lamp and reaches for the baby, I see that I've been holding him so tight my fingers have left marks on his arms. 'Be careful,' I whisper. 'He's sleeping – don't wake him up.'

'Are you mad because I'm late?'

'No.'

'Ala Moana was great. Nice relaxing little curls. Jenny came out with us.'

'I took the baby to the doctor today; it wasn't time for his regular visit but I took him anyway.' Peter sits down with Hans Lucas in his lap. 'The doctor said he'd never seen a baby so blond. Then he stuck him with a pin and told me he was mentally retarded.'

'Retarded? Retarded my ass.' He slams his fist on the sofa. 'He's never met the family, how does he know? I can't believe you took him seriously.'

'Why do you think I *went* to the doctor?' I'm almost

screaming. 'He should be sitting up by now. He's *nine months old*. He should *know* people, his own mother, he should be able to feed himself a cracker, and be *afraid* of strangers.' I pound Peter's arm. 'It's because he's a Hollander, that's why you can't believe it – you're just like M.S.'

'He knows me,' Peter says. 'I'm sure he knows me.' He puts out his hands, big plausible hands, and holds the baby's head. 'I'm just not sure he knows anybody else.'

'Why can't you believe there's something wrong with him? Look what happened to Jenny, and she's a Hollander.'

'There's nothing wrong with Jenny now; if anything, she's better than ever.'

I get up and begin to walk, not going anywhere. 'That smell he has – it's something to do with his metabolism. He wants to send Hans Lucas to a specialist, but he's not sure they can do anything. You know what he told me, you know what he said? That he may never recognize us, who we are or anything, and we'll probably have to put him in an institution. And when he gets older, he'll get sexy and sit around playing with himself, or put his hands on little girls.' I fall on my knees, crying. Peter goes down the hall to put Hans Lucas to bed.

When he comes back, he picks me up. 'We'll take him to the specialist,' he says. 'We'll do whatever we have to.' He's wearing an old white shirt, open at the throat, the V as full of meaning as Churchill's upraised fingers in the war. Pressing hard, I lay my cheek against his neck as if I can stamp its magic into my skin, make it work for us.

42

PETER: I get up just before dawn. Kate is lying on her
stomach, eyes closed, her mouth squashed against
the pillow like something battered in the rain. Last night she
couldn't get to sleep, and I held her while she talked: 'What I
don't understand is, if there's something wrong with him, why is
he hungry all the time? I hated to watch him tonight. He'd just
been given a death sentence, and I've never seen him eat more.'

I leave a note saying I'll be back by eight, and in a T-shirt and
trunks I drive down to Ala Moana. But after I park the car I
don't go for a swim, just sit on the beach watching the torches on
the reef. The sky behind the mountains is beginning to show a
little color, but the sea is still dark. Before dawn or after dusk
you can always see fishermen on the reef, the reflections of their
torches floating on the water. Keoki took me out there once, and
showed me how to use the two-pronged spear. You could see the
sleeping fish drifting in the current like the pennants the
Japanese float on Boy Day. Up to my thighs in life and water, I
liked the idea at first, but right after my spear thonked into the
fish's body, the mullet seemed important, not just a few quick
seconds of life, but something I should take care of forever, and I
didn't want to kill it.

When Kate first told me about Hans Lucas, I couldn't believe
it, but this morning when I saw her face on the pillow, I knew it
was true. Not only that, but I think I expected it, as if deep down
I knew that the shit that started with Jenny's leg is still coming
out, and it's going to go on coming out till whoever or whatever
it is that pushes the buttons hits the one marked 'Stop'.

Out on the reef they're still stabbing fish. Already M.S. has
probably been up for over an hour. When I was a kid, I used to
like to get up when she did, have breakfast with her before the
rest of them got her attention. Slitty-eyed, she'd drink her coffee,
and I knew she was planning our day, every minute accounted

for, so we couldn't do anything else if we wanted. As I remember, there's something intense about her in the early morning, as if she knows how to pick up fire or water in her fingers. If I go to see her now, I can tell her about the baby before the others get up.

43

KATE: 'You look like a fruit peddler,' M.S. tells me, 'under
            that umbrella.'

'But it's so hot for him, strapped on this thing. I don't want
him to get heatstroke.' One of Hans Lucas's hands is lying in the
sun, and I pull it back under the umbrella.

'It's just good honest sunshine and he might as well get used
to it. He's old enough now to – '

'Maybe you can explain to Rosemary how they turn the surf-
boards,' Geneva interrupts. 'I haven't a clue how they do it.'

Geneva's brought a friend from Louisville out to Palikai, and
I'm grateful to her. M.S. has done nothing but complain since
the day I started using the umbrella. I know she thinks it looks
bad for a Hollander to take shelter under anything, but I don't
care. For almost four months I've been lugging Hans Lucas to
specialists who stick him and pinch him and X-ray him and take
his blood. 'Not a single organ is where it ought to be,' my doctor
tells me when all the reports are in. 'We'll just have to keep an
eye on things and wait.' Twice a week I take him to Shriners,
where they show me how to exercise his arms and legs. His
muscles have no elasticity, and flab like bread dough. They say
his spine is so curved he'll never sit up unless he's strapped to a
board. The theory is, if he lies on his stomach, every time he lifts
his head he'll straighten his back. When I go shopping for
groceries I carry him on his board, and wheel him alongside me
in another cart.

They tell me I can unstrap him at night, but sometimes when
I take him off it he cries, so I bring in a book and sit with him till
he calms down, falls asleep in his crib. I'm always tired, maybe
numb is a better word, and sometimes I just sit there, hoping
and dreaming, like a young girl in love. I still have expectations.
There isn't a mother who doesn't have them, and I think they
keep me going. But dreaming takes a lot of energy, and when

mine falters, I think about the bills. Some of the doctors, because they're nice and know we don't have any money, send very small bills; others ask practically as much as Peter makes in a year. M.S. would pay the doctors, but he never asks her. In the ways you'd think they'd be close, they aren't.

Jenny and Keoki are coming down the beach from his shack. I don't see her as much as I used to, because whenever she isn't working at the hospital or surfing she's off with Keoki. And I'm staying home a lot more, alone with Hans Lucas. I like to turn on some music, keep him safe close by, out of the hands of doctors. When he's awake I carry him from room to room on his board in case he wants me, and sometimes he lifts his head. Every day I have some kind of project for getting the house cleaner or neater. I figure the more I square things away, the less can happen to me. Lately I've started to believe that in order to stay alive, you have to be tidy. Life is all one piece, but death is an explosion – a flying apart – the most untidy state of all. And yet the doctors obviously believe that there's something in between, because they've relegated Hans Lucas to an unknown, unsigned, liminal world, neither tidy nor untidy, a place where only he exists.

'Hey,' says Jenny, coming up to me. 'It's small and glassy, and Keoki says its perfect. What do you think?' She's been wanting to surf Palikai since the day Eric went out with Peter.

'Why not?' Axel says. He's just arrived, carrying his board. 'With stuff like that you won't have so much trouble with the rip.'

'What do *you* think, Kate?' says Jenny. M.S. has stopped talking to Geneva and is waiting for my answer.

'I think you should do it,' I say, wondering why she's asked me. Probably because ever since I told her about Hans Lucas she's been looking for ways to make me think about something else. ('He's a wonderful little baby,' she'd said, kissing both his hands. 'And there's nothing wrong with him they can't fix. He's going to be neat.')

M.S. goes on explaining to Geneva's friend about the surfing. 'Do you do it too?' Geneva says to Axel. 'It looks so frightfully dangerous.' But he's listening to M.S. and doesn't answer.

The day Axel first met M.S., he didn't seem to notice her much, but I don't think he ever stopped being conscious of her after that. If she asks a question, he's the one who answers; if she wants something, he goes and gets it. He stops by almost every day to check out the stove, the plumbing or the car before anything even goes wrong. He's only six years older than Peter, but up at Alewa he seems like the man of the house. He has a lot of energy, not free-floating like Barney's, but violent and specific, as if it's being forced out of a narrow opening. He was driving around drunk once, with Peter and Keoki in Keoki's jeep, and when Keoki turned a corner he fell out on his head. Peter said it was a really bad fall, but Axel got up laughing; later we found out he was dizzy for a week. Punchy, he surfed Palikai, decked or got decked on Hotel Street, and ran errands for M.S. 'I don't ever want to let your mother down,' he told Peter.

I never hear him have a conversation with her; in fact, she hardly talks to him at all, except to ask him to pick up Jenny, or cut the grass. She lets him stay to meals sometimes, and then he does all the dishes. One night he won a *kapa* in a crap game out at the barracks, one of those Hawaiian cloths made of bark that they stain with berries. I think it was old, the loveliest I've ever seen. He came right up to the house and gave it to her, but as soon as he left, she rolled it up and threw it on the floor of a closet. Maybe it was because he didn't warn Peter about the inside break that first time at Palikai. I could tell those bloody marks on Peter's chest really set something off in her.

'Let's go,' Jenny says to Keoki.

'I swear, you look so noble,' says Geneva's friend as Keoki picks up their boards. 'Are you related to King Kamehameha?'

'No,' he says, showing his teeth. 'But my great-grandfather ate Captain Cook.'

Sitting next to me, Axel finishes his cigarette. Close inside, Peter is swimming laps. 'I never saw anybody look so good in the water,' Axel says. 'Probably because he never comes out.' He glances at Hans Lucas. 'Well, maybe once or twice.' He flicks ashes in the sand as Mark takes off on a tiny wave. 'Look at that,' he says to me. 'You see the way he craps out in the ten-footers, but look at him now: in this little stuff, he gets right down and dances on the nose, shitty little hot-dogger. He knows how to play grown-up when company comes to dinner, but after they leave he's afraid to go to bed because of the bogeyman.'

'Where does he go wrong,' I say, 'in the big stuff?'

'He can't get his tiny toes forward like he's doing now.' He waves a hand in Mark's direction. 'Because he's too busy trying to keep his flying board from cutting off his head. He loses his board more times than all of us put together, because he's got no judgment. You shouldn't take waves you're not sure you can make, and you ought to be able to tell the difference.' He leans back, cigarette between thumb and forefinger. 'He's so scared that he takes dumb risks, rides waves he doesn't understand, while the rest of us who don't mind admitting we're scared, who know we could end up one day face down and floating, are better surfers. We use our heads, we don't try to hide anything; we put our energy into staying alive in the water, not trying to fake out the people on the beach.'

'I don't think he can help it,' I say. 'M.S. brought all her kids up not to show fear. Peter's the same way.'

'Maybe. But in the water he doesn't pull any shit. He respects what it can do, and he says so, to me and Keoki.' He buries his cigarette in the sand. 'No mother wants her kids to funk it. Especially,' he glances at M.S., who's still talking to Geneva, 'a real feminine woman, who gives up her life for her kids. But Mark doesn't know how to play the game, and I guess maybe she knows it. All you have to do is to watch him in anything over ten foot; he paddles and backs off, paddles and won't pull down into it. If he makes a mistake and catches it, he doesn't even prone it out, just gets under our feet.'

He shades his eyes with his hand, watching Mark walk the nose. I've seen Axel take spectacular wipeouts, and I know how different they are from Mark's. Not just because they're fewer, but because you can hardly miss them: spinouts going backward down the wave; drops as straight and hard as a boulder off the edge of a cliff. But when they happen he's always trying something new. Sometimes he puts himself in the most critical position and takes a direct hit from a fifteen-footer, just because he knows the chances and contingencies, the configurations and the odds.

Jenny is scratching for her first wave. Since Keoki taught her how to balance, she rides standing up. Kneeling, she holds on to the rails, and when the board slips into its momentum, she hops into a standing position between her hands. To turn, she drops back on her knee, sticks a hand in the water; or, lying on her belly, throws her leg over the side. Keoki rides with her on the same wave, big body turned toward her as if they're talking and walking down the street.

Every time she stands like that I wish Barney could see her. We just had a letter from him, and a lot of it seemed to be meant for me. 'Mostly, I'm happy in Cambridge,' he wrote. 'I never thought I could like snow and dead leaves so much. But the people are certainly different. They look like outpatient T.B. cases, and the women all read Christina Rossetti. I've checked out the surf on Cape Cod (non-existent), and once I even got down to Newport. Not much to tell except the water is the color of factory smoke, nothing like the homeland. Haven't had time to think or dream about anything but particles and light – speed of, not the dawn's early. And I'm really stoked on wave theory, which has nothing to do with hot curls. To relax, I go to a little moviehouse and watch horror shows until midnight. You'd love it. With a big bag of popcorn, you can last a long time.' When Peter finishes the letter, he tosses it on the table. 'If he comes over at Christmas like he says, the surf'll be up at Palikai. I hope he can handle it. With those bum eyes of his, when he says, "Is that a wave, or is that a wave?" it's not a rhetorical question.'

Jenny and Keoki are coming in. I brush some kind of insect off Hans Lucas, and he smiles a little, still asleep. The sky hangs over the mountains like a bright drop of water, and I want to cup the afternoon in my hands, admire the beautiful slow beat of its wings. I'm glad that when I wrote to Barney I didn't tell him what the doctors said about Hans Lucas.

Axel and I stand up to watch them paddling out again, this time the two of them on Keoki's board. 'Darling, I've got to go,' Geneva says to me. 'I think Rosemary has had a moderate sufficiency, and Davis will be in a frightful tizzy if we're not home in time for drinks. Give me a ring tomorrow.'

'I bet,' says Axel as she walks off with her friend, 'if you wake up a limey in the middle of the night they don't talk like that.'

44

CHARLOTTE: I open the magazine the English woman left behind, and pretend I don't see Keoki putting Jenny on his board. Best to ignore whenever you can. Like the way Kate fusses over that baby. Nothing wrong with the kid that a good diet and temperate sunlight won't clean up, but the way she acts you'd think he was on pure oxygen, behind glass walls. I guess we're lucky the obstetrician didn't try to botch him; Kate told me he was Japanese, and who knows whether the Japs – any more than the Hawaiians – like delivering white babies. When the locals call me '*haole*', I want to stick a fork into their faces like you would into a roasting goose, let all the fat drip out, dry up their greasy smiles. My skin crawls whenever the landlord's daughter touches Hans Lucas. If Kate would let me take him back to California, he'd be sitting up and talking in no time. I'd give him decent meat, aged meat, not this stuff that tastes like it's still running around. And I'd feed him recognizable fruit and vegetables whose value has been acknowledged for centuries by the western world. Even the pineapples over here have a hard-nosed Oriental look. The only thing wrong with Hans Lucas that I can see is that he's a little listless; so much humidity can't be good for a baby. All around the island the palms droop; and the coconuts, ambitionless, let go. I miss my house in the San Francisco dunes; in a high wind, the sand hides us more completely than any snow. Sometimes after a storm, we've been cut off from the city, and the road had to be dug out before anybody could reach us. I love every bump and crevice of the California landscape. But this little turd flushed out into the Pacific only pretends to be real, when everything about in fact is tiny and phony and lazy, and much too pretty to be practical. There's an appealing monstrosity about California, in its doomy hills and deserts, its fogs, its sulky beaches. California is a place I can understand.

I've tried to talk to Kate and Peter about my feeling that we should all go back to San Francisco, but Peter won't listen. If Hawaii gave him nothing but Palikai, it would be plenty for him. It's harder to tell about Kate. She never talks about herself, except maybe to the English woman. And since that doctor put a flea in her ear about Hans Lucas, she's been losing weight; her voice is cold, and she watches the baby all the time. But, still, she has the best of Peter, fires herself up with his guts and glamor. Their phone rings a lot now. Surfers who've come over from California want to ask him about Palikai and the other beaches. There was an article in the *Star-Bulletin* about him and Axel and Keoki 'rediscovering the old Hawaiians' favorite surfing spot', and a photograph of the three of them standing by their boards. But you didn't notice anything but Peter's blond hair, the grave lines of energy in this arms and legs. And whenever she wants, Kate can feel that beauty, run her fingers through it like a cache of fine coins. Kate, totally ordinary Kate, with a vein of depression near her heart that's always threatening to burst. During the day she'll gnaw at a book, but if anybody comes to the house she hides it. At night she has Peter – his nakedness, his undefended thoughts – all to herself. I wonder, do they ever talk about me? In bed, do they say things? In the dark, hips working together, do they whisper my name?

I don't like to go to their house. Everything in it has the mark of their private use, the print of their invisible life together. Two weeks ago, I told Jenny I never wanted to set foot in there again. Jenny and Eric had gone in ahead of me, and as I shut the car door, I heard Axel's voice. He'd been up at Alewa an hour earlier, and had washed the big picture window in the living room. Every day I look up from whatever it is I'm doing to find him standing there. He likes to take a good look at me before going off to do something in the house or yard. Like a Filipino houseboy, he's tidy, diffident and discreet. It doesn't matter why he's there, as long as he doesn't ask for any of my time or attention. Let him worry about his reasons. Peter's apartment is on the first floor, and I could see Axel watching me from the window. I was almost at the steps when the toe of my sandal caught on a paving stone and I fell forward into the grass. My ankle was twisted so I couldn't get up. 'Stupid sons of bitches,' I whispered. 'Can't even build a sidewalk.' And then Axel kneeling beside me: 'Are you all right?'

'Don't be an asshole,' I said. Kate came out, holding the

baby, then Peter and Jenny. 'Just give me your hand,' I said to
Peter. But Axel closed his fingers around my ankle, slid his hand
gently up and down. 'Maybe you shouldn't walk on it,' he said.
My children watching, he picked me up like a cripple or an
invalid. 'Get your hands off me,' I hissed, but nobody seemed to
hear. Jenny and Peter were smiling, and I closed my eyes so I
wouldn't see them. His shirt was stiff and clean, a military shirt
that might have blood on it before the night was out; he smelled
of strong soap, Lifebuoy maybe, or some G.I. stuff. As he
carried me through the door, the others were right behind, and I
wondered if they could see up my dress. (When I'd run away
from the nigger in the grass everyone could tell that my
stockings were wet; one of the dogs had begun to sniff, and Papa
had carried me to the buckboard, his jacket sane and full of a
familiar rectitude, my eyes shut tight against his chest.) Inside
the apartment, Axel put me down. 'You better check you didn't
get a hernia,' I said. 'And from now on, remember: I don't like
to be saved, not even by the Marines.' When I took a step my
ankle didn't hurt at all.

If I lower the magazine a little, I can see that Keoki and Jenny
are in the lineup now, and Keoki is turning the board. Some
little swells are coming through and, as they start the slide, he
gets to his feet, pulling Jenny up; when I realize what they're
going to do, I close my hands into fists. Keoki bends over and, in
a kind of rolling motion, Jenny is on his back. Light as a
ladybug, she pulls herself up, hooks her leg into his armpit and
perches on his shoulder. Deep into the slide she stretches her
arms over her head as if waking from a perfect sleep. I can hear
the excitement behind me as the board comes closer to the
beach, and I want to put my finger down my throat, bring up
my anger. I'm dizzy: Kate, the baby, the umbrella, the cars
parked under the palms – everything looks round and smooth
and made of gold; and glittering in the water. Jenny and Keoki
are dense and compressed, as if their edges have all been rubbed
off. I close my eyes, but when I look at them again the truth is
still the same: my daughter, on the shoulders of a black man, has
become a circus freak.

45

PETER: A flamingo with a kink in its neon bill buzzes over the door of the little bar in Kaimuki. 'I found this place the day I got here,' says Axel, leading the way into a tiny room. 'You can order something to eat, and they'll bring it to the table.' Axel shakes hands with the man behind the bar. 'This is Joe Hiroki,' he says to me. 'His wife makes the best tempura east of Japan.' Mrs Hiroki comes out to be introduced, then waits, smiling at Axel. 'How about a double order of the shrimp,' Axel says, 'three sides of fries, a bag of chips, a Primo and the biggest bottle of ketchup you have in the house.'

'Just a Primo for me,' I say. Inside the bar I can still hear the crackle of the electric bird.

Gray-painted walls and tables, plastic chairs. 'Joe got a deal from a paint contractor for the Navy,' Axel says after we take a table at the back. 'and for the first few minutes I always feel like I'm belowdecks.' Mrs Hiroki brings out beer on a flamingo-colored tray. 'It's early yet,' he says, as two women come in. 'It gets pretty crowded later.' He yawns and sips his beer. 'Christ. Last night, down at the Club Hubba Hubba, soldier built like a brick shithouse, throwing bottles around. When we get there he's running down Hotel Street, pissing on the whores.' One of the women sits down at the bar, and he narrows his eyes. 'Nice little close-cropped ass there; fits right on the stool with nothing left over.'

The woman looks pissed off and I think maybe she heard him. I smile at her and she smiles back. 'After that wipeout you took today,' I say, 'have you got the energy to do anything about it?'

'Man, I'm so horny I could screw a faucet.' He glances at me. 'You look like you could use a little yourself.'

'I've got to keep an eye on the time. If I'm more than a couple of minutes late, Kate stands by the door, waiting for me. I can't figure her out, she's unpredictable.'

'Has she always been like that?'

'Ever since they told her that shit about the baby.' I pick at the Primo label. 'It's changed me, too; made me ask for a lot less than I used to. You know the best thing about Palikai on a big day? When you make it in with your ass in one piece, and you're walking up the beach, and you know you've got another twenty-four hours – another night, and another day, another chance to see the sun come up. Right now that's about the most I can expect.'

Axel pulls a picture out of his wallet and tosses it on the table. 'A buddy of mine from Schofield took this of us out at Palikai last month. Remember that day? When we paddled out it was about twelve, but this shot of you, I figure an eighteen-foot set sneaked through and we didn't even know it. Next winter we're going to be taking bigger and bigger humps, and we better start concentrating on the important stuff, forget everything else.'

'Like what?' From the kitchen, a strong smell of frying fat, and I drink some beer to get the traces of it out of my nose and mouth.

'Like getting in shape for the twenty-footers, and forgetting about the hot-dog stuff. Leave that to Mark. Listen, man – you crap from a great height, you got to expect a big splash. Worry about handling a twenty-five-foot wipeout.'

'The first time Keoki and I saw Palikai, it was breaking all the way across, dumping like cement from a truck. A strong onshore wind, and it drops right over. It'll close out at twenty or twenty-five, so the problem won't come up.'

Mrs Hiroki brings two more Primos with Axel's order. 'From Joe, on this house,' she says with a little bow. Axel hands me a couple of shrimp. 'Yeah, but it's mostly a northwest swell; too much west, then maybe you've got a closeout.'

'Ten bucks it won't hold up over twenty. I was thinking today: we're mapping that place, finding out stuff nobody else knows. Maybe a hundred years ago they had it wired, but not now. In a wipeout last winter at middle break, I damn near hit bottom, and it looked like a couple of manholes down there. I don't know what it was. And I'm sure there's a sandbar building out at the point. All this stuff, we're the only ones who know it.'

'Nobody else is asshole enough to surf that place. Listen, I think we should set up a buddy system. Anything over ten foot, nobody goes out alone.' He drags a shrimp through the ketchup on his plate. 'You, me, Keoki and Eric: we look out for each other. Agreed?'

'Maybe. Okay. I'll talk to Eric and Keoki.'

Axel smiles. 'Don't take offence, man, but I think Keoki and Jenny are getting pretty friendly.'

'I guess they are.' I pour beer from a fresh bottle into my glass.

'They're alone in his shack a lot, and when they come out they have a certain look. Okay, let's shitcan that – you've got enough on your mind.' He puts shrimp, ketchup and fries on a napkin, lays it in front of me. 'I can't scoff it all, and the missus Hiroki will make me take it home.'

'What if the doctors are right about my kid?'

'Then you'll have a kid who needs a lot of attention. It's easier in a place like Hawaii that's small and warm and the people are nice, and you don't have to take him out in the snow.'

'I keep thinking, if he doesn't have a brain, he'll fall into the hands of women; they'll pat him and kiss him and change his pants for the rest of his life.'

'In the beginning and the end everybody's at the mercy of women anyway – mothers or nurses, what difference does it make?' Axel tips his head, drops two fries down his throat. 'My grandmother was the best woman in the world, but my mother was a whore. Since then I haven't found much in between. Anything good comes from my grandmother; she loved me, she took care of me. Every morning she read me the Bible. I know the Bible better than any preacher. On the reef off Tarawa I remembered a lot of it, not just in my head – I figured I needed something I could feel, something to mark me off from the water – and not out loud, which would've wasted energy. I whispered it – Genesis, Proverbs, Psalms, the New Testament – and I kept the rhythm even, ticking like a clock. No question, it regulated my heart and my breathing. When they pulled me out I was still going, on Ecclesiastes, and all I needed was a little sleep.' He tilts his chair and rubs the back of his neck. 'Jesus. I don't know what to tell you about the kid.'

'When Kate was pregnant she read in the paper about a baby being born with a tail. The tail had fur on it. She said, If that ever happened to me, I'd jump off the Pali. I said, What's so bad about a tail, and anyway it says the doctors cut it off. She went into the bathroom and threw up. I wonder what she'd say now, if she could choose between a tail and an empty skull.'

46

KATE: 'How about some tea?' I'm trying to get Geneva to
stay. Peter's not home yet and I don't feel like being
alone.

'Thanks, lovey, but I'd rather have a drink.' She rearranges
the pillows on the *punee*. 'Where's Peter?'

'Sometimes he stops off for a beer with Axel.'

'I have to be home by six-thirty,' she says. 'Soiree tonight at
the university – what's the matter?'

'Can you make the drinks? I don't know how because Peter
always does it.'

'Have you got any limes? Yesterday, I had some of the
trustees' wives to lunch. While we were having coffee, I took out
my sewing, a little chemise I picked up at the thrift shop. You
can find some wonderful things – Diors, Balenciagas – if you
don't mind the way they smell of other people until you can get
them cleaned. Where's your tonic? I'd hardly put thread to
needle when one of them said, "That looks like my dress – let me
see." And there was her name on a tiny label right inside the
neck. She thought it was funny, and so did I, but I daren't tell
Davis; he's always on at me about my lack of pride.' She hands
me a glass and stretches out on the *punee*. 'Why do you keep
craning your neck like that?'

'I'm listening for Hans Lucas. He wouldn't take a nap today,
and I'm hoping he'll sleep through the night.'

'Well, sit down and don't worry. It says they do that. I've
been reading a child-care book I found in the library, so I'll be
au courant when you talk about him.'

'The other day I was wondering what I'd do if you weren't
here. I don't like to worry Jenny. She's happy now, and anyway
she's always with Keoki.'

'Drink your drink; it's good for you. How do you get on with
Peter's mum?'

'Okay, I guess.'

Geneva reaches into her glass, squeezes the lime and licks her fingers. 'She's a perfect cunt, my dear. I wonder how you stand her.'

'She's amazing in some ways. I used to want to be just like her.'

'And now?'

'One of us has changed. She's different since she came to the islands, or I'm seeing her in a different light, I don't know which. But whatever it is, Peter's my husband now, not just her son, and I'm going to make her see that if it kills me.'

'Being a member of that family doesn't seem to have done anybody any good. The baby, Jenny's leg. And you said you got sick on your honeymoon.' She pours some more tonic into her drink. 'Aren't you afraid for Peter when he's surfing?'

'More at Palikai than anywhere else. Even the Palikai locals are nervous about that place. Once, when Peter and Eric were out in storm surf, a bunch of firemen waded out with megaphones and hipboots, and yelled at them to come in. One of the firemen got knocked down in the shorebreak and couldn't get up because his boots were full of water. He was still yelling "If the waves don't get you, the sharks will – you're going to drown" when Peter and Eric paddled in and rescued him.'

'Do you think about going back to the mainland?'

'I love it here.'

'But it's such a crazy place. I think about going back to England sometimes, but Davis would never leave. I don't like the humidity, and though I grant you the Hawaiians can be charming, I don't think they're very civilized. Davis asked me once what my definition of civilization was, and I told him, a place where things get done. Do you realize that in the last election, the votes from one of the outer islands were sent to Honolulu by *carrier* pigeon?'

When Geneva finally leaves, I cut up lamb for a casserole, and make a salad, but at a quarter to eight Peter still isn't home. If he's with Axel he can't be much longer because Axel has to be on Hotel Street in fifteen minutes. Hans Lucas hasn't made a sound since I put him down for the night, but lately he's been having nosebleeds, and I keep checking to see whether he's all right. In the house I always go barefoot, so I don't make any noise when I come into his room. He's lying on his back, his breath slipping uneasily through the crust of blood in his nose. His eyes are shut, but I don't think he's asleep. I shut my own eyes, trying to imagine what he sees on the backs of his lids: primary shadows and underlights, or just a blank screen? I imagine a dark arena, sunless and moonless, a headlife without questions or images, and reason flat as a line. I kiss his little belly. Since they've put him on a special diet, the smell is gone, and his skin is tight and sweet, like an apple fresh from the tree.

I turn the heat down under the lamb, and take the custard out of the refrigerator. Mrs Kanazawa has taught me how to make *haupia*, but I don't like splitting the coconuts, warm furry animals. I'm standing near the door when Peter's key scrapes a couple of times in the lock. Outside I can hear Axel laughing. 'I'd sure hate to be a virgin you were trying to screw,' he says. But Peter comes in alone.

'You smell good,' he says, 'or is that dinner?' He's smiling, but his eyes are red and tired. 'Axel thought you'd be mad I'm late, so he walked me to the door.'

'I am mad,' I say. 'If you're not surfing, you're off drinking somewhere.'

'When I'm home, all you do is worry about the baby. Why don't you try to enjoy him?'

'How can I enjoy a baby who doesn't even know I'm in the house? It's like living with a stranger, a pissing, shitting stranger, who's completely indifferent to you but you worry anyway, because even for a stranger you want to do the right thing.' I sit down at the table. 'All the time, I wonder what I did wrong when I was pregnant – or before I was pregnant – to make my baby turn away from me like this. I must have done it to him; I'm his mother. Every day I wake up thinking, maybe today I'll find out the magic thing I have to do to make him all right – give him a little more egg or banana or something. Or maybe his mattress is too hard, maybe that's it. If I just find out that one thing, it'll fix whatever I did wrong.'

'That's crazy. You worry so much you don't have a personality any more.'

'He's so beautiful,' I say. 'I keep thinking that: he's beautiful to throw us off the track.'

At dinner Peter laughs about a couple from the midwest, tourists, who hate salt water and come every day to swim at the pool. I think he's a little drunk. When I'm doing the dishes, he cups my fanny in his hands. 'You don't eat much,' he says. 'You're losing weight.'

He takes a shower while I finish cleaning up the kichen. As I pass the baby's room, I hear Hans Lucas rustling in his crib, but his breathing is quiet. I leave our door open so I can hear him. On the bed Peter is asleep, his arm across his eyes, the open hand naïve, but his shoulders as fierce and fabulous as a painting on a church wall. I sit down hard on the edge of the bed, hoping he'll wake up. When he falls asleep, he's as good as dead. Right after we got married, I never wanted to close my eyes, afraid that sleep would divide us, trap us in separate cages, no longer together, no longer in love. Sleep is a risk. Ideally, you should be awake all the time, protecting thought and property, body and breath.

I read for a while, and when I turn out the light, I can smell plumeria, acid and sweet. In the morning the petals will be as white as a sunrise in the Himalayas. It's hard to believe that a tree like that could be mine without asking, without paying a dime. In the petals of a plumeria is a yellow eye, solid but speckled, steady but whirling, and whenever I look into it, I fall down into the fragrant grasses of my own imaginings. I turn on my side, put my cheek against Peter's arm. The scent of plumeria is palpable, almost a liquid. I shut my eyes, trying to picture the green and perfectly growing things around us, but all I can think of is our baby growing badly in the next room. I hear a noise, a soft thumping or banging. I sit up. An even beat, then silence; a thrumming, and it's quiet again. I get out of bed and go down the hall.

Without turning on the light I bend over the crib. I can see the outline of his body on the sheet, his hand tapping against the wooden slats. It's the humdrum beat of boredom, or maybe a wordless prayer for sleep. For the first time I understand how lonely he must be. Every night while Peter and I fit ourselves together in animal love, or at least warm each other's dreams, he can never be certain of seeing anybody again. Waking or sleeping, he can only hope. What guarantee does he have that I'll be there in the morning, that I'll love him, change him, pick him up? How can any mother not be frightened at the intensity of such a trust? And how can any baby born without it live more than a day?

As I touch his cheek, something moves, itches and skitters under my fingers. When I turn on the light I see the blood running out of his nose. I shiver and he smiles. Five or six cockroaches are drinking it, tracking it across his face. As I stare, another one crawls up the side of his cheek, where the blood has dripped down. I pick them off with a Kleenex and flush them down the toilet. With soapy water, I clean his face and neck; strip the sheet, and see cockroach spoor on it like a faint pattern of roses. I'm kneeling, scrubbing the side of the crib, when Hans Lucas laughs and I see Peter, naked, looking down at us.

'What the hell's going on?'

'Cockroaches. Guzzling his blood.'

We take Hans Lucas into our bed. 'One of us has to stay awake,' I say, 'or we might roll over, crush him in our sleep. I'm not tired, so I don't mind.' In the end, we both stay awake, propped on our elbows, whispering across Hans Lucas.

Peter says, 'Tomorrow I'm going to spray hell out of his room.'

'Spraying isn't going to help,' I tell him. 'Whatever it was happened much earlier. Maybe in the woods one of us was thinking the wrong things, but nobody tells you what you're supposed to think while you're getting pregnant.'

47

KATE: The water is as clear as a ray of light, but there's a
        strong onshore wind, so Peter and Keoki stay on the
beach with me, waiting for it to drop.

'We better talk,' says Keoki. Ground swells are hitting the
outside reef, and the waves hang crookedly, toppling with the
density of icebergs.

At the tone of his voice, Peter says, 'About what?' He glances
at me.

'Your mother,' Keoki says, 'no like the *kanaka*.'

'Maybe,' says Peter. 'But a lot of Hawaiians hate *haoles*,
which is just as bad.'

'In war, G.I.s get drunk and fuck our sisters.'

'And dumped them – right?'

'With plenty *keiki* bastards.' From his fist, Keoki trickles a
thin stream of sand over his big toe. 'Your mother, she no like
me and Jenny.'

'Look, I don't know what M.S. has been saying. But as far as
I'm concerned, what you and Jenny do is your own business;
you don't have to clear anything with me.'

'I could do all kine things, like G.I.s, but your sister my
wahine.'

'Hey, that's great – I mean it,' Peter says, and they both look
at me.

'Did you guys just figure that out?' I say, turning a page.
'Jenny's known for ages.'

Keoki claps Peter on the shoulder. 'Wind drop; let's go.'

'I got a great ride at Waimea yesterday,' Peter is saying as
they wax their boards. 'Perfect fifteen-footer. I'm in the hook,
under the falls, white water hissing over my head like a nest of
snakes; it curls around me without spilling a drop, and I'm
happy as a flower in a greenhouse. I'm locked up in there only
about two seconds, but it's really fantastic.'

Keoki nods. 'My father he say: "You ever get where wave curl, clap over your head, you gon' find *ke ohe*, one fine tube. You no *on* wave, you *inside* it." ' He looks up as Mark carries his board down to the water. 'Sets coming look good – I get one big ride. But Mark, he gon' bust his *okole*.'

Later, as one of the long set begins, M.S. arrives. 'Jenny isn't coming,' she says. 'She's working at the hospital.'

Keoki is paddling into the first line of the set; two strokes and he's lifted as easily as a flea on a dog's back. It's a pretty good size wave, but he takes a gentle drop, his wake down the wall lengthening evenly. This is the first time they've been able to surf Palikai in two weeks. Lots of storms and chop and closeouts. The surf that autumn started big and stayed big, from early September on. Peter would paddle in with red eyes, fingers wrinkled like someone who's sat in a tub too long. He didn't even eat the sandwiches I brought, but sometimes he came to sit with me. (A typical conversation: 'Did you see me take gas?' – 'No, I missed it.' – 'Jesus, I can't believe you didn't see it.') Bug-eyed buses parked on the dirt road so that the restless middle-aged, sniffing for treats, could snap pictures of the surfers before the tourguide bundled them off to the sugar mill, the pineapple fields or the Mormon temple.

At middle break, Mark and Eric pump for the third wave of the set. Eric is first down the wall, inside, and Mark follows a fraction of a second later. The wave begins to curl over Eric's head and he's locked in, but it looks like he's going to make it. Mark's on his left, a little above him. Just before it peaks, the wave shines and rattles like a piece of tin.

Mark is too close. The speed, the double-edged wood, water guiding the board in a lateral swipe: if it hits Eric it could slit his throat. The board bucks, and Mark leans too far into the wave. He must have dug his rail in, the way he stops short and shoots right off. But once he's in the air, his trajectory, the curve of his body, seems deliberate, as if it's a dive he's planned and he doesn't want to hurry it. He enters the water almost without a splash, as his board spirals forward, cracks Eric on the back of the head. Eric nods once and, without shape or grace, half sitting and half standing up, drops straight down into the water.

Mark comes up right away, and starts to swim for his board. 'Oh God,' I say when the next wave passes over the spot where

Eric went down. Caught in the soup inside, Keoki grabs his own
board and turns turtle until the wave passes overhead. 'Oh
God,' I say again. I'm wringing my hands. M.S. folds her
newspaper, pressing the crease harder and harder, back and
forth. Out at middle break, Peter has just taken the drop. Keoki
is searching now, his hands parting the water like grass. In the
air, a fleshy smell of salt. Keoki's shoulder flexes, he raises his
arm, and I can see Eric's hair clenched in his enormous fingers.

I fall on my knees, my face almost level with M.S.'s. Up close
I see that she has begun to look like the women at Waikiki, her
skin thickly tanned, dry and grooved as the bark of a tree. 'Why
do we live like this?' I say. But she doesn't look at me, and I
repeat the question to myself. Why do we sit around like this,
just waiting for something to happen, aimless in the sun?

We both stand up, while Keoki paddles Eric in, while he and
Mark carry him ashore. Eric takes a few steps on his own and
sits down on the wet sand, the backwash circling him on its way
out. Neither of us makes a move to go down there. Peter tosses
his board on the sand and kneels beside Eric who, holding his
head in his hands, leans forward to vomit. Mark says something
and Peter laughs.

M.S. unstraps Hans Lucas from his board. 'Please,' she says,
'I want to hold him.' She's never said 'please' before.

By the time I go down to see how Eric is, he's already thrown
up again and they're all standing in the water. 'There it goes,'
says Mark. He and Eric are laughing. 'A sacrifice for da big
kahuna,' he says to me. 'Out at Kaena Point. He grows
pineapples with the shit of scared surfers and picks his teeth
with smashed boards.'

M.S. is up by Keoki's shack now, Hans Lucas clamped to her
shoulder. In the water Eric's puke is shipping out, and I wonder
if it will make it to Kaena Point.

48

KATE: A rooster runs across the road, but Peter brakes in
time. We've driven past the canefields without seeing
another car, and now we've come down into Haleiwa, where the
rooster flies into the window of a grocery store, and a woman in
red shorts and pincurls yells at it in Japanese. Further up the
street the Haleiwa theater – imperial and racy with lights on a
summer evening – comes across ramshackle in the cutting edge
of the early sun. I can smell pineapple, and the people in the
street are smiling and quiet, as if everything important has
already been attended to so there isn't any need to talk.

Keoki's grandmother lives on the bank of a stream. We turn
off onto a dirt road and the car noses into its first pothole, jogs
past the wooden houses on stilts – some on land, some half in the
water – past cheerful crazy clothes drying from tree to tree, and
men rummaging under cars. On fragrant porches, old people
watch us drive by. 'It's like fifty years ago,' Axel says.
'Plantation workers never left home except to go fishing or into
the fields, or cash their checks at the company store.' Papaya
and plumeria bending right over the car, palm and pandanus;
the leaves are green and shiny and growing so fast you can
almost hear them making a grab for the sky. I reach for Peter's
hand. I've left Hans Lucas with Amy Kanazawa, and when I
kissed him goodbye, I was sure he watched me all the way to the
door.

It's the last house on the road. Keoki's mother, an immense
woman in a muumuu with purple flowers on it, is supervising
the preparation of an *imu*, a wreath of ilima binding her hair.
When she hugs me, it's like bathing in the source. 'Hi, Auntie
Lilia,' I say. I've been out to her house in Nanakuli several
times.

'You pretty-pink today,' she tells me, lowering several pikake
leis onto my shoulders. 'Kini no come wit' you?'

'She's coming later, with M.S. and Eric.'

'Come see da *pua'a*,' she says, taking my hand. And so I help put the pig in the pit at Jenny's engagement luau.

Keoki isn't allowed to help. One of his nieces in his lap, he sits under a tree drinking beer while we load the *imu*. His grandfather got the oven ready early that morning, layering paper, kindling and guava wood around a stake; piling stones on top. Now everything has dropped down to the right degree of smoulder, and with a hoe he levels the bottom of the pit. At the same time two girls using special stones rub the singed hairs off the pig. I never knew a dead porker could make anybody giggle so much. Using tongs, Auntie Lilia and one of her daughters drop some of the red-hot stones into the pig's belly, and the men lash it together with chicken wire. I kneel with the others at the edge of the *imu*, help them cover the cooking stones with shredded banana leaves. Helping at the luau, I don't feel I'm just playing house the way I do cooking fancy things for Peter. Hawaiian food is so sure, so grown-up in its plainness, like a woman who knows she looks good in a black dress, that any other kind of food seems superfluous. When the men have lowered the pig onto the leaves, we lay down sweet potatoes, laulau, breadfruit and taro. Waiting to help, Keoki's aunts line up in straw boaters, big and venerable as Easter Island statues. 'Now we covah it, deah,' says Auntie Lilia, pinching my cheek. Ti leaves are packed down, slim and aristocratic as the feathers of a cockatoo; more banana leaves; lauhala mats, then dirt shovelled over. Keoki's grandfather gives me a pail of water, lets me sprinkle it on top to seal any little openings.

'Chow in five hours,' I say importantly, sitting next to Axel and Peter on the dock. Axel has started on the pineapple swipe. 'Nobody'll be on their feet by then,' he says.

Peter hands me his bottle of beer and puts his head in my lap: 'Speak for yourself.' The stream is quiet under my dangling feet, its blue and green reflections locking together like tiles; all around us the sexy breath of tropical wind and fruit and trees. I try to picture the mainland, what they'd be doing on a Sunday morning in October. But when you live on an island you think you're at the center of the world, and now it's hard for me to conjure up California. When I lived in San Francisco I always knew there were a lot of other places out there, but here in

Hawaii I can't imagine any place else. I've begun to think that as well as being the best place to live, an island would be the best place to die. More fun to be buried with the Hawaiians and their ghosts in this porous rock than to be packed unromantically in the airless dirt of the mainland. And when you're dead and buried on an island, the living are never far away. The first few days I was in Hawaii, I couldn't believe anyone ever died here. A veil of light hangs from the sky, so intense and southern and pure you almost think it could stop the shiver of death. (Death is dull and metallic, and comes from the north.) Suddenly, clearly, I see Barney in Cambridge: bourbon and football; the early lamps and slippery bricks, the leaves hanging down in clusters, like bats.

A car door slams and Axel looks up at the house. 'M.S. and Jenny are here,' he says. Peter stirs in my lap and I stroke his cheek. I know we should go to meet them, but I want to stay here, feel his breath on my hand, consider the simple pig cooking in its pit. I hear Jenny laughing. 'Come on,' Peter says, sitting up.

Eric is pinching the petals of his lei; he sniffs his fingers. Two other leis sliding on her arm, Auntie Lilia kisses Jenny and drops one of them around her neck. Jenny is on crutches. I haven't seen her wearing the leg since she's been in Hawaii. M.S. looks just a fraction less important without Mark at her side. He's gone back to the mainland, giving Georgia as his reason, but I think M.S. said something to him after his board hit Eric. He lost it again a few days later, smashed it on the reef.

I've never seen M.S. wearing a muumuu, and I wonder if she's done it for Jenny. Her braid on the flowered cloth looks out of place, as formal as an epaulette. In that little knot of people anyone would pick her out; self-conscious and intense, she's surely apart, as if she alone knows the real reason why we're here. And yet, hands clasped on the handle of her bag, she seems almost timid, anxious not to attract any looks. Of expensive black leather, the bag looks unfriendly in that climate, like some kind of mainland reminder of the proprieties, a doctor's satchel maybe, discreetly warning us to lower our voices. Her hands are rough. Summers in Redwood Creek, she'd washed three batches of dishes and all our clothes, cleaned the floors, the john and the sinks, with water heated in a so⌐

kettle. I can still see some of that work in her hands; they're hard and flagrant like those sculptures of the poor that artists get rich on.

'Mom,' says Jenny. 'This is Auntie Lilia.'

Auntie Lilia opens her arms, but M.S. holds out her hand. 'Me, my husban', we love Kini,' Auntie Lilia says, taking M.S.'s hand to her breast.

'So do I,' says M.S. 'And her name is Jenny.'

'She one fine *wahine* foah Keoki.' Auntie Lilia hoists one of the leis and M.S., who's a few inches taller, has to bend forward so she can slip it over her head. But M.S. straightens up too soon, it catches on her braid, and she has to pull it down herself. For a second Auntie Lilia brings her face so close to M.S.'s, I think she's going to kiss her. She's looking into M.S's eyes, concentrating as if listening to some vital news somebody's telling her in a whisper. M.S. flinches, and something slithers out from between her feet. Born in M.S.'s shadow, a lizard, poised and brown and wavy as a hair. Auntie Lilia sees it too. '*Auwe*,' she says, and the lizard whips across the road into the grass.

Jenny pulls at M.S. 'Come look at the *imu*.' And when Axel takes her arm to lead her across the lawn, M.S. doesn't seem to mind.

Auntie Lilia is crying. '*Ino ino*,' she says, and Keoki squeezes her shoulder. '*Hauna ele*,' she wails. She wipes her eyes.

For the rest of the afternoon, M.S. stays close to her kids, and the only stranger she talks to is Auntie Lilia's yellow dog. Just before we eat the pig, I see Jenny pounding something with a pestle and mortar. A little brown girl comes up to her. 'You fix,' she says, pointing to a strap on her sunsuit that's come undone. Jenny ties a reef knot. Crutch under her shoulder, she picks up the little girl and kisses her on the nose. I'm shocked at how strong she's become.

Jenny sits with me in the grass. 'What are you making?' I say when she begins pounding again.

'   kui nuts and rock salt. It's kind of a relish.'

'   here it's coming from. One of the kids kept
           o Peter and me, but Axel said it was a laxative,
           it.'

'   ive if you eat too much.' Jenny grins. 'But I
           u.'

'Oh, we're go*in*' to a hukilau, huki *hu*ki, huki *hu*ki, huki *hu*kilau. . . .' Down on the landing somebody has brought out a uke, and over the deep throng of Hawaiian voices, the words in Eric's mouth are precise and sweet. Not far from the singers, Keoki, one bare foot on the ground, the other propped against a tree, is talking to Axel. I've noticed before how he always looks around for Jenny, and how happy he is whenever he finds her. Right then he's looking for her, and I know that, unlike me and Peter, there'll never be anything for them to stumble over, nothing in their lives they won't be able to see.

'You're so lucky,' I say to Jenny. 'Did you ever think,' I wave my arm in a dreamy half-circle, 'that you'd be doing this?'

'Grinding kukui nuts? Sure. Auntie Lilia likes the way I bash them. Dumb-dumb,' she says, tugging on my hair the way she used to. 'No, I know what you mean.' Clink, the pestle against the mortar. Clink, like bamboo chimes. 'When you and Peter went to the prom, I stayed awake all night. My eyes were wide open. I saw every step you took, and I hated you for being there. I hated both of you. I hoped something really bad would happen. Now I hate myself whenever I see you worrying about Hans Lucas.'

'Well, don't. I used to wonder how you got through it all, and now I know. By hating me. What are best friends for?'

'Come on, bruddahs and sistahs, *kaukau*; let's eat da piggy.' Keoki's father is waving his arms.

'Kini, Kini, there you are. Come wit' Keoki, get da firs' bite of da *pua'a*.' Auntie Lilia calling Jenny.

'Why is it,' I say as I follow Jenny to the *imu*, 'that every Hawaiian I'm around acts like a doting parent?'

'I know what you mean,' she says. 'We're not used to people liking us so much right away.'

Keoki's father and brother shovelled the dirt off the *imu*, lifted the mat. From the steaming casket of earth, a smell as original as bread. Women reaching into the pit, cooling their hands in buckets of water. Circle of rapt humid faces. When the stones like dying eggs are taken from the belly of the pig, the women suck their fingers before dipping them into the pails. The pig is lifted up, shy and healthy-looking from the heat, snout turned without anger to the sky.

After the men ease the pig into a tub, the chicken-w

offered to Jenny, who picks off a piece of skin. She hisses when it burns her fingers, waves it like a little flag before popping it into her mouth. Lips shiny, she reaches for more. I remember the story of the Chines boy my mother read me: pigs trapped in a fire, he tastes one of them, discovers roast pork.

Peter and I take our plates to a fern-covered table. At the *imu*, Axel is stacking meat on a plate for M.S. Both hands on her bag, she watches him incredulously, as if he's an employee she's about to sack. 'Was Auntie Lilia crying,' says Peter, 'when Jenny introduced her to M.S.?'

'Yes. And she said something to Keoki in Hawaiian.'

'What do you think it meant?'

'I'm not sure. But Davis told me some Hawaiians can read people like the gas man reads meters.'

After dinner Keoki and I are alone for a few minutes at the table while everybody else is watching the dancing. Auntie Lilia is sitting between M.S. and Jenny, her body a prayer, still and metaphysical. 'Auntie Lilia is different from the rest of us,' I say.

'For her, all same time; for her, always morning. She see everything like that. Never night for her.' A dry pulse of music, steady as the warning of crickets in autumn. 'She say Peter so clear she see through him to birds and trees on other side. She know all kine stuff.' In a breeze from the water, the torchfires tremble and I think how easy it's always been for a light to go out. 'But she say M.S. got one big black tail, and it follow her around like the tail of comet in sky.'

49

CHARLOTTE: 'Are you coming?' I say to Jenny after the
               hulas are over.
   'Luau no finish yet,' Keoki says. He takes Jenny's hand.
   'My ass,' I say. I know they'll probably disappear, just the
two of them, for a long time in the dark. I see that Peter is
leaving with Kate, and I follow him to his car. 'I'll see you and
Kate up at the house,' I remind them.
   'I don't think we'll come up to Alewa tonight,' he says. 'Kate
wants to go home to Hans Lucas.'
   'We'll drop by then. First I have to make a phone call.'
   I find a drugstore that's open in Waikiki, and tell Eric to wait
in the car. 'Give me lots of change,' I tell the clerk, handing him
two tens. Out of sight in the phone booth, I touch my cheek to
the cold metal box, and then scrub at my skin with a Kleenex.
Public telephones are filled with the spit of strangers, but if I call
up at the house the kids will be around. I don't want them to
hear, and I don't want them to know the horrible scenes I
imagine: Jenny-one-crutch in a sarong, hopping down the aisle;
Keoki's arm, big and rubbery as the wheel of a tractor, around
her waist; on her wedding night – one leg crooked, beckoning
him – my daughter lying down like a whore. Or Jenny pregnant:
will she have a panda or a hippopotamus? In my dreams now, I
stand over all my kids and, feet apart, suck them back up, one by
one, into my womb.
   The coins feel too light to pay for what I've got to tell him, so
I toss them loose as stones into my bag and call collect. Sole
and unresilient, the operator's voice is entombed; the cable,
silly in the water as a piece of string, yet guiding my voice
through its tiny airless walls, bringing it in safe under the
Golden Gate at one-fifteen in the morning. San Francisco
dark, its thousands of eyes gone out, the long muscles of its
hills shifting in the fog.

Hank picks up the phone with a clatter as if he's lunged for it. 'Are you here in the city?' His voice is not quite sure of itself.

'No. I've just been to a picnic – Jenny's going to marry that Hawaiian.'

'Christ, can't you stop it?'

'I'm thinking of ways.' I squeeze my handbag.

'I've lost ten pounds since you left.'

'Get a woman in to cook.'

'It's not that.'

I can feel his need, the phone exuding his dampness into my hand. 'Screw your secretary then; other men do.'

Cloth or his skin brushing the mouthpiece. 'I can't get to sleep without you. The house smells funny when I come home; it's cold and I don't feel like sitting down.'

'Then come over here.'

'I can't right now, you know that. Too much work piling up. Do you miss me?'

'Yes.' He can sit on the beach with me, we can talk about the kids; I'll rub lotion on his back so he won't get those nasty spots. 'If she does marry him, you'll have to fly over.'

'Will you come home after?'

'I can't even think about that right now,' I say, my lips close to the mouthpiece. 'But if you come over we can make a week of it.'

'At the hotspots in Waikiki?'

'No. In my room up at the house.'

Peter's apartment is lit, but the light at the front of the building hasn't been turned on. 'Careful,' murmurs Eric. 'It's pretty dark.'

As I go up the front steps, somebody opens the door. There's no direct light in the hall, but I can see whoever's standing behind the door is black. Memory-warning-dream: sun hammering, loud noises, like the kids used to make banging on my pots and pans. Bunt, I'm going to have to bunt. Last time I fouled, down the left field line. Cross my legs, my drawers are dry and they haven't seen me. Hank and I are reflections cast on the water by two people who no longer exist; we'll have to be on guard. They should have dropped the bomb on Hawaii, sent all that flesh up, deadly nightshade unfolding its petals against the sky.

Behind the door, the shadow turns on the light. A nigger steps forward, its body shrinking to a stick, its head round and shiny: a black sun on the body of a lollipop. My palm stinging, I lean against Eric. He grabs my arm. Somebody begins to howl, and Kate comes out into the hall.

'Amy? Are you all right?'

Sniffing and crying, the big girl swings her head up and down. 'I held the door open for her,' she says, pointing at me.

'And M.S. slapped her,' says Eric.

Kate puts her arm around the girl. 'Amy's my babysitter. Why did you hit her?'

'What was she doing behind that door?' I brush Kate aside. 'I'm really sorry, Amy,' Kate is saying. 'Eric, can you take her home?'

'What's up?' says Peter, as I come into the apartment. He's in the kitchen making a sandwich. Axel, who's sitting at the table, gets up to give me his chair, even though there's nobody sitting in the other one.

'I don't know why you let Kate have those people in the house,' I say, 'touching your baby.' Peter and Axel glance at each other, and I slam my fist on the table. 'Not only do you have no guts, you're too dumb to see danger when it's everywhere. It can begin in the smallest ways, with the laying on of hands.' Is there a small spot of dampness between my legs after all? Maybe I drank too much out at Haleiwa.

Kate comes into the kitchen. 'I don't know what you think you were doing,' she says, 'but you better call her and apologize.'

I have to smile. I think she's trying to threaten me; something in that enigmatic body finally arching, feathering, pulsing up. 'Calm down. I want to talk to you.'

Axel touches my shoulder. 'Been kind of a big day, maybe I should run you home.'

I jump up. 'I don't need a goddam chauffeur.' I move in on him so close I can feel the buttons of his shirt through my ridiculous Hawaiian dress. 'You're just a hick Marine who's trying to cash in on my son's publicity. Scheme all you want, but they're better than you and they always will be. Just like I'm older than you and I always will be, thank God.'

Peter glances at Axel again and the two of them go outside. 'That food made me thirsty,' I tell Kate. I run myself a glass of water. 'Now we can talk.'

'I don't want to talk,' Kate says. 'Hans Lucas is crying and you've made a mess of everything.'

'The only thing I care about is you kids, and I don't want anything to happen to that baby. We girls took care of Lucas. We'd never let anybody else touch him, except maybe Mama sometimes. Lucas wasn't my son, only my brother, but even then I knew that a baby is as much your own image as your shadow or a snapshot or your face in the mirror. That's the whole secret, that's what I'm trying to tell you: if you take care of your baby you don't have to worry about yourself, because you've got something that's going to do the work of being you. Whether you're dead or alive, when that kid grows up he's going to be your voice, your footsteps, your fingerprints, your name. We would never have left our brother with a dirty girl like that.'

'Amy's not dirty.'

'They're all dirty; you just can't see it. You notice they don't wear white because it shows the dirt.'

'That's a lie. And Jenny's going to *marry* a Hawaiian.'

'Nothing in this life is certain.'

'Axel went to check out his buddies on Hotel Street,' says Peter, coming back into the kitchen. 'Off-duty, he gets nervous.'

'Hey Kate, how about some coffee.' Eric walks in and picks up the pot. 'Can I make it?'

'Yes,' she says, hurrying off to Hans Lucas.

Peter sits down next to me. 'Do me a favor,' he says, 'and don't call Axel a hick. Another thing: he's not trying to cash in on anybody. He was surfing Palikai before we even saw it.'

'He's trying to run the show. He tells you Palikai can or can't be surfed at twenty or thirty or forty, and you take it like a baby sucking its bottle. Why don't you find out for yourself?' Eric is sitting on the floor with a page of the comics. When I raise my voice, he looks up like an animal smelling a predator on the wind.

'When I want to surf, I surf; where and how I want to surf. It's got nothing to do with Axel.'

'You look pretty cautious to me, just like the Sunday surfers you laugh at. This buddy system is all his idea to make sure you don't do something on your own, to make his nuts look like custard. He took your wave right out from under you the other day.'

'It wasn't my wave; the wave doesn't give a shit who rides it.'

'By God I'd like to show you. It's not because I'm forty-eight years old that I'm not going out there, because I don't believe in getting old. Old age isn't a natural process, it's some kind of disease, and when you get it, your resistance breaks down and you get all sorts of other diseases, and I'm goddamned if I'll have a stroke, cling to life like a limpet to a rock, so some doctor can poke me with a stick. It's not because I'm old that I'm not going out there to show you, it's because raising you kids I haven't had time to train. But if I'd been given a prick, I'd know how to use it. Something you never learned. You couldn't even take care of the other kids when we went camping. Couldn't kill the snake, could you?' I lean forward and my handbag falls to the floor. 'Don't you care about staying alive? Killing something that could kill you makes you feel *good*. Surfing, it's the same: those waves are trying to kill you; they're murderers, just like people. I really believe that. There are a lot of simple but important things most people don't understand.'

On the rise, the coffee has started to perk. Plop hush plop, all the rains of my childhood falling in that single sound. Eric turns down the flame, and by the light of the stove I can see the bumps on his fingers. He's got warts, like Danny's grandson, and for a second I think I mind these low-class pustules more than all the drama of Jenny's leg. 'You don't need that leatherneck,' I say. 'Kill or be killed. Go out alone.' I lean forward. 'I can see you're not listening; why am I wasting my breath?'

'What's this kill or be killed? I'm not a bullfighter.'

Plop plop plop plop. Prairie rain. Whenever I could tell a storm was coming, I'd run over to Francie's. Sod house, dirt walls three feet thick, flowers planted on top. From a distance it looks like a tall garden. Nice and cool inside and Francie's mother has tacked up muslin on the walls and ceiling to keep out the field mice. Francie and I sit by the window, muslin falling around us as gracefully as the folds of an Arab's tent. Holding hands, we watch the twisters twirling on the flatlands and hope they'll come our way. I close my eyes, tired of Peter's excuses.

'Learn to fly solo,' I say, as Kate calls anxiously from the other room. 'Get rid of the Marine.'

'What did Kate want?' Eric is pouring milk from the bottle into his cup when Peter comes back into the kitchen.

'Nothing. She thought the baby . . . but now he's okay.'

He picks up my bag, which is still lying on the floor. As he hands it back to me, the clasp snaps open. Between my wallet and keys, he can see the slim fish wavering under the change. 'Is that a knife?' he says.

'If you know it's a knife, why ask? Damn,' I say. 'I should have had the clerk give me back my bills.' I begin scooping out money, tossing nickels, dimes and quarters onto the table. 'Here, Eric. Present for you.'

'Why are you carrying that knife around?' Peter says.

'You have to be ready to defend yourself, especially in a foreign city.'

'This isn't a foreign city. You don't even need a passport.'

'Well, there are plenty of foreigners, and you can never tell when one of them will take it into his head to attack you.'

Without looking at me or my bag open on the table, Eric stuffs the coins into his pockets. 'Nobody's going to attack you, for Christ's sake,' Peter tells me. 'But with that knife in there, you're going to cut your fingers to ribbons. Let me take it.' As he reaches into my bag, I snap it shut.

'Mind your own business.' I squeeze his fingers in the clasp. 'Big baby. Grow up, be a man, and leave your mother alone.' I rip open the bag to let his fingers out, and if he hadn't grabbed me, I'd have fallen over backward. 'I'm going home,' I say. 'But first I want to see Hans Lucas.'

'Kate's just got him to sleep.'

'Well, she'll have to wake him up – I want to say goodnight to my grandchild.' I get up and leave, but outside the kitchen door I wait a minute, listening.

'What are we going to do?' says Eric.

'About the knife? Nothing. If we take it, she'll get another one. I just hope to Christ she doesn't use it on some poor pake or Hawaiian. We better not mention it to Jenny or Kate – no sense in getting them excited.'

What they don't understand is, I'm not going to use it on anybody if they let me alone. If that Hawaiian lets Jenny alone, and Kate stops fussing with Hans Lucas. If we can all just go home.

50

KATE: The guy waiting on me is in love with my hair. He
        keeps lifting his hand like he wants to touch it, and
when I bend over to look at a plate or some glasses, he bends too.
My hair always attracts attention; I guess nobody's immune to
a really good head of hair, it doesn't matter on which sex. As a
matter of fact, the salesman is probably homosexual. With Peter
he's diffident, aware of his own special knowledge, anxious not
to inflict it on possibly hostile strangers. When he talks to me, he
pats his own cheek, gentle little slaps as if he's trying to keep
himself awake.

'Did you check on Hans Lucas?' I say, turning to Peter.

He nods. 'Ten minutes ago. Sleeping peacefully.'

We've come to this expensive place so I can pick out a
wedding present for Jenny and Keoki. They're going to be
married on New Year's Day, and Keoki went out this afternoon
to buy his first pair of shoes. We wanted to make a ceremony of
it, but Keoki insisted on going alone. 'If no can buy da kine
shoes, no can marry Jenny. Time for be grown up.'

Instead I persuaded Peter to go shopping with me. But we
couldn't get a babysitter, so we've had to bring Hans Lucas.
Peter has parked the station wagon under some trees a few doors
down from the store. We locked the doors and rolled down the
windows a little to let in the cool breeze. On his board he was
taking a nap, but I was afraid he'd miss me and kept turning
back every few steps. It's getting harder to get me to go
anywhere without Hans Lucas.

The night we came home from the luau, I said, 'Did you see how
Hans Lucas lifted his head when I picked him up?' I unbutton
my dress and pull it over my head. 'It was beautiful out there
today; I couldn't stand going back to the mainland now.' Peter

is lying on his back, looking at me. Underneath my dress I'm naked. 'I wish I'd known you didn't have any pants on,' he says. 'We could have had a little easy fun in the dark down by the dock. Why didn't you tell me?'

'I wanted to be the only one to know. The flowers, the water, the pig in the pit – Jenny and Keoki, all the hugging and the kissing and the music. I just wanted to think, with a couple of twists of my buttons I can step out of my dress, I can lie in the sand or jump in the water.' I kneel on the bed. 'Let's have another baby.'

'Today wasn't perfect.' He takes my hand.

'When M.S. slapped Amy? I think she was drunk.'

'I'm talking about later. When you thought Hans Lucas was having a seizure.'

'Maybe he wasn't,' I say. 'Maybe he was just tired.'

'I saw him. Arched like a bridge, and his eyes rolled up.'

'And he made a funny sound.'

'You better tell Dr Fulton.'

'But just before it happened he held out his arms. He seemed to know who I was, and want me to pick him up. I'm sure he's going to be all right. I want another one. I want to be the mother of a hundred golden sons.'

'Suns as in moon, or sons as in man? You're beginning to sound like M.S.'

'Please,' I whisper. Kneeling between his thighs, my hands under his hips, serving him up.

'I won't let you do it,' he says. 'I don't want to destroy you. Let's get Hans Lucas through this first, lets. . . .' He groans. 'Your mouth is so wet . . . healthy . . . sweet like . . . syrup . . . on my prick.'

I lick my lips and sit up. 'Get him through what?' I spread myself, ease down on him in a slow circle.

'Let's get him a little more grown up. . . .' he says. 'Sweet Jesus.'

I'm drawing him in: there's no way out except straight up. If he gives in to the shudder, the twitch, I'll have my way. Twitch of life, twitch of death: one led to the other, and to the incoherent spasms of Hans Lucas in between. His come would shoot up bright and shiny, a coin flipped into a midnight sky, but I can't believe that this time it will bring down another dead mirror of himself, a face that doesn't look back.

'Stop it; wait a minute.' He rolls over, throwing me off balance, and reaches under the mattress. 'I'm not going to let you be crazy – you've got to let me use a rubber. Maybe in another year. . . .'

'You don't love him the way you keep saying, or you'd want to.' My voice is pale as a moonstone. I slip my legs under the sheet and turn away. 'The day is over now. I want to get some sleep.'

The salesman picks up a glass. 'Too gaudy,' I tell him.

'I know what you mean,' he says. 'What do you think of this one?'

'I love it – it looks like it should be in a palace.' I hand the glass to Peter. Cold and sharp and deeply cut; a circle of six-pronged stars encased in diamonds, palmettes flying near the rim.

'It's nice,' Peter says, and I try to imagine it in Keoki's shack, in the same room as the rusty sink, the snaggled chairs, the *punee* with busted springs. 'It's nice,' he murmurs. 'Why don't you get it?'

'Do you have six of these?' I ask the salesman. 'Or,' I say to Peter, 'should we make it eight?'

'Anybody here own a blue Ford station wagon?' says a policeman from the open door.

'I do,' says Peter.

The policeman shakes his head. 'You better step outside.'

'What is it?' I say. 'Ask him what it is.'

A small crowd is standing around our car. A family of Japanese – mother, father and three children – heads bowed as if at a funeral or in the presence of an honoured guest; a *haole* couple, honeymooners probably, shuffling packages; two cops, a fireman and a couple of M.P.s. One of the M.P.s is holding the back door of the station wagon. Somebody has ripped it off its hinges. 'Is this your car?' he says, balancing the door against a lamp-post.

'Yes,' says Peter.

'You son of a bitch.' The young honeymooner hands his packages to his wife. 'Tying up a kid like that. Do you torture animals too?' He backs Peter against the car, as the cop and the M.P.s close in.

'It's to straighten his back.'

'Maybe I should straighten your jaw.' He shoves his hand against Peter's chest and Peter braces himself against the car. 'Poor little kid.'

The honeymooner's lips are greasy and well-pleased. Above her bags and boxes, his wife glances at the Japanese to make sure they're watching. I look up into an avenue of sky. They think we torture our child. The Japanese love children even more than the Hawaiians do, and yet there's no anger in their faces. In the newsreels the survivors had the same look of composed despair, and the faces of the ones near the blast calmly rotted in stepped-up time, their bodies like broken pedestals under the heads of once-great men. 'It really is to straighten his back,' I say, pleading with the Japanese. Parts of those faces would never be found; particularly the eyes, easiest to be blown out and misplaced. The honeymooner slams Peter's head on the top of the car. 'Stop it,' I scream. 'Make him stop it.'

'Okay, that's enough,' says one of the cops, pushing the honeymooner aside. Peter lifts his head. A few warm drops of rain lick our faces, although there aren't any clouds.

The salesman has come out of the store, still holding my wineglass; blushing, he watches us, as if he'd not only known what was going to happen but had actually caused it.

'Call Dr Fulton at Shriner's,' I say to the cop. 'He'll tell you.'

Over the heads of the crowd, the salesman says, 'You can use my phone.'

'Okay, lady, I'll call him. But he better tell me something pretty good.'

Peter drives slowly past Ala Moana. 'Let's eat out,' he says. 'I don't want to go home.' He's thrown the unhinged door in the back. A breeze comes in through the hole where it's been torn off.

'What about Hans Lucas?' I'm holding the baby in my lap.

'We'll take him with us; they have special chairs for kids.'

'Why did you let that creep hit you? You should have smashed him one.'

'With the cop going ape-shit, and the two M.P.s? Anyway, I knew he wasn't going to hurt me.'

'How did you know that?'

'Just something I figured.' He taps his fingers on the wheel. 'I never think anything can hurt me.'

The restaurant is one we both like, down by the yacht harbor. A family restaurant where children play in the aisles under the feet of their parents and the tolerant waitresses. The manager brings us a high chair for Hans Lucas. 'He isn't sitting very straight,' I say when we're alone. 'I thought his back was getting better.'

A few days after the luau, I took Hans Lucas for one of his check-ups, and Dr Fulton told me that the reason he was holding his head up more was not that he was becoming more alert, but that the board was strengthening his spine. 'There's been some improvement in his gross motor development, but you're being too optimistic, I'm afraid. Hans Lucas isn't making any progress upstairs, and I don't want you to have any unpleasant surprises.' He leaned forward, considering me. 'I'm a little worried about your health. Try to get your husband to help you carry the baby; he's getting pretty heavy. Can I be honest? If he hasn't shown any improvement in, say, six months, I'd strongly recommend that you put him in the state home. You're both too young to have your lives crushed before you begin.'

'He painted a pretty bleak picture,' I said when I told Peter. 'Do you think they can take him away from us? If they're sure he's not going to get better, can they *make* us give him up?'

'Of course not.'

Hans Lucas had cried for an hour that night, and right after I came back to bed I had a dream. I heard my own groan, a long spiral pulling at the roots of my hair. When Peter shook me I gasped and opened my eyes. 'I dreamed I was underwater, and there were all these little red fishes. Barney told me once how the harbor turns red like that when a Hawaiian chief is going to die.' I put out my arms and Peter held me. 'I still can't get my breath,' I whispered on his shoulder. 'I wanted to get my head above water so I could see who it was, who was going to die, but the fish kept jumping down my throat. I was choking,' I said, 'and now I can't stop.'

A waitress brings our menus. 'Can we get a small plate of food for the baby so I can cut it up?' I ask her. Hans Lucas is bent over, his forehead almost touching the tray of his chair, and I tie him loosely upright with the belt of my dress. 'Jenny came by this morning,' I say.

'What did she want?' Hans Lucas is tugging at his own face. Gently I loosen his hands. Red marks splay his cheeks as if he's been scratched by a cat. 'Why does he do that?' Peter says.

'He doesn't know he's doing it; it's a habit like biting your lip.' I let go, and Hans Lucas begins pulling again with both hands, as if trying to stretch a sweater that's shrunk. 'She was on her way to the state hospital to see one of her crippled kids. This kid was moved out there because they found out he was retarded too.'

'Is this the place Fulton was talking about?' says Peter, as the waitress comes back. 'I'll have the ulua steak – "All You Can Eat For a Dollar" – and a bowl of saimin.'

'Can you give me a plate of ulua with mashed potatoes and peas for the baby? And I'd like a cheese omelette.'

Hans Lucas has started to slump over again, and the waitress says, 'Wait a minute.' She brings out a pillow, tucks it between him and his chair. 'There. So he doesn't rattle around so much in that big thing.'

'Jenny took me with her,' I say, 'and I met the woman who runs it. It's not as depressing as I thought. Lots of linoleum – and the toys are a little shabby, and some of the blankets on the beds are worn. But it's clean, and that woman cares. She showed Jenny a letter she's sending some parents who had to move back to the mainland, all about how Santa came and brought presents to their little girl, and how excited she was. Their "little girl" is thirty years old.'

'Why did you go?'

'I told you; Jenny wanted me to.'

'I wish you hadn't. I'll never let them have Hans Lucas.'

'I'm not saying *I'd* let them have him. I'm just telling you what it was like. The kids grab you around the knees and try to pull you down so they can look at you. Some of them are just smart enough to know something's wrong with them and that's why they can't go out into the world. One funny thing: a father was visiting his daughter – she's the only *haole* in the hospital right now – and one of the helpers said, "Hey, you Peachie's daddy? She one smart keed." '

'Don't tell me any more.'

'Why not? We're going to have to face up to it sooner or later. Mrs Kanazawa told me today that the reason we can't get other babysitters is that they know there's something wrong with him. And, if M.S. hits Amy again, we won't even be able to get her.'

'Why do you have to keep talking about it, point out all the things that can go wrong?'

'Why do you act all the time like everything's perfect? Why can't you ever admit that he's retarded? Because you think if he's retarded he's not masculine, that's why. Why do men always have to equate everything with their own virility?'

'That's a crock.'

'Maybe it is a crock. But you don't have to live with it like I do. I never used to think that every little sin gets noticed, but I'm beginning to wonder whose screw-up we're being punished for.' I take his hand. 'I'm sorry,' I say. 'It's not you. It's just that I don't even like to go to sleep any more. I don't know which is worse, the dreams, or getting up when he cries. Why does he do it? Does he know just enough to realize he's helpless, and *that's* why he cries? He's never been hurt, and he doesn't know about dying, so what *else* can he be afraid of?'

51

KATE: Henry Hollander came over for the wedding, but we
        didn't see him much. He stayed for a week, and most
of the time he was off somewhere with M.S.; sightseeing, I
guess. When I came down the aisle ahead of Jenny, all I could
see up front were Keoki's shoes. Very black loafers, flat and
unwrinkled. Even the tux wasn't such a shock as those shiny
harnessed feet. They went to Lahaina for their honeymoon, but
I did most of the mooning, imagining how romantic Maui must
be. At two in the morning, with Hans Lucas crying in my arms,
I needed something nice to think about.

One day in March M.S. calls to see if I want to drive out to
Palikai with her; she's bringing Jenny a toaster. The university
is having its spring break, so I call Geneva and ask her if she'll
look after Hans Lucas. 'Of course, ducky. Come and have a cup
of tea.'

'Let's take him off that frightful board,' Geneva says, when I
bring him over. 'We're out on the *lanai*, and I thought he might
like to play in the grass. Go on out – Davis has something to
tell you – while I just finish in the kitchen. By the way, the
recipe for chocolate mousse I gave you – the one you had
trouble with? Well, I think maybe you let it come to the boil.
Actually, it should only heave and bubble a bit, as if it's having
an orgasm.'

I put Hans Lucas on the lawn and Davis kisses me. 'How is
he?' he says.

'His back is better, I think.'

'I'm glad, sweetie, I'm really glad. You know those words you
asked me about? What the Hawaiian woman said when she first
clapped eyes on your mother-in law? I finally saw Bob Jamison
at the Bishop and he said – wait a minute – I have it written
down here. Yes. "*Hauna ele*" is a disturbance, or stinking
darkness; it can also mean an ill wind that bodes no good. And

"*ino*" means wicked, or maybe contaminated; to think evil, or do harm. "*Ino ino*" just emphasizes the meaning.'

'No wonder she cried.'

'What do you know about this woman?'

'Just that she's Keoki's mother, and they come from the big island. I love Auntie Lilia, and so does Jenny, but it's scary she said that about M.S.'

'If it's something bad about your mother-in-law, I'm all for it,' says Geneva, bringing out a cake.

'Could she be a *kahuna*?' I ask Davis.

'She could, but most of them have gone underground. She could just be extraordinarily prescient. I told you before – a lot of Hawaiians are. They look at things differently, explain them differently. We all have to pick our own explanations, or we'd go crazy. There's a thing called Occam's razor: if you're faced with two solutions, two answers to a question – both equally reasonable – choose the one that's simplest, and that's the one most likely to be right.'

'I don't know how Auntie Lilia knows that things always go sour around M.S.,' I say, 'but for me the simplest answer is that she just knows.'

Geneva's been watching Hans Lucas. Lying on his stomach in the grass, he lifts his head, but he doesn't look at us. 'Has he ever tried to crawl?' she says.

'I take him off the board more than I'm supposed to because I want him to have the chance to try. I just don't tell the doctor I do it.' I kneel on the grass by Hans Lucas. 'But he never seems to care about anything except what goes on in his own head.'

'And what,' says Davis softly, 'might that be?'

'Stop it, Davis.' Kneeling beside me, Geneva holds out her arms to Hans Lucas.

'If you keep him you're going to be destroyed,' he says. 'My aunt Tina had a child like him. My cousin, I guess, but I never thought of him that way. He didn't seem like a person.' Davis stands up, casting his shadow on both of us. 'She had another child, a normal girl, and she ruined the girl's life for the sake of that idiot. I watched the life go right out of her while her mother cleaned up his drool and his bowel movements. My aunt raising money for retarded kids, and her daughter growing up silent as a tree. And, finally, I was the one who found her: sixteen years old, with her head like a roast in the oven.'

'He shouldn't have said that,' Geneva says, when Davis goes into his study. 'But I think he was very fond of her.' Hans Lucas is in her lap, and she's feeding him little pieces of cake. 'And he's also worried about you. We both are. You look very tired these days. Obviously one can't ask if everything is all right because it isn't. But is it something more than the baby?'

'It's Peter and me. Things are different.'

'Probably not as different as you think. Things don't change, darling, only our illusions. The longer we live, the fewer our illusions – and when every one of them is gone, then we're probably dead.'

'I don't have any illusions, and I love him as much as ever, but since that day with the baby and the cops and the guy banging his head on the car, he doesn't tell me what he's thinking.'

'He probably wants to – it seems such a simple thing to tell you how he feels – but I'm sure it's that gory mother of his. She's so ballsy I'm amazed she could even *produce* a child.'

'When he's sleeping I watch him, and sometimes when I wake up in the middle of the night he's watching me. But I never let him know that I know he's doing it.'

Geneva comes out of the house as I'm getting into the car. 'I used to wear this when I was younger,' she says, 'and it saw me through a lot. . . .' She hands me a bottle of Joy. 'No matter how miserable one gets, my dear, how poor or depressed, it's vital to have a bottle of really good scent.'

In the late sun Keoki's shack is the color of a nice piece of toast. He's shored up the porch so it doesn't sag, and patched the hole in the front steps. On a line at the ,back, an old muumuu of Jenny's swells in an updraft, and two pairs of chinos waggle their knees. Underneath, several hens and a rooster are scratching in the red dirt. M.S. slams the car door so hard I think I've said something to make her mad, but there's no expression on her face. She doesn't speak as we go up the steps, and she pulls open the screen door without knocking.

My wineglasses are laid out in a neat circle on the coffee table

Keoki has built. Jenny has put them on a flowered tray and they look pretty in the speckled light. On the lauhala mat the shadows of leaves are shifted by the wind in the poinsettia outside. A *kapa* cloth covers one wall, and over the kitchen door is a swag of old lobster net. In a corner are a couple of Keoki's long fishing spears. The shelves are full of octopus lures, basalt sinkers, scraps of paraffin wax, coils of line and whale-bone hooks as sharp as a new moon. There's almost no furniture, and the lampshades are either full of holes or missing, but for a wedding present Keoki's father has replaced the old rusty sink with a brand-new stainless steel one. Inside you can smell the salt air, and everything is very clean.

The door to the bedroom is open. 'Jenny?' I call. 'Just a minute,' she says, and I see her pulling up the sheet. Keoki comes out buttoning his pants. 'Hey, Kate, you skinny *wahine*, you have one Primo with me?' He glances at M.S. 'You want coffee, da kine beer?'

M.S. points to the toaster under her arm. 'A present,' she says. 'For Jenny. So don't try to give it back. You haven't got a pot to piss in, and if I want to give her things I don't want you telling me *you're* supporting her. With what? Fishing and making leis?' In a halter and shorts, Jenny comes out of the bedroom. 'I guess you know about lays all right,' M.S. says, handing the toaster to Jenny. 'I'll have a beer.'

Jenny touches my arm. 'I have to feed the chickens – come with me, Kate.' Outside she says, 'Sometimes I could kill her.' Supple and upright on one crutch, she scatters the feed. The surf that day is a mild blue, unstained by storms. In the spring all you can hear out here are the trades, and the whitewater swirling, bubbling like milk. But now the window is open and we can both hear M.S. '. . . out of this shanty and into Honolulu, Jenny could have a better life. I realize you don't know what a better life is, but if you marry a white woman you're going to have to find out.' I don't hear Keoki's answer, but Jenny does. She just hands me the feed and leans against the shed.

When we go inside, one of the kids from Lo's Groceries is waiting. 'You daddy call,' she says, pointing to me. Keoki doesn't have a telephone, and they bring him messages all the time. 'You daddy say he got b-i-i-g squid,' she spreads her tiny arms, 'and you come fix kaukau for ever'body.'

'Some man at the club brings Peter fish,' I say. 'Come on, you guys; we can't eat it all alone.' M.S. makes a face.

We go back over the Pali, M.S. leading the way, Keoki and Jenny in the jeep behind us. Just before we get to the top, Keoki honks for us to pull over. Jenny loves to stop and look at the view. M.S. opens her door, but I say, 'I'll stay here,' and push the lock down on my side. In a strong wind, cars and people have been blown off the Pali, and I don't like to get out. How do you know a wind won't suddenly come up? I think I'm an inept learner. If I once get a crazy idea, I can't get rid of it, like a dumb calligrapher who begins wrong and repeats the same bad stroke over and over again. Since we found out about Hans Lucas, even the most ordinary things seem either grisly or fatal. I see blood in the baby's eyes and bowels, in Peter's mouth, my own urine. At night I turn on all the lamps so the corners of the room are clear, full of yellow light, where nothing rotten can hide. It's worse when Peter's away. I see death in a cut I get from opening a can of tuna; on a piece of meat with mold at the back of the fridge; in the baby's sobs when he doesn't want to take a nap; in the taut uncountable spasms of my pulse. Sometimes late in the afternoon I whimper like a dog who wants to be let out.

As M.S. goes up to Jenny and Keoki, I'm conscious of the sun setting behind us, and even though I can't see it, I can feel it swaying, chiming, a big brass bell. M.S. must feel it too, because for a second she turns to look behind her. Off to the left, the light strikes Kaneohe, and Keoki points, showing his kingdom to Jenny. A few steps in back of them M.S. raises one arm, lowers it, raises the other, like the goddess Parvati dancing; there's a sweetness in her movements, a womanly rhythm. But when she lifts both hands together, I cover my eyes, as if the sun has toppled from its belfry and landed at my feet.

M.S. doesn't stay for dinner, so it's just the four of us. On the way back from the Pali, she said, 'Keoki's getting too big for his britches, or should I say loincloth. He actually thinks he's going to stay in that shack with Jenny, when I *told* him I'd pay for something nice in Honolulu. Wouldn't you like to have Jenny close by?'

'Not if she's happier out there.'

'In Nebraska we'd use it for a privy. I'll give her another month, no more.'

My hands are shaking as I cut up the ginger, pour sake over the squid. In the other room Jenny and Peter are doing imitations of tourists at 'Wah-kicky', but Keoki isn't talking. When he comes out to the kitchen, I'm chopping garlic. He touches my shoulder, and we look at each other like two lovers afraid to confess their love. I put down the knife. 'I saw it,' I say, 'didn't I?' (The arms no longer passive, but snakes of gold stiffened to hiss or strike.) 'M.S. tried to push you off the Pali.'

'She number one bad *wahine*.'

'Did you tell Jenny?'

'No tell Jenny; M.S. no get what she want, we no tell Jenny or Peter.'

I don't know how he knows I'm not going to tell Peter. But I'm not. 'No,' I say. 'No need.' (The Pali rising like a continent, a chopping block, and Jenny holy but precarious. M.S. bends her knees, sinks her Hindu hands like fangs into Keoki's back.) 'But what if it happens again?'

'No happen again; she just plenty *huhu* that Jenny in bed with me. Brothers and sisters been on this island for long time, and no *haole wahine* gon' shove me off Pali. No *haole* buggers gon' push me out of here.' (M.S. leans against Keoki as if she needs him, but the heels of her hands dig in and that's how I know. A fast cloud whirls overhead: something has been let loose and I'm the only one who sees it. Old bones at the foot of the Pali, and around us mountains as sharp as dinosaur teeth. But Keoki doesn't give under her hands, his shoulders a sign, a witness. He turns, takes her wrists, wags them back and forth as if teasing. Later, Jenny snaps a picture of them sitting on the wall, but I won't let her take one of me.) 'You no worry,' Keoki tells me in my kitchen. 'But that *wahine hooinoinoia*.'

While we eat the squid, I take the word apart in my head: *ho-o-ino-ino-ia*. I don't ask him about it, because it sounds like what Auntie Lilia said, and I know it can't be anything good. But it's such a beautiful word, and I see what Davis means when he says, 'Hawaiians choke on the white man's language, on the noises *haoles* make.'

52

KATE: In July I hurt my back lifting Hans Lucas, and Dr Fulton decides to take him off the board. His spine is a little stronger, but as soon as he gets tired he still curves like a crescent moon. I spend a lot of time on the lauhala mat showing him how to crawl, and Peter says my knees are getting ugly, they're so red and scratched. Whenever I hold one of Keoki's nieces, hot, heavy children who knee your belly to be put down, Hans Lucas seems incomplete, as if the marrow has been sucked from his bones. He looks around a lot, checking things out, but his head flops wildly and I don't know how much he takes in.

Sometimes I lie down and put my lips to his, the way you give someone mouth to mouth resuscitation. I say things slowly, letting him get the feel of my lips, my teeth, my tongue. The world is a murmur, a haze of signs, and I need someone to talk to. Peter is silent these days, and Hans Lucas either cries or goes 'Mmmm' sometimes when he's going to sleep. The only other noise he ever made was the little gasp or sigh when he had the seizure. He turned two last April, and last summer he started to press his lips together in a way that made me think it might be the beginning of something. But then he just seemed to forget it, and I guess I got a little desperate because, when you get right down to it, life is nothing but calls and answers, and I wasn't getting any answers. How do you know somebody is out there if he doesn't let you know? Looking at people doesn't tell you anything; they're not real until they say something. And if they're not real, how do you know whether or not you exist? The silence I live in is like total darkness.

I get the feeling that Hans Lucas and Peter only need each other, that there's nothing they want from me. And since M.S. believes that she still performs all the important offices for her children, all the necessary acts, it's as if morally or genetically I have nothing left to give. While I was nursing Hans Lucas, I could tell she didn't like the idea of a Hollander sucking foreign love and milk. I watch her on the beach at Palikai and, just as in the days when she sat around the pool in Redwood Creek, she never relaxes. Even lying in the sun, she's full of plans; life is succulent and satisfying, designed to gratify her by gratifying her children.

In October I notice that Hans Lucas is beginning to have that smell again, as if he's been thrown down a coal hole or buried under a pile of wet leaves. Dr Fulton makes another change in his diet. 'I've put your name on the waiting list for the state home,' he says. 'If a place comes up, you don't have to take it – but I hope you'll think about it.'

I don't tell Peter for two days. The winter surf has started to hit the north shore, and I wait till late Sunday night, after he's been out at Palikai all day. 'Dr Fulton doesn't think Hans Lucas is getting any better,' I mumble when he's on top of me. 'He's putting his name on the list for the hospital.'

'Shut up about it,' he says, and pins my wrists together over my head.

In the beginning, everything was given to the Hollanders, and now, little by little, it's being taken away. After we found out about Hans Lucas, I knew nothing would be whole-heartedly given to us again. Somehow we'd defaced what we had, squandered it. People who have less – Axel, the Kelways, the Kanazawas – are safer; life doesn't cost them in the same way. When I married Peter, all my dreams came true, and when your dreams come true life is harder, because you have something to lose.

Once Peter said, 'First Jenny, now Hans Lucas. What next?'

'You forgot me,' I said. 'I got sick the moment I married you.' I've started to watch M.S., Peter, Mark and Eric. But nothing shows in their voices or faces, no sin or secret that could have brought down my world. And even though I don't buy the idea of retribution, I wonder about Henry Hollander. He's a man without malevolence, pathetic, his needs daily pinched back by his family. I think that in the war, deputized, he used his wits on the bomb as carelessly as a monkey uses its fingers to catch fleas. But careless men suffer accidents, not the design of tragedy. M.S., on the other hand, isn't careless. She looks good, important; she puts her children above everything else. On the surface it seems like unselfishness, but most people are unselfish out of humility, while she is arrogant. There's a line from *Murder in the Cathedral*: 'The last temptation is the greatest treason, to do the right deed for the wrong reason.'

Hans Lucas is due for a regular check-up today. I've given him a bath, scrubbed every defenseless little crevice, but the mossy smell still clings to him, and I'm beginning to think I smell it on me. As I put him on the *punee* I notice two pale spots, like splashes, on the floor. I rush to the kitchen to get a rag, but none of my powders or cleansers touches them; it's almost as if something's taken the finish off. Then I notice that when I bend to the side the spots are gone, but when I straighten up, there they are again. It's the sun. I've been scrubbing the sun.

M.S. comes in without knocking. 'Hi,' I say, hurrying to hide the rag under the sink. She puts what's left of the coffee on to heat and sits down with Hans Lucas. He's looking at the ceiling and doesn't notice when she takes his hand. 'Jenny's pregnant,' she says in a loud voice. 'Knocked up by that nigger.'

'I'm glad,' I say. 'She really wants to have a baby. But I wish you'd shut up about Keoki. And for God's sake, it makes me sick, stop calling him a nigger.'

'He's so big and fat, having it'll kill her.'

'You're crazy on the subject of Keoki,' I say. 'Jenny'll be fine.'

She picks up Hans Lucas and lays him on her knees. Right then, he looks so much like her that I wonder whose baby he really is, whether I actually had him, or whether the hospital played a joke on me. There are moments when I feel that I've never had a say, that he was born in spite of rather than because of me. 'You don't know how lucky you are,' she says. 'You have a perfect baby, and she'll have a pickaninny.' Taking both his hands, she pulls him up, but his head falls back under its own weight. 'Peter told me what the doctor said about putting him in a home.'

'The coffee's boiling,' I say. I heat some milk and put a spoonful of sugar in the cup, the way she likes it. I can't believe Peter told her. We haven't really talked about it ourselves; it's still private and undecided, but he's told her.

M.S. has put Hans Lucas on the floor; elbows on her knees, she sits watching him. 'Any day now,' she murmurs, 'he's going to crawl.' He lifts his head for a second, then lies cheek down on the rug. She looks disappointed, and I hand her the coffee. 'Do you keep him clean?' she says. 'What's that smell? Maybe you should bathe him twice a day, the way I did with my kids.'

'I explained it to you. There's something wrong with his metabolism, and they're trying to treat it with diet. I'm taking him to the doctor today.'

'I've brought up five kids, including my brother, and it's time I told you. Somebody has to. You spend too much time taking that kid to the doctor. Doctors are just assholes who try to run your life. They're like priests, they want you to fall on your knees and tell them everything. Thanks to me, Lucas never went near a doctor, and he was the healthiest kid you ever saw.'

'Then why is he dead?'

'You skinny little twat.' She bangs down her cup. 'I've been watching you, how you're trying to ruin Peter, and kill this baby. Nothing you can do is going to stop him from being the best damn surfer in the world. Nothing. And I'm not going to let you take Hans Lucas to the doctor so he can help you get rid of him. No child of mine is going to a nuthouse.'

'He's not yours, and Peter's not yours, because I'm not going to let you have them. One by one, you maim us. Wreck our lives. Sometimes I think you were never young, never innocent; that you've always been around, making bad things happen, since the beginning of the world. And we're the ones who're paying for it.' I pick up Hans Lucas. 'Please go,' I say. 'Finish your coffee and go.' I put Hans Lucas in his crib and hide in the bathroom. I don't know what else to do. In a few minutes I'm going to have to leave for the doctor's and I don't want to see her. While I'm combing my hair I hear footsteps. I slip the lock. She jiggles the knob a few times and goes down the hall. I wait, listening; she dashes past. As I come out, the front door slams and I hurry to Hans Lucas' room. He isn't in his crib.

By the time I run outside, she's started the car. I grab the handle of the passenger door, but she just takes off, dragging me a little way until I let go.

53

PETER: 'Let's try it again, Nancy,' I tell her as she climbs
out. 'Your head wasn't down enough and your feet
weren't together.' The poor girl's so fat that every time she dives
I'm afraid she'll displace the entire pool. But her mother's
determined, and watches the lessons from a chair under the
trees. 'Come on,' I say. 'I want you to concentrate.'

Nearby, Lucy Delano dangles her still fancy legs in the water,
but her body's a bundle of scraps and cords, dry and whispery
as hay in a wind. Now that her grandchildren have finished with
their lessons, she comes three times a week anyway just to swim.
I don't mind as long as she doesn't try to talk to me all the time,
or interrupt when I'm giving a lesson, and she's pretty good
about it. One time, she offered to babysit Hans Lucas, but Kate
said no in a tone that didn't encourage any more offers.

Nancy's in the middle of her spring when the pool attendant
tells me Kate is on the phone. I wait until she swims over, her
stroke like the blades of a lawn mower on the blink. 'Your feet
were a little better that time,' I tell her. 'I'll be right back and
we'll try it again.' My head and shoulders wet from the fallout, I
pick up the office phone.

'Peter? M.S. kidnapped Hans Lucas.'

'What do you mean, kidnapped?' I say, trying not to laugh.
When Kate is upset, she gets really melodramatic.

'She came here accusing me of all sorts of things, of trying to
kill Hans Lucas, and then when I locked myself in the bathroom
she snatched him out of his crib. I almost got him back, but she
kept on going and I couldn't hang on to the car.'

'Are you okay?'

'I'm going to go crazy if I don't get him back.'

'I mean, did she hurt you?'

'No. Please take the car and find him right away.'

'Stay by the phone, and I'll drive up to Alewa. It's probably just some mother-in-law trick to keep you in your place.'

Lucy Delano hears me talking to Nancy, and when I leave she follows me out to the car. 'What kind of family emergency? Can I help?'

'No. Kate's just worried about Hans Lucas, but I don't think it's anything serious.' As I drive off, she looks like she's going to cry.

M.S.'s car isn't in the driveway, but Axel's is. He's sitting on a stool in the kitchen, one of M.S.'s rush carpets over his knees. 'Where's M.S.?' I say. 'Has she been here?'

'I haven't seen her, man, but Eric might know where she is. Right now he's in the head.' With a sailmaker's needle and palm he's sewing together the squares that've come undone.

I lean against the sink. 'Kate had some kind of hassle with her, and she's run off with Hans Lucas.'

'Don't sweat it. She's probably taken him out for a drive somewhere. It's like her own kid, and she wants to do things for it. I don't think she can hack being a grandmother; she ought to have had more kids of her own.' He drives the needle in and plucks it out the way a diving bird scoops up fish.

'But where the hell is she?' The knife a thin silver trail, at the bottom of her purse, fickle as smoke or mercury. At the time I really wanted to tell Kate about it, see what she thought. Now I'm glad I didn't.

'Christ, give her a chance; she'll turn up. She puts her kids above everything else. I've never seen a woman work her tail off for her family like that.'

The faucet's leaking, and I shake the drops out. Axel's next project, maybe. Except for my own prints, the faucet is shiny, not a mark on it. On the sink a dishrag is folded exactly in half – maybe by Axel, maybe by M.S. Their approach is pretty much the same: everything squared off, as if they're getting an operating room ready for surgery, or an altar for Mass. Once I came up to the house when they were both hard at it – Axel scrubbing the floor, M.S. vacuuming – each one in a different room. She hardly ever talks to him, so you'd think they'd duplicate each other, but the system seems to work. One day Axel was an hour late getting out to Palikai. 'What are you,' I said, 'a goddam maid?' Axel went on untying this board from his car. 'None of her kids ever gets off their ass,' he said, jamming it nose down into the sand, 'and she could use some help. Okay?'

'Hi.' Eric tosses a copy of *Reader's Digest* onto the table. 'Why aren't you down at the club? I was going to stop by on my way to work.'

'M.S. ran off with Hans Lucas, and I'm looking for her. You haven't seen her, have you?'

'No.' Eric blinks and glances at Axel. 'Jenny called this morning, and she left right after. Would she. . . ?'

'No – forget it.' I interrupt because I'm afraid he's going to mention the knife. 'I'm going to call Lo's and get a message to Jenny.'

I tell the kid from Lo's it's urgent, and I don't know what he said to Jenny, but she's on the phone in a couple of minutes. 'I haven't seen her – God, what's going on? Why did she take Hans Lucas?'

'I don't know, but if she shows up out there, call me right away at the club.'

I get into the car and drive down into town, look for M.S. at the market where she usually shops; talk to Dr Fulton at Shriner's, in case she decided to take the baby there and get nasty; check out the parked cars at Ala Moana and Waikiki. Back up at Alewa, the house is empty and I call Kate. 'I think she's probably taken him for a drive around the island,' I tell her, 'and she'll bring him back before dinner. Just sit tight – I'm going back down to the club.'

When I get home Kate has laid only one place at the table. 'You don't expect me to *eat*,' she says. 'I think we should call the police.'

'And say what? That his grandmother took the kid out for a ride?'

'With*out* asking *me*. Anyway, she's crazy.'

'What do you mean, crazy?'

'Don't make me tell you things I don't want to. But if she doesn't bring back my baby pretty soon, I'm going to call the cops and tell them plenty.'

Eric calls around eight to say he's just heard from M.S.: she's going to be very late, and he should eat the ham at the back of the refrigerator. She hangs up before he can ask her any questions. 'She sounded just like she always does,' he says.

'You see?' I tell Kate. 'There's no need to panic.'

I fall asleep on the couch till after midnight. When I wake up I go into the bedroom, but there's no sign of Kate. I find her on the kitchen floor, curled up, her cheek against the stove. 'Come to bed,' I whisper. 'You can't wait out here.' But she stays there, huddled by the stove, taking comfort I guess from her appliances, her tame enamel animals, the guardians of her house.

54

PETER: 'Want another beer?' Axel opens the screen door and
          the light angles across the sandy boards of the porch
over to where I'm sitting at the top of the steps.

'Sure.' The door slams and M.S. puts 'Frenesi' on again. I
think I heard it for the first time just before the war. I was ten or
eleven, and M.S. was having a party. Over the cigarette smoke,
the sawdust smell of bourbon, Artie Shaw's clarinet – snobby
and calm and smart. M.S. dancing, her face sweaty. When she
put me to bed I could smell her pleasure.

'I brought three,' Axel says. 'You're drinking fast.'

Earlier he'd called me from Hotel Street. 'Just got back from
Palikai. Man, it's starting to line up out there like a fleet of
razors. Try to get out to Keoki's and I'll see if I can knock off
around midnight, finagle a twenty-four hour pass. I think I can
swing it – a couple of guys owe me.' But first I took Kate to a
movie. 'I've never left you and the baby alone at night before,' I
said. 'But Axel thinks we should go out as soon as the sun comes
up. I've got to be at work by nine-thirty, and I'll stop by the
house on my way back.'

I wipe the sweat from the bottle on the sleeve of my shirt.
'Hear it? A rising northeast swell, my favorite sound –
Beethoven doesn't come close. Tomorrow we're going to see
something beautiful and well-defined: great big critical ass-
licking walls.'

'About twenty-five,' says Axel, 'with a lot of chop. That's my
guess. Tomorrow we're going to ride the wildest stuff we've ever
seen. We're going to map this place like you said. We're going to
set all the records, and then we're going to break them.'

'Eric's not too happy. He's got to be at work early tomorrow.
Bunch of tourists from the Moana.'

'He shouldn't mess with this stuff, anyway.' Axel leans
against the top step and looks up at the sky. 'Keoki's not going

out either; he told me he doesn't want Jenny to get excited.
What's the matter with her, do you know?'

'Kate says she started to bleed, so she's got to stay in bed. If
she moves around too much it could happen again.'

'She's lucky she's got her mother to take care of her. But if
M.S. is going to stay out here, Keoki should find something
better than that broken-down *punee* for her to sleep on.'

'He hasn't got any money. And M.S. doesn't give a damn –
she just wants to be with Jenny.' I glance behind me at the light
on the porch floor. 'She must have played that song six times
already, and she's putting it on again. She found it in some little
junk shop down on King Street.'

'Maybe she misses your father, or the mainland, or the days
when you kids were little. She looks poorly, like she's not eating
or sleeping.'

'Kate's still mad at her for taking Hans Lucas. She stayed in
the kitchen all night, wouldn't come to bed until M.S. brought
him back. Around daylight I hear M.S. come in. "Here he is,"
she says to Kate, "and I hope it teaches you a lesson." We still
don't know what the lesson was or where she took him.'

'Wait.' Axel holds up his hand. 'There's a new note, kind of a
splintering sound. Like when I was little, before my mother left,
and she used to get drunk and throw lamps and dishes around.
When it gets bigger, it goes into another gear, and if you're
sleeping on the beach, the noise pounds your head into the
sand.'

'Kate didn't want me to sleep out here tonight. Between her
and M.S., I've got two nutty women on my hands.' Behind the
shack, palms clatter in the wind. 'Something's wrong with Kate
and me, and I don't know what to do about it.'

'Maybe you just need a little exotic nookie to keep the home
fires burning.'

'I don't talk to her, I never tell her anything, and it's getting
worse. We go around like two people with contagious diseases,
holding our breath so the other one doesn't catch it.'

'Sounds pretty much of an asshole lash-up.'

'I think better than I talk, and she puts a lot of importance on
words. She's just going to have to trust me.' I spread my fingers
and look at my hands. 'I've known her since she was a kid. And
now when I look at her I think, which one is the pimply little

friend of Jenny's? The wise hot woman in my bed, or the other one, who twitches in her sleep and sobs till I have to shake her? She's got a bottle of horse-size pills the doctor gave her to make her sleep, and two of them don't even touch her.'

'It's the kid. It has to be the kid. It's her kid, she had it, and she's got these female instincts. She wants it to be perfect, and it isn't – and she can't eat it like a cat eats a bum kitten.'

The palms are chattering nonstop, and Axel goes inside. When he comes back out, I've already started on the extra beer. 'I brought another one,' he says. 'It's the last.' He sits down next to me.

'If that's what's wrong with her,' I say, 'I don't know what I'm going to do. I can't make him walk or talk. It's weird but I don't mind him the way he is. I'd like him to have the same chance as other kids, but I don't mind it the way she does. I don't know what to do about her.'

'Talk to her, man. That's what you've got to do with people who are scared. What the hell do you think we're doing right now? We're talking because we're not sure we can handle it tomorrow if it's really big. When you're dying, a priest or a doctor or some nurse comes and talks to you. Talk to her.' He reaches behind himself, pulls out an empty bottle and stands it on the railing.

'I always think I am, and then I realize I haven't said a goddam thing.'

'I don't know where I get off giving you advice.' M.S. has stopped playing her music, but the water is louder and he raises his voice. 'I haven't been doing so hot myself. Little chippie I picked up Friday – drove me and my board out to Makaha in her husband's new Buick. The surf didn't look too good and I'm banging her in the back seat, but her box is so big I can't feel a thing. I'm looking out of the window and, no shit, I see a perfect set stacking up. I stop in mid-poke, and she says, "What's the matter – I make a boo-boo?" and I'm grabbing my board and paddling out before my pecker's dry.'

'Give me a sip of that,' I say. I finish the bottle.

The moon is almost down, but in the gray light, I can see the set of long lines, uncountable and very close together; perfectly

formed, they're evenly spaced as columns. 'We better stay close
to the trees,' Axel says as we unroll our sleeping bags on the
beach, 'or we'll drown in the spray. I love the smell when they
break like that, hot and salty, everything good stirred up from
the bottom. Better than tail.' He holds out his leg. 'I've got feet
like fucking rakes; when I'm drunk or somebody hits me I never
fall down.'

I slide waist-deep into my bag. 'Every wipeout I ever took is
running through my mind right now. One time last winter I got
pushed down so far it was like midnight – I come up and all
these fish are floating around, knocked unconscious. It'll be nice
when we're old and we don't have to risk our asses any more.'

'We don't have to now.'

'Yeah, but we do.'

'*You* do,' he says. 'I just have a good time.'

'Right. Because you can swim against the rip faster than I can
swim with it.' The moon has dropped, but there's a faint mist of
light as if it's snagged on something just over the horizon. 'This
sand is as hard as a cowboy's ass.' I round out a hollow to fit the
shape of my bag. 'I shouldn't complain. The only time you're
ever really comfortable is when you're dead – so you don't want
to get feeling too good. But it's funny: I'm not sure how I'd feel
surfing this place if I didn't *know* I could die out there.'

'You wouldn't like it. Your head is so full of shit I'm surprised
you can still stand up. Just try getting down the bastards as fast
as you can and forget the catechism. Open your hand.'

'What's that?'

'Salt. Put some on your tongue and take a swig of this.'

'Jesus.' I wipe my mouth on the sleeping bag. 'I either love it
or hate it. What is it?'

'Tequila. It lights a good fire, puts you to sleep and you're still
smoking in the morning.'

I take another swallow and hand the bottle back. 'Does it
seem to you that they sound bigger?'

'That's because they are bigger.' Axel drinks from the bottle,
caps it and zips himself into his bag.'Out at Makaha the other
day I saw a guy come down an eight-foot wall with more moving
parts than a whore on a Saturday night. There must have been
fifteen of us; it's getting as bad as Waikiki. When he pearled, his
board was slamming into people all over the place. In a couple

of years there's going to be so many coast *haoles* over here there won't be an inch of empty water. Except at Palikai: they won't be surfing middle break.'

'You know something that worries me?' I say. 'One time I was *positive* I was on a twenty-foot wall out here – and I did everything perfect, but I still got wiped out. So maybe it can't be done. Maybe twenty or over, it can't be done.'

When the next set starts to come through, I hear an echo right under my bag. Somebody, Davis maybe, told me there are lots of lava tubes on this side of the island. Later I can't tell if the sounds I hear are real or in my dreams. The night is cool, but it's humid, and my whole body is wet. In my old Ford I'm kissing Kate. Windows up, we're parked out at San Francisco beach. The sound of the shorebreak is very dim, like the chime of a distant clock. Kate buttons up her blouse and before I start the car I roll down the window. I can hear the shorebreak better now: the fanning hiss, the pause, the running down; the suck-out, faint as rain.

I sit up, my bag soggy with spray. Awake for sure, I can pick out the silent swells tracking down from the top of the world. The water has a foreign look, as if I've never seen it before; as if I've never set foot on it, pissed in it, puked it up. I fold up my sleeping bag and, using it as a pillow, lie down again in the sand. Eyes shut, I see the lines being born in the Aleutians, black against snow and ice; in a night wind, they pick up speed and roll driverless down the empty street between the continents.

'Aren't you going to get your asses out there?' M.S.'s bare feet a few inches from my face. Eyes closed and counting, I've just clocked a sixteen-second interval between the waves.

I sit up. 'I don't know yet.' An overhead shorebreak. Outside, waves hitting the reef, shining like axes.

Axel rolls up his bag. 'It's a west swell now,' he says. 'I'm not sure.' Squatting in the early shadows, he watches a set come through.

'This is what you've been waiting for.' In her nightgown and flowered housecoat, M.S. is yelling over the shorebreak, black purse swinging by its strap from her arm.

'They're surfable,' I say.

'Maybe we can handle them, but I smell close-out.' Axel seems to be talking more to M.S. than to me. 'Can we afford a close-out in this stuff and risk getting caught inside?'

'It's worth a try,' I say. 'Where's your sense of humor?'

'This is boneyard stuff.' He gets to his feet. 'I can't figure out what you're trying to do.'

'Look, I'm not going to hold you to this buddy system. If I want to go out, you don't have to come.'

'He can't stop you,' says M.S. Her braid is fuzzy and some of the hair has pulled loose.

'Go on back up to the house,' I say.

'I want to watch.'

'I'm not going anywhere until you go back up to the house.'

She starts up the beach and turns around. 'I mean it,' I say.

Pulling at the skin of his jaw, Axel watches her. 'This is the first time I've seen her make a mistake.'

'She didn't make a mistake. It's surfable.' When she's at the slope that leads up to the shack, she waves. 'Got any wax?' I hold out my hand.

'Don't be an asshole.'

We start walking, going higher up the beach. 'What are you going to do?' I say. 'Tie me up? Otherwise I'm going out.'

Axel stops. 'Look, man, I'll go toe to toe with you if I have to. I know tricks about fighting you never even heard of, and I'll have you on your ass before you have time to curl your knuckles.'

I can't see his face, just a corona of sunlight, the outline of his head and the short hair; the shoulders like mesas, and, underneath, the dark rock. Axel's breath, so thick from sleep it's almost visible, and my own, meeting like ghosts. 'I made a lot of plans,' I say, 'and I took a lot of chances – with my life and with Kate's – so I could get here on a day like this, and I'm not going to pass it up. I'm going to do it because right now it's the only thing I can do something about. I can't change anything else that's happening to me.'

'Christ, I don't know,' says Axel. 'If I deck you, you're out there as soon as you can walk; if I don't, you're out there anyway, and probably a dead man, because of some complicated shit in your head. But there's no way I'm going to let you pump all that beautiful juice by yourself, so let's go.'

'Maybe I'll change my mind,' I say, when we're waxing our boards. 'Look at the rip now.'

'Like my grandmother used to say: don't go all meat and potatoes on me.'

'What?'

'Don't get into a stew.'

'I'm scared shitless,' I say, the wax softening in the heat of my hand. 'It's like one summer, when Mark and I were kids, we fooled around with each other's dicks, you know, to see what feelings we could get. But afterward . . . Jesus, we were guilty and scared. Right now, looking at that stuff, I feel about the same way.'

In a lull, we push out. 'Probably the last one,' says Axel. Outside, the horizon is smaller, as if the world has blown up and chunks of water are exploding into the sky. Thirty yards offshore our boards pick up speed. We've entered the rip. If we're lucky, it'll carry us right out to the lineup. The suck takes us into the channel which ordinarily doesn't break, but straight ahead, some fuzzy dumb things are beginning to hump up; big and undeveloped, they shuffle along, a different species from the smart-lipped peaks out at the point. If one of these swells crests and we can't get over the top before it breaks, we'll have to bail out, abandon our boards and try to swim in against the current. To hold on to your board in soup like this is asking to have your brains bashed out. The rip is losing its momentum and one of the big-footed freaks is padding toward us. A whistling above and below me, a muttering in the wind. In a sprint I'm up and over, dropping maybe twelve feet down the back, my fingers digging into fiberglass. Cool tunnels to my right: the insides of middle break. Axel on my left, the muscles of his shoulders rising and falling like the water. Seven or eight more swells are coming. As we hit each one, the water takes on a deeper color, like grass when a wind bends it at the roots.

'Thank God for small mercies,' Axel says, as we turn our boards in the lineup. 'One more of those, and my arms would have cramped solid.'

I pound my chest. 'I think I'm having a heart attack.' By Keoki's shack a spot of white: a stone, my mother, or a puff of dust? A burn between my shoulders, as if I've just been branded, and, out at the point, the water beginning to mound again. 'I think that's M.S.,' I say.

'Yeah, but I wasn't going to mention it.' As we rise on a swell, Axel points to a yellowish stream offshore. 'The rip – looks like a giant took a piss in it.' Watching, judging, choosing, we move our boards into position.

'Outside,' Axel yells.

It's started to break out at the point, not in sets but in infinite regularities, wall after wall, as if all other forms have been exhausted. No longer waves, they're abstractions – philosophies, explanations, answers to questions we're too dumb to ask. Axel tries to pull down into a wall, his board bucking in the wind. Caught in a strong gust, it noses up like a dolphin and he's blown back out of the wave. I stroke on the eighth rise. Hovering, teetering, I'm in the lip, the bottom as far below as early history. Crouching in the cross-chop, I bounce twice as the wave throws out spindrift like smoke from a burning city. The drop is sudden, my body in spasm as if from electric shock. Smooth, no resistance, angling now, hissing down into darkness. The biggest wave of my life, and on its belly no pleasure. I've asked but I haven't been given. Blowing offshore, the sweetness of plumeria. No joy driving down hard into shadow, only a faint regret. Lean into the wall, not in intimacy, but in self-preservation; if I don't pull out and the wave collapses, I won't be able to hang onto my board. Jamming down hard onto the tail, I bring the nose up, turned almost backward into the wave. A shudder like a plane that isn't going to take off, then the nose lifts into the sky. Curve back into the shoulder and down into the trough: one movement. Sprint-paddle up the face of the wave behind.

It's closing out. Long lines of whitewater dumping on the outside reef. Another lurch down into critical shadow and I'm on top again. Axel has taken off, board bumping in a three-foot chop at the crest. The sun is low but strong, and after the drop, the wave behind him hangs straight and shiny as a mirror. Trying to stall, he steps on the tailblock, and, in a silly unrelated gesture, puts a hand over his eyes like Kate at a horror movie. As I slide into the trough I see him spin out, his board bouncing like a penny on cement. Top of the next swell: it hasn't completely closed out yet, some waves still navigable. No sign of Axel or his board. It was the sun; he'd been shielding his eyes from the sun, and the bright wave had turned out to be a blind man's path. Thirty seconds is the longest anyone's ever stayed down in a wipeout. But in surf like this, twenty-five would be enough if you got a lungful of soup on your way up. Twenty seconds. I take the plunge, still counting. Try to head seaward as long as I can. Holes: on the bottom, I've seen them. Blurred by fifteen feet of water, as if they haven't yet taken their final shape. Underwater holes. Inside, no scorpions or vipers – maybe not even squid; just empty holes. Throttling chambers. Swooping up the next crest, my arms begin to fade. An empty sea. Trip down its mineral back, too fast this time, headfirst, halfway off. Forty. Legs overboard, checking my fall. Top of another rise. Sixty-five. On the fiberglass rails of my board pockmarks, a slight inconsistency, the panicky impressions of my fingers; I've busted through to wood. Paddling up again. Over two minutes. A drab shape inside the wave coming toward me: Axel's body, sucked up straight, drawn up by its hair to the lip, arms cloudy, reaching for the glass horizon.

55

KATE: Barney came over for Christmas, but I didn't get
        much chance to talk to him until just before he left. He
surfed every day with Keoki, and slept on the porch out at Palikai.
After the drowning Peter didn't mention Axel to anybody except
Keoki, but by the time Barney came over he was a little better.
There was a lot I wanted to tell Barney, but mostly he talked to
Peter. If I tried to start a conversation he wouldn't look at me, case
me the way he used to, whenever I said something he liked. Didn't
wield his hands, paint atoms and particles, the books he'd read; or
swing his unfocussed eye. 'Lot of parties in Cambridge,' he said.
'Lot of people – but not a lot of friends. They're not as serious back
there. Californians are cleaner, more excited, as if they've just been
baptized or something.'

The day he came by I was in the kitchen running water, and I
didn't hear him knock. I like to bathe Hans Lucas in the sink
because it's easier to hold on to him; in the bathroom he
thrashes around so much he hits his head on the edge of the tub.

'Lucky kid,' says Barney. I'm soaping Hans Lucas, cleaning
the creases between his legs.

Not quite sarcastically, I say, 'It's good to see you.'

'I've got to pick up some things for Jenny, and I borrowed the
jeep. I'm leaving tomorrow, so I came to say goodbye.' I keep
my head down and don't answer. 'I seem to do this a lot,' he
says. 'Come to say goodbye.'

'First, you might try saying hello.'

'I know, I'm sorry. I didn't mean to come skulking round
when Peter was gone. Well, maybe I did – I've been wanting to
talk to you, but I've been postponing it because from the look of
things, I didn't think I'd like what I was going to hear.'

I pour a few drops of baby shampoo on Hans Lucas's head.
'Hold him straight, will you, so I can wash his hair. And what
do you think you're going to hear?'

'I don't know . . . Christ, he's slippery. Why do you keep looking away like that?'

'I don't.'

'You do – my God, you've got a black eye.'

'Hold him tighter, he's sliding down. He had another convulsion, and when he was waving his arms around, one of them connected.'

'You mean he's had one before?'

'He's had three, but I didn't tell Peter about the last two.'

'Didn't he notice your eye?'

'I guess not. He didn't say anything. You can let go now; I can do the rest myself.'

'Then I can't sidle up to your bony little hip. You've lost a lot of weight, but I can still tell where all the goodies are.' I lift Hans Lucas, and Barney holds his hands under mine, as if I might drop him. 'What are you going to do?'

'About Hans Lucas? There's nothing we can do. Anyway, I can't discuss it with Peter now. It's too close to Axel.' He follows me to the bedroom where I put Hans Lucas on our bed.

'I don't remember you being like this,' he says, looking around. 'Everything squared off. Makes me scared to step on any cracks. I noticed when you were giving him his bath, you washed his face three times.' He swings his face at me. 'Ritual, superstition? But it didn't do you any good, because here I am, the evil eye.'

I pull at a tiny button, trying to do up Hans Lucas's shirt. A dappling of stains on the powder blue: my tears, splattering like rain on dusty pavement. 'A long time ago you said we control our own atoms and we're each our own god. I don't feel like I control anything any more, especially me. Every night I get the feeling my brains are leaking out onto my pillow.' I put one hand on the baby to keep him from rolling off; with the other I rub my eyes. 'Just when I think I'm beginning to have control again, something else happens. So, I straighten up the house, try anyway to keep the dead things in their place. I cook all the time, so I can put something together instead of watching it fall apart. Whenever I bake cookies I count them when they're going into the oven, and I count them again when I'm taking them out. And when I put them away I count them, and if anyone eats one I count what's left.'

Diana Cobbold

'Here.' He lifts my other hand to my eyes. 'Do a good job of crying and I'll hold the kid.'

'I don't even read any more,' I say. 'Right after Jenny's leg, Peter told me that whenever anything awful happens, he isn't surprised. That he almost sees it coming, but he doesn't know why. Now I'm beginning to feel like we're the plot of a book or a movie, but we're the only ones who can't tell how it's going to end. I go around looking for clues, so I can piece together what the plot is, what's going to happen next.' With one of the baby's socks I scour the corners of my eyes.

'You can't be in a book,' he says, 'or I'd be saying, "Let me take you away from all this." You know that wave theory stuff I wrote you about? Basically it says that on the subatomic level some things are statistically more likely to happen than others. And there's another theory that the minute you observe what's going on at that level, you automatically effect those possibilities. There was even an idea that this holds true in everyday life. So maybe by connecting yourself with Peter's family and watching from the sidelines you made all the shit more likely to happen.'

'You mean I'm the *cause* of it? Thanks a lot.'

'Not the cause, maybe – you just weighted the possibilities.' With the tips of his fingers, he strokes Hans Lucas on the belly. 'I get the feeling Peter is even more raving-ass desperate than you are. You've got to get him back in the water.'

'It's been almost two months since Axel, and he won't go near it.'

'If you think you've got troubles now, they're nothing to what they're going to be if you don't get him in the water.' Taking both my hands, he lays them back on the baby. 'I can see a time coming,' he says in front of the mirror where he can watch me behind him, 'when I might hang up my board. It won't be easy. There's a lot to be said for surfing only the big stuff – kind of like climbing Mount Everest every day. If you're scared shitless most of the time, life seems short and nothing can bore you. On the face of a big wave there isn't any make-up or wigs or elevator shoes; no soft lights, no deodorant, no cocktail parties, no way to fake it. Every foot of every wave measures you exactly. On the other hand, there's a lot against it: like you have nightmares about drowning and wake up fighting for breath; like when you hit a certain age you probably have to cut down on your drinking to stay in shape; like it's hard to take a piss and stay afloat at the same time. And there's always a chance you'll take ultimate gas, especially if you think about doing something crazy – like trying to ride inside the wave, in the tube, just because Keoki says it can be done. In my case I could quit if I had to because most of the red-hot action goes on inside my head. I just surf to scare my body with something real, instead of all the theoretical crap my brain throws up. I could just as easily be a snake handler, and get the same effect with a lot less effort.' He picks up Geneva's bottle of Joy. 'But his *home* is in the water. He doesn't wrestle with it like the rest of us; he just drops in for a piece of cake and a glass of milk.' He pulls out the stopper and sniffs it. 'I'll put it another way: I think he could survive better without blood than without salt water.'

'Don't Hans Lucas and I matter?'

'You're in the best position to answer that.' He shakes perfume onto his finger, rubs a few drops on the back of his wrist. 'But if appearances mean anything, I'd say your're right up there. You, the kid and Palikai: mother, son and frigging Holy Ghost.' Sniffing, he shuts his eyes. 'And I have to settle for this.' He puts his wrist to his mouth and licks it. 'Do it, Kate. Get him into the water, and then you can fix up the rest of your life.'

'M.S. did this to him,' I say. 'Why, I don't know. I think I understand her less now than I did when I first met her. She's important to me because she's Peter's mother, but I don't know why it's so dangerous to be around her. Somehow I think maybe she didn't finish with her life in Nebraska, that she carries it around like a rotten knapsack on her back. I know one version of what's happening to us, but M.S. knows the other, the real one. I think I've always been fighting her for Peter whether I knew it or not – but I never had the feeling I was playing with a full deck. I was missing something, some important piece of information that might give me the upper hand. She almost *wills* things to happen, I think, and the rest of us are helpless.' I stop and take Barney's hand. 'Thanks,' I say, 'for listening.'

In the kitchen I give him a cup of coffee and a piece of passion fruit pie. 'You ought to go out and see Jenny,' he says before he goes. 'M.S. is driving her crazy, sticks to her like a duenna. And yesterday Keoki's mother came out to heal her. Now *that* was a sight to see.'

'What do you mean, heal her?'

'I don't know what else she was doing. I'm having a beer with Keoki, and a shadow as big as an ocean liner falls across the floor. There's Keoki's mom in an orange muumuu, and some kind of gourd hanging from her wrist. She gives Keoki a couple of juicy kisses and goes in to see Jenny. I can tell M.S. is having a shit-fit, and when Jenny asks can she talk to Mrs Keoki alone, M.S. stomps out of the bedroom, but she leaves the door open. Keoki's mom is making these sounds in Hawaiian, kind of like the noises you make when you're doing something nice in the dark with somebody else. I sneak over to the bedroom door, and M.S. gives me a dirty look, but she doesn't say anything. Keoki's mom's got a whole bunch of stones, about the size of cherries, all spread out on a mat. She goes right on chanting, or praying, and she knows I'm watching. A couple of times she makes a face.' He pulls his lips tight against his teeth, pops his jaws open in a rush. 'Like that. Made Jenny spit on a ti leaf, dropped it in the gourd. M.S. is standing next to me by this time, and when she sees Jenny spit, she goes crazy, rushes in there and kicks the stones all over the room. Keoki's mom sweeps out, swinging the gourd like a billy club. Fierce shiny face, more than a match for M.S. – I got a good look at her. I sneaked in later and talked to Jenny. She said she felt incredible with the chanting and the stones and stuff. Incredible was the word she used.'

'I wish I'd been there,' I say. 'A friend of mine thinks Keoki's mother might be a *kahuna*.'

'Well, don't knock it. I've never seen a face like that.'

Hans Lucas in my arms, I go with him to the door. 'They offered me a great job in Georgia,' he says, taking the baby's hand. 'But when I asked the guy if there was any surf there, he said no. So next year I'll be over in Berkeley. A lot of the exciting stuff is being done there, and anyway I didn't really want to leave California. Are you and Peter going to stay here in the islands?'

'I don't know. There are lots of things I love about this place. Weird things, like everything in the house except the lauhala mats had to be brought over in a ship.' Hans Lucas gives a little shriek and flaps his hands as if he's trying to fly. It's a cry of pleasure, a long psalm, but it makes me think of rape and murder and the torture of innocents.

'Don't look like that,' says Barney. He puts his hand in his pocket. 'Call me if you want to talk. Here's my number. Any time, collect.' He starts down the hall. 'There were some other things I wanted to say,' he calls over his shoulder. 'I forget what. But it's kind of hard making a pass at the Pietà.'

I start listening to weather reports. On Sundays, whenever I hear what I want, I make Peter take me for a drive. He hasn't untied his board from the top of the car since the day Axel died, and everywhere we go the board goes with us, rocket-nosed, aimed out over the hood, so we look like an outdated weapon, something left over from the war. On bright January mornings we drive out to Sunset, Makaha and Haleiwa. Sometimes I take a picnic lunch, but Peter makes us eat it in the car. If we sit on the beach, he keeps lifting the corners of the blanket as if he's looking for something, as if he doesn't like being in the sand. I never say, 'Why don't you go out?' But he knows that's why we're there. He stays away from Palikai, and I don't push it. Hans Lucas in a little hanging seat between us, we glide around the island, the tight nose of the surfboard shielding us from the sun.

Until now the idea of losing Peter was like the idea of death when I was very young: it couldn't happen to me. He's not sick, and I know there isn't another woman. So how can I lose him? But late at night, when the *kona* wind scrabbles around in the crotons under our window, I'm sure of it. Although we both go to bed at the same time, we've begun to sleep different hours, Peter from midnight until dawn, while I usually don't get to sleep till early morning. About three or four, I slip down into a dark green sea of dreams, where long convulsive shapes catch the light close to the surface. I learn after a while that these shapes are really sounds, the gasps Hans Lucas makes when he begins to cry. But after I've gone to him, the sleep is always lighter.

Peter is awake one night, hands behind his head. 'Cockroaches?' he says.

'I don't know what it was. Anyway, he's gone back to sleep.' I get into bed facing him, the crook of his arm a few inches from my lips.

'You're up three or four times a night now,' he says. 'It can't go on like this.'

'Do you want to do it?'

'I tried, but you wouldn't let me.'

'I have to go and see if he's all right.'

'Why can't I?'

'It isn't the same – I have to see for myself.'

'I'll never make a woman pregnant again. I promise myself that.'

'What about what I want?'

'I can live like this, but after a while you won't be able to. You need something more, something he's never going to be able to give you. For me, it's different; for me, he's not just a baby, a tiny replica of you and me, he's something more beautiful. Like Billy Budd. Beautiful and smart in a way we don't understand.'

'Like an animal?'

'The things he knows aren't the things we know – they're more sensational.'

'And I'll be his caretaker for the rest of his life. I'm not married to you, I'm married to him. But most of the time I'm not married to either one of you, because neither one of you knows I'm alive.'

'You seem pretty alive to me.'

'In bed, maybe. Do you think if I got pregnant again, the same thing would happen?'

'I don't know, so I'm not taking any chances.'

I don't think he has any idea what I want. He doesn't believe in signs between people, only what he can feel. He trusts more what he does, packing himself into me so tight that in my shimmied-out state I never know until he lets go what curve his own excitement has taken. No sound or word to show me where he is, only a slow rolling tremor, spread out, as if a closer configuration might hurt him.

'Why don't you make any sounds?' I say.

'Have I got to grunt to show you I'm having a good time?'

Geneva told me once that every woman wants a man who demands something from her. 'Maybe it's men who've made us that way, but secretly we need to feel virtuous, and the only time we can feel virtuous is when we're giving.' I sleep with my fingers tucked into the opening of his pillowcase. If what Geneva said is true, the only time I'm virtuous is when I'm lying down. The times we're closest, the times I make him feel the best, are when I'm lying down. And lying down I had given him Hans Lucas.

I don't take anything for granted: even a love that lasts is transient and finally cancelled. His sex in mine, no matter how well-locked we are – mouths and bellies, tongues and teeth, hands and breath – there's going to be a last day. Marriage is an impossible state. You're told you're a corporation of two, a single impermeable being, but you know that sooner or later your heated friendship is going to end in death or desertion, so you can never tell which one of your days together is going to be your last.

Keoki calls me on a hot and humid Sunday morning. 'You and Peter,' he says, 'you better come out here. M.S. drive me *pupule*, she all-time push me out of way. In night she come in our room. Jenny more more tired, jump like frog; M.S. give her da kine pill for sleep, I gon' tell M.S. that Jenny go with me Nanakuli. Auntie Lilia, she take care of her till *keiki* come. That way more near you and Peter.'

'I'll bring something out for dinner,' I say, feeling guilty, 'and give everybody a break.' In spite of what Barney said about Jenny's needing me, I haven't been out to Palikai for weeks.

As we get into the car, I decide this is the day to make the big push with Peter, and once we're whipping along the Kam Highway I open up. 'Face it,' I say. 'You've got to get back in the water.' On top of the car, the board is flat as a dead fish, drying out in the sun.

'I'm fine the way I am.'

'You're not – that's my point. You give up the one thing you love, the thing you do best, because of some phony guilt. There's no way you can take the blame for what happened to Axel.'

He looks at me for such a long time that I think the car, undirected, is going to skip off the road. 'It's not guilt – I'm afraid.'

'Of what?'

'That in a wipeout I'll see those big feet of his sticking out of one of those holes.'

'Barney told me they go down really deep,' I say. 'Thirty or forty feet.' And wish I could take it back. Lips together, Hans Lucas goes 'Mmmm', like somebody eating a gooey dessert. I reach in back for his fluffy rabbit and close his fingers around it, squeezing them shut. Every day, carefully, I feed toys into his shaky fingers, but it's like putting coins into a busted Coke machine: they don't connect, and fall right through. 'Dr Fulton called yesterday,' I say. 'A place opened up at the state home, and he wants us to think about putting Hans Lucas there.'

'No.'

'He had a couple more fits I didn't tell you about, and Dr Fulton says the seizures are going to get more violent and I won't be able to control him.'

'I won't give up my son.'

'You're gone all day, you just come home and admire him at night. I lift him a thousand times, change him a thousand times, listen to him cry. When he gets older – and believe me, he's going to get older – lifting him and changing his pants is going to get worse. I'm failing with him, and I'm failing with you. He came from us, but he doesn't exist, so it's like a great big part of us died. And you don't want another baby – so what's left?'

'M.S. could come and help you.'

'I'd rather be dead. She's making Jenny miserable, practically sleeping with her and Keoki, and I have enough trouble getting close to you as it is. Maybe we should put him in the home to save his life.'

'What do you mean?'

'She might try to kill him because he isn't perfect. Just like she tried to push Keoki off the Pali because he's a Hawaiian.' I'm not looking at him, and I'm mumbling, but I go on. 'I'm sorry,' I say, 'but she did. You can ask Keoki. For everybody's sake, I've got to tell you.'

We're going seventy and he starts to bang his head on the steering wheel. The car shoots toward the center of the road and I reach for the wheel, but he sits up and straightens it out. 'She was beautiful,' he says. 'When I was a kid I thought she didn't fart or shit or screw my old man. But things happen, and when I knew she did, I thought there couldn't be anything worse to find out about my mother.'

In the distance, mountains with the long sharp backs of

lizards are cooling in a mist, but down where we are the sun is hot on rows and rows of pineapple plants, delicate as sketches. 'I don't want to see you for a while,' I say. 'I can't take it. What you don't say, and what your mother does do. I'm going back to the mainland for a couple of months, maybe stay with my parents.'

'Are you going to take Hans Lucas?'

'Maybe, or I might do what Dr Fulton said – put him in the home for a few months, see how it works out.'

'I don't want him to leave the island. If I can get M.S. to take care of him, I'll keep him with me.'

'You're crazy.'

'Why not? She's good with kids, she wouldn't hurt him.'

'I won't leave him with her.'

'Are you going to come back?' A hand on the wheel, he looks at me, his head at an angle so I see mostly the underline of his jaw.

'I don't know.' With a Kleenex I wipe a ball of spit from the corner of Hans Lucas's mouth. 'That first summer at Redwood Creek, you said I watched all of you like some kind of government agent making a report. Well, my report isn't encouraging, especially the one on M.S. Everything she touches dries up around the edges. Most of the time now I get the feeling that something terrible's going to happen – I just don't know what it is. The only way I could ever feel safe with her around is if I was a turtle and could pull every part of me in.'

As we turn off the highway onto the dirt road that leads to Keoki's shack, he touches my cheek. 'If you leave, you're not going to be with me any more or less than you are right now. Somebody close to you like I was at the beginning of your life is still going to be part of it at the end. You better think about that. You and me and Jenny, all of us growing up – the cabin at Redwood Creek, you learning to swim, Billy Budd – all those memories aren't going to take us anywhere if you give them away cheap to somebody else.'

He helps me unload the car, carry in the dishes of food. When I go back out to get the diapers, I notice that he's untied his board. I don't see him, so he must have moved fast. Still carrying the diapers, I start down the hill to the beach, and halfway I see him running on the unbroken sand. I call, but he lifts his board and throws it like a spear into the water.

56

PETER: I turn my board shoreward and notice that a rainbow, tender as a baby plant, is sprouting from the Koolau Range. The water's still warm, the sun high; but pretty soon it'll start to slip down toward Kaena Point. From out here Kate and Keoki are practically invisible in the jumble of shadows on Keoki's porch – in the distance, the long sweet distance. I take out my thoughts now there's nobody but me to read them. 'Making the decision is what takes guts; the action's just an animal reflex.' Axel on big wave surfing. It's true: he didn't die from any action, he died from making a decision. About me. I bow my head. 'You turned your back,' I whisper. 'At the last minute you turned your back, arms waving like a baby, dancing in the lip. Wouldn't let me see in your face what we'd done to you.'

The first wave of the set is coming. Fuck it. Maybe just blow out my breath, leave nothing in reserve; slide down, wipe out, take gas, see his big duckfeet. Gas equals water. Mouth open, I'll suck it in till my lights go out. The family's always been a knot, and Kate an extra piece of string looking for a loose end to tie onto; let her go, she'll be all right. But what about Hans Lucas? A creature so vulnerable gives you your only chance to play God – but a just god. No other role to choose: power without mercy is murder. Kate doesn't want to play God; maybe women don't, except for M.S. Kate's always scrubbing Hans Lucas, wiping him, covering his traces. In public she hides him with her body from the eyes of strangers, and in private, naked, searches herself for the cause. Regret: my son'll never be drunk, never be sober; never see a tree dip its head.

Running toward me a glassy swell, pane of ice and heat and light. I take off a fraction past the peak. Step on tail, slow board; wave beginning to throw out over my head. Go for it. *Inside* the wave, not on it. What was it Keoki said? '*Ke ohe*, one fine tube.'

Let it curl over, make me invisible to bad angels. Possible? Or smother in a circle of water, a tunnel of love. Bail out, take no chances. Too late: water slammed shut. Inside the circle I'm standing, breathing, sunlight blasting through the wall. Blue and green and yellow: summer day for a child. Tuck shoulder, shift weight, steer clear of the falling lip. Magic. An easy fifteen – shoot straight through it standing up. The song begins. A groaning – of tunnels, of water, of people calling in early morning streets, of couples twined in early morning sheets. Behind me the tunnel collapsing, charge of air and water firing past. Board lifting, screaming, flying, in the vacuum left by the sucked-out air. Tubing, being tubed, gravity curving around me like a sleeve. Make it through to hard daylight, and they'll let me keep Hans Lucas. No power will ever be mine that's not mine now; I'll never be stronger, never be wiser, I'll only know there are many ways to fail in the genius of the sea. I lift my arm and with the tips of my fingers hold up the wall. Wall of feathers, wall of cries. I'm in the peacock's tail.

57

CHARLOTTE: 'Talking to Kate's got you all excited.' I
                crank down Jenny's bed. 'Here. Swallow one
of these and see if you can take a nap.'

Renting a hospital bed has turned out to be a good but
expensive idea. In the morning before he goes fishing with his
father, Keoki puts Jenny in the new bed, cranks it up. After he
leaves, Jenny and I are alone together for the rest of the day.
Sometimes a vagrant – a Filipino or a Hawaiian – comes to the
house, but so far a couple of choice words and a slammed door
have been enough to run them off. I slip a hand under Jenny's
mattress. More practical now to stash the knife in the hospital
bed than to carry it in my bag. I never leave Jenny's room
during the day except to crap or take a meal. And, if you give
him a simple list, Keoki can be sent out for groceries, so I never
have to leave the shack.

In the kitchen getting dinner, Kate's talking to Keoki. 'I'm
starving,' Jenny says. 'Kate said she brought some good stuff,
and right now I'd rather eat than sleep. I'm only tired because
I'm fat. I've felt much better ever since Auntie Lilia, but then
you started making me take those pills. If you just leave me
alone, everything'll be fine.'

'The pill will make you drowsy, so you can rest. Anyway
Peter isn't even in yet – you can eat later.' Under the thin
nightdress Jenny's belly is round and mobile in the last
stages of pregnancy. Healthy and smooth and clean and quiet,
she closes her eyes, and it's easy for me to imagine her a child
again, untouched in spotless sleep. No thanks to Keoki's
mother, who's been trying to take over, work her ignorant
spells. Next thing, she'll try to hypnotize Jenny, make her dance
naked round a fire, eat shit.

In a straight-back chair, I sit at the foot of the bed. No
mending, no knitting, no book; I don't need anything to do.

Jenny and I will deliver the baby together, alone in this Christ-bitten shack. No doctors, no damp porous Hawaiians, no twatty little nurses; just the two of us to fetch the baby into the world. Jenny might have trouble delivering – she's missing a lever, a pillar, to pass the baby through. But not if I'm here helping, the first one to see the baby's head, turn it, twist it if I have to, with my bare hands gouge it out. Another Hollander, beautiful like Hans Lucas. Jenny's half of the baby too strong to be cumbered by that barbarian's slippery black genes. Hands crossed, rising and falling on her breathing belly, Jenny's asleep. I bend closer. Aching with the toothy pleasure I've always taken in my children's bodies, I stroke my daughter's shoulder, the juicy knobs of her elbows, her knee. A sigh, mouth open a little, and Jenny turns toward me; a glimpse of tongue, fresh and sweet, firm as an eel behind her lips. Dazzled, I long to spread my legs like wings again, giving birth. Pretty pain opening me up, oh how I loved it, spewing out life, my cunt as red as Mars.

'I gon' talk with you,' says Keoki. He's sneaked in here without my seeing him.

'What do you want?' My hand on Jenny's shoulder reminding him who's in command.

'Tonight, we go Nanakuli. . . .'

'Keep your voice down,' I hiss. 'I've given her a pill.'

'I take Jenny with me,' he whispers. 'We go Nanakuli, stay with Auntie Lilia till *keiki* come. Kate and Peter gon' take us in car.'

'I'm not letting my daughter near that crazy old bitch,' I say, my voice lower than his.

'She come with me.'

'Try it and see what happens.'

'All time you tell Jenny, do this, do that. She my *wahine*, she come with me.' He pulls open a drawer, takes out Jenny's nightgowns, her slips and bras and panties.

'She's got to stay in bed.'

'Auntie Lilia's gon' take care of her Nanakuli.' A pile of Jenny's underclothes on his upraised arm, he looks like a waiter balancing a tray.

'Jenny's staying with me.' He looks so funny, squeezing his fist, like black Sambo watching the tigers. In a scatter of underwear he storms out of the room, but I'm just as fast. Right behind him, I shut the door, jam a chair under the knob.

Moist and heavy, Jenny's voice: 'When are we going to eat?'

'Soon. Go back to sleep.' Kate knocks on the door, telling me to open up, but after a minute she goes away. It's hot, hotter than it's ever been. God, how I hate it. Rotting fruit and wind, sweat running down like poison. In houses, hotels, restaurants, the stiff cunning of orchids, their bright-colored, lightly laughing mouths – clever, sneaky, eating flesh in the jungle at night. Bomb it till the maggots crawl, let them eat rice.

I snap on the light by Jenny's bed, but the bulb blows and a crackle of green light jags the room.

'Old man Hoffman's taking us into town so the girls can pick out the cloth for their Easter dresses.' Mama puts a hand on my shoulder. 'You're the oldest. I depend on you to take care of Lucas while we're gone.'

'Yes, Mama.'

'He's just had that bad cold, so make him rest in the house. Maybe you can read to him a while.' Mama puts on her hat, gives it a couple of turns, screwing it down tight. 'Now.' She kisses Lucas, takes Corinne and Abby by the hand. 'Lucas, you do what Charlotte says. We'll be coming back with Papa in the buckboard.'

I run upstairs to look out of my bedroom window, and watch old Mr Hoffman's wagon till it's out of sight. Fourteen years old, and this is the first time my mother's left me to take care of Lucas alone. Dust flying up behind the wagon, hiding it, as if they've gone through a puddle. It wouldn't matter now if none of them came back. For at least five years I've known that if my mother died I could run my father, my brother, the house. And, more important, that even if I was left alone in the world, I could take care of my brother and me.

The rooms are tall and quiet now that everyone is gone. I come downstairs slowly, enjoying the strength of my hand on the banister, the breeze coming through the open door. The first really nice day, and the smell of my skin is sharp and intimate from being outside in the sun. In the dining room Lucas is playing with the buttons Mama saves in a bottle, lining them up like soldiers on the floor. Click, click: two big buttons from Papa's brown overcoat, starting a new row. Click, click, click, click: Abby's first birthday dress, flakes of mother of pearl – snows left over from babyhood, tiny and dead and dry. Set loose with the button bottle, Lucas won't want me to read.

*If they never come back, what will I fix him for supper. I go into the
pantry. Bacon. And I'll slice some potatoes, fry some onions. Apple betty
for dessert. We'll sit here neat, the two of us, faces and hands washed, feet
together under the table. No grace. Tomorrow I'll walk into town, bring
back some beans, dried beef, flour for bread, and lard. I'll raise chickens so
I can send Lucas to college.*

A strong breeze blowing in at the kitchen door; soapy and crisp, it smells
like sheets on a line. It's been a winter of heavy snow, and I haven't been out
to Cathedral Rock for months. I find two lemons, take some cookies from
the stone jar. When the lemonade is ready, I call Lucas. 'Let's have a
picnic,' I say.

'Mama said not to go out because I might get the pneumonia,' he tells
me, coming into the kitchen.

'Take that button out of your nose. If you put on a sweater it'll be all
right. It's warm out, and I want to walk to Cathedral Rock.'

'Mama told you to stay with me. Why can't we have the picnic in the
kitchen?'

'Nobody has picnics in the house.'

'I want some lemonade.'

'Well, if you want some, you have to get it at the rock.' I swing the
basket on my arm. 'Get your sweater and let's go.'

It's too early for most of the wildflowers, but the goldenrod is out,
lighting up the path to the fence. As we leave the house and the barn behind,
Lucas takes my hand. 'What will Mama do if I get sick again?'

'You won't. Anyway she can't do anything because I won't let her.' I
squeeze his fingers. 'I'm the one who takes care of you, remember? Mama
popped you out, but you've been mine ever since.'

'How come I was in her belly and not yours?'

'Because Papa planted you there.'

'Why didn't he plant me in you?'

'I guess he didn't think I was old enough.' I lift his hand and kiss it.
'But maybe he was wrong.'

Lucas stops, halfway to the rock. 'I don't want to go,' he whimpers.
'Mama says people get lost out here.'

'She means in winter: in a blizzard people can get so confused they die
fifty feet from their house. But that can't happen now.' He sits in the grass,
but I just smile. When I want somebody to do something, when I will it, I
always get my way. Out here the wind is picking up, the wings of a hawk
rocking unsteadily as it banks over our heads. Lucas jumps up. 'A blue
racer – there. I saw it, but it ran off in the grass.'

'It's too early for snakes.' I take his hand, pull him on. Coming at us the central tower of Cathedral Rock, dark and smoky-looking, the stack of a haunted furnace. 'When we get there,' I say, 'I want to climb up on top. You can be the guard, take care of the picnic basket.'

At the bottom of the cluster of rocks I tuck my skirt into my bloomers. 'I'll tell you what: I'll let you come with me halfway, and then you can sit on one of the low spots while I go on up to the tower. Just put your feet in the places I show you.' With one of my stockings I tie the picnic basket to his arm. 'There. Now you won't drop it.' Halfway I say, 'All right. Now you sit here, and I'll call down to you from the top.'

He shrinks from the edge and won't look over. 'Rain's coming,' he shouts as I begin to climb. Above us a big triangular cloud, a band of greenish white around it like the edge of a new dollar bill. 'Don't worry,' I tell him. 'It's a while off.' The cloud itself is pale as mist or mirage. I tear a hole in my bloomers hoisting myself over the top. My hair rattling like plumage in the wind, I squint, turning slowly to the cardinal points of the compass. Nothing missing, nothing changed. The prairie is the same, always the same – but even if something is different, it's too small to be seen. Somewhere the eagle is watching.

'Can you hear me?' I call down.

'Yes.' His voice is trembling a little.

'I'm God,' I say. 'You better bow down to me.'

'Girls can't be God.'

'Do you want me to tell Mama you came out to the rock with me? Maybe I'll ask her to beat you.'

Going down on one knee, he crosses himself. 'Will you have to go to confession,' he says, 'for making believe you're God?'

'Of course not. Stay kneeling and I'll bless you.' I hold out my hands, palms up. 'Blessed are the meek, for they shall inherit the earth – and bless you, my son.' Freighted black clouds are thronging the prairie. 'It's my turn,' he says when I climb down. 'You have to kneel.'

'If you're going to be God, you have to get yourself up there.'

'I don't know how.'

'Put your foot in my hands, and grab the part that sticks out. After that there are a couple of holds and crevices; it's not hard. Keep going, that's it.'

The weather is coming breakneck. Further up the prairie rain is falling in long strokes, although here the sun is still a warm circle on my face. But it's windy, and if we were in the house the curtains would be blowing straight out, drops of water spattering the floor. I like to be the one to shut *the windows, sport my power when it rains. 'Go on,' I call, 'wedge your foot in the crack and reach your hand up.'*

'I can't find it.' He sounds whiny, and I know he's going to balk.

'There. By your knee.' In the distance the leafless trees are turning gray, like dirty instruments.

'Don't like it. Want to come down.'

'You're such a terrible baby.'

'Mama said not to bring me out. Storm's coming and I want to come down.'

'Not until you show me you're not afraid.'

'I'm not.'

'Yes, you are. You can't even make me kneel.'

'I can if I want to.'

'Up on top you can.'

He grabs a jet of rock. A few miles upwind lightning flickers, a gleam in an evil eye. He's standing on top. 'You kneel,' he tells me. 'You said you would.'

On my knees I'm laughing. Lightning flashes and the first drops fall, singly, tapping the rock like diamonds, then in heavy chains that slip off and bend the grasses below. He doesn't give the blessing, but his arms are straight out, hands together, as if he's going to dive. Slam of a cellar door: thunder. 'Lucas,' I call. A draft. My skirt flies up; my hair. The sky cracks open like an egg, spurting light and water. When he falls, he passes down me like a shiver, something I cannot control.

58

KATE: Signalling with a red towel, I run down the beach –
but I can't see Peter in the water. Both he and his
board have vanished. A big quiet wave, heavenly pale in height
and width and color, is breaking straight across, dead straight,
with a couple of feet of whitewater piloting it into the beach.
Worried as I am, I'm sorry Peter has missed it. I wonder if he's
paddled out around the point, because I can't understand how
he could have come in without us seeing him. Inside the belly of
the wave something flashes like the tip of a fish's nose, and then,
just before the wave collapses, before it dumps right over, Peter
shoots out the end of it. Crouched on his board, arm straight, fist
clenched, he looks as if he's punched his way through. It's
miraculous. One minute he's wrapped up, completely hidden in
the wave, the next he comes to light.

I flap the towel again and he sees me right away. He doesn't
wait for another wave but paddles in to the beach. He must
know something's wrong because I've never done anything like
this before, but he looks peaceful, happy, and, in a way,
apologetic. 'It's M.S.,' I say. 'She's locked herself in with
Jenny.' He drops his board and, as we run up the hill, I say, 'I
don't know what that was you just did out there, but congratulations – was it a tube?'

Inside the shack, Keoki's listening at the bedroom door. 'She
no say nothing,' he says.

I squeeze his arm. 'Did you get Jenny to talk to you?'

'I no dare. That *wahine*, she might do something.'

'Open up,' calls Peter. He shakes the door by the knob.

'Get out of here,' shouts M.S. 'He's not taking Jenny.'

'I want to talk to you.'

'That bastard's just waiting for me to open the door.'

Peter nods toward the kitchen and Keoki tiptoes out of the
room. 'He's gone now. Open up.'

'Leave us alone,' she says. 'We've got things to do.' Jenny murmurs something and I move closer to the door. 'Not unless they get out of here,' M.S. is saying. 'I don't want them looking up you when the baby comes.'

Peter goes into the kitchen to talk to Keoki, and I pick up Hans Lucas, who's half-sitting, half-lying on the floor. Keoki has given him an old octopus lure, a cowrie shell without the hook, and he's still holding on to it. I hug him tight, listening to the whispers in the kitchen, and he rubs his fist back and forth against my cheek. The shell is cool, as if it's been lying in the shade, but his hand is sweaty. I wonder if, now that he's learned how to grip, he's worried about what comes next. What are common reflexes for other children are for him almost moral choices, followed by conscious deliberate acts. When Peter and Keoki come out of the kitchen, the shell vibrates with the wash of feeling in the room.

'We gon' bust down that door,' Keoki tells me in a low voice.

'Can't you do it some other way?' I say, afraid of the noise a shattering door might make, a curtain ripped open to show the violence onstage.

'I don't know,' says Peter. 'I don't want to give her any more time in there with Jenny.'

The knob rattles and I can hear a chair jump and skitter.

M.S. opens the door. Her hair is dirty, loose strands ravelled, as if twisted and untwisted in a bad sleep. In the hospital bed, Jenny is watching from under a light quilt, handmade – morning glories sprouting from blue and purple squares – a wedding present from Auntie Lilia.

Keoki brushes past, his big body pressing M.S. against the wall. As he bends to pick up Jenny, M.S. grabs his arm. 'Put her down,' she says.

'Let go,' says Peter, but she yanks at Keoki with both hands. 'Come on,' he says, reaching out. 'Let him go.'

'Don't be silly.' She slaps at Peter's wrist as if he's a lover taking liberties.

I'm standing just outside the door, and when Keoki lifts Jenny, I see M.S.'s hand spark. I think she got him just below the elbow, but the blood surfaces so fast, laying down thin branches on his arm, it's hard to tell. It must have hurt, but Keoki doesn't stop or jerk his arm. With the drag of the blade still on his skin, he carries Jenny out of the room, shifting her weight to his other arm. M.S. follows them. 'How have I endured any of this,' she says, peering into each of our faces, 'when it is so unendurable?'

'Listen,' says Peter. 'Give me that knife. You can't see Jenny till after she has the baby. Understand?'

'I want Jenny. Make him give me Jenny.'

'No. You've got to let her go with Keoki.'

'That's what you think.' Swaying up to him, she looks directly into his eyes. 'I know who you are,' she says. She rubs his cheek, roots with her fingers in his still wet skin. 'I made your goddam heart, your feet, your teeth.' Absentmindedly, she hands the knife to me.

'You're not going to do this anymore,' says Peter.

She turns to Keoki and shakes his arm, as if trying to make him drop Jenny. When Peter grabs her, she loses her balance and falls back, her loose hair curving over his arm, like Rita Hayworth's did when she was dancing with Gene Kelly in *Cover Girl*. As he catches her, his face is utterly calm and smooth, the way it was when he came out of the water. He's so close I can smell the salt drying on his skin. (Not too long ago, mouth open, I had lapped the sweetness of his hair.) 'Jenny's going with Keoki to Nanakuli,' he says, 'and you're not going to do anything to stop them.' From a corner of the *punee* Hans Lucas whimpers. Peter picks him up and starts to rock him, whispering in his ear, but all the time he's watching M.S. Something is bubbling, slow at first and then it gathers speed. For a minute I think one of my pots on the stove has come to a boil; but she's doing it in her throat. 'Please Mom,' Jenny says. 'Stop it. I'll talk to you later, okay?'

The screen door bangs and Keoki carries her down the steps. Somewhere a faucet is dripping, and I see that little piles of sand are growing in the corners of the room.

I go into the kitchen and turn off all the burners, shut the knife away in the drawer. When I come back out, Peter is still holding Hans Lucas, the light from the window as pale as the water had been when he'd disappeared inside the tube. 'I'm taking Hans Lucas home,' I say, holding out my arms.

'Not necessarily,' says M.S., but Peter steps between us and hands him to me. I open the door.

'Are you coming?' I say to Peter. M.S. picks up the stack of diapers I've left and, arms crossed, holds them against her chest. I think she wants me to fight her for them.

Peter says, 'Give the diapers to me.' As he reaches out to take them, I can feel her anger like a pulse. Her pupils are an autumn shade of red, and I know that she's someplace that I will never go.

She follows us out of the house, but she doesn't come down the steps. When Peter gets into the car, she says, 'Where the hell do you think you're running off to? You always were gutless – couldn't kill the snake, could you?'

As we drive off, I'm the one who looks back. I wonder how I'm going to remember Hawaii: for the rest of my life will I see a dream, a radiance in the path of the Pacific, mountains hissing in bright mythical waters? Or only a scrap of land, an unimportant resort, a place where things either get lost or die, where they've locked up Hans Lucas on a long public hall?

M.S. is sitting on the top step. Skirt hoisted, knees slack, she's braiding her hair. She had thought that she loved us, she brought us all up. What does it mean about the way we will be?

Arena

☐ The History Man	Malcolm Bradbury	£2.95
☐ Rates of Exchange	Malcolm Bradbury	£3.50
☐ The Painted Cage	Meira Chand	£3.95
☐ Ten Years in an Open Necked Shirt	John Cooper Clarke	£3.95
☐ Boswell	Stanley Elkin	£4.50
☐ The Family of Max Desir	Robert Ferro	£2.95
☐ Kiss of the Spiderwoman	Manuel Puig	£2.95
☐ The Clock Winder	Anne Tyler	£2.95
☐ Roots	Alex Haley	£5.95
☐ Jeeves and the Feudal Spirit	P. G. Wodehouse	£2.50
☐ Cold Dog Soup	Stephen Dobyns	£3.50
☐ Season of Anomy	Wole Soyinka	£3.99
☐ The Milagro Beanfield War	John Nichols	£3.99
☐ Walter	David Cook	£2.50
☐ The Wayward Bus	John Steinbeck	£3.50

Prices and other details are liable to change

ARROW BOOKS, BOOKSERVICE BY POST, PO BOX 29, DOUGLAS, ISLE OF MAN, BRITISH ISLES

NAME...

ADDRESS..

....,.........

....

Please enclose a cheque or postal order made out to Arrow Books Ltd. for the amount due and allow the following for postage and packing.

U.K. CUSTOMERS: Please allow 22p per book to a maximum of £3.00.

B.F.P.O. & EIRE: Please allow 22p per book to a maximum of £3.00

OVERSEAS CUSTOMERS: Please allow 22p per book.

Whilst every effort is made to keep prices low it is sometimes necessary to increase cover prices at short notice. Arrow Books reserve the right to show new retail prices on covers which may differ from those previously advertised in the text or elsewhere.